When The
Ravens Die

ALSO BY CAMERON KENT

Make Me Disappear

The Witness Files*
Seduced and Betrayed*
Twist of Fate*
Nightrangers*

*Films

To Gretchen —
Hope you're
Royally entertained!

When The Ravens Die

All the best —
Cameron Kent

CAMERON KENT

Alliance Books

an imprint of Harlan Publishing Company

Greensboro, North Carolina USA

HARLAN
H
PUBLISHING

Published by Alliance Books
an imprint of Harlan Publishing Company
5710-K High Point Road #280
Greensboro, NC 27407 USA

Visit our web site at: http://www.harlanpublishing.com/alliance_books

Book design by Jeff Pate

FIRST EDITION

Library of Congress Control Number: 2002107353

ISBN: 0-9676528-7-1

Printed by R.R. Donnelley & Sons Company

01 02 03 04 05 06 07 08 09 10

To my parents, who taught me always to seek the truth and to love the British Isles, and to Bynum Shaw, who taught me that a writer writes.

As long as there are ravens in the Tower of London, the Monarchy will survive.

— English legend

Chapter One

Even as he slept, Malcolm Bride knew someone was watching him. He cocked open his right eye and saw the young mother and her son staring him down, gathering the courage to ask him a question.

"Can I help you?" asked Bride with a genuine intent to do so.

"I was wondering, if it's not too much trouble, if you wouldn't mind moving so we could sit together. I mean, the flight's so long—"

"Say no more," interrupted Bride, flashing a warm smile that immediately dispelled their worries about asking a perfect stranger for such a discomfiting favor. "Where is your other seat?"

"34-F."

"Fine, just give me a moment," said Bride as he collected his belongings from the seat pocket in front of him. He even hoisted the young woman's heavy carry-on luggage with one swift movement into the overhead compartment as he relinquished his claim to a precious window seat.

Within moments the fifty-seven year old college professor was struggling down the aisle with his charcoal gray herringbone overcoat under one arm, a scarred brown leather valise under the other, and enough reading material stashed in between to last him the full eight hours it would take to fly from Boston to London's Heathrow Airport.

He purposefully tracked down a flight attendant who was busy slamming compartment drawers and fastening locks in the galley in the midsection of the airliner.

"Excuse me, Miss?" he ventured between slammings.

"Yes?" she answered with the forced smile and simulated polite tone of voice acquired from years of dealing with passengers who do anything other than sit down and go to sleep.

"I need to let you know that I'm switching seats with the lady in 11-A. The name is Malcolm Bride. I'll be in 34-F now."

"Fine," she replied as she resumed slamming and hasping.

"Don't you think you should write that down?"

"Write what down?"

"The change in the seating arrangement."

"It's fine, really."

"But shouldn't there be some sort of official record?"

"Why?"

"In case of emergency, in case we should crash. I should think investigators would appreciate an accurate listing of who was sitting where as they sift through the rubble. I've heard cases where it took days, perhaps weeks, for them to sort out the victims. They had to bring in dental records, relatives of the deceased, a real mess, all of which could have been avoided had someone kept an accurate seating chart."

Bride had finally captured the young woman's complete attention, but the plastic smile had evaporated into disbelief.

"First of all, if this plane goes down, any such list and subsequent changes to it will go right down with us. Secondly, I don't have time for this, so if you would kindly take your seat, whatever one you decide on, I would greatly appreciate it."

Bride felt an obligation to pursue the matter. "Perhaps I should speak to the captain," he said politely, turning and heading back toward the front of the aircraft.

"Okay, okay, you win," said the flight attendant with an exasperated shake of her French-knotted hair. "I'll make a note of the seating change."

"Thank you," said Bride with a smile. "That's Malcolm Bride, now sitting in 34-F."

"Fine. Now then, the sooner I see you in that seat, the sooner I can make the necessary adjustments to our archives."

Bride decided to let her sarcasm pass and head aftward to his new home. After all, this wasn't about winning or losing a debate, it was simply about being correct, about making sure the record reflected the truth. An insignificant point to most, including one antagonized flight attendant, but no less than a matter of principle to Malcolm Bride.

Bride squeezed his six-foot-two-inch frame into 34-F, a cramped opening in the middle row that posed as an airline seat. His broad shoulders, built during his teens by racing a scull up the Charles River and maintained by a regular exercise regimen, poured over the edges of his seat and into the shoulders of his adjacent passengers.

"Ruggedly handsome" was the way Bride had heard himself described on several occasions when nobody thought he was listening. He took that characterization as a compliment, even though he understood that his square jaw, angular nose, and untamed brown hair put the emphasis more on the rugged than on the handsome. Put a button-down shirt, khaki pants, and wingtips on an Australian bushranger and you had Malcolm Bride.

The features that left a lasting impression were his eyes, light brown and gentle like maple sugar. He could be physically imposing standing in the front of his classroom, but those eyes let his students know he loved the subject he was teaching and he was approachable with any questions they might have.

Seated to his right was a middle-aged businessman whose furrowed eyebrows made it clear he was still angry at his company for failing to fly him first-class and therefore in no mood for casual conversation with the proletariat in coach. To his left, an earthy young woman in her twenties who was taking up more than her fair share of the common armrest. They exchanged polite nods as he struggled to fit his long frame into a space ill-designed for that purpose.

His seat belt finally buckled, his overcoat folded gently in the overhead compartment, and his valise neatly tucked under the seat in front of him, Malcolm Bride was finally settled in for what would be the journey of his life.

Even though he had traveled the world for most of his adult life, Bride still took a moment to study the "emergency landing" instructions. His earnings as a professor of history at Amherst were hardly a King's ransom, but enough for a bachelor with muted tastes for material possessions to indulge in an extended vacation every summer.

The scrapbooks wedged into his bookshelves of his study contained the souvenirs of forty-seven states, three junkets to South America, a cruise of the Norwegian fjords on a working fishing boat, a hiking tour of the Italian Alps, two weeks of scuba diving off Australia's Great Barrier Reef, and a month long photographic safari in sub-Saharan Africa. If the world were meant to be a banquet, then Malcolm Bride owned a voracious appetite and had tasted nearly every dish on the menu.

Despite a passport that bore more stamps than a Secretary of

State's, Bride had never been to Great Britain. Perhaps England wasn't exotic enough and therefore less of a challenge. Perhaps it was too similar to New England, and would disappoint his insatiable hunger for greater knowledge and understanding of the world. Or perhaps he had never before summoned the courage to go, for fear of what he might learn about himself.

It was over an hour into the transatlantic flight before Bride awakened and realized he had even taken off. The businessman to his right was sleeping with headphones, still scowling even in slumber.

The young woman to his left was engrossed in a crossword puzzle but clearly on the verge of giving up with a third of the squares remaining unfilled.

"Paseo," volunteered Bride without inhibition.

The woman was mildly startled by the intrusion. "Excuse me?" she replied.

"Fifty-three across, the parade of bullfighters, it's called a 'paseo'. Conjures up images of Hemingway's *Death in the Afternoon,* doesn't it?"

She checked to see if it fit. "So it is. Thank you." She scribbled it in and resumed biting nervously on her pencil.

"And that would make eleven down, 'tetrastich', a four line poem."

This time her voice resounded with a tinge of annoyance. "Gee. Thank you again." The woman filled in the appropriate blanks, as Bride craned to get a closer look. In a polite way of saying "I don't want your help", the woman casually closed her magazine and tucked it into the seat in front of her.

Bride was immediately sorry. "Oh, now I've gone and spoiled your fun, haven't I?" he said with contempt for his own behavior. "I apologize. I shouldn't have butted in, it's just that I saw you struggling and I thought I could help."

"No, no, I'm just tired, that's all," she replied, lying to protect his wounded sensibilities.

"You're just being nice. I know when I've overstepped my bounds. Believe me, this isn't the first time."

Bride eased back into his seat and closed his eyes, establishing that imaginary barrier that frequent fliers like the man next to him are so adept at creating.

Now the young woman felt miserable about her own impulsive reaction. She searched for the right words. "Actually, now that you're awake, I was hoping you might be in the mood for conversation."

The imaginary barrier was slowly vanishing.

"Really?" he said disbelievingly.

"Yes. You look like an interesting person," she said as she turned to face him. She pulled one leg up onto the seat and glanced at her watch. "And you have exactly six hours and forty seven minutes to tell me all about yourself."

A smile crossed Bride's face. As one prone to talk, on any subject on the table, he was never one to turn down a willing audience. "What would you like to know?" he inquired as he turned to face the young woman more squarely.

"For starters, how'd you get to be so smart?"

He chuckled with genuine modesty. "I'm a college professor. American history."

"Married?"

"Bachelor."

"Lifelong?"

"So far."

She laughed out loud, warming up to his charm.

The flight attendant made her way down the aisle, none too pleased to cross paths again with the man in 34-F.

"Something to drink, Mr. Bride?" she asked, her smugness again seeping out.

"Scotch and water, single malt if you have it, and actually, it's Doctor Bride."

"I'll make a note of that," replied the flight attendant as she bit her lip to keep from snapping, *For the record.* "Something for you, Miss?"

"Mineral water."

The flight attendant poured the drinks as hastily as possible and moved on.

"Ironic, someone with the last name of Bride who isn't married."

"I suppose it is," he said with a nod.

"Okay, so what takes you to England? Academia?"

The boyish excitement on Bride's face quickly vanished. He narrowed his eyes and stared straight ahead. "Your question is more difficult than you know."

The young woman could clearly tell that she'd struck a nerve. "Oh, now I'm the one who's intruding. Look, you don't have to tell me if you don't want to. We can talk about something else."

He shook his head and turned back to face her, more intent than before. "The truth is, I'm not sure why I'm going over there. I suppose it's some kind of quest, although I don't know what I'm going to find, and I'm not even certain where to begin looking."

The young woman was confused but sincerely interested. "Quest? Quest for what?"

"My ancestry. My lineage, my genealogical heritage, my pedigree if you will. My beginnings. My roots."

Bride again stared off into space. It was as though it was the first time he himself had come to grips with his impending mission to the Isles.

"Your ancestors were of British descent?" asked the young woman, trying not to pry too deeply into his obvious pain.

"My mother was born there. Unfortunately, that and her name are about all I know about her. And that, to answer your question, is what is taking me to England."

Bride sat back in his chair and crossed his arms, the lonely passenger on his own train of thought. The conversation was over, but the quest was about to begin.

◆   ◆   ◆

Weary from travel and time zones, Bride dragged his suitcase through the teeming masses at Heathrow Airport, pulling on his overcoat as he muddled through the crowd. The hair on the crown of his head stood up two inches higher than normal from a night of restless sleep, while the stubble on his face begged for a clean shave. His bloodshot eyes focused on a sign by the exit that said "Gatwick Express," which seemed to check with the scribbled set of instructions he held in his hand.

Within minutes, Bride was on the railcar, finally capturing a coveted window seat. The English countryside whirred past him as the train picked up speed, numbing his senses. Why had he come? What would he unearth about his past? He drifted off, suddenly uncaring about anything other than sleep as his head bobbed against the windowpane.

"Victoria Station!" bellowed the Conductor as he ambled down the aisle of the train. "Next stop, Victoria Station!"

Bride sat up in alarm. The Conductor's call had tugged at his memory even as he slept. He again referred to his handwritten instructions, then grabbed his suitcase and valise and scrambled for the exit.

Even in late May, the London air was filled with reminders of the cold and damp of winter. Bride buttoned the top button of his overcoat and worked his way down to the taxi stand. A black cab raced up to the curb.

"Where ya headin', sir?" the driver shouted over the din in a polite tone that makes even the most common of Londoners sound as if they're of noble peerage.

Bride referred again to his notes.

"Uh... the Dunbarton in Bloomsbury," he called back.

"Bloomsbury," echoed the cabbie, subtly correcting the American's pronunciation. "On Gower Street?"

Bride was suddenly infused with enthusiasm over the man's recognition of his destination, obviously unaware of the navigational prowess of even the most ordinary of London cabbies.

"Yes, yes! You know it?"

"Just so 'appens I'm headin' that way," said the driver with a friendly wink. "'Op in."

Bride scooped up his bags and climbed into the back of the spacious black taxi. After an exhausting journey to this point, the man behind the wheel felt like salvation to Bride. Although thousands before him had occupied this same seat, Bride had the sensation of being in the lap of luxury. A courteous cab driver who actually knew more about where he was going than his passenger. This would never happen in Boston he thought to himself.

Bride wanted to resume his intermittent nap, but the sights and sounds of London wouldn't permit it. Legions of businessmen in dark suits and tan raincoats filled the sidewalks, all walking with the purpose of someone with appointments to keep. Double-decked red buses circumnavigated the roundabouts, flowing into traffic like streams into a mighty river.

He caught a glimpse of Westminster Cathedral as the taxi drove up Victoria Street.

At the corner of Victoria and Millbank, he could see Westminster Abbey, the Houses of Parliament, and Big Ben against the backdrop of the River Thames. North along Whitehall came the National Gallery and Trafalgar Square.

The bookstores on Charing Cross Road piqued Bride's interest, and he knew he would find his way back to them after a shave and a night's rest.

The old gentleman at the newspaper stand on the corner of Tottenham Court Road and Oxford Street was tacking up a new blue and white headline sheet for the *Evening Standard*. It read:

GRAY LADY DOWN

The headline made no sense to Bride as he caught a glimpse from the back seat.

"Excuse me," he said as he leaned forward to the driver.

"That paper said 'Gray Lady Down'. What does that mean?"

The cabbie was no less than stunned by the question.

"Well that would be the Queen, of course! I thought you Americans kept a close eye on our Royals."

"I guess some of them do. I've never been one to revel in the gossip that seems to follow them around. Is she ill?"

"I should say so. Had the pneumonia all winter. Hadn't been out of the palace in months. Pity, really. Like her, I do. Best Queen of England we've had, if you ask me. Held this country together through a little thick and a lotta thin."

Bride didn't want to contradict the driver, but correctness had become virtually a knee-jerk, involuntary response for the professor. "Pardon me, but you referred to her as 'Queen of England', when in fact, isn't she the 'Queen of Britain'?"

"England *is* Britain," shot back the cabbie with assurance.

"Not to the Scots and the Welsh and the Irish," argued Bride.

"Well now, I can't help that, now can I?" he answered back, turning up his radio to signal that this brief debate was now concluded.

The driver turned the corner and hunched down to get a better look at the row of townhouses along Gower Street. He came to a gentle stop in front of an Edwardian townhouse with a carved wooden sign over the bay window that announced it was the Dunbarton.

"We're here," whispered the driver in a voice just loud enough to rouse the professor, who had finally given in to his weariness.

Bride sat up at attention, pretending to have been cognizant the entire time. "Yes, yes of course. We're here. How much?"

"Seven pounds, twenty."

Bride pulled out a ten pound note without hesitation.

"Here's ten quid for a job well done."

"Thank you, sir, and good luck to you here in London."

"I'll need it."

Bride collected his baggage and stood for a moment on the sidewalk, admiring his new quarters. The Dunbarton would apparently fill Bride's three requirements for lodging: clean, convenient, and cheap.

A tiny bell jingled as Bride pushed open the substantial oak door, made even heavier by at least a dozen coats of forest green paint. A Persian rug led down a narrow hallway that was crowded by an antique Hepplewhite sideboard along one wall. A vase of freshly cut daisies cast a silouetted shadow onto the open guest register underneath.

Bride took several steps along the creaky maple floor and examined the register, dismayed to see that the most recent entry was nearly a fortnight before his arrival. Had he made a grievous error in selecting his accommodations? There was still time to back out and alter his plans. He had remembered seeing a modest inn called the Wayfarer just a few blocks back. Perhaps they might have a vacancy. He picked up his luggage and took one creaky step toward the door. He would not know until later how fortunate he was to be intercepted.

"Professor Bride!" echoed a thick London accent from the mouth of one Peter Rumpole.

Bride stopped dead in his tracks, gracefully rearranging his luggage to make it appear as though he was still moving forward into the warmth of the Dunbarton.

A bowlegged swagger carried the gray haired innkeeper down the Persian runner. The man's thin ruddy face, threadbare corduroys, elbow-patched wool cardigan, and reading glasses that dangled on a chain around his neck reminded Bride of some of his professorial colleagues at Amherst on their days off.

"We've been expectin' ya!" cackled Peter, as he took both of Bride's hands and shook them with the excitement of a man who had found a long lost friend. "Hope my directions from the airport were good enough."

"They were...fine," said Bride, finally reclaiming his hands.

Rumpole opened the Hepplewhite sideboard and fished around for a room key. "Here 'tis. Room One. We saved the best of the lot for our distinguished American guest, Dr. Malcolm Bride," he announced proudly.

"You don't appear to be all that busy," said Bride, gesturing to the underworked guest register.

"Oh that. Not to worry. The IRA sets off one bomb in Harrod's and ole Peter Rumpole here loses fifteen American tourists. It'll pick up in the spring, always does."

Bride's immediate inclination was to remind his host that spring was nearly over, but for once he bit his tongue before the words escaped. After all, the man had remembered to acknowledge his doctorate. A smile and a gentle nod were the best he could do.

"Do you need a credit card, some kind of advance?" asked Bride.

"Nonsense!" chirped the innkeeper as he collected his guest's bags.

"We're all family here at the Dunbarton. You just settle up when you leave, and after a taste of me wife's cookin' and a coupla pints of London lager, I'm bettin' you won't want to! Off we go now!"

Bride followed the old man down the hallway to the first door on the right; Room One.

"I'm bettin' you're a bit road weary, so I'll let you grab a stretch and see you in the morning. You need anythin', you just call on Peter Rumpole." He set the luggage inside the door and vanished down the corridor as quickly as he'd arrived.

The room was more than adequate for a man who had more than once made an airport floor his bed for the night. Bright chintz curtains, a snow white comforter, and a tasteful mix of Victorian and Empire furniture. A lamp with a fringed shade stood on the carved wooden desk added to the inherent warmth of the room.

Malcolm Bride laid down on the bed and nestled his head against the feather pillow. His mind felt too busy to go to sleep, but his body was too tired to keep up. The last clear thoughts were of his rebirth.

Chapter Two

*J*ohn Martelli was nineteen years old when he discovered the people he knew as Mother and Father were not his natural parents. The news had come in an unusually abrupt fashion, with no one there to issue sorrowful prefaces or repentant explanations.

In his junior year at Columbia, Martelli applied for a passport for a semester abroad in Venice. When he went down to the Federal Building to pick up his new passport, he also received a photocopy of the birth certificate mailed in by the people he knew to be his parents, Alfred and Maria Martelli. Young John had always been told he was born in Boston's North End, the only son of an older couple who had finally been blessed with a child after so many years of trying. His birth certificate reflected that version of reality, with one notable exception; place of birth was listed as London, England.

Surely there was some mistake, thought John, as he set out to correct what was clearly a governmental clerical error. The overbusy woman on the other end of the phone assured him it was not and hung up, having no idea of the pain seeping out from the voice on the other end.

When John Martelli returned to Boston for Christmas, he showed his parents the photocopy and asked pointedly what they knew about it. The betraying look on their faces vanquished any hopes they might have had of hanging on to their secret.

What was to follow was a tale that John could never have imagined, and one that the Martellis had hoped he would never have to.

It had been the late spring of 1945. War World II had just ended. Alfred was recuperating in a British hospital from a German bullet that had lodged in his thigh when Maria sailed over to help bring her husband home.

As the steamer headed west across the North Atlantic, Alfred was confined to the ship's clinic while the only doctor on board fought to clear away clotting in his leg.

As Maria stood by his hospital bed, a young woman and her infant child were brought in and put in the bed next to Alfred. She was deathly ill, bleeding profusely from between her legs. The doctor couldn't find the cause or the cure.

As the woman moaned herself into a restless sleep, Maria held the crying infant close to her warm heart and let the rhythmic pitch of the steamer lull the young boy to sleep. The young mother's silent nod let Maria know that her kindness was appreciated.

By morning, the baby would be orphaned. The young woman was wheeled away to make room for another patient.

She was properly buried at sea. No final words, no last rites, just an anguished look from an overworked medic who couldn't seem to get used to the face of death no matter how many times he stared into it.

Before he had been sent overseas, Alfred and Maria had tried for five years to bear children. He was the last of that line of Martellis, and they had forever wanted a son to carry on the family name. They also wanted to share their true happiness in marriage with someone else, and complete a joyous household with the laughter that only children can bring. Therefore, it was almost without consultation, without a second thought, that Maria clutched the infant to her bosom and immediately accepted him as her own.

In the span of a week, the Martellis would move from a cramped one bedroom apartment on New York's lower East Side to an airy three bedroom unit in north Boston. There they would all grow and prosper, in laughter and in love. They were a family.

In hindsight, it all made sense to John. He had often wondered why he displayed not even the slightest physical resemblance to his parents. His voice was different, his mind processed information in a way distinct from those who raised him, and his mannerisms were uniquely his own. It also explained the yearning that had heretofore been inexplicable. Why had he forever sensed that there was something or someone else out there with a spiritual connection to him? Even as a young boy, he had always felt as though a part of him was missing, and now he knew why.

John returned to New York that same night, crying himself to sleep on the train, enjoying the numbing sensation of riding the rails.

He would make the trip to Venice that spring and brood for hours over coffee in St. Mark's Plaza, surrounded by hundreds of people but feeling very much alone.

Young John Martelli couldn't remember the exact moment it had happened, but the disconsolate young man slowly realized that his anger was no longer consuming him. He had taken the step that so many have been unable to take and completely reversed his outlook on the situation. He suddenly saw a brighter light, heard a sweeter chorus, walked a higher road. Had it not been for Alfred and Maria, would he have arrived at the same point? Would he have stood a chance in this world as a parentless child destined for some orphanage? Perhaps, but not likely.

His innate yearning had in fact had a positive effect, giving him an unquenchable thirst for knowledge and adventure. He had enjoyed a happy childhood, achieved the distinction of Valedictorian, been granted a full scholarship to an Ivy League school, raised with the underpinnings of morals and values, and most of all, he had been loved by two people with an infinite capacity to give of themselves. Yes, he wished they had told him the truth, but all things considered, life had not been so bad for young John Martelli.

When he returned from his spring abroad, John traveled home to Boston. It had been six months since he had last communicated with Alfred and Maria, but they looked as though they'd aged by a decade. When they came to the door, he spoke not a word, but wrapped them both up in his powerful young arms. They stood under the transom, crying together. They were a family once again.

All had been forgiven, but John would have one request; that he be permitted to adopt his given name. Allison Bride was the name they recalled from the young woman's medical chart hanging on the end of her cot on the ship. She had called her baby son Malcolm.

And thus, at the age of nineteen, Malcolm Bride was born.

Chapter Three

The breakfast room of the Dunbarton was alive with the aromas of fresh Viennese coffee, Earl Grey tea, steaming hot porridge, and smoked sausages, all competing for olfactory attention. Bride followed the scent as a night's rest and a clean shave added a fresh element to his athletic gait.

"Top of the morning to you!" called out Peter Rumpole as Bride walked in and joined him at the breakfast table. "Sleep well?"

"Like the fox that escaped the hounds," said Bride. He closed his eyes and savored the fragrant cloud that wafted over the table.

Fionnuala Rumpole entered from the kitchen with a tray of freshly baked biscuits just begging for a complement of butter and jam. Fionnuala was just turning gray, but enough of her chestnut brown hair remained to highlight her natural good looks. Had she been a woman of means, with access to boutique makeup and designer clothing, she might have been considered a raving beauty. As the working wife of an innkeeper she would have to settle for pleasantly attractive, quick with a smile and kind word.

Bride stood up with the politeness of a gentleman when the lady entered the room.

"This here's me wife," said Rumpole proudly. "Fionnuala, say good morning to Dr. Malcolm Bride."

"We're so happy to have you!" she said with a natural warmth that reminded Bride of his own mother. "Course, these days, we're happy to have most anyone!" Her hearty smile filled the room as she laughed out loud. "Sit down, sit down!" she commanded.

Bride obeyed, more pleased than ever that he hadn't been allowed to escape from the Dunbarton. "Fionnuala...what kind of name is that?" asked Bride in a tone of voice that let her know he meant it as a compliment.

"Why, it's a first name, sir," was her candid reply.

"Where did you get it?"

"From me mum, I suppose."

"No, I mean of what origin?"

"Oh. Well now, I don't really know."

"Fionnuala isn't a name you hear everyday. Haven't you ever wondered where it originated?"

"Can't say that I have. At the end of the day, what would it matter? Biscuit?"

Bride returned her smile and accepted her offering. He was starting to learn when to leave well enough alone.

"So what's on the agenda for today, Professor?" interjected Rumpole. "Sightseeing?"

"Perhaps, but my main objective this trip is for research."

"Research? Research into what?" asked Fionnuala.

"Well...research into me, I suppose."

The puzzled look on both their faces let Bride know he needed to provide further explanation.

"I've come to England to search for my ancestors," he announced. "I was born here in 1945 to an unmarried young girl named Allison Bride, but aside from that, I haven't the foggiest as to who preceded me."

"And why are you wantin' to know that?" said Fionnuala.

Once again, what appeared to be the simplest of questions forced the professor to sit back and take stock of his mission."I don't really know," he admitted, as much to himself as to the two innkeepers. "It's history...it begs to be discovered and recorded, otherwise it's as if it never happened. And I suppose it has something to do with knowing the truth, whatever it may be. The same reason an innocent man hires a five hundred dollar lawyer to fight a twelve dollar parking ticket. That's the best I can tell you."

The two Rumpoles nodded quietly, perhaps not fully understanding but accepting their guest's words as explanation enough.

♦ ♦ ♦

The enormous leatherbound volume thumped onto the mahogany table, echoing throughout the cavernous reading room in the London Hall of Records. Here were assembled the various personal milestones of the millions who had lived in the old city and surrounding environs since before the days of the American Revolution. Every birth and death, marriage and divorce, were contained somewhere within the pages of the vast collection of musty record books.

Bride stared at the giant tome in front of him, three times as thick as the Boston phonebook. Two decades of anxiety were bubbling up inside him as his fingers drummed across the title,

BIRTH RECORDS - 1945

There was that fear again, the same fear he'd experienced from the time he had made a conscious decision to discover his past. For a man of letters whose entire life had been spent in the exploration of new worlds and the pursuit of greater knowledge, the fear of what he might learn was irony of epic proportion. Bride's determination finally won out over his trepidation and he opened the book to the letter *B*. Somewhere between Babcock and Bynum he would search for his mother, Allison Bride.

He could feel the pulse in the very tip of his index finger as he drew it slowly down the pages—past the Brewers, the Brians, the Briars, the Briarcliffes, the Brickmans—but with a jolt his finger ran into the Bridwells. No Brides on record in 1945.

He was stunned and baffled. He had never once taken into consideration the possibility that it wouldn't be there. However, Malcolm Bride was not a man prone to giving up without a battle, and one unsuccessful pass at a book of record wasn't about to stop him. There must have been a mistake, and he was determined to rectify it.

He would check and double-check the volumes for 1943, 1944, 1946, and 1947. He would scan the Bridges, the Bridgers, even the McBrides. He delved into marriages and deaths, and births from three decades before, but not an Allison Bride among them.

His eyes ached from five hours of small print and dim light. His heart ached even more. He returned the feckless volumes to their resting place and walked slowly away. Bride couldn't recall ever feeling more deflated. He had taken years to summon the courage to make this journey, only to learn that his final destination did not exist.

An air of gloom hung heavily over the supper table at the Dunbarton as Bride silently nibbled the feast Fionnuala had prepared. His host and hostess sensed their guest's sadness, but were ill-equipped to find the words that would soothe his troubled face.

"It's as if I wasn't even born," muttered the professor to nobody in particular. He laid his fork down on a half-eaten meal and stared into the nothingness of the white linen tablecloth.

"Odd that your mum would have a first name for a last name and a last name for a first, isn't it?" Rumpole offered casually between bites.

"What do you mean?" said Bride, looking up.

"Well, I don't suppose it's any big thing, it's just that most of the Allisons I know use it for a last name. I can think of my school chums Darby Allison and Michael Allison off the top of me head. And most of the women I know use the name Bridget for a first name, you know, like Fionnuala's friend Bridget Parker out in Essex."

"Yes, but my last name is *Bride*," said the American as he launched another attempt to eat something.

"Right. Bride is short for Bridget, you know, like Bob is short for Robert and Jack is short for John, although I never really understood that one. Doesn't seem that much shorter to me."

Bride had stopped listening halfway through Rumpole's sentence. He sat thunderstruck, his fork stopping halfway up to his open mouth. He suddenly dropped his utensil with a clank onto the bone china plate and sprang up from his chair. He was out the door before anyone could catch a breath to ask him where he was going.

"See there?" said Fionnuala. "You've gone and upset the poor man!"

Rumpole stared back in disbelief, not knowing what he'd said to generate such a spontaneous reaction from the American. He had no way of knowing he had given his lodger new life.

As a way to release a torrent of energy swelling inside him, Bride ran the seven blocks to the London Hall of Records. A trip that had taken him nearly twenty minutes earlier that evening now took him only five.

It was half past seven when the night watchman at the Hall of Records answered Bride's furious pounding on the front door.

"We're closed!" he bellowed to the breathless man standing on the front stairs. "Come back tomorrow!"

He started to slam the giant door shut when Bride shoved his foot in the way. "You have to let me in!" wheezed a winded Bride.

"Oh I do, do I?" retorted the night watchman. "And why would that be exactly?"

"My mother's in there!" he gasped.

It had been a repeated blessing for Bride that he was born with a face that reeked of sincerity. It had won him extensions on term paper deadlines, convinced more than one young lady to accept his social invitations, and eased the way for apologies when he sometimes forgot to keep them. As the night watchman gazed down from his position of power, that sincere face was about to pay off again. Within moments Bride had given the man an abridged version of his tale and was being politely escorted back into the grand sepulcher of record books.

Bride slammed the 1945 volume back onto the table, barely able to contain himself, for now he knew what he was surely going to find. He flopped open the pages to the *A* section and quickly rummaged forward. And finally, there she was, rising off the page as if illuminated. His mother, Bridget Barrow Allison. Triggered by Rumpole's casual musing, his suspicions had been born out; Alfred and Maria Martelli had inadvertently transposed the name Bride Allison after reading it on the medical chart with the last name listed first. A single missing comma had nearly stood between Malcolm Bride and the truth.

Bride was experiencing one of those rare instances when you are so overwhelmed with joy that you want to hug someone, anyone, even a perfect stranger. But there he stood, all alone to share this watershed moment with no one. And yet, he was not alone anymore. Bridget Barrow Allison had found her son.

In all of his excitement, he hadn't immediately noticed that there was more information next to his mother's name than he had anticipated. There were in fact two names listed on the ledger beside Bridget Allison's, two sons born to her on March 16, 1945. Twins, one Malcolm Barrow, one Michael James.

Any sudden hopes that Malcolm Barrow Bride had a twin brother out there somewhere were quickly dashed when he scanned the recorded deaths for that same year. On a single day in March of 1945, baby Michael James Allison had known three worlds—his mother's womb, a birthing room, and the life hereafter. Bride's tumultuous happiness over his original discovery was now balanced by the grim news of his sibling. In the space of a few minutes, he had found his mother and lost a brother.

Chapter Four

*T*icking bombs are the most cowardly of weapons. They offer absolutely no chance of defense. No time to react, no opportunity for last second heroics.

They don't even provide the victim the dignity of staring at his killer face to face. It is the element of total surprise that makes the ticking bomb so effective. When its time is up, so is everyone else's within its sudden and deadly grasp.

On this rainy London night, the pub known as the Strangers' Bar of the Commons was living up to its reputation as the Kremlin because so many Members of Parliament from Britain's Conservative Party were gathered there. The Tory powerbrokers seemed to accomplish considerably more over a few pints at their favorite watering hole than over the roundtables at their headquarters.

A dozen of the most influential Conservatives were huddled in a corner of the pub to discuss strategy for the upcoming national elections. The Tories had finally decided to put aside their bitter infighting and present a united front to the voters. In recent years, the Conservative MP's had spent so much time destroying each other to gain control of their own party that they were decimated by the Labourites and Liberal Democrats in the run-up to the general election. This time it would be different. The man they felt had the best chance of leading the party to victory would be decided upon right there and then.

Three men were logical candidates for the job and all of them were there. One by one, all eyes focused on Reg Bottomley of Gloucester, currently the party's spokesman for domestic affairs. His reputation was pristine, his record as a modernist lawmaker impressive, and his courage to stand up to the hated Labour Party was unchallenged. In the midst of clinking pint glasses and thick cigar smoke, the matter was settled; Bottomley had been anointed. He would run unopposed in the upcoming party vote and receive solid support in the general election as the Conservatives tried to regain their grip on power they had held for so long but now enjoyed by the ruling Labourites.

Bottomley hoisted his mug of Federated Ale and saluted his colleagues. It would be his final drink.

Without warning, a massive explosion ripped through the Strangers' Bar of the Commons, destroying hardwood, glass, and the immediate future of the Conservative Party.

Chapter Five

As an unabashed lover of life, wandering in graveyards wasn't something Malcolm Bride particularly enjoyed. Contrary to his affection for history, cemeteries tended to remind him of his own mortality and that was a notion he would just as soon postpone until he was certain his time was up.

In fact, he had often wondered why cemeteries were necessary at all. Why spend so much money and attention on the dead when there's so much that needs to be done amongst the living?

Perhaps he was simply overreacting to his surroundings. For the last two days, from dawn to dusk, he had trudged through what seemed like every burial ground and plague pit from Chigwick to Chiswell. He had read epitaphs at Highgate and Kensal Green, and discovered the graves of Blake, Freud, and Thackeray, but the search for his brother's final resting place had up to this point been futile. As he entered the iron gate surrounding the graveyard behind St. Bartholomew's Church, dusk was quickly giving way to darkness and he had no reason to believe he wouldn't be in for a third day of searching come tomorrow.

Bride wandered through the marble and granite headstones, searching for clues. In an obscure corner of the lot, underneath the sprawling branches of an ancient yew, stood a weatherworn marker. The head of a lamb had been carved into the top of the simple stone, but the remaining slate was blank.

This headstone had fared better than most around it, perhaps protected by the waxy needles of the overhanging yew. But even in the fading light of nightfall, Bride could tell it had periodically been scrubbed to remove the lichens and industrial soot. Someone still cared about the person who was laid to rest in the earth beneath his feet.

Bride discontinued his search for another day and walked slowly toward the front gate as the last glimpses of daylight faded into the London night. As he turned his collar up against the light fog that was rolling in, he knew that his weary legs would sleep well that night. Tomorrow he would try again.

The random timing and juxtaposition of life's little events so often have a profound effect on one's future. Had you left the house fifteen seconds earlier, you might not have been rear-ended by the careless man reading a map in the car behind you. Had you not missed your first bus, you might never have struck up a conversation with the charming young woman on the next bus who would later become your wife. Malcolm Bride was about to become entangled in the collision of two unrelated events that just happened to occur at the same moment in time.

He pushed on the cemetery's heavy iron gate to let himself out, but nothing in the way of an exit made itself known to him. His next instinct was to pull on the gate, but again he remained caged within the confines of St. Bartholomew's graveyard. He went so far as to lean over the railing to look for some hidden latch that he hadn't bothered to notice during his entry. Still, he was on the wrong side of the fence. He pushed harder, then pulled harder, then searched again for the phantom latch. It was only after a full minute of fumbling in the dark and thickening foggy mist that Bride suddenly realized he had been wrangling with the wrong side of the gate. With embarrassment that only he had to endure, he slid four feet to his left and pushed on the gate. It magically flung itself open and delivered its prisoner from his own private purgatory.

Bride laughed to himself over his ineptitude and started to walk through the open gate when suddenly the headlamps of a car bathed him with filtered light.

A long, black limousine came to a stop on the gravel service road in the rear of the cemetery. He watched silently as a figure climbed out of the rear passenger door and entered an obscured gateway in the rear of the graveyard. Bride could tell it was a woman simply by the graceful manner in which she moved.

Silently, he moved back inside the fence to get a better look at the strange visitor. As he crept between the headstones, his footsteps were muffled by the carpet of heavy grass and the blanket of fog that had so swiftly engulfed the burial ground. As he approached to within thirty feet, still undetected, he stopped as the mysterious woman knelt by the unmarked grave in the corner where Bride had been just moments before.

He peered through the murk as she laid a fresh bouquet of flowers by the headstone. He could detect their gentle aroma in the air as his heightened sense of smell compensated for his limited vision. The woman murmured what sounded like a short prayer or Bible verse, followed by the unmistakable sound of someone crying to release the anguish of a deep and intense sorrow. Bride saw a flash of white against her dark topcoat as she pulled out a handkerchief to dry her eyes. She slowly arose from her kneeling position and the white handkerchief disappeared into her pocket as she started to leave.

Suddenly, she turned back and returned to the area surrounding the marble headstone, bending down and rummaging through the grass as if searching for something she'd dropped. Bride inched closer to get a better look. A twig snapped under his foot, betraying his voyeurism.

The startled woman spun around, peering into the blackness.

"Who's there?" she called out in a refined British accent.

Bride stealthily ducked behind a large marble obelisk, simultaneously panicked and embarrassed over his secret intrusion. What was he going to do? He could make a run for it and hope the gate would be kinder to him this time around, or he could hold his ground and pray that the shroud of night and fog would keep him hidden from further detection.

"Is someone there?" she cried out again with a higher pitch in her voice that indicated a tinge of fear.

Bride remained in hiding behind the obelisk, his heart pounding so loudly that he was certain it would give him away, perhaps even wake the dead around him. He silently prayed that the mystery woman would give up on him and provide a merciful end to this impromptu misadventure. By either divine intervention or mere coincidence, his prayer was immediately answered as someone climbed out of the parked car just outside the fence.

"Is there a problem, ma'am?" said a man with a guttural Scottish tone that emphasized his concern for her well being.

"We'd best be going," she quietly responded as she slipped back through the rear gate and quickly made her way back to the waiting car.

Bride heard two doors slam shut. The car roared to life and spit gravel as it rapidly departed the scene. By the time Bride dared to venture from his hiding place, the red of the taillights had vanished into the evening fog.

He moved swiftly back to the unmarked grave where the woman had been kneeling. A handful of freshly cut violets lay peacefully at the base of the headstone. Bride held them up and smelled them, noticing that they were virtually odorless. He now realized the enchanting aroma that lingered in the air was the scent of the mystery woman herself. It was forever burned into his memory.

Addled by the strange events of the last few minutes, Bride shook his head and replaced the flowers. He took two steps and felt something hard under his foot. His hand reached into the thick, moist grass and retrieved an enameled box, about the size and shape of a deck of cards. This was clearly what the woman had been searching for in the dark, he thought, most likely dropped when she reached for her handkerchief.

It suddenly occurred to him to vacate the premises as quickly as possible, partly out of fear that the lady might return, and partly because his dislike of graveyards in the broad of day was trebled with the coming of night.

Chapter Six

Lithesome young girls twisted and writhed to the pulsating music as they dangled in chrome cages from the ceiling of The Crypt, the flashpoint of London's underground club scene.

It was a futuristic Babylon trimmed with black leather, throbbing lights, and a full spectrum of hair color. The senses were bombarded by the sight of women in black lipstick and teardrop tattoos, waiters wearing women's lingerie, and earrings protruding from assorted facial features including tongues and eyelids. The stench of alcohol and the residue of narcotics stained the low slung couches spread among the low light of the corners. It was an orgy worthy of high praise from Bacchus himself.

The most famous and among the most frequent visitors to this high-tech opium den known as The Crypt was Prince John of the House of Windsor.

If every family has a black sheep that causes it constant duress and embarrassment, then Prince John was an entire flock. John had been dubbed "Black Jack" by the Fleet Street tabloids for his brooding demeanor and style of dress, a title he thoroughly enjoyed and helped to perpetuate.

The youngest of the Royal children and the second of the sons, his existence in the grand scheme of the monarchy was to be nothing more than second in line to the Crown, described in the papers in unflattering terms as "the spare to the heir." He had no official responsibilities and therefore assumed no personal ones other than to torment members of the palace staff with his rude and childishly indolent behavior for no other reason than he could.

His position as a member of the Royal Family not only gave the servants no recourse but to obey his whims, it also sent family members and Royal publicists scrambling to cover up several decades of decadence.

Prince John had been quietly expelled from Gordonstoun, which was explained away as "a return home to receive private tutoring." He was caught cheating in his one and only year at Cambridge, but received only a slight reprimand in a closed-door session. The Crown avoided further disgrace when John was on the verge of a dishonorable discharge from the Marines for using illicit drugs and insubordination among other crimes. The Queen's personal physician stepped in with a sudden diagnosis of some obscure liver disorder, which granted the Prince a medical discharge. It obviously wasn't the truth, but it was an explanation the British public could live with.

John's only self worth was found in indulgence in the seamier side of life, or more correctly overindulgence. From the time he was kicked out of boarding school at the age of sixteen, his apartment at Buckingham Palace had become a haven for drug dealers, underground rock stars, groupies, and prostitutes of both sexes.

In day to day matters regarding her youngest, the Queen had chosen simply to look the other way because John made no attempts to hide his uncontrolled appetite for sinful living. The only measure she had taken to prevent her youngest child from completely self-destructing was to cut back on his substantial allowance. This maneuver had forced John to finance his vices in more creative ways, and selling information was one of them.

Prince John broke away from his circle of miscreant friends and made his way toward the back of the enormous room. No one along the way seemed overly impressed with his celebrity. This collection of the dark side of humanity was the closest thing John had to a family and he delighted in his status as one of their equals.

He entered a small room with black walls and huge pillows scattered across the carpeted floor. The two couples already inside were paying no attention to the bank of video monitors blazing in the corner. The only other person in the room was a man who looked freakishly out of place in a poplin suit and knit tie. He was Nigel Banks-Finch, a reporter for the *Sun-Times* tabloid. This prearranged rendezvous was clearly not the first time these two had met under clandestine circumstances. The pasty and slightly rotund reporter pulled out a pad and paper as they sat down on some pillows in the corner.

"What have you got for me today?" asked Banks-Finch.

John leaned in closer to keep his remarks between them. "Lord and Lady Hibberley are getting a divorce. Apparently he's developed quite a fondness for their new nanny."

Banks-Finch shook his head in dismay. "Who cares about them? Nobody cares about minor Royals. What else?"

Prince John instantly deflated. He had hoped that morsel about his very distant cousins was going to be enough to satisfy Banks-Finch, but the competition among the tabloids for sordid details was so rabid that only the most startling revelations carried any weight anymore.

Like his journalistic confederates, however, John wasn't above making up a story when the truth wouldn't sell any papers. He was about to fabricate a bold-faced lie, knowing full well it would be headlines the next day.

"Well," he began, glancing around as if to insure their privacy. "I'm not supposed to know this, but I hear that Mother is quite a bit sicker than anyone is letting on. They keep saying it's pneumonia, but I think it could be cancer."

"Really?" gulped the reporter as he scribbled feverishly on his pad. "Now this is something I can use. You're certain?"

"Would I make up something like that about my own mother?"

"This is good. This is very good."

"Do you want any details?"

"No, I can fill it in from here. Try to pinch a copy of her medical reports if you can."

"Absolutely. Now then, payment?"

"Yes, yes of course."

Banks-Finch closed his notepad and tucked it away. From his breast pocket he pulled out a brown paper bag and handed it to John.

The Prince opened the outer wrapping and revealed a plastic bag of snow white cocaine. "See you Thursday," he said with a gleam.

"Indeed," replied Banks-Finch as he departed.

Both men would leave the meeting with a measure of success. Banks-Finch with an ounce of truth, Prince John with an ounce of narcotic, and neither with an ounce of remorse.

◆ ◆ ◆

John Hackney looked like a character out of Charles Dickens' London. He could have been Marley or Fagin with his bony facial features, scraggly gray hair, and a moth-eaten wool sweater.

He pushed his bifocals tighter onto the bridge of his hooked nose

and narrowed his beady eyes. In forty-seven years of owning his jew-
elry store on the North side of Leicester Square, he had never seen
anything like it. A pillbox with blue Celtic enameling and bone inlay,
highlighted Brazilian topaz on the corners and solid gold push pieces.

"Hmmm," murmured Hackney as he inspected every detail.

Bride leaned over the glass counter, waiting for the verdict. "Well?"
he inquired impatiently. "What do you make of it?"

"Where did you say you got this pillbox?" he asked Bride.

"I found it."

"Found it?" he asked with a hint of suspicion.

"That's right," said Bride, slightly indignant over the veiled accusation.

"Well, what you have here appears to be a wonderfully crafted
forgery," announced the jeweler.

"It's a fake?"

"Has to be."

"Why does it have to be?"

Hackney held up his index finger and nodded his head, to let Bride
know a substantiated answer was forthcoming. He rummaged through
a stack of catalogs under the cabinets in the rear of the shop and finally pulled out the one he wanted. Like a barrister presenting evidence to the court, he flopped the catalog onto the countertop and
thumbed through the pages. He stopped on a page with a dozen or so
photos of pillboxes and pointed ceremoniously to one that looked
exactly like the one Bride had found in the cemetery.

"This is the genuine article here—a Cartier pillbox, and a rare item
indeed. They made only a handful of them back in the 1860s, and as
far as I know they're all in either museums or private Royal collec-
tions. Worth somewhere in the neighborhood of fifteen thousand
pounds, so hardly the kind of thing a tourist might up and find on a
jaunt through the park, know what I mean?"

"I see," said Bride.

"Don't be too upset, though. It's an excellent piece of workman-
ship for a forgery, and might fetch you a few quid at auction."

"No thanks," said Bride, putting the pillbox back in his pocket.
"It'll make a nice souvenir of my visit. Thanks for your time."

Bride ambled out of the shop, feigning disappointment. He made
his way through the morning throng and found a park bench.

He pulled the pillbox out of his pocket and examined it once again,
but now with a greater reverence, because he alone knew this was no
forgery. The question before him now was "Who was the mysterious

woman from the night before?" He was beginning to think he knew.

The giggling of two schoolgirls echoed from behind the curtain of the photo booth in Covent Garden as Bride waited patiently outside for his turn. With a national treasure worth $50,000 clutched in his hand, he was suddenly now much more conscious about drawing any attention to himself. The girls finally emerged from their photo session and collected their miniature polaroids from the receptacle outside. Bride nodded politely to the girls as they squealed their way down the sidewalk, then casually slipped inside the booth.

This was ideal for his purposes. He dropped his money into the coin slot and pressed a button, then quickly straightened the hair hanging over his forehead, as if aesthetics played any role in all of this. He held the pillbox next to his cheek like a commercial spokesman selling a new brand of toothpaste and waited for the four camera flashes to capture him on film.

Seconds later, his photos were dropping into the receptacle outside the booth. Bride quickly scooped them up and walked away as they developed before his eyes. He decided that the third shot was far and away the best, and would be the one he would present when the time came. He tucked them into his breastpocket and strode calmly away as if he'd just pulled off the white-collar crime of the century.

A polite crowd of nearly two hundred gathered on the sidewalk outside the newly opened Kensington Animal Refuge. A light rain didn't deter them because they were waiting to catch a glimpse of Britain's most beloved Royal, Princess Catherine. In an age where scandal and embarrassment had rocked the House of Windsor, Princess Catherine had always managed to remain above the fray, escaping the growing criticisms of the Fleet Street journals and the biting intrusions of the tabloids.

Catherine was a study in contrasts. She carried herself like the royalty she was, but one could easily picture her gallivanting through the hay in the barn like a young farm lass. She vacillated between her public image as the demure and lovable Princess, and a shy, insecure schoolgirl, always stopping at mirrors to see if she'd done as much as she could do with the modest natural beauty that God had given her.

She had just marked her 61st birthday, but gray had not yet mingled with her auburn hair, and a pleasant smile smoothed over the wrinkles she had accumulated from years of public scrutiny and personal tragedy.

Professor Bride was among the crowd gathered for the dedication ceremony, but his purpose in being there was undoubtedly different from all the others. Taking advantage of his relative height, Bride peered over the blanket of umbrellas. With little fanfare, Princess Catherine walked onto a makeshift stage and stood comfortably behind the podium.

From the instant he saw her graceful movements, Bride knew this was the same woman he had seen in the cemetery. His only question now was "what was she doing there?" and he intended to find out. As he pushed his way to the front of the crowd, he caught only snippets of her speech that contained references to "all creatures great and small."

After several minutes and a cascade of "beg your pardons", Bride had forced his way up to the velvet ropes in front of the stage, five feet from where the Princess was speaking. He was close enough to detect a hint of her perfume, and immediately recognized it as the same regal scent he had savored in the cemetery at St. Bartholomew's. Catherine's traitorous perfume had no loyalty to the Crown, and unknowingly confirmed all of Malcolm Bride's suspicions.

Catherine closed out her remarks with a polite wave and a warm smile for the gathering and descended the stage. As she exited, Bride boldly leaned over the restraining ropes and begged for her attention.

"Your Highness!" he called out above the applause. The words sounded strange to him, having never before passed his lips.

She was paying no heed to his call as she shook hands with various dignitaries from the RSPCA, either by choice or from years of ignoring thousands of subjects clamoring for her undivided attention.

"Excuse me! Your Highness! I need to speak with you!" he yelled with more volume.

Something suddenly clamped down on his arm, powerful and numbing, like a tourniquet. It was the meaty right hand of one Trevor McFarlane.

"Is there a problem, mate?" he scowled as he tightened his grip.

Before he even saw his face, Bride immediately recognized Trevor's thick Scottish accent as belonging to the driver of the car at the graveyard. He turned to see a stocky man nearly a head shorter than himself latched onto his bicep like a bear trap.

If you were going to engage in a barroom brawl, Trevor McFarlane would be your first choice for someone you would want on your side. Nearly as wide as he was tall, his arms burst out from his trenchcoat, bulging with the kind of muscles you can only get from hard work.

Trevor's physique was developed as a youth spent rowing a barge along the Thames, and in a way he reminded you of the mighty river—strong, powerful, always moving, and never quite sure what lay beneath his surface. And like the river, he could at once be your best friend or your worst enemy if you dared to tangle with its swift current.

He had no formal training as a bodyguard but was supremely qualified to perform as one. He had faced death countless times and refused to succumb to it as a Sergeant in the Royal Scots, a regiment known in the theater of war as "The Ladies From Hell" in reference to their kilts.

Squaring up to a boisterous tourist was almost a pleasure for Trevor McFarlane. His face twitched and his nostrils flared as he stared at a very startled Malcolm Bride. "I asked you a question! You gotta problem?" he said with hair-trigger temper.

"No, not at all!" said Bride. Trevor relaxed his grip a notch. "Well, actually, yes, I do," he continued. Trevor's squeeze grew tighter once again. "I want to speak to the Princess."

"Don't we all," sneered Trevor.

"It's not that I necessarily want to, although I do want to, it's more a matter of I *need* to speak to her. Confidentially, of course."

"Oh, of course!" said Trevor with a sarcastic grin. "And then maybe ya would like to go on a picnic in the Berkshires." His eyes flared with renewed anger. "My advice to you, mate, is go home and learn some proper manners, or else I'll have to teach you some on the spot!"

With that, Trevor released his grip on Bride's arm and backed away. Undaunted, Bride reached into his pocket and produced one of the pictures from the photo booth. He held it straight out so Trevor could plainly see the image of the Cartier pillbox.

"Perhaps this might change her mind," said Bride.

Trevor's steely eyes widened in shock. He took three swift paces forward and snatched the photo out of Bride's extended hand.

"I'm staying at the Dunbarton. My name and phone number are written on the back."

Trevor didn't say a word as he pocketed the photograph and instinctively moved closer to Catherine's side. She had been completely unaware of their exchange, but Bride felt confident that his mission had been accomplished.

♦ ♦ ♦

Fionnuala Rumpole was just setting a steaming mincemeat pie on the supper table when the telephone rang.

"I'll get it," she told her husband and their American guest as she vanished into the front hallway.

Bride held the dish in place as Rumpole sliced through the thick mincemeat, his mouth watering.

"Nothin' like the wife's mincemeat pie, I tell ya. God put that woman on this earth to cook," said Rumpole.

Fionnuala came back into the dining room, checking out her one and only lodger with mock suspicion. "It's for you," she said to Bride.

"Me?"

"'At's right. And, it's a lady."

"A woman?" asked Rumpole.

"Not a woman," she retorted. "A lady."

Bride shrugged his shoulders as if he had no idea who could be calling him, hiding his suppositions.

"Excuse me," he said politely, dabbing the corners of his mouth with his napkin as he stood up from the table and departed for the phone in the hallway.

"Now that's a piece of piss," muttered Rumpole. "The man's in town for less than a week and already he's got some bird trackin' him down. I should be so lucky."

Fionnuala whacked him across the crown with a tea towel. He grabbed her apron strings and reeled her back onto his lap, then wrapped his arms around her and bussed the only woman he had ever loved.

In the hallway, Bride wiped away the beads of perspiration that had made a sudden entrance on his forehead as he pressed the receiver up to his ear.

"Yes, yes, I think I know the place. I'm sure I can find it," he said to the voice on the other end. "Ten o'clock tomorrow is fine. Ten in the morning, right? Yes, of course. You have my promise, not a word to anyone. I'll see you then." Bride stared straight ahead, dazed as he hung up the telephone.

"Who was that?" asked Rumpole as Bride made his way back into the dining room.

"Oh, that?" said Bride, stalling for time as he attempted to restore some semblance of normalcy to his ruffled outward appearance.

A dilemma had invaded the conversation. Bride knew that of all the answers he could give, the truth wasn't one of them. There were questions of privacy and security to be considered. A vow of secrecy had been made. But Bride couldn't remember the last time he had told a brazen lie. He vaguely recalled a wild story he'd once told his high school wrestling coach to explain why he'd missed practice, but in Bride's mind that had actually been less telling of a lie and more a reorganization of the facts to his advantage. Lying simply wasn't one of the colors on Bride's palette, but if he was going to work his way out of this corner into which he was painted, he was going to have to blend the hues that were there until they could cover his tracks.

"That was the clerk at the Antiquarian and Second Hand bookstore," he boldly announced. "She was calling to let me know she's tracked down a volume of Walt Whitman's *Leaves of Grass* that I wanted."

"Well that's lovely, it is," said Rumpole. Bride didn't see his disbelieving wink at Fionnuala.

Bride filled his fork with mincemeat pie and guided it into a mouth that was already opened by a subtle smile. For his first real lie as an adult, he thought, it seemed to go rather well.

Years ago, when the evening meal was finished at the Dunbarton, the tradition for the guests was to retire to the sitting room for either a good book or a lively conversation. By now, the sitting room was called a den and the activity there had been reduced to watching television.

"According to the most recent figures from the Henley Center for Forecasting" said the BBC announcer on the screen, "the economic picture appears bleak. In the three year span from 1999 to 2002, there has been a 300% increase in mortgage repossessions in the Commonwealth. In the first quarter of this year, there have been over 3,000 business failures in London alone. Conservative Party spokesman Robert McGuire said today that these figures show the economic policies of the Labour Party are failing, but with the Labourites widening their gap in the most recent polling, it would appear that few voters agree with him."

"You have an election coming up?" Bride asked Rumpole.

"Next month, though I don't know why we bother. I can tell you right now what's going to happen."

"What's that?"

"Labour will win again, they'll make Philip Roth Prime Minister again, the Tories'll pound on him again for another five years and once again nothin' will get done. Jolly ole England, where nothin' ever changes. Bloody hell."

Rumpole became so disgusted as he looked out across the political landscape that he jumped up from the couch and shut off the television.

"Goodnight, Dr. Bride," he said as he abruptly left the den.

"Goodnight, Rumpole."

Bride remained alone in the den, appreciating the sudden quietude of the room. The absence of distractions allowed him to focus on his meeting the next day with the lady on the telephone. He had that curious mix of excitement and fear like a teenager on his way to his first real date. His mother would call it "journey proud" when he was too excited to sleep before going off to summer camp. He wondered over and over what an authentic Princess would be like.

Indecision was about to make Bride late for the most important meeting of his adult life. He had already cost himself nearly ten full minutes from a nervous razor hand that had left his face badly nicked and covered with bloody bits of toilet tissue. A debate between the blue tweed and the brown herringbone blazers had taken another fifteen, and now he was paralyzed as he weighed the virtues of the knit club tie against the red silk foulard. Thank goodness he had only packed powder blue dress shirts or he might never have escaped the Dunbarton's Room One.

It was a rare sunny morning in London as Bride stepped quickly down the sidewalk, having finally decided on the blue blazer and red tie. Within moments he had arrived at Bedford Square, a circular grove of towering sycamores in the heart of Bloomsbury, surrounded by a tall iron fence with sharp spears along the top.

It was only fitting that difficulties with a balky fence gate had led to Bride's initial encounter with Princess Catherine because a similar situation presented itself as he arrived several minutes late for his scheduled rendezvous. The small sign on the gateway said "Private Park", a small detail Her Highness had neglected to mention on the phone the night before. When one has unlimited access to a city, he thought, one probably forgets such things.

His watch already read six minutes after ten o'clock, which ruled out any chance of gaining entry to the hallowed ground by applying for membership and securing a key. With scarcely a moment's hesitation, Bride found himself scaling the fence, carefully negotiating the spikes on top. He couldn't recall any other such blatant act of civil disobedience, but then again this was no ordinary situation and therefore demanded whatever drastic measures necessary.

He landed on the other side with a resounding thud and brushed off traces of rust from his blazer.

It was under a gazebo in the west end of the park that the professor came face to face with the Princess. Trevor, her stocky driver and bodyguard, stood watch from the shadows of the branches across the park, motionless except for his piercing eyes that followed Bride's every move.

"I don't see your car," blurted Bride. It was out of his mouth before he had a chance to think of something more profound.

"Good drivers are well practiced at hiding their vehicles. They have always been confederates in the indiscretions of their riders."

Bride nodded his head, unable to think of any intelligent rejoinder. He could tell that things were not off to a rousing start. "It's nice to meet you, Your Highness," he finally offered.

"And good morning to you, Mr. Bride. Please, sit down."

"Thank you," said Bride as he sat on the bench as far away from her as the side railing would let him. "And actually, it's Dr. Bride, but you can call me Malcolm. Well, you can call me anything you like. May I call you Catherine?"

"No, you may not," she responded quickly but politely. "Are you a physician, Dr. Bride?"

"Uh, no. Doctorate in American history."

"I see," said Catherine with a hint of remorse.

He nodded without real purpose, just to fill the silent void. It's not often that a man goes from being an ordinary history teacher to having a private audience with a member of the Royal family, and the normally talkative professor discovered he was ill-equipped to carry on small talk under the circumstances. The sweet fragrance of her perfume was distracting enough without the external pressures thrust upon him. Not wanting to cut his visit short, but at a complete loss for words, Bride went straight to the business at hand. He reached into his blazer and pulled out the Cartier pillbox.

"I'm returning this. I feel certain it's yours."

Catherine said neither yes nor no, but simply extended her delicate hand and allowed Bride to place the box into her open palm. Without ceremony or hesitation, she put it in her handbag.

"Thank you," she whispered.

"I'm sorry I opted for such a clandestine method of going about all this, but I wanted to make certain I had the right owner, and I didn't want you to have to worry about it falling into the wrong hands."

"I appreciate your kindness. I suppose now you want to discuss remuneration for your troubles?"

"Oh, no, no, absolutely not!" he replied with urgency. "The box belongs to you, and that's that. I wouldn't consider monetary compensation, not even for a minute."

"Your honesty is noble."

"Well, before we go about knighting me, there *is* something I want."

"Oh?"

Bride pondered for a moment the best way to approach such a delicate matter. He proceeded cautiously. "I would like to know, if you can tell me, why were you so frightened in the cemetery that night?"

"Graveyards frighten me."

"So why would you go to one at night?"

His question was not well received. Catherine gazed off in the opposite direction, the gentleness disappearing from her face. "Dr. Bride, I was polite enough to not ask what you were doing lurking about in the graveyard spying on me, so suffice it to say that I don't feel any obligation to explain my presence there."

Bride felt perfectly awful, but even in the company of Royalty, his need to know again superseded his attention to etiquette.

"Ordinarily, I wouldn't pry into your affairs, or anyone else's for that matter, but the grave you visited, the one where you left the flowers... I was just curious as to why a member of the Royal family would make a pilgrimage to an unmarked grave. Who's buried there? Can you at least tell me that much? Is it someone famous?"

Even a woman trained to brace herself in the face of any national crisis could not completely hide her trembling. Bride's words had clearly struck a nerve deep within her, and he was immediately sorry he'd proceeded so far with this line of questioning. Catherine clutched her handbag and rose to her feet, visibly shaken. Bride stood up to face her.

"You have done me a great favor by returning my property, Dr. Bride. I'm sorry that I'm unable to repay you."

With that, she walked briskly across the park to the gate. Bride stood motionless by the gazebo, watching as her long, black limousine appeared from nowhere. Trevor suddenly leapt from the driver's seat and opened her door. Even from fifty yards away, Bride could sense the driver's anger towards him. In an instant, they were gone. It had not been the happiest of endings to Bride's first encounter with nobility. As Catherine's scent lingered in the air, he prayed he would get another chance.

Chapter Seven

Colin Crowe was smart enough to be a doctor, clever enough to be an attorney, handsome enough to be an actor, and gregarious enough to be a first-rate salesman. With all of his natural attributes, it's no wonder his parents were more than a little disappointed when, at the age of eighteen, he announced that he wanted to be a radio broadcaster.

Through diligence, countless early mornings, and a bit of luck, Crowe was one of those rare few in this world who proceeded to do exactly what he originally set out to do. In the fourteen years since his graduation from Cambridge, Crowe had steadily risen through the ranks at BBC's Radio 4. A career that began as an assistant to an assistant on *Farming Today* had led to positions as studio manager, tape editor, acting editor for *Kaleidoscope*, writer on *Start the Week*, and finally political correspondent for *The World at One*.

Crowe's journalistic wanderings and ever-changing schedule had allowed him to develop several talents. He could handle any story, from animal husbandry to global economic summits, with equal aplomb. He had used every precious spare minute to study and make himself into an expert on British history, the monarchy, and parliamentary procedure. He could last seemingly for days without a solid meal or a good night's sleep. And best of all, he could get out of bed, shower, dress in his standard jacket, starched shirt and tie, and be out of his flat in Marylebone and on his way to BBC Broadcasting House in just a tick over thirteen minutes, shaving in the car on his way there.

The pace at which Crowe drove himself also had its drawbacks. He had never shared a romantic relationship with a woman that lasted more than two months, and his chain smoking was legendary. But all things considered, Colin Crowe led a good life. He was well liked by his colleagues, respected by Members of Parliament, and adored by legions of faithful listeners on Radio 4.

His most recent promotion was the prestigious post of anchoring *The World at One* every Friday. Crowe enjoyed the constant buzz of activity in the long magnolia halls of Broadcasting House, but he was most alive as a field reporter.

He filed his live reports and actualities from the back of a black taxicab that had been converted to a mobile sound studio. The power would go on, the giant antenna mast would go up, and Crowe would take his place behind the microphone to deliver his latest nuggets of political intrigue. It was one thing to read the news, but quite another to actually go out and uncover it. It made him feel less an observer and more a participant in the spin of the globe.

Crowe split time between Parliament, 10 Downing Street, and the pubs on the West End. He figured that somewhere between all these places he could distill the essence of what was really important in the modern political world. He loved lively conversation on virtually any topic and thought nothing of buying a perfect stranger a pint or two just for the privilege of listening to what the man had to say.

It was natural curiosity that put Crowe on the trail of Malcolm Bride. Even on Saturday, his day off, he was chasing down a hunch and hoping to turn it into a story. He had no idea what the story might be, but his sixth sense told him it would be worth the trouble to track down the American professor.

Crowe stood across the street outside the Dunbarton for over an hour, the butts of nine cigarettes at his feet. Finally, Bride emerged.

It has to look coincidental, Crowe reminded himself as he followed behind at a safe distance.

He tailed Bride for nearly six blocks, almost losing him in a sudden burst of people exiting from the underground on Tottenham Court Road. Bride finally reached his destination, a bookstore on Charing Cross. Crowe jaywalked quickly across the street and followed Bride inside.

The bookstore was crowded and Crowe didn't immediately see Bride. He meandered through the stacks, searching for his prey, occasionally picking up a book at random to give the appearance that he actually had business there. He finally spotted him, browsing through the section marked 'Historical Reference'. The reporter subtly worked his way through the 'Travel' and 'Gardening' sections until he stood nearly abreast to Bride. He pretended to scan the pages of a paperback with a picture of the late Prince Albert on the cover, casually glancing sideways to read the cover of Bride's selection, *House of Windsor.*

"Fascinating, isn't it?" offered up Crowe without taking his eyes off his open text.

"Excuse me?" replied Bride, apparently unsure if he was the intended target of conversation.

"Oh, I was just thinking out loud about all of the great figures of history, and how they all have at least a dozen books written about them. I don't suppose I shall ever reach a status that would warrant much more than a paragraph in the obituary section."

"You could always write an autobiography," joked Bride.

"Yes, I suppose. But who would publish it? Let alone read it!" laughed Crowe as he returned the Prince Albert volume.

Bride kept reading, unwilling to add any more to the conversation with the intruding stranger.

Crowe took the initiative again. "You're an American, am I correct?" he continued.

"That's right."

"Wonderful country, America. I've visited New York City, and spent a night in Raleigh, North Carolina, but sadly that's been the extent of my travels there. I would love to see the Mississippi just once, flowing at full bore. I've heard it puts our Thames to shame. Have you seen the Mississippi?"

Bride quietly closed his book and returned it to the shelf. He turned slowly to Crowe and raised one eyebrow. "Is that why you followed me all the way from my hotel? To talk about the Mississippi?"

Crowe instantly blushed a deep crimson. He'd been checkmated at his own game. He reached for the security of a cigarette.

"No smoking," admonished Bride, pointing to the sign above the door.

Crowe returned his cigarettes to his pocket. He took a deep breath, trying to compose himself after this unfortunate turn of events. "And you let me go on with my charade. I don't know which of us should be more embarrassed."

"I should think you."

"Yes. Quite."

"What are you after? Are you trying to sell me something? Are you representing some harem of prostitutes? Because if you are, I'm not interested."

"No, no, no, mate, nothing of the sort! I'm a reporter. Colin Crowe, Radio 4." He extended his hand. Bride reluctantly shook it.

"So what's newsworthy about me?" asked Bride.

"That's what I'd like to know," answered Crowe. "There's a pub just 'round the corner. All I'm asking is fifteen minutes of your time, then I'm on my way. What do you say?"

Five minutes later Crowe and Bride were taking a seat at the bar in the Marlborough Arms. It was filled with cigarette smoke from the noontime crowd and Crowe quickly added to the haze. He flagged the bartender's attention.

"Coupla Scotches here, Mick," Crowe called out. The hulking bartender nodded and quickly set up two Glenlivets on the rocks. Bride nodded his thanks and clinked glasses with the reporter.

"Cheers," said Crowe. "Now then, I don't mind drinking with strangers, but I prefer the company of friends, so why don't you start by telling me your name?"

"Bride. Malcolm Bride. How'd you know I was a Scotch drinker?"

"We Scotch drinkers all have an unmistakable air about us, don't you think? Worldly, ruggedly handsome, a certain erudition," said Crowe with a wink and a healthy sip from his glass.

Bride couldn't help but smile. "You have fourteen minutes left to tell me why a reporter from BBC Radio 4 is following a simple professor on vacation."

"Well, you've helped frame my question. You see, a few days ago I'm doing a favor for a lady friend of mine who produces one of our programs, *Woman's Hour*, which led me to covering the ribbon cutting ceremony at the new animal shelter in Kensington. One never knows when one of the Royals might actually say something important, but once again I was disappointed. Until, I observed from a casual distance, a commoner trying desperately to seize Princess Catherine's attention and immediately being fended off by one of Her Majesty's bodyguards.

"Subsequently, this same man with the American accent handed the bodyguard a slip of paper or something of the sort, the contents of which had a profound effect on the aforementioned bodyguard. So then, my question to you, is why a self-described 'simple professor' on holiday is accosting a member of our Royal family, and what could you possibly hand to an ex-marine that would make him turn as pale as the white cliffs of Dover?" Crowe took another long draw on his Scotch as he waited for a reply.

"How in the world did you track me down?" asked Bride.

"I watched you hail a taxi and I wrote down the license number. I later contacted the driver and for five quid he was more than happy to tell me where he'd dropped you off. Now then, I've answered all of your questions, so how about answering mine?"

Bride sipped his Scotch to buy some time, for he suddenly found himself in the middle of another moral quandary. On one hand, he felt strongly about a free press in a democratic society and believed in a reporter's right to know the answers to his questions. After all, he was only searching for the truth. On the other hand, he felt an inexplicable yet undeniable loyalty to Princess Catherine. In their fleeting rendezvous under the sycamores in Bloomsbury, he had sensed her pain and knew there was greater meaning to her visit to the cemetery than he could presently understand. To tell this reporter sitting next to him the true purpose of his foray to the animal shelter that afternoon would be tantamount to announcing Catherine's graveyard visit to the entire world, and at this point he could not betray her, even in his ignorance to her purpose. Therefore, he was again left with only one loathsome option; he must lie to Mr. Crowe.

Having reached that decision, Bride realized that this would be easier thought than done. Crowe was obviously a clever man, more so than he would let on, and not prone to accept any shallow fudging. What could Bride possibly say to throw him off the scent? This entire debate between good and evil, philosophy and practicality raged within Bride's mind for several awkwardly long moments. He swallowed his Scotch.

"The truth is," he stated with conviction, "the truth is, I had found Princess Catherine's driver's license."

"What?" bellowed Crowe, nearly spitting out his drink. "Her driving license?"

"Exactly, which is why her bodyguard was so shocked. I mean, imagine my own surprise when I looked down at my feet on a gravel road in Berkshire and there it was! I thought about keeping it as a souvenir, but my conscience wouldn't allow it, and so I returned it to its rightful owner."

"Princess Catherine can drive a car?"

Bride sensed his fish had been hooked and he was ready to bring him to the boat. "Of course! You mean you didn't know that?"

"No, I've never heard anything about—"

"Now what kind of reporter doesn't know a simple thing like that? I've seen dozens of newsreels of her back in the states driving her Range Rover around. A five speed, no less."

"Get out!"

"Now I suppose a lost driver's license is something your listeners might find newsworthy, but then again, you'd probably have to mention that you didn't even know Her Highness could drive. It's entirely up to you."

Crowe frowned and gulped down the rest of his drink. He shook his head, ready to close the books on the whole idea.

"I suppose you're right. Looks like the old Crowe has pulled his nets in empty again. It was nice to meet you, Dr. Bride. Have a good holiday."

Bride heaved a sigh of relief as Crowe departed the pub. Given his lack of experience at telling outright lies, he felt pretty good about his most recent effort.

When Bride returned to his room at the Dunbarton that afternoon, it was as if his sudden loyalty to the Crown had been rewarded.

"This came for you mid morning!" called out Rumpole as he charged down the hallway with a parchment letter held over his head. "Delivered by someone looking very official, I might add."

"Thank you," said Bride as he examined the missive.

"You mind tellin' me what's goin' on here?"

"What do you mean?"

"Women ringin' ya up, men in limousines droppin' little notes off to ya. You're not CIA, are ya?"

Bride laughed with astonishment.

"As a matter of fact, I am. Sent here to assassinate the Prime Minister."

Rumpole's ears pinned back. He found nothing amusing about the American's joke.

"I'm kidding, Rumpole! This letter is probably from a professor friend of mine I'm planning to visit in Scotland. He tends to have a flair for the dramatic."

Bride opened the letter and quickly glanced over its contents. His smile slowly evaporated as he realized it wasn't at all what he was expecting. The handwritten note was unsigned, but the letterhead bearing the Royal Crest and the faintest whisper of Catherine's perfume were all the proof of authorship it required. It read:

> *Dear Dr. Bride,*
> *I would like to apologize for my unmannerly behaviour and the abrupt ending to our recent meeting. You performed an unselfish act for the Crown and for me personally and you should be duly thanked.*

Allow me to express my appreciation for your thoughtful gesture with an invitation to dinner. A driver will pick you up at six o'clock tonight. Proper attire for the evening will be delivered to you at your lodging.

Bride read the note again in disbelief, then tucked it into his coat pocket.

"Well?" asked Rumpole. "What did it say?"

Bride cleared his throat, preparing to blatantly lie for the second time that day.

"A note from the lady at the Antiquarian. Walt Whitman has finally arrived."

"Oh," said the innkeeper, sharing his disappointment.

Bride felt guilty for lying to dear old Rumpole, but in this case, the truth was completely unbelievable.

◆ ◆ ◆

Bride stood outside the front steps of the Dunbarton with his overcoat buttoned to the top to cover as much of his tuxedo as possible. He had sneaked past the Rumpoles to avoid any questioning and therefore any more falsehoods.

At precisely six o'clock, a black limousine pulled up to the curb. Bride hopped in as quickly as possible, taking a leap of faith that this car was sent for him. He hoped the driver knew where they were going because he certainly did not.

In just over an hour and a half of driving directly out of the city, Bride's chauffeured transport reached its destination: Windsor Castle in Berkshire. He stepped out of the limousine at the end of the lane and was immediately whisked away to a horsedrawn carriage.

Bride liked to think of himself as a man of some refinement, but as the carriage rolled to a gentle stop in front of the illuminated battlements of Windsor Castle, he suddenly realized that heretofore the most formal occasion he had ever attended was a rehearsal dinner for the daughter of the university president. He hadn't worn a tuxedo since his senior prom.

Inside the walls of the castle, Bride felt very much an imposter, like some gate crasher at the Oscars. The sheer enormity of both the structure and the occasion nearly overwhelmed him. He was surrounded by well-heeled gentlemen and proper ladies, all politely nodding to one another without really saying anything of substance. Most of the men were in some sort of gaudy uniforms with sashes, medallions, ribbons, and a host of tiny medals jangling above their breast-bones. If war broke out, this would be the best-dressed army in military history. Bride thought the medals were a bit overdone, but realized each one probably represented some act of great chivalry. At least he hoped it was the case.

He presented the official invitation that had been delivered along with his tuxedo and proceeded cautiously into the main dining room. The opulence took away his breath.

The 160-foot mahogany table had been waxed to a blinding sheen earlier that day by servants gliding across the patina with pillows underneath their knees. Each of the 160 chairs was precisely equidistant from the edge of the table. The dining room twinkled with the light of chandeliers dancing off the 800 Starbridge crystal goblets engraved with the seal of Queen Victoria, each one hand polished and painstakingly set into place above the silver gild cutlery. Twenty centerpieces of yellow orchids rested neatly among the place settings of 18th century Royal Menton china. It had all the appearances of an enormous birthday cake and it seemed a shame to cut into it.

Bride was ushered to his seat and knew enough to remain standing until the guests of honor were ushered into the room.

The giant doors at the end of the hall slowly swung open as brass trumpets ceremoniously signalled their arrival.

Princess Catherine entered first in a teal blue satin gown and white sash. Three strands of pearls encircled her slender neck. A small tiara rested naturally on her head as if it had always been there.

Next was Prince John, dragging behind like a schoolboy forced to scrub behind his ears and sit through church services. He made no pretense that he would rather be somewhere else, anywhere else, than where he was at that moment.

Prince George entered last, waiting just that extra second or two for dramatic effect. He was flanked by French President Mirrou, but the diminutive Frenchman all but disappeared in the electrically charged atmosphere surrounding the Crown Prince. Like one of the Golden Age movie stars, when George was in full ceremonial dress he created an aura that made it impossible for those around him to look away.

His own eyes were piercing, deep brown and swirling like steaming coffee in a white china cup. His face was angular, with a slender nose and high cheekbones rising out of a chiseled square jaw.

George was King in every way except title. Impeccably tailored, every crease standing at attention. Each brown hair on his handsome head was in perfect order, no doubt out of fear of being plucked out and washed down the drain for insubordination. George walked with a certain style that commanded attention to his aristocracy, upright and erect to make his six-foot-two-inch frame appear even more imposing. With his feet pointed slightly outward, he moved slowly with a definite heel-to-toe pattern, deliberately locking his knees with every step. He exuded confidence and self-control.

The eldest son in the Royal Family had been increasingly looked to for leadership as his mother's recent failing health limited her public appearances, and he made it clear that he was equal to the task. All eyes were on him as he glided to his chair. He relished the stage.

As the guests took their seats, George studied the room. There were no less than 160 guests, but Bride was quite certain that the Prince had visually singled him out as not belonging. It came in the form of a brief narrowing of the eyes and slight cocking of the head, imperceptible to anyone else in the room but nonetheless an unmistakable indication to the American that made him feel as though he was one of the unwashed.

Prince George remained standing until everyone was comfortably in place. A respectful silence fell over the room.

"I wish to welcome all of our guests this evening, with a special welcome to President Mirrou," said George in a robust and sturdy voice. "At this time, I would like to offer a message from the Queen. Mother apologizes for not being able to attend tonight, but she wants everyone here to have a wonderful time and asks only in return that you pray for her speedy and full recovery. With that, enjoy the evening."

A general murmuring and nodding of heads rippled across the banquet hall. As Prince George sat down, an army of servers emerged from the woodwork and the great feast was in progress.

Bride soon discovered himself entrapped in something of a moral dilemma. On one hand, his liberal political mind viewed the display of conspicuous consumption as approaching vulgarity. There were enough diamonds and furs seated around the table to retire a sizable portion of the national debt, and certainly enough food to nourish a legion of starving homeless.

On the other hand, he couldn't help but delight in the fact that he was sitting in the same room where the great Kings and Queens of Britain had dined for centuries before him, perhaps even eating out of the very pudding service Queen Victoria herself used.

The situation reminded Bride of a day in his early youth when he first stepped onto the parquet basketball court of the Boston Garden where Celtic legends Russell, Cousy, and Havlicek had gone before him. He knew he was trespassing on hallowed ground but for that moment in time he felt as though God would forgive him. After a lengthy internal debate, Bride decided he would try to enjoy his evening at Windsor Castle, but not to excess.

Bride found himself sitting between the wife of the Earl of Marshal to his left and Lady something-or-other to his right. They both seemed more fond of conversing with the dining partner to their other sides, which was just fine with Bride since he had only limited knowledge of blueblood pursuits such as fox hunting and dealing with a temperamental Welsh corgi.

He drank just enough Bordeaux to calm his nerves but not enough to dull his senses. He wanted a clear head to soak in the surreal quality of the evening and more importantly to avoid any embarrassing social faux pas.

In between bites of quail's eggs and European turbot, he glanced down the table and observed Princess Catherine. She conversed politely with the two gentlemen beside her who were decked out in full ceremonial military uniform, but it was obvious to Bride that she wasn't enjoying this any more than he was. She was simply better trained to hide it. Their eyes met through the hum of activity. She served him a genuine smile, which was enough to carry him through his veal and peaches Tuscan.

At the conclusion of dessert, Prince George and the French President stood in a receiving line at the end of the banquet hall and greeted each of their guests as they exited, accepting their warm wishes like a country parson after a particularly rousing sermon.

Bride finally reached the head of the receiving line and found himself face to face with the Crown Prince of England.

"Good evening, Your Royal Highness. I'm Dr. Malcolm Bride," he said as he extended his hand. "How are you this evening?"

Prince George had an intimidating manner of looking at someone for an uncomfortable period of time before responding to even the simplest of questions. He often carried a facial expression that exposed his condescending amusement with whatever had been said. He was particularly loathsome of the Americans, seeing them through the eyes of his ancestors who relegated them to the role of provincial Colonists. Apparently the fact that England actually lost the American Revolution did nothing to sway his opinion. His disdain for Americans was superseded only by his utter contempt for the French, whom he regarded privately as a "nation of overemotional handholding pseudo connoisseurs."

In public, of course, he lauded the French as Britain's economic partner, in much the same way that people are charming and friendly at family reunions until they get into their cars to go home, then the gossip and backbiting can begin.

"Very well, thank you," said George. "Thank you for coming. Now if you'll excuse me." With that, George made a swift exit and marched down the castle corridor like a man with real purpose.

Bride worked his way through the throng milling about in the entryway until he joined Catherine, who was busy shaking hands and exchanging pleasantries. He lingered a comfortable distance away until finally they had a moment of privacy.

"So what did you think?" she asked with a smile, still waving politely to Counts and Barons across the way.

"When you ask someone to dinner, you really ask them."

"I hope you weren't overwhelmed by it all."

"Not completely, but it did leave me wondering."

"Wondering about what?" said Catherine, turning to face him.

Bride hesitated, then continued.

"It just left me wondering why? I mean why all of this opulence, this luxuriance? And who pays for it?"

His ruminations were clearly offensive to Catherine's sensibilities. Her smile immediately vanished.

"All of this may appear to be extravagant to you, but it represents a thousand years of British tradition," she said in what sounded like a speech she'd been forced to deliver to the grossly uninformed on numerous prior occasions. "The Monarchy is the only constant in a world that is perpetually muddled with political and social upheaval. We provide moral leadership for the Commonwealth, stability in times of national crisis, and cohesion from one generation of subjects to the next. What you see as extravagant we view as necessary."

Catherine bid Bride goodnight with an abrupt nod and left him standing awkwardly alone, regretting his lack of tact. However, his embarrassment was supplanted by rapidly surfacing emotions that he vaguely recalled from his days as a smitten schoolboy. One of the sweetest nights he could remember was fast coming to a close, hours before Bride was ready to let it end.

◆ ◆ ◆

A recently restored study chamber of Windsor Castle would serve as host to a meeting where secrecy was vital. Following the fire that had gutted a significant portion of the castle, Prince George had overseen the restoration of this particular chamber himself, knowing that its soundproof walls would someday serve his purposes.

George dismantled the ceremonial garb that enveloped him and poured a snifter of Louis XIV brandy, pausing to inhale the rich fumes of the burnt wine.

Joining George in the nocturnal summit was his General Secretary, Elliott Wiggs. Wiggs was eighty-four years of age but still possessed a calculating mind that remained as clear and sharp as a freshly cut diamond. The Oxford graduate had devoted a lifetime of service to the Royal Family, starting his career at Buckingham Palace just prior to World War II as the equerry to George's late father.

Though Wiggs regularly insisted that he had never campaigned for the role, he had come to be viewed by George as a father figure. With George's real father away on travels during much of the Prince's youth, and emotionally distant with his children even when he was home, much of the paternal responsibilities were left in the comforting lap of Elliott Wiggs.

His encouragement through letters and visits had helped young George survive the rigors of a tough Scottish boarding school, and in the summer months Wiggs's estate in Cornwall had provided the young Prince a safe haven where he was free to be a boy without the intruding eyes of the media around him. From the time George put his first sentences together, Wiggs became his sounding board and confidant, advising the young man on everything from personal grooming to the best way to cope with capricious young girls. Even before George's investiture as Prince of Wales at the age of twenty, Wiggs had been preparing his surrogate son for Kingship, teaching him the proper way to walk and speak.

Wiggs's loyalty and devotion to the Crown Prince had remained above reproach over a half century and the young boy who once looked to his mentor to comfort a skinned knee had grown up to be the statesman who sought his advice on national affairs.

Standing guard in the rear of the room was Nick Crumrie, a solid figure of mixed Anglo and Asian descent whose square jaw was pocked from several bouts with shingles and an unfortunate meeting with the advancing end of a fixed bayonet.

At one time, Crumrie had been one of the proud men of the 2nd King Edward VII's Own Gurkhas, a lethal fighting regiment similar to the American Army's Green Berets. It was the same grit he had used to survive the mean streets of Brixton and the hellish nature of basic training that would eventually end Crumrie's ascension through the ranks.

The careless musings one night of a drunken officer on the subject of ethnic purity within the elite military unit caught the young Gurkha's ear, and the diatribe ended with Crumrie's elbow smashing through the officer's nose like a cricket ball through a wicket. Regardless of the circumstances, assaulting an officer was tantamount to professional suicide, and Crumrie's Gurkha cap badge was forever tarnished.

The case came to the attention of Wiggs, who exercised his considerable powers of influence with stunning swiftness. After one closed door meeting with Wiggs, Crumrie was immediately plucked from his unit and installed at Buckingham Palace. The jingoistic officer that Crumrie had assaulted was last seen getting his papers ready for his reassignment to the Falklands.

Crumrie's loyalty to his savior Wiggs was unquestioned. His official title was obliquely described as 'Personal Assistant to Secretary Wiggs', but his unofficial duties consisted of virtually anything Wiggs needed him to do. He was responsible for everything from security to transportation and on this occasion, Crumrie stood in the corner of the room like a chiseled statue to provide a healthy dose of intimidation.

The focus of the secret meeting was Robert McGuire, a stout man who overflowed from his chair. McGuire was a career politician who had risen to a high position of leadership in the Conservative Party in the late 1970s but since passed the torch to younger men in recent years.

McGuire appeared eternally weary from battling the Labour Party for decades, and was now facing stiff competition from the revitalized Liberal Democrats. And now he was without the young lions of his Conservative party, all of whom had been simultaneously wiped out by one well placed IRA bomb in the Strangers' Bar of the Commons. It was only by the grace of God and a miserable English headcold, which kept him home in bed the night of the bombing, that McGuire was still alive.

McGuire was a man who desperately wanted to retire to a cottage in the Lake District, but couldn't bring himself to walk away and leave the future of the nation in the hands of the Labour MP's he despised so much. That's why he was ready to listen to the extraordinary proposition Prince George and Elliott Wiggs were about to lay out before him.

"There is less than one month before the national elections, but you have a party with no leadership," began George. "I am a Prince with no power. If you're interested, I think I have a way to solve both problems."

McGuire raised the corner of one of his bushy gray eyebrows. He leaned back in his chair and nodded. "Continue, sir," he told George.

"The world is changing faster than ever, and England needs to realize some real change just to keep from falling farther behind. What I propose may seem radical, but I see no other solution."

"And what exactly are you proposing?"

George glanced over at Wiggs, who responded with one gentle nod of his head. It was a signal to put all of their cards onto the table. "You have the power to make me the head of the Conservative party. We use my good name, my considerable financial resources, and your political organization to defeat the Labourites in the general election. Simple as that."

Even for a veteran of smoke filled rooms where deals were cut like a deck of cards, this was a lot for McGuire to absorb. He downed his snifter of cognac and breathed heavily through his nostrils. "You're serious?"

"I don't think we'd be having this meeting if I weren't."

"But it's...it's...unthinkable! The Crown Prince of England running for political office like some—"

"Some ordinary person?"

"Well...yes," admitted McGuire.

"There was a time when the earth was believed to be flat. There was a time when scientists thought the sun orbited around the earth. But things have changed. There is a new world order, and there are new problems facing Britain. New problems require new solutions. That's what I'm offering."

"But you're going to be King of England one day!"

"That could be decades from now, if ever. And then what? What power does a modern King have to lead a nation? There is work to be done, and I desperately want to be at the forefront."

McGuire bit his bottom lip, still unconvinced that such radical measures were needed.

Wiggs could see McGuire's uncertainty but also sensed his willingness to listen. The aging Secretary General took over the conversation. "We have before us the rare opportunity to change the course of history, and the time is now." Wiggs leaned in closer. "Your opposition hasn't been this vulnerable in years, and if you don't seize the moment, if you don't reach out and embrace this opportunity, you can expect to take a back seat in Parliament until the day you draw your last breath. Consider carefully what we're offering you, and then think about your other options. There aren't any."

"When do you need an answer?" asked McGuire, his eyes narrowing as he mulled over the possibilities.

"Take your time," said Wiggs. "Think it over. We just need to know before you leave tonight."

McGuire tugged nervously on his ear as Prince George and Wiggs intently stared. He knew the other Conservative MP's would abide by his decision, but he still didn't know what his decision would be. He felt like Christopher Columbus setting sail, not knowing if he'd find the New World, or fall off the edge of the earth. The only thing McGuire knew for certain at that moment was that he needed to have another drink.

◆　◆　◆

Bride's limousine ride back from Windsor Castle was nearly at its end, but he wasn't ready to call it a night. The professor was still floating from his visit to Windsor to see Catherine and he wanted someone, even the company of strangers, to share the glow. He leaned forward to talk to the driver.

"Could you do me a favor? Could you drop me off at the Marlborough Arms? It's a pub just another block from here."

"All the pubs is closed, mate. It's after eleven o'clock."

Bride looked at his watch in dismay, noting that it was long after midnight. "So it is. Is there anything still open?"

"There's a wine bar I know about, not far from here."

"Would you mind?" asked Bride.

The driver smiled with amusement. "Would I mind? Tonight I work for you, sir. It's whatever you say."

"In that case, I say the night is still young!"

"That it is, sir!"

Bride was remembering Colin Crowe's sage advice that the true pulse of England can be found sitting on barstools when he meandered into The Parisian, just north of Victoria Embankment. The wine bar was still alive with customers.

He took a seat next to one Andrew Shore, who was using the bar to prop himself up because his own legs had long since grown weary of the task. His hand was wrapped around a nearly depleted pint of lager, and his bobbing head was glancing around the room as if he hoped someone would come up and talk to him.

Shore was a tax attorney in everyday life, but on this day he had been involved in a mission of mercy. As part of a fundraising event for a local hospital, Shore and at least two dozen others had spent the day visiting a pub at every station on the London underground's Circle Line, some twenty-five stops in all. Only in Britain would the medical community think to raise money by sending young men out to consume mass quantities of alcohol.

When he finally focused on Bride sitting next to him, Shore was ready to talk about anything.

"Glenturret on the rocks," called out Bride to the bartender. "Buy you a drink?" offered Bride as he turned to Shore.

"No no, nothing more for me," slurred Shore. "I know when I've had enough, and I crossed that point about four hours ago."

He laughed at his own joke, banging the bar with his fist and nearly losing his tenuous grip.

It was nearing closing time, so Bride cut right to the heart of the conversation. "As an American, I'm curious as to what an average Englishman thinks about the Royal Family."

"As individuals, or as a concept?"

"Both, I guess."

"I can start by telling you this...England wouldn't be England without the Royals. I know you Americans have this caricature of Brits in your mind where you think we're all very cute and quaint with our pomp and circumstance, but it's part of our national identity."

"You're saying that you wouldn't be British without a Queen?"

"No, what I'm really saying is that without our Queen, we'd all be Germans." Shore laughed again.

"How's that?" asked a puzzled Bride.

"World War II...the Germans took Poland, they took France, England wasn't far behind. We were taking a mighty pounding and lesser stock might have given up, but I remember my grandfather telling me the one thing that held us Brits together was our Queen. She stood out on the balcony at Buckingham Palace, pregnant with Prince George no less, and vowed that her children and her children's children would know free British soil. Once our lads in uniform heard that, well, the Nazis didn't stand a bloody chance.

"You can talk all you want about Winston Churchill, but at the end of the day, it was Alexandra that pulled us through it. That's why it burns me up when I hear all these republicans and so-called modernizers talking about doin' away with the monarchy. They tried to do the same thing to Queen Victoria, and where would this country be if they'd knocked her off the throne? The monarchy's a national treasure, like you people and your bald eagle. It's part of our fabric, and we can't just toss it aside like a wet Mac."

"What about the Royals themselves? Do you like them?"

"Well, even the most diehard Royalists like myself would have to agree that this latest lot is somewhat less than perfect. Queen Alexandra is a real lady, but I think she lost control over some of her children."

"Like Prince John?"

"Oh, dear God, don't get me started on that one. I've never seen someone start with so much and make so little out of it."

"What about Prince George?" asked Bride.

"George, he's alright I suppose. Hard to read him, really. You see him on the telly and he looks like the fine sort of bloke you'd want representing your country or even dating your sister, but then you read all these sordid things about him in the tabs and it makes you wonder which is the real George. Lately I think he's gotten a little too involved in politics. He should stick to ribbon cutting and polo matches." The drunken gentleman shook his head, trying to clear up the focus in his eyes. "You know, you look a bit like the Prince. Anyone ever tell you that?"

"Nobody sober, no," joked Bride.

Shore laughed heartily, then took a deep breath, somewhat winded from talking so much on top of the rest of his day's activities. Bride took a sip of his drink, preparing to ask the one question he really wanted answered.

"So then, what about Princess Catherine? What do people think of her?"

Shore stared off into space and gently smiled, like a man remembering his first true love, or his first taste of fine brandy. "Ah yes, Catherine. Now there's a Princess we can all be proud of. A bit on the shy side, but sweet as orange marmalade. Done nothin' but good things for Britain, from top to bottom. I feel a bit sorry for her, I do."

"Why's that?"

"Just everything that's happened to her, and for having to put up with all of those aristocratic twits around her. She just doesn't seem to fit in with all the others."

"Drink up!" hollered the bartender as he rang a brass bell on the end of the bar.

"Cheers, mate," said Shore as he allowed himself to stand freely for the first time. "Just remember one thing... when you realize that regal spelled backwards is lager, England makes a lot more sense." Shore downed his last swallow, and wiped his frothy mouth with his sleeve. "Now then, I better get home and see if I'm still married."

The wayward traveler stumbled away, well before Bride was prepared to finish their conversation. He was at least happy to know that he wasn't the only one who saw Catherine in the same pristine light.

As Bride headed for home down the dark sidewalk of Gower Street, he sensed someone following him. He quickened his pace and now there was no mistaking that someone was hot on his heels. Bride abruptly stopped and whirled around to face his pursuer.

"What are you after?" he yelled without fear. He found himself staring face to face with a rather sheepish Colin Crowe. "Evening, Dr. Bride."

"Why do you insist on stalking me? Why can't you just use the telephone like everyone else?"

"In London, phones aren't a good idea when you want to keep something a secret."

"I don't have any secrets."

"Oh, I'm not so sure about that one," said Crowe as he lit up a cigarette.

"I don't know what you mean."

"Well, allow me to enlighten you. Ever since our meeting at the Marlborough Arms when you fed me that rubbish about finding Princess Catherine's driving permit, I knew you were hiding something. It's *what* that I can't figure out."

"You don't believe me about the license?"

"Dear God, man, that was one of the worst attempts at lying I've ever heard. Drunken husbands stumble in with better stories than that tripe you unloaded on me."

"But you pretended to believe it."

"Naturally. I knew then that you must be sitting on some tasty bit of information and if I just allowed you some free rein you would eventually lead me directly to it. Unfortunately, I've been a little busy as of late working on another story, but I haven't forgotten about you."

"I can see that."

"So then, my honorable American friend, what in the devil is going on between you and our fair Princess?"

"What makes you think anything is going on?"

Crowe pulled out a well-worn notepad and held it up to the dim light of the nearest street lamp. "At precisely thirty one minutes past four this afternoon, a tuxedo was delivered to you at the Dunbarton. At precisely six o'clock, a driver pulled up and whisked you away. Two hours later, you were dining on veal at Windsor Castle." Crowe snapped shut his notebook and tucked it away like a gunfighter holstering his weapon after a demonstration of his marksmanship.

"Please don't tell me that all of this was arranged by your travel agent as part of the new European plan," said Crowe as he stared at Bride, waiting for a straight answer.

Bride took a deep breath, debating whether or not to continue his ruse or come clean. The intensity that burned in Crowe's eyes like a hound that was locked onto the scent told him that it was time to surrender all pretense. "You didn't specify the sauce that came with the veal."

Crowe reached back into his pocket for his omniscient notebook, but Bride waved him off. He walked over to a park bench and sat down, joined by Crowe.

"How in the world did you find out all of that?" asked an impressed Bride.

"In Britain, information is a precious commodity, especially when it's anything pertaining to the Royals. It's harvested, bought, and sold by virtually everyone you see around you. All one has to do is ask the right questions of the right people and back it up with a few quid and you can find out virtually anything you need to know."

"Well then, with all of these moles lurking about, why haven't you been able to put the whole story together?"

"Good question," nodded Crowe. "I've encountered one roadblock after another on this one, which has made me even more determined to find out what's going on."

Crowe lit another cigarette, took a lengthy draw, then leaned back against the lamppost and struck a philosophical pose. "You see, Dr. Bride, you and I are cut from the same cloth. We seek the truth, the verities of life. We can't accept anything at face value, or shrug our shoulders at the unknown and simply walk away. It's a bit of a curse, really. A hunger that can't be satisfied until every morsel of information has been uncovered and digested."

"Am I that transparent?" asked Bride with a hint of sarcasm.

"Not really, but as a mutual sufferer, I've learned to recognize the symptoms. Knowing this about you, coupled with considerable experience in these matters, I have come to the conclusion that either you have learned something about Catherine that she doesn't want revealed, or she's keeping some secret that an inquisitive chap like you is desperate to discover. More than likely it's a combination of the two. Would that be a fair assessment?"

The intrepid newsman had hit the bullseye, but Bride allowed only a wry smile to crease his weary face.

"You certainly have an active mind. Goodnight, Mr. Crowe."

Bride patted the reporter on the shoulder as he turned and headed for the safe haven of his lodging.

"She's beautiful, isn't she?" said Crowe as he stared straight ahead into the invading fog.

Bride stopped and nodded. "Yes. She is."

Bride made it to the door of the Dunbarton. He glanced back down the street as he put his key into the lock, but Crowe had already disappeared into the shrouded London night.

Crowe's words reverberated in Bride's mind as he stretched out to sleep in Room One of the Dunbarton. Catherine was indeed beautiful, but only to those with the more studied eye.

There was nothing overpowering about her that immediately drew people's attention, yet her charms were undeniable to those who took the time to recognize them.

She was not the Grand Canyon, but rather the delicate flower that grows on the rim. She was not the crashing wave, but rather the fragile white shell glistening on the beach. She was not the Mona Lisa, but rather the painting that hangs next to it, and no less a masterful work of art.

And if any one aspect of Catherine's composition made her more intriguing, it was a mystique that seemed to keep her separated from the world around her. Bride had sensed it from their first encounter in the park. He didn't know if it was born out of some personal experience, or simply a defense against life under the microscope, but it was clearly there.

Despite all of her grace and politeness, she kept an emotional distance, as if she had something to hide and refused to let anyone approach close enough to learn her deep secrets. Bride's curiosity into the inner workings of the enigmatic Princess were getting the better of him, and his final thoughts as he drifted off to sleep was that when daylight arrived on the streets of London, he would do something about it.

Chapter Eight

Prince George stepped quietly into Queen Alexandra's bedroom in Buckingham Palace and forced himself to walk closer to her as she slept. For years he hadn't been comfortable in her company and he'd always been uneasy around the sick and the dying, so the combination of the two made each step difficult.

The room was dimly lit by a porcelain lamp on the marble mantle on the fireplace. The bulb put out a light no brighter than a single candle but doubled its efforts by reflecting in the huge mirror over the fireplace. It was just enough to illuminate the crystal pendants in the enormous chandelier that hung from the vaulted white ceiling.

As he reached the foot of her canopied bed, George felt a genuine twinge of sadness. The monarchy had been a symbolic position ever since the days of Charles I in the 1600s, but what a rich symbol it was with Queen Alexandra on the throne.

For the last half-century, Alexandra had been the cornerstone of Great Britain, the foundation on which everything else was built. She was small in stature but a courageous tower of strength, a bulwark that withstood every storm that swept across the kingdom. In a nation often divided by political schisms, Alexandra had been the voice of reason and compromise, a symbol of national unity. She had been a rampart against fascism, communism, and more recently terrorism. In the body of England, Queen Alexandra was the heart. Above all, each step along the way was taken with a pristine grace that endeared her to everyone from world leaders to the unemployed chimney sweeps of East London.

But now she lay helplessly in her bed, brought down by her own weak heart that never seemed to pump quite as strongly after her husband passed away. She also felt deeply the pain that came with each tragedy and each embarrassment of her three children. The palace medical staff was divided on how long she had to live but all agreed that inner resolve and God tipped the scales in Alexandra's favor.

For most of the winter and early spring, the newspapers had been reporting the palace whispers that George rarely visited his mother during her infirmity and so he had recently made a high profile effort to see her more frequently. But today was not a public relations visit. He had come to resume a conversation they'd been having for several years and one that he had accelerated in recent months.

"Mother?" said George as he shook the end of her bed.

"Good morning, George," came her feeble reply.

"Sleep well?" he queried politely.

"No. I go to bed every night worrying about the people. I feel as though I'm letting them down."

"I'm sure they understand," said George with cursory reassurance.

Alexandra put her hands down next to her hips and pushed herself toward her headboard, propping her gray head onto one of the overstuffed feather pillows behind her.

George pulled a mahogany Queen Anne side chair from the writing desk over next to the bed and sat down with his hands clasped in front of him. His eyes riveted on the floor. The polite small talk was over. It was time to get on with the real reason for his visit. His forehead was furrowed in serious thought as he searched for the best way to begin. "Have you thought any more about it?" he said quietly.

"About what?"

"Mother, please don't play games. This is too important. I need to know."

"Well, if it's a straight answer you seek, then it's a straight answer you shall have." George tilted his head up a few inches and raised his eyes to meet hers. He could barely contain his anticipation over her response. She looked squarely at her son and said, "the answer is unequivocally no."

George's shoulders slumped as disappointment rushed through his soul. Even before she had become ill, he had been trying to persuade the Queen that it was time for her to step down from the throne and allow him to ascend as King. He had been waiting in the wings for fifty-seven years and his station in life hadn't changed. Even though abdication was considered a dirty word in Royal circles, he yearned for his chance to wear the crown and his patience had finally worn out.

"Mother, you are being unreasonable!" bellowed George as he jumped to his feet and paced the floor next to Alexandra's bed.

"What you seem to fail to understand, George, is that there is no choice to be made here. The path is clear. Being crowned is like getting married—it's supposed to be for life. One doesn't get promoted to the throne, one gets anointed. From that point forward, it's a sacred trust."

"But you have to consider what's good for the country! Frankly speaking, Mother, you are bedridden, and I am in the prime of my life. Now which of us is better equipped to lead Britain?"

"Believe me, George, I have the country's best interests at heart. I am the head of the Church of England. I am the Defender of the Faith. Because of that, abdication would be nothing less than heresy! The people look to the monarchy for continuity and tradition, and I will not let them down. So I will not be stepping aside and I trust there is no further discussion necessary on this particular topic." Alexandra closed her eyes, drained from the unpleasantness. When the Queen placed her handbag on the dining table it was a signal to everyone that the meal was over. When she closed her eyes, it meant the conversation had ended.

George stood fuming in the middle of the room, his dark eyes swirling with anger. "Very well. If that's the archaic, anachronistic position you have chosen, there's nothing I can do but wait for my *anointment*." He spoke the word *anointment* with sarcasm that bordered on sacrilege but under the circumstances he felt he was doing well not to launch into a violent tirade. "In the meantime, I shall push forward with my own agenda and believe me, Mother, tradition will have *nothing* to do with it."

"What are you talking about?" said Alexandra, opening her eyes with concern.

"You will see. You will see what men do when they are left with no choices." George stalked out of the bedroom and slammed the door behind him. Another piece of her heart left with him.

◆　◆　◆

It's one of life's odd paradoxes that the brain often operates more efficiently while at rest than it does during the height of the day. Lucid dreamers are often blessed with nocturnal gifts that provide inspiration for music or literature, ideas for new inventions, or solutions to nagging problems that couldn't be worked out on the drawing board.

As he pulled back the sheets and placed both feet on the cold wooden floor of Room One at the Dunbarton, Bride suddenly realized he'd been visited by a possible solution to his problem during the night, something his waking mind had failed to even consider. Perhaps it was encased in a brief dream of Catherine, in which Bride imagined himself holding her hand, a hand that had never known the calluses of manual labor.

At least two people must know who was buried in the unmarked grave at St. Bartholomew's; Princess Catherine, who clearly wasn't going to tell, and the man who actually dug the grave and laid the body to rest. Would he tell? Could he tell? Did he even know? Probably not, responded Bride's rational mind to all three of his own questions. But the glimmer of optimism, and the lack of any other illuminating avenues, spurred him to seek out the gravedigger and at least pose the same series of inquiries. Bride sprang out of bed like a ten-year-old on a summer Saturday and got dressed.

Bride's new path to discovery would also turn out to be unmarked. He naively assumed he could buzz right down to St. Bartholomew's, check back into the employment records, and research the names of anyone who had ever been in its employ as a digger of graves. But after a brief conversation with St. Bartholomew's current minister, who seemed to know about such things, Bride sadly learned that no such written employment record existed.

About halfway through their conversation, Bride began to sense that he wasn't the first person to come poking around with such an odd question. It struck him funny that the reverend wouldn't want to know *why* Bride wanted to know the name of a former gravedigger. Although the smiling reverend acted as though he was sincerely interested in helping, his clipped and somewhat vague answers indicated to Bride that he was trying to extract information from a stone wall wearing a clerical collar.

Bride's suspicions were confirmed further when the young reverend couldn't think of a single member of his Congregation who might be able to help the curious American professor in his quest for knowledge. Bride didn't want to let his imagination get away from him, but the word *conspiracy* entered his mind more than once. "Oh well, guess that's that," said Bride with feigned resignation as he politely thanked the reverend and exited the sanctuary.

He entered the cemetery outside where the bizarre episode had unfolded a few nights before, pondering his next move. He wasn't going to give up that easily, but it might require another night of heavy dreaming before he came up with the next logical step. Then again, maybe it was time to resume the task that had brought him to St. Bartholomew's in the first place—to seek out his own heritage. Why had he veered so far off course in his journey to England? Was he subconsciously avoiding some awful truth about his parentage?

It had been days since he'd even thought about Bridget Allison, the woman who bore him and remained his only link to his unknown past. Indeed, decided Bride, it was time to put his cloak and dagger in the closet and uncover his lineage. But having made that decision, Bride's legs didn't move. Something about that unmarked grave stirred him, and he simply needed to know more.

As he stared at the graying headstones, his mind wandered. He remembered hearing a homicide detective on television once saying "the only person in a murder investigation who won't lie to you is the victim." His conscious mind finally kicked in with a contribution. Bride glanced back to make sure the reverend wasn't observing him, then he moved quickly among the grave markers. He was looking for something specific, a headstone from the mid 1900s, and one with a peculiar surname that would make it easier to track down relatives of the deceased when he got out the London phonebook.

Up and down the rows of graves he wandered, searching for the perfect candidate. Something seemed to lead him to the south end of the cemetery, some unseen force, like a restless spirit taking him by the arm. Near the end of a row, dwarfed by the more stately sepulchers around it, Bride found it. The gravestone of the poor dead soul who would tell him what he wanted to know. His entire lifetime was summed up in three chiseled lines on the dingy marble:

Barrie H. Mawhinney
Born June 1, 1915, Died June 6, 1944
in service to Her Majesty the Queen
Survived by his wife Rachel and son Noel

Bride committed the information to memory and moved quickly away.

As he flipped through the telephone directory in the bright red phone booth on Clerkenwell Road, Bride was shocked and dismayed to see just how many R. Mawhinneys were listed in Greater London. He began pouring ten pence pieces into the payphone as he systematically began calling each one in hopes of eventually reaching someone connected to the gravestone.

He had brief and fruitless conversations with Raymond, Robert, Regina, and Royce Mawhinney, before he finally reached the home of one Rachel Mawhinney, the widow of the late Barrie H. Mawhinney.

The date of June 6, 1944, the day of Barrie Mawhinney's death, stands out in the mind of any professor of American history like a lighthouse on a craggy coastline. It was D-Day, the invasion of Normandy. Every day of a war is long and June 6, 1944 was the longest day of them all. Using that knowledge and combining it with the inscription on the headstone that Barrie had died in service to the Queen, he launched the first chapter of a tale that would far surpass the biggest lie he'd ever told.

"Mrs. Mawhinney?"

"Yes?"

"Rachel Mawhinney?"

"Speaking."

"Mrs. Mawhinney, my name is Malcolm Bride. I'm visiting from the United States and wondered if you might be able to help me out. My father knew your husband during the war, and told me if I was ever in London that I should try to get a hold of you."

Bride closed his eyes and bit his bottom lip as he waited to see if she believed him.

"Your father knew my Barrie?"

He was in. Bride was hoping to extract the information he wanted over the phone, but Rachel insisted on seeing him in person. He jotted down directions to her house in East London and immediately started to work his way there.

He took the District tube line all the way out to Dagenham East. He checked the address on the piece of paper in his hand and knocked on the door of a modest flat.

Rachel Mawhinney answered, pulling off her apron and smoothing back her wavy gray hair."Won't you come in, Mr. Bride?"

This was one time when he wasn't going to insist on having his doctorate recognized.

"Thank you," he said as he entered her humble home.

Bride remembered a time in Boston when people thought nothing of inviting strangers into their homes for conversation and refreshments. It was nice to think that London hadn't been caught up in the modern paranoia that every unfamiliar face is somehow out to get you. Or perhaps it was, and Rachel Mawhinney was simply a special person.

"I've just taken some biscuits out of the oven. Can I bring you some with a cup of tea?"

"That would be wonderful," said Bride with remarkable sincerity as he decided how best to lay out the next few chapters of his fabricated story.

He was trapped in an odd paradox. In order to get closer to the truth, the more he found himself spreading untruths. Before this week, he could have counted the bold-faced lies he had told in his lifetime on one hand, yet now he was involved in a level of deceit that seemed to him to be approaching pathological. But the truth remained an addiction for him, and the addict will stop at nothing to fulfill his need.

Rachel brought in a tray of steaming biscuits and a pot of hot tea and set them down in front of Bride. The table was set for good conversation.

"Now then, tell me about your father," she said.

"What would you like to know?" said Bride as he spread butter on jam on the open face of a fresh biscuit.

"What was his name?"

"Anthony," began Bride. "His name was Anthony."

"Anthony," she nodded. "I seem to recall Barrie talking about a chap named Anthony. Of course, that was a long time ago. Did he know him from Portsmouth?"

Bride's confidence immediately surged. Rachel had provided him with the wind to fill his sails as he ventured into uncharted waters.

"Yes! Portsmouth! That's exactly where they met!" said Bride with enthusiasm as his story started to take shape.

Bride's grand fabrication about his father's friendship with Barrie Mawhinney was based partly on historical facts that the professor knew in rich detail, partly on Army anecdotes he'd heard from his adoptive father, and the rest he simply drew from his imagination.

He spoke about their days of training together in Lincolnshire, of spirited rugby matches between the Yanks and the Brits, of late nights of singing salty chants in timbered pubs, and quiet reflections on the girls they left at home. He recreated the hours before the invasion of Normandy, when Anthony and Barrie said goodbye as their units boarded ships and set off to storm the beaches of Omaha and Utah.

The more he talked, the easier it flowed and the better the story became until this *Anthony Bride* character he'd invented was becoming larger than life. If this soldier he described had really existed, he would have been awarded several Medals of Honor, been elected President, and played himself in the movie about his wonderful life.

After nearly an hour of weaving his fantastic yarn, Bride finally worked his way around to the real reason he had come.

"I was wondering if by some rare chance you would happen to know the name of the man who—"

Bride suddenly stopped short. It dawned on him that there was no delicate way to ask someone if they knew the name of the man who dug their husband's grave.

"The man who what?" asked Rachel.

Bride's confidence was waning. He felt like a bank robber who had finally cracked the vault but was having trouble stuffing the money into his valise.

"The man who what?" she repeated.

He was starting to panic under the pressure. It occurred to him to blurt out "never mind" and politely say goodbye. But there was "the truth" dangling tantalizingly in front of him and he needed to summon the courage to snatch it. He pulled himself together and tried a different avenue. "This is awkward for me to say, but my father believed there was another one of his friends buried in St. Bartholomew's. I looked for his headstone, but couldn't seem to find it. I was wondering if perhaps you knew the name of the man who would have tended to the cemetery at that time."

Rachel sat pensively, trying to recall events of more than a half century ago. "I can see his face, but the name eludes me. No, I don't think I remember," she said as she shook her head.

Bride's heart sank. All of that effort was wasted. He would have to trudge back to the cemetery, find the name of another lost soul, track down his relatives, and develop yet another falsehood. He stood up to say goodbye.

Suddenly Rachel's head popped up with inspiration. "Wait! Let me check something!"

She vanished into the back of the flat. Bride could hear cabinets being opened and closed and squeaky drawers being pulled out.

Within moments, Rachel returned with an old scrapbook. "We took some photographs the day of the funeral. I can't be sure, but there were a lot of people from the church there that day."

She sat down on the couch and opened the scrapbook. The pages crackled at their first sighting of light in many years. Bride sat down next to Rachel and held one side of the album while she lifted the pages.

It was a much better account of Barrie H. Mawhinney's brief time on earth than the three lines that had been carved on his tombstone. A wedding photo, pictures of a young couple holding an infant son, and a handsome soldier in uniform, all helped to color in the sketchy lines of his life.

The last page of the scrapbook contained photos from the day Barrie was laid to rest in St. Bartholomew's. The photographer had captured on film the family members, the reverend who gave the eulogy, the casket draped in a Union Jack, and a brave young boy trying to understand why Daddy wasn't coming home again. And in the corner of the last page was a picture of a man in an ill-fitting wool jacket. He had the grim visage of someone who had seen too many funerals.

"I think this is it," said Rachel.

She peeled back the black and white photo from the yellowed paper. On the back, in Rachel's neat handwriting, was a vital piece of the puzzle that Bride was trying to put together.

Patrick Butterfill
Sexton, St. Bartholomew's Church
June, 1944

Bride trembled visibly with excitement, but under the circumstances he knew he had to mask his true feelings.

"I remember now," she said as her memory freshened. "I recall seeing Mr. Butterfill on Sunday afternoons when I would lay flowers on Barrie's grave. I thanked him on more than one occasion for taking such good care of the cemetery, particularly my husband's resting place. Butterfill always struck me as a patriotic sort. Seemed to pay special attention to the war veterans who were buried there. For some reason I don't think he was able to serve in the Armed Forces, slightly crippled I think, and that was his way of serving his country. A likeable fellow as I recall."

"Do you know where I can find him?"

"Seems to me he moved up to Yorkshire, not long after Barrie passed away. He told me something about starting up a kennel, something like that. It's just been so long."

It was enough of a clue to keep Bride on the trail. He was anxious to leave and resume his investigation, but needed one of those lulls in the conversation that signals when it's an appropriate time to conclude matters. This was clearly not the time as Rachel sat forward and turned the pages of the scrapbook back to the photo of the handsome soldier. Tears began to fill her eyes.

"What do you remember your father saying about my Barrie?"

Bride suddenly felt absolutely awful about being there and betraying Rachel's trust. He considered his answer carefully as he attempted to salvage some dignity from the situation. "He said he was the bravest soldier he ever knew. He always said Barrie Mawhinney was a good man."

"He was," said Rachel as she nodded and brushed aside a tear. "He was a good man."

Bride gave Rachel a gentle hug and thanked her for all of her kindness.

He sat silently as he rode the tube back to Bloomsbury, jostled back and forth by the whims of the track below. The railcar's journey through the London underground seemed to parallel his own, pressing forward through the blackness of the subway tunnel toward an unseen destination.

Bride felt increasingly bad about lying to someone like Rachel Mawhinney. Worse than that, it broke his heart to think that she had never remarried during all these years. She had pledged her love once, and though they parted in death, once was going to be it for Rachel Mawhinney. It made Bride sadder still to think he had never known a love like that. The only saving grace to all of this was that if she *had* remarried, she would have changed her name and he would have never been able to track her down.

As the Northern line pulled into the Goodge Street station, Bride shook his head as if to rid his brain of the misdeed he had just performed. What was done was done and he intended to use his ill-gotten information for some higher purpose. He would head home and begin to look for the mysterious Patrick Butterfill.

Chapter Nine

It was precisely 12:59 on Monday afternoon when Bride turned on his Grundig travel radio and spun the dial to BBC Radio 4. He wanted to listen to *The World at One*, curious to see what golden nuggets of information Colin Crowe was mining on this day. As the clock struck one o'clock, Bride would soon discover that Crowe had tapped into a major vein and would be the first of his colleagues to witness its splendor.

"This is Ronald St. James," began the announcer on the radio with a baritone voice that carried the strain of uncertainty. "And this is *The World at One*. We begin our broadcast this afternoon with a news bulletin that will change history as we Brits know it. For an exclusive report on this story, we now go live to Radio 4's Chief Political Correspondent, Colin Crowe, stationed just outside of Parliament."

Bride reached over and turned up the volume and stared intently at the Grundig radio as if that would help him hear better.

In the shadow of St. Stephen's gate outside of the Houses of Parliament was the black taxi that had been converted into a mobile broadcast unit. Crowe was crouched behind a microphone as the generator hummed with the power to spread his word to the masses. He adjusted his headphones and loosened his collar as he prepared to unleash the report that would surge to the top of the world's headlines. He wanted to make sure he was flawless in his delivery, knowing in advance that it would be one of those moments that everyone would always remember exactly where they were and what they were doing when they first heard the news.

"BBC Radio 4 has just learned that in an unprecedented move, Prince George, the Prince of Wales and Duke of Cornwall, has stated his intention to seek the leadership of the Conservative Party. This startling revelation is according to a highly placed and unimpeachable source, but is yet unconfirmed by the Prince or his spokespeople in the House of Windsor. If his bid to assume leadership of the Conservative Party is successful, he would be in line to take over the position of Prime Minister should the Conservative MP's sagging fortunes reverse and they win a majority in the impending national elections. What we are witnessing is history in the making. Never in the modern era has a member of the monarchy crossed over into the political arena, a step argued by many to be unconstitutional."

Bride didn't get to hear another word of the historic broadcast as he was interrupted by the clatter of Fionnuala Rumpole's heavy leather shoes thundering down the staircase outside of his room.

"Peter!" she hollered down the hallway. "Peter! Turn on the telly! Turn on the BBC!"

Bride emerged from his room as Fionnuala disappeared into the basement to search for Rumpole, more intent on sharing the news flash than on gathering any of the details.

Bride became aware of a growing rumbling outside. He walked briskly down the hallway and opened the door to Gower Street. The sidewalks had suddenly become alive with activity, as people moved nervously about with no real purpose. It was the kind of human whirlwind that Bride could only recall after the assassination of John Kennedy when people found themselves spontaneously heading outside to seek the comfort of strangers in a world that had suddenly been turned upside down.

On Gower and every other avenue in England, Brits were tossing up window sashes, bursting out of doorways, and climbing out of cars to confirm with each other the incredible news.

The air was now clogged with a cacophony of radio and television broadcasters, all scrambling to catch up with Crowe's stunning scoop. Bride could only wonder if this were part of the secret that Princess Catherine was so intent on keeping.

♦ ♦ ♦

The House of Commons was frenetic with activity. Members of Parliament jumped up and down, vying for recognition from the Speaker in hopes of obtaining the floor and joining in the heated debate spawned by Prince George's stunning announcement.

It's difficult to say exactly when the British monarchs lost their power to rule. The decline probably started with Charles I in the 1620s when Parliament forced him to sign the Petition of Right, a document that limited Royal power. Not that Charles I obeyed the agreement, but the erosion of power had begun and was clearly complete by the time Queen Victoria took the throne in 1837.

One Victorian essayist summarized the sovereign's three rights in a constitutional monarchy as "the right to be consulted, the right to encourage, and the right to warn". No further interference was tolerated by the Prime Minister and his Cabinet.

In theory, the modern British monarch has the power to dissolve Parliament, veto legislation, and appoint or dismiss ministers, including the Prime Minister. But in reality, the King or Queen's role in politics has been reduced to little more than influence. Whereas the sovereign used to choose the Prime Minister from the ruling party in the House of Commons, the task has evolved into merely endorsing the candidate already elected by the party members themselves.

Ironically, the gradual loss of power of Kings and Queens had actually served to strengthen the institution of the monarchy and made it possible for many to see past the 125 million pounds required annually to maintain it. Queen Alexandra was a glowing example of someone who had remained far above the political fray and as a result had developed no enemies. She could speak on any topic and nobody could accuse her of trying to curry votes.

The problem that Prince George was now creating stemmed from the fact that England doesn't have a written constitution, relying mainly on centuries of tradition and customs to lead the way. Suddenly George was challenging those traditions and there was a wide range of thinking on how to deal with the unthinkable: nobility entering the ignoble world of politics.

The grand chambers had never witnessed a more emotionally charged battle of words. Blood vessels were bulging with passion as the MP's waged a verbal war with the fervor of evangelists.

"It's unconstitutional!" stormed Labour MP Jonathan Heseltine of Harrogate. "The members of the monarchy are to be nothing more than ceremonial figureheads and should under no circumstances be actively involved in anything important regarding the leadership of this nation!"

A thunderous mix of applause and roars of disapproval drowned out Heseltine's final words on the subject.

Amid the din, the Speaker recognized the Conservative's Michael Bottsford of Warrington North, sitting on the opposition side of the party benches that were exactly two drawn swordlengths apart.

"My honorable colleague will note that there is not one word in our constitution, *not one word* mind you, that describes the duties of the Prince of Wales. Constitutionally, he doesn't even exist! There's absolutely nothing that says he can't take on an active political role and I say the time is now!"

Both sides of the issue again responded in boisterous fashion, but Bottsford held fast to the floor.

"We need a true leader to put the 'Great' back in Great Britain, and we have a man who can do just that waiting in the wings at Kensington Palace!"

"It's not a matter of 'can' or 'can't' yelled Prime Minister Philip Roth, dispensing with all parliamentary formality. "It's simply that he shouldn't! History has proven to us time and again that monarchs are not equipped to run a country, and it's for that very reason that the responsibility was shifted to the Prime Minister in the first place!"

"Order!" barked the Speaker as he furiously pounded his gavel, but Roth pressed on.

"The fact is, Prince George can't handle the job! He has absolutely no experience, and I assure you that his adventure into politics would have a devastating effect on this country!"

"Can he possibly do any worse than Labour?" retorted Robert Stanton of Vale of Glamorgan. "Has my right honorable friend forgotten that the Labour Party has given us the worst record of unemployment, investment, and growth of all the G-8 countries? Our country is on the brink of economic collapse and social despair and it is the ruling party that has dragged us there! I ask you, how could anyone possibly do any worse?"

Roth and his Labourite colleagues had no substantial reply to Stanton's stinging indictment as members of the Conservative Party stood and cheered with raucous enthusiasm. The Speaker abandoned all hope of restoring order, tossing his gavel aside and sitting back to witness the one sided celebration.

"It's blasphemous, 'at's what it is!" blustered the rotund man in a thick Cockney accent as he wobbled back and forth on the milk crate that served as his podium. "Bloody blasphemy!"

Despite a light afternoon rain that was falling, the crowd that gathered at Speaker's Corner in the northeast corner of Hyde Park was larger than usual because finally there was a topic that concerned everyone.

The rotund gent's debating partner stood on a similar perch a few yards away. "I don't see why everyone's gettin' their knickers in a bunch over this. We live in a democracy don't we?"

"Politics is no place for the Royals! Georgie Boy should stick to saving old buildings and whales."

"What about change?" charged the smaller man.

"We don't need change!" fired back his opponent.

"Neither of us has had a job in six months! Yeah, things is just bloody lovely, they are!"

"Listen, mate, you don't just jump into politics without some experience, just like you don't jump off Tower Bridge without knowing how to swim."

"And I say that it's about leadership. Leaders are born, not made. If the Italians can elect a former soccer coach to lead their country and the United States can elect an actor as their President, then we can elect a Prince! Why don't we give him a chance? I mean, he can't bloody well do much worse, can he?"

A ripple of cheers floated through the crowd. The unthinkable was starting to actually make sense.

In the ornate chambers of the House of Lords, not a word was being spoken. The men of peerage sat ruefully in the faint light that bled through the stained glass windows, collectively realizing that Prince George's bold step meant irrevocable change in the way things had always been done. A thousand years of British tradition were in danger of being swept away in the avalanche of modernization, and the only remnant of the House of Lords that stood to rise from the rubble was the dust of powdered wigs.

Ordinarily, Prince George's presence at the opening of new facilities at the Kettering General Hospital in Northhamptonshire would have drawn scant media attention. The Prince's official photographer, a few local reporters, and perhaps a feature editor from *The Times* would have been the only ones on hand to record the event. But today, the media swarmed to the event like invading Panzer units.

Colin Crowe was among them, one of several correspondents dispatched from Radio 4. Outwardly, he looked the same as always in a rumpled London Fog overcoat, and inwardly he felt the same exhaustion that had become a normal part of his journalistic existence. But Crowe realized this was not simply another day on the job. As he walked among his colleagues, he sensed a chain reaction taking place. There were whispers among the other reporters as he approached, many nodding and taking a reverential step backwards as if he were the Allied Commander inspecting the troops on the front lines.

Crowe had always received professional respect, but after breaking the news story of the decade, he had suddenly catapulted into stardom. Whether he liked it or not, the radio man had become nearly as large as the story he had broken.

The Prince pretended as though the event was just another ceremonial duty on the docket. He said all the right things about the need for better medical care, acknowledged all the right people, and smiled at all the right times. He had performed this ritual a thousand times before and all he had to do was fill in the blanks.

The crush of international media had been kept at bay behind a hastily erected wire fence several hundred yards away and steadily grew more impatient as the nonnewsworthy portion of the day lingered on in a light drizzle. Crowe chewed on the end of his pen, anxious to get cracking on the followup to his scoop.

A hearty round of applause from the VIP's gathered around the Crown Prince indicated to the reporters that the routine business had concluded and it was time to get on to more pressing items. They readied their tape recorders and camera gear like Marines preparing to hit the beach.

George had all but ignored the throng of newsmen and women up to this point, virtually pretending they weren't there. As if he suddenly now noticed them, he veered from his usual exit to a waiting limousine and strode confidently toward the gathering for his first encounter with the media as a politician.

Normally a candidate would be hit with a barrage of overlapping questions shouted from the crowd of reporters and the wise man would sort out the ones he wanted to answer. But on this occasion, nobody knew quite what to say or do. They all looked at Crowe to lead the way. He sensed the mantle of responsibility thrust upon him and asked Prince George the most basic of questions.

"Why are you doing this?"

George smiled as he clasped his hands behind his back and rocked back on his heels. The motordrives on the cameras whirred, capturing every movement.

"Football," said George.

"Football?" replied Crowe.

"Football," nodded George, relishing the mystery of his answer.

A buzz of murmuring and snickers rolled through the throng of reporters.

"Would you care to elaborate?" said Crowe.

"England invented football. For a century and a half, we dominated the sport. It is *our* game. Yet we haven't won a World Cup since 1966. We failed again in this last go round. It's time that overpaid coaches are sacked and pampered players are replaced with new blood...the fighting blood of true England. Do these things, and the Cup will come home, where it belongs. And that, ladies and gentlemen, is why I am doing this."

The crowd of journalists stood in collective silence as the Prince allowed his metaphorical statement of purpose to soak in.

"I would love to talk more, but I'm afraid I've got other pressing engagements. I'll be outlining the details of my candidacy in a speech within the week."

The Prince's eyes momentarily locked onto Crowe's with a look that said "put that in your pipe." With that, George turned and joined his gauntlet of bodyguards and equerries for the short walk back to his limousine, ignoring the sudden burst of questions that emanated from the reporters.

Crowe wasn't sure how the Prince's foray into politics would end, but he was certain that it was off to an impressive start. The ordinary Conservative candidate would have launched into a shopping list of everything the other parties were doing wrong and how a vote for him would be the lesser of three evils. Divide and conquer at the ballot box. But the Prince of Wales had seized the moment to strike at the very heart of what ails every Brit, Scot, and Welshman from Portsmouth to Inverness.

The star of Great Britain no longer shone as brightly in the global sky. Even countries it had helped to defeat in the war like Germany and Japan were now bigger players in the world theater. Crowe could see the handwriting on the wall and the penmanship was in Olde English; George's entire candidacy would wrap itself in the Union Jack and tug at the fierce national pride of the once mighty island. The campaign strategy would be to unite the voters in principle, and eventually unite them as one giant voting bloc that backed the now fragmented Conservatives.

It all revolved around an enormous paradox—it was time for Britain to find new ways of doing things to rediscover old glory. Brilliant, thought Crowe, as the scenario accelerated through his mind. And quite possible.

George loosened the Windsor knot on his necktie as he found a comfortable position in the back of his limousine. Elliott Wiggs sat next to him, stroking the handle of his cane.

"I thought that went rather well," beamed George.

"Your delivery was spot on...you didn't leave out a single word. Hopefully the chaps on Fleet Street will get it right."

George sank back into his seat and closed his eyes. His journey into political history was now fully underway.

Chapter Ten

It was a full day's train ride from London to York, a walled medieval city not far from the border of Scotland. Bride had called every kennel in Yorkshire except for James Herriot's until he found one bearing the name Butterfill. It had taken him less than thirty minutes to pack and find his way to a British Rail station as the search headed north.

The trip would fit well into Bride's plans to visit an old friend in St. Andrews and also permitted a generous amount of sightseeing along the way.

The train rumbled through time as it passed through thatched English villages that evoked thoughts of Shakespeare, Hadrian, and the Knights of the Round Table. Bride wouldn't have been the least bit surprised if Robin Hood and his merry band of outlaws had come galloping alongside.

Every turn in the track brought something new to see, from the crumbling remains of stone walls and medieval towers dotting the Yorkshire countryside to fields billowing with the yellow flower of oilseed rape. These were the sights that Americans traveling by car were normally prone to miss because they're completely focused on driving on the left hand side of the British motorway.

Bride wondered how many of his British ancestors had traveled these same hinterlands before him.

He found lodging at a bed and breakfast along the Shambles in York, just inside the 13th century stone wall that encircled the city. From his window he could see the imposing towers of the York Minster, bathed in floodlights to show off the cathedral's full majesty. It seemed almost sacrilegious to Bride that he was going to shut his blinds to block out the light, but he knew he needed a good night's rest. What he didn't know is that his search for the truth was about to take a bizarre turn.

The next morning, a taxi shuttled Bride from Duncombe Place to his destination in Moor Monkton village on the outskirts of the city, still within the sound of the bells of the Minster. A hundred yards off the road was a tidy farm. The sign outside the driveway read:

BUTTERFILL FARMS

KENNEL AND CATTERY, BEDDING PLANTS

"This is it," Bride told the driver. "You can let me off right here."

The cabbie drove away with a generous tip as Bride stood on the side of the road, legislating in his mind over how best to approach the task at hand. He was about to ask questions he really didn't know how to ask, and would be hard pressed to sufficiently explain why he wanted them answered. The absurdity of his quest finally struck him. He had traveled to England to trace his own roots, but his personal quest had since been forgotten as he entangled himself in the mysteries of Princess Catherine. Worse than that, he couldn't explain even to himself why he was continuing this quixotic pursuit. But he had blindly come this far, and if for no other rational reason, that investment of time was enough to keep him going. He took a breath of clean Yorkshire air and headed for the main building.

Bride hadn't gone fifteen yards when a chorus of Airedales announced his arrival on the scene.

A young girl of about nineteen emerged from a storage shed adjacent to the main house. She wiped her sweaty brow with the back of her wrist, then used her checkered apron to clean off a generous amount of potting soil on her hands.

"Help you?" she called out to the approaching professor.

Bride referred to a piece of paper in his hand.

"I'm looking for the owner...a Mr. Patrick Butterfill. Does he live here?"

"Paddy?" she asked with surprise. "Yeah, he's here. Out back with the dogs."

The girl motioned with her head toward the sound of the barking Airedales. Bride nodded his thanks and headed that way.

He was fully expecting to meet a gentleman farmer, someone who had known the education of the city but had been seasoned with the salt of the earth. As he entered the kennel, Bride was shocked to find a man decidedly different from the country squire he had envisioned.

Paddy Butterfill was eighty-six years old and looked even older. His cheekbones jutted out from his weatherbeaten face like those of someone suffering from malnutrition. His clothes were ragged and spotted with permanent stains. Arthritic fingers protruded from the unraveled tips of ancient wool gloves. Worst of all, his spine was so badly curved from years of grave digging that he stood less than five feet tall. Sadly, that handicap was now serving him well as he hunched over to perform his primary duty—sweeping up the excrement of three dozen Airedales from the cement floor of the kennel.

Bride edged closer as he slowly overcame his initial shock of seeing this broken man, coupled with the raw stench of the kennel and the agitated bark of the penned up dogs.

"Mr. Butterfill?" he called out. The old man didn't respond as he continued to sweep. "Mr. Butterfill?" he said louder. Again no response. Bride felt certain the old man was aware of his presence, but there was no acknowledgement. He moved forward, now close enough to touch him. "Mr. Butterfill? May I talk to you a moment? I wanted to ask you some questions."

Butterfill glanced up at Bride but said nothing. He swept the final remains of the Airedales onto the shovel with his gloved hand. He lugged the full bucket outside to a compost pile, muttering unintelligibly as he walked like someone speaking in tongues. Bride was nearly consumed by the powerful odor as he followed a few steps behind, but Butterfill didn't seem to notice. Here was a man who seemed to have dulled his senses to the point that only the bare minimum of external input was getting through to him. Bride attempted to break through once again. "Mr. Butterfill, I've come all the way up here from London to ask you a few questions about St. Bartholomew's."

The mere mention of the word *Bartholomew* immediately struck panic into Butterfill's face as he stopped what he was doing and spun around to look at Bride. His eyes danced with fear as he rapidly shook his head in denial. His muttering grew quicker. He dumped the bucket of excrement and scurried away as quickly as his withered legs would take him.

Bride started to follow him, but was stopped by the sound of a woman's voice. An angry woman at that.

"Who the bloody hell are you?" bellowed the voice from the house.

Bride turned around to see an elderly woman coming swiftly towards him with an over-and-under shotgun in her arms. He held up his own hands in the surrender position to let her know he meant no harm to anyone. He'd never been held at gunpoint before, much less by an octogenarian, but he knew enough not to make any sudden moves. The young girl emerged from the house to watch.

"I'm Malcolm Bride. I came up from London to talk to Mr. Butterfill."

"Paddy doesn't talk to anyone," said the woman.

"Why not?"

"I suppose that's his business and not yours." The old woman gripped the shotgun tighter to underscore her point.

"Fair enough," replied Bride with a disarming shrug. "Perhaps then you might be able to answer a few questions about his days working at St. Bartholomew's?"

The same word, *Bartholomew*, clearly cut deeply into her consciousness, but the old woman was quick to cover it up. "Don't know what you're talking about. Now then, you'll kindly take your leave of this place before I call the constable and have you cited for trespassing." She gripped the shotgun a little tighter to let Bride know the conversation was over. With his hands still raised in the air, he slowly backed away toward the gravel driveway. Out of the corner of his eye, he saw Paddy Butterfill mutter by, oblivious to the episode being played out in front of him.

The woman didn't lower the shotgun until Bride had walked fifty yards down the road, heading back to the city limits of York. He was leaving the Butterfill Farm with a lot more questions than answers.

Bride would have ample time to mull over the baffling situation as he continued north to Scotland. He traveled by train to Edinburgh, then by motorcoach up the eastern coast to the village of St. Andrews, standing up bravely to the whippings of the North Sea winds from the Firth of Forth.

It was in McIntosh Hall on Abbortsford Crescent that Bride would find his old friend Donald Lawrie, a professor of anthropology at St. Andrews University. The two had become fast friends five years ago when Lawrie was on sabbatical at Amherst and they had kept in touch ever since.

Lawrie looked every bit the part of a Scottish professor, with his thick, black framed eyeglasses, a wool cardigan, bow-tie, and a pipe protruding out of his thick salt and pepper beard. He was so absorbed in the book in front of him that he paid no attention to Bride's entrance.

"Dr. Livingstone, I presume?" said Bride.

Lawrie looked up, his surprise quickly changing to delight.

"Malcolm, my boy! You're early!"

The two men exchanged friendly hugs, beaming at the sight of their respective soulmates.

"My day in York was unexpectedly cut short, so I hopped on the next train and here I am."

"Welcome, welcome to St. Andrews. Let's go across the street and have a drink," said Lawrie as he picked up Bride's bag and led him out the door.

Bride was quickly learning that virtually all business and conversation of any import in the British Isles was conducted in a pub, and since he had a few significant items to discuss, not to mention a thirst from his journey, he gladly followed along.

The two men pulled up stools in the downstairs bar of the Homelea Hotel, Bride with his Scotch and Lawrie with a frothy pint of molasses colored Guinness Stout.

"What a time you picked to travel to the UK, eh, Malcolm? History in the making and Prince George was kind enough to let you be here to witness it."

Bride nodded politely, his mind wandering back along the trail of foggy graveyards and Yorkshire kennels.

"He's got a better chance than the oddsmakers would have you believe. He's a charismatic one, that George, and his timing couldn't be better. I think people are fed up with the whole Labour lot, and they're tired of supporting a Royal Family that doesn't do anything but cut ribbons and pose for pictures.

"And of course, what's George got to lose? Right now he's just waiting for his mother to die. And if the Tories can convince the voters that—"

Lawrie stopped in midsentence and carefully studied the American professor. "What's troubling you?"

"Hmmm?" said Bride, snapping out of his shallow trance.

"I've been talking about the biggest news item to hit Britain since the Battle of Hastings and you've scarcely acknowledged any of my sterling observations on the subject."

"I'm sorry," apologized Bride.

"Now then," said Lawrie with a rich Scottish accent, "what is it, mate?"

Bride took a stiff drink and a deep breath and began.

"I've gotten myself involved in something, like a maze with one dead end after another, and I can't seem to find a way out."

"Can you be a bit more specific?"

"Frankly, I'm not sure what it is, but there's something going on and my natural curiosity won't permit me to walk away from it."

Lawrie shifted in his chair, leaning in to capture every word. He could tell from Bride's troubled look that this was something weighty, and he didn't want to miss a single word.

"You want to start from the beginning?" asked the Scot with sincerity.

"As I wrote in my letter, I came over here to do some research on my roots. One evening, actually nightfall by the time it was all over, I was traipsing around in a graveyard at St. Bartholomew's church in London."

"Not familiar with that one."

"Doesn't matter. Anyway, I'm just about to leave when lo and behold, who pulls up for a visit to the cemetery?"

"Couldn't hazard a guess."

"Catherine," said Bride with dramatic flair.

"Catherine who?"

"Which Catherine do you think? Catherine."

"You don't mean...Princess Catherine?"

"The same."

Lawrie's mouth hung open and his eyes narrowed. He studied Bride's face to determine if this was some sort of ruse, but the American's stalwart expression told him it was not. The Scot quickly gulped down the remainder of his stout and pulled his chair closer to Bride. "Go on."

"She knelt down next to an unmarked grave and said a prayer. I was hiding a short distance away, but she sensed someone was there and she ran back to her car and sped away."

"You're not on any medication, are you?" said Lawrie, searching for some other explanation than the plain truth. "No recent head trauma, anything like that?"

"You know me, I wouldn't make up something like that."

"I mean, I believe you, I just can't believe that would happen. It's unfathomable! What the bloody hell is the Princess Royal doing in a cemetery at night?"

"That's what I wanted to know, but she wouldn't tell me."

"Wait...you asked her?"

"I found something that belonged to her in the cemetery, that's how I knew for certain it was her. When I returned it to her, I asked her what she was doing there. All I managed to do was upset her."

Lawrie shook his head as he attempted to make some sense of it all. He glanced around, then motioned Bride out the door. "We need to talk, but not here. Come on."

Within minutes, Bride and Lawrie had walked to the end of South Street and cut over to the rocky shoreline overlooking the ruins of the Castle of St. Andrews, the crumbling remains of an ancient kingdom.

"Who else knows about this?" whispered Lawrie with gravity, his voice barely rising above the crashing of the North Sea waves on the headland below.

"Nobody."

"I'd keep it that way if I were you. You may have stumbled onto something you don't want to know any more about."

"What are you talking about?"

Lawrie nervously glanced around, as if spies were hiding behind every pillar.

"Do you know the name Robert Nolan?"

"Dr. Robert Nolan? He was Princess Catherine's husband, wasn't he?"

"That's the one," nodded Lawrie.

"He was killed somehow, wasn't he?"

Lawrie's eyes widened as he nodded more slowly this time. "Do you remember, about twelve years back, Prince George's wife and Sir Nolan both disappeared while skiing in Austria?"

"I vaguely recall something like that, but you know us Americans...news of the Royal Family all seems to run together."

"They were supposedly swept away in an avalanche on the back side of the mountain. They found her the next day, but Nolan's body was never recovered, even after an exhaustive search that lasted well into the summer. What makes their deaths and his mysterious disappearance even more compelling is that they were skiing with Prince George at the time of the avalanche. George, as you can see, escaped unscathed."

Lawrie nodded as he waited for the factors of the equation to soak in to the professor. Bride's eyes grew wider as he began to grasp the connection between their two stories.

"You think that the missing body of Sir Robert Nolan is buried in St. Bartholomew's?" said Bride.

"Pure conjecture at this point, but I must say, it adds up, doesn't it?"

"But why?"

"Perhaps his disappearance wasn't an accident."

"Are you suggesting Nolan was murdered?"

"Your shock tells me that obviously you haven't followed the history of the British monarchy over the centuries. Murder is as much a part of the Crown as the Star of India. I know it may sound a little farfetched in a modern society, but I'm not the first one to whisper about it."

"But you're also saying that Prince George killed his own wife."

"It's no big secret that they weren't the happiest of married couples. This way he's rid of her without a divorce, which keeps him in line to be King and Defender of the Faith and makes him a tragic figure in the minds of his public."

"Let's just pretend for a minute that all of this is true. Why would he kill Nolan?"

"Who knows. Perhaps he stumbled onto the plot, or maybe he was having an affair with Prince George's wife. Throughout the ages, people of Royal blood have usually disappeared for one of two reasons...either they couldn't give birth to a male heir, which is clearly not the case here, or they posed some real threat to the Crown. It wouldn't surprise me one bit if Nolan had something on George and the bonnie Prince did him in, then buried him in London as a concession to his sister."

"But wouldn't Catherine say something if she knew?"

"I can think of any number of reasons why she wouldn't. First of all, Catherine knows that if anything should happen to Prince George, that would put Prince John in line for the throne and heaven help us all if that lascivious twit should ascend. Secondly, and above all else, a member of the Royal Family doesn't bring scandal to one of its own. You keep mum, whatever the cost, for to tarnish the Crown is to threaten your own livelihood.

"The monarchy is in a precarious enough position already and a revelation like that would send the Crown tumbling down Fleet Street. And of course, if our outlandish ruminations have any grain of truth to them, then Catherine has to be concerned about her own safety. Power can be intoxicating, and a thousand years of Kings and Queens have proven time and again that they'll stop at nothing to wrest the crown. Richard III smothered two young boys for his chance at the throne. Which is another way of saying, my good friend, that this is not a matter you should be investigating. This very conversation could be construed as treasonous. Better to leave well enough alone."

Bride nodded as if he agreed, but he couldn't help but think to himself that there was nothing "well enough" about any of this. He started sorting out some of the pieces, and the more he thought about it, the more Donald Lawrie's wild musings made sense. Robert Nolan had been murdered by Prince George and quietly laid to rest in St. Bartholomew's where his grieving wife could visit him in an anonymous grave.

One nagging question that had been in the back of Bride's mind from the moment he met crazy Paddy Butterfill was how could a former gravedigger afford to own a thriving enterprise like the one he'd seen that morning? When he plugged the question into Lawrie's wild hypothesis, one possible answer actually made sense. What if Butterfill really *did* know who was buried in the anonymous grave at St. Bartholomew's? And what if he had been paid handsomely for his patriotic silence, which allowed him to buy the farm in Monkton Moor village? Had the pressure of maintaining such a dangerous secret slowly driven him mad?

The scenario that was developing seemed absurd upon initial inspection, but then again, who would have ever believed America's own Watergate scandal upon first glance? And it was certainly no less feasible than any of a number of conspiracy theories surrounding the Kennedy assassination. Considering the bizarre theater of the British monarchy, the likelihood of such a modern-day Shakespearean plot seemed all the more possible.

Why else would the mere mention of the name St. Bartholomew evoke such a sharp response from an elderly woman and a man who was otherwise devoid of human emotion? It was the same kind of frightened backlash he'd felt when he had asked Princess Catherine about her visit to the cemetery that night. A muddled picture was gaining at least a shred of elementary clarity; there was something in the graveyard at St. Bartholomew's that a lot of people wanted to hide.

Bride would take the first bus out of St. Andrews the next morning in his eagerness to return to London.

Chapter Eleven

Bride stepped into the lobby at BBC Broadcasting House, looking for the only man he knew with a curiosity more voracious than his own. As he waited nervously, he translated the Latin inscription above the elevators:

> *Good seed sown may bring forth good*
> *harvest, and that all things foul or*
> *hostile shall be banished hence.*

He did his best to believe that the inscription was some kind of good omen, put there to convince him to stay his course.

Crowe came out to meet him after a buzz from the receptionist. "Well, well, well, Malcolm Bride," he crackled as he lit up a fresh cigarette with the dying embers of his last one. He motioned Bride to follow him back into his office. "Been out of town, have we?"

"And I suppose you know what I had for breakfast?"

"Sausage and eggs."

Bride stopped in his tracks. Crowe was right.

The reporter couldn't help but laugh. "You have some egg in the corner of your mouth. Don't worry, mate, my spies aren't *that* good."

Bride wiped away the residue of Fionnuala Rumpole's soft-boiled eggs and continued on into Crowe's office. From the chair railing up, the walls were covered with plaques and awards for broadcasting excellence. Most of them were dusty and hanging slightly crookedly, indicating that they meant more to the people who gave the awards than to the man who received them. Crowe was not a man who cared about ornamental honors or salary increases. He was content with the respect of his peers and the satisfaction of putting out a good story.

"So why has the fox come seeking the hound?" said Crowe.

Bride took a deep breath, for he knew he was at a crossroads that might effect the course of modern history, and one step down that forbidden path meant no turning back. "I may have a story for you," he began.

Crowe instinctively plopped his notepad onto the desk and sat poised to take notes.

"No notes," commanded Bride in a serious tone. "This is not the sort of thing you want written down."

Crowe sensed the seriousness of the situation and obeyed Bride's instructions. "Fair enough," he said.

"Right now I just have a theory, with only a hint of evidence to support it."

"I'm listening."

Bride took a deep breath and narrowed his eyes to amplify his seriousness about the theory he had developed with Donald Lawrie. "What would you say if I told you that the skiing accidents of Prince George's wife and Robert Nolan were not accidents at all."

"I'd believe you," replied Crowe unflinchingly. "I've thought that for years, but going about proving it, that's another matter indeed."

"Okay, what if I told you I think I know where Robert Nolan is buried?"

Crowe's glib expression evaporated from his face as he slowly extinguished his cigarette. "How could you know a thing like that?"

"I saw Princess Catherine visit his grave. It's an unmarked plot in the corner of St. Bartholomew's."

Crowe had no reason now to doubt the validity of Bride's theory. After all, he had always known the American professor had a connection to Her Highness and now it was becoming clearer.

"Catherine knows you saw her at the cemetery, and she invited you to Windsor Castle in appreciation for your silence." Bride gave Crowe a half nod. "So, what's happened that has you talking now to me?"

"I guess I didn't realize what I'd stumbled on. I suppose now I feel like someone ought to know about all of this, or at the very least I need to know for myself if it's really true or if this is just my imagination running rampant. Actually, I'm rather hoping that it is."

Crowe carefully pondered the information presented to him, his lips pursed as he attempted to balance the equation. Suddenly he shook his head, as if to dismiss the notion entirely. "No. Sorry, old boy, doesn't add up."

"What doesn't add up? Why not?"

"Catherine's marriage to Sir Nolan was arranged, and despite her best foot forward in public, people close to her tell me that love was not one of the ingredients of their relationship. In fact, I imagine Nolan's death, however untimely, was actually somewhat of a relief to her. It doesn't make sense to me that she would risk so much to visit the grave of someone who was in truth not much more than a business partner."

"But he was in fact her husband, and there must be *some* grieving there. Besides, how much of what these people do on a daily basis makes sense anyway?"

Crowe bobbed his head from side to side to demonstrate his concession on that point of debate. "Well... there's only one way to find out, isn't there?"

"How's that?"

"We do some digging. I'll pick you up tonight."

Bride nodded and stood up to leave. Crowe fired up another cigarette as he showed him into the hallway.

"These are very dangerous waters you're navigating, Professor. How do you know you can trust me?"

"I guess I don't."

"Well, don't worry. You can. But nobody else must know, and I'm not speaking as a journalist who wants to hold onto a good story. I'm speaking as a man who wants to continue breathing. Do we understand each other?"

"I understand."

Bride walked out of Broadcasting House and saw All Soul's Church across the street. He hoped that somewhere, somebody was praying for him.

When Colin Crowe had indicated the necessity for *digging*, Bride had not interpreted him as literally as he should have. As they rumbled down the road in Crowe's vintage Triumph, the protruding wooden handles of two shovels battered their shoulders with each turn through the city.

Bride had scarcely had time to really consider the actions he was about to undertake, other than the fact that he was taking another giant step in his recent descent into civil disobedience. In the space of one week, he had gone from scaling fences at private parks to telling bold-faced lies, and now he was only minutes away from graverobbing.

This was not an endeavor he would have even imagined on his own, but Crowe had such a confidence about him that this was the only solution to the mystery before them that Bride couldn't help but follow his lead.

"We take Nolan's skullbone," said Crowe to Bride in a hushed tone, "then compare it to dental records, and when they match, the guilty will go punished."

Bride admired Crowe's resolve and purpose. No mention of awards or personal fame and fortune, but simply righting wrong without regard for the high station of the guilty party.

Crowe killed his headlamps as he pulled onto the gravel road adjacent to St. Bartholomew's. They sat for a brief moment of silence, then each grabbed a shovel and stepped out into the lurid surroundings of the graveyard. A half-moon glanced through intermittent clouds.

There wasn't a sign of life anywhere near the cemetery, but the two men moved with the quick and quiet of trained commandos. Bride silently led Crowe to the unmarked grave underneath the yew tree in the corner of the cemetery.

"That's it right there," confirmed Bride.

Crowe raised his shovel, ready to strike the first blow into the ancient soil. As if on divine cue, the steeple bells of St. Bartholomew's rang out, splitting the silence and nearly shattering the already jangled nerves of the two trespassers. Eleven clangs of the bell rippled across the brisk London air, then mercifully permitted the silence to return.

Crowe raised his spade one more time and without hesitation thrust the cold steel into the defenseless ground. He had tossed away four shovelfuls before Bride could bring himself to strike just once. He was frozen in place, unable to continue. His mind raced wildly, measuring risk against reward, the treasures of courage against the prudence of retreat. There was still time to turn back.

"Come on!" whispered Crowe with anger. "Show me some of that American backbone!"

"I'm afraid," answered Bride in a hushed voice.

"Afraid of what? Ghosts?"

"I'm afraid we'll find what we're looking for. Have you stopped to imagine the consequences?"

"So? This won't be the first Royal George you Yanks have brought down."

Bride remained in limbo as Crowe resumed digging. It was a metaphor of his life. He had always lived safely on the surface, reluctant to uncover the next layer. When he came to the fork in the road, he always chose the path more traveled. Throughout his adult life he had essentially existed with one job, one house, and zero romances. In fact, his trip to Britain to discover his roots was his first real journey into the unknown and the unsafe, and now he was managing to avoid even that.

He watched Crowe tossing dirt aside and admired the intrepid nature of a man who dug deeply beneath the surface every day of his life. Risk and reward, of which Bride knew little of either. In that instant, he made a decision that would change his life and eventually the lives of many others. Bride hoisted his shovel and pitched in, and together he and Crowe joined in the unenviable task of unearthing the mystery that lay six feet beneath the surface of St. Bartholomew's.

They dug at a feverish pace, feeding off the adrenaline generated from a myriad of fears. Bride's natural aversion to graveyards was exaggerated tenfold by the nature of their mission. He felt like one of the bodysnatchers of old.

The steeple bells clanged twelve times but by now the two men were so involved in their work they scarcely noticed.

The dirt was getting harder to dig through and their muscles were aching from the torrid pace. It was becoming painfully clear to Bride why poor old Paddy Butterfill was so stooped in stature. They pressed on until well after midnight, gradually lowering themselves deeper and deeper into the sacred ground of St. Bartholomew's, one shovelful at a time.

It was Bride's tool that first struck the top of a casket with a hollow thudding sound. The eyes of the two graverobbers met, then instantly they were energized with a second wind as the steeple bell signaled the arrival of 1:00 AM. Their shovels worked around the outline of a coffin until finally they could coax their tools underneath it and gently lift it out of the grasp of a burial ground that seemed unwilling to part with the dearly departed.

Crowe whisked a screwdriver out of his coat pocket and quickly pried open the lid. He paused as their eyes met again in the wispy light of the moon, then with great ceremony, Crowe flung open the top of the casket like Pandora opening her box.

It was not at all what they had expected. There were human bones inside the coffin to be sure, but these were clearly not the remains of the late Robert Nolan. They belonged to a newborn, no more than twenty-one inches long.

Bride and Crowe stared at their find in stunned silence. A sense of dread fell over the pit as they discovered they had made an awful miscalculation.

"Well," said Crowe as he hurled a handful of dirt in defeat. "It certainly isn't Sir Nolan, is it?"

Bride stared at the skeleton of the child, mesmerized by the sight. "He or she," he said in a melancholy tone.

"What? He or she?"

"*He* or *she* isn't Sir Nolan. Not 'it' isn't. This was a person. Like the brother I lost. This child had a name and was living and breathing, even if just for a few days or weeks. But now, nobody knows where he or she is. Just like my brother. Who knows, this could be him."

"I don't mean to sound insensitive or disrespectful, but I don't think the Princess Royal would be coming to visit the grave of your brother. I mean, you understand what I'm saying, don't you?"

Bride gently nodded his head. "Yes. Just...wishful thinking, I guess."

"For all we know, this could be a girl."

"Right. For all we know."

"What I *do* know is that if Princess Catherine comes back anytime soon, people are going to be visiting us in jail. Let's get this back in order."

Bride nodded in agreement, finally snapping out of his mild trance. Without so much as a word between them, they slammed shut the lid and replaced the coffin in its original position.

They were exhausted and frightened, but summoned enough strength to fill in the hole with blinding speed. In less than half an hour they were stamping on the wet sod on top of the grave, pressing it into place to cover their crime.

They ran swiftly back to Crowe's car and sped away as the steeple bells unleashed two haunting clangs that seemed to chase after them in their escape.

Bride and Crowe were still sweating as they sat in the reporter's car outside of the Dunbarton. There was an uneasy quiet between them.

"Now what?" said Bride, the first words spoken between them in almost an hour.

"I don't know, I don't know! What the bloody hell is going on here?"

It was the question of questions, and to a weary and frightened Malcolm Bride, the answer seemed more elusive than ever. "Who do you think it is?" whispered Bride.

"Could be any of a number of possibilities," replied Crowe with a dismal shake of his head. "Some illegitimate child perhaps, difficult to even guess. Knowing Princess Catherine's penchant for adopting strays, it could just be some waif off the street that found a place in her heart. Although I doubt it's as simple as that. This could be big, really big, terrifyingly big."

"So what do we do now?" said Bride. "Do we just walk away?"

"I don't know," said Crowe. "I need some time to sort this matter out a bit. This isn't going according to plan, and right now I don't have any fresh ideas. I'll call you tomorrow. In the meantime, speak to no one you don't already know, and trust no one that you think you do."

Bride nodded as he exited Crowe's car and hopped up onto the curb. He froze in his tracks as a stranger walked by with an umbrella tucked under his arm. Suddenly everyone seemed suspicious.

The sight of the infant's bones in the coffin hours before had an unsettling effect on Bride. As he pulled his weary body into his bed, he couldn't remember feeling this alone in his life. He stared into the infinite darkness of Room One, thinking about the mother and brother he never knew, and trying to come to grips with the likelihood that he might never find another trace of their existence. The idea of not knowing what happened to them bothered him more than he had ever imagined. His trip to England had been intended to give his family matters some closure and to bring him a sense of wholeness. The journey was having a decidedly different effect.

If there was anything positive that had come out of his experience, Bride finally understood why people went to visit the dead.

Chapter Twelve

The pounding at the door of Room One at the Dunbarton jolted Malcolm Bride from a fitful night of sleep.

"Who is it?" he bellowed with the annoyance of someone whose usual pleasantness had not yet caught up with his physical being.

"It's Mrs. Rumpole!"

"What do you want?" said Bride as he buried his head into the feather pillow.

"You 'av another message and I think it's important!"

Bride sprang to his feet as awareness cleared out the cobwebs in his head. He pulled on a robe and quickly opened the door.

Fionnuala Rumpole took a step back in shock when she saw the professor. "What in God's name 'appened to you?" she blurted out.

Bride was taken aback by her reaction, especially so soon after waking up. "What do you mean?"

"Look at yourself! You look like a dog that's been digging for bones!"

Fionnuala had no idea how close she'd come to the truth. Only now did Bride catch a glimpse of himself in a hallway mirror and saw the streaks of sweaty dirt crisscrossing his face. He looked like a chimney sweep just finishing a long day's work. His hands were even worse, with a generous amount of St. Bartholomew's acreage lodged up under his fingernails.

"I uh...uh..." began Bride.

"Don't even bother, Mr. Bride. You're about the worst at making up stories I've ever met."

"It's *Doctor.* Dr. Bride."

She paid no attention to the correction as she handed him an envelope with his name on the front and a red wax seal on the back,
unmistakably a missive from Princess Catherine. "And no need tellin'
me this is another note from your friend at the local bookstore," said
Fionnuala.

"How do you know it's not?" replied Bride as he quickly tucked
the envelope away in his robe pocket.

"'Cause most messengers from the local bookstores don't drive
Bentleys, I suppose."

"Good point."

Fionnuala grinned as she glanced down either side of the hallway,
then leaned closer to Bride and spoke in a hushed tone.

"There's nothin' to be shy about. You know, you're not the first
American to have a romantic flirtation with an English lass."

"Oh?" said Bride, gladly realizing the innkeeper was unknowingly
getting him off the hook.

"We're sassier than you thought, aren't we?" she said with a wink.

"If you say so."

"Who is she? Can you tell me? No, never mind, I'm not one to go
puttin' me nose in other people's business. But judging by the quality
of that envelope and the car that brought it, I'd say she's a real lady."

"She is. Very much so."

"I knew it! I know these things. But she still took you for quite a
roll in the hay, didn't she!" said Fionnuala as she poked Bride in the
ribs. "I mean, just look at you!"

"Yes! Quite a sight I must be. Well then, I suppose I'll be cleaning
up now. You have a good morning, Mrs. Rumpole."

"I already *had* a good morning, Mr. Bride," she said as she headed
back down the corridor. "I'm workin' on me afternoon now!"

Bride closed the door and checked his watch on the nightstand.
He was stunned to discover that it was almost one o'clock. Bride
couldn't recall a single morning in the last twenty years that he'd slept
past 8:00 AM; but then again, the past week had offered one surprise
after another.

He eagerly grabbed the note in his robe pocket and quickly tore it
open. It was Catherine's handwriting, inviting him to watch polo. The
Royal Windsor Cup was to be contested that afternoon at Windsor
Castle. A driver would be arriving at 1:30 to take him there.

Bride scrambled into action, racing down the hallway to the com-
munal shower to wash away the incriminating dirt from the previous
night's activities.

As the stone walls of the Berkshire countryside whizzed by out-side the limousine that was taking him to Windsor, Bride chewed his fingernails. Partly to remove the last bits of dirt, but more to feed his nervousness. His mind was racing and he didn't like what he saw at the finish line. Why had he suddenly been invited to watch polo? Prin-cess Catherine hadn't mentioned anything about it before now, but suddenly she was summoning him to join her on the very day of the event.

There was only one logical conclusion—she must know what he and Crowe had done in the cemetery at St. Bartholomew's just hours before. Crowe was right. There *were* spies everywhere in London. Why else would an American commoner be whisked out to Windsor Castle? She had definitely repaid her debt for the return of the pill-box. And certainly a woman in her position wasn't in need of com-pany. No, there could only be one explanation.

Catherine knew. But how could she know? They had been sure nobody had seen them. Had Crowe broken their vow of secrecy? Out of the question. But somehow she knew. Why else was he going to Windsor? She knew. Absolutely. She knew.

He chewed his fingernails down to the quick.

By daylight, Windsor Castle was even more imposing than Bride had remembered. The massive Gothic structure dwarfed everything in sight, even the river Thames, which Bride only now realized flowed nearby.

He felt as though his heart were pounding visibly underneath his tweed jacket as he walked from the limousine to the viewing area. What would he say to the Princess? How could he possibly explain his activity in the graveyard?

With panic seeping rapidly into his mind, Bride considered flee-ing the scene. He turned back to the circular driveway, only to see his limousine pulling away.

"Dr. Bride?" came the gruff voice a few yards away.

He turned to see Trevor McFarlane walking his way with a scowl on his face. Bride did his best to glean some information from Trevor's expression but found it impossible because the same angry scowl was always there.

"Yes?" he replied with the feigned innocence of someone greeting an approaching policeman who's about to cite them for speeding.

"The Princess would like to see you in her box."

"I'm sure she would," he murmured.

Bride followed Trevor like a convict following his executioner to the gallows. For the first time in his life, the professor wished he were a better liar, because he was going to need the fabrication of a lifetime to extricate himself from this mess.

"So good of you to come, Dr. Bride!" exclaimed Princess Catherine as Bride entered her private box. She looked as regal as usual in her butterscotch herringbone suit, Wellington boots, and broad brimmed straw hat. He was surprised to find her alone.

"It's good to be here," he replied with caution. "It was unexpected, to say the least."

"I apologize for the short notice, but I tried to reach you by telephone late last night and heard you were out. Did you find something interesting?"

She definitely knew, thought Bride. There was that inner resolve of hers again, toying with him. The Princess had raised her binoculars to her eyes and trained on the field of play, but Bride knew her attention was still focused on him. She wanted to watch him squirm, to sink deeper into the quagmire. So be it, decided the professor. If this were to be a game of cat and mouse, he would at least take a turn at being the cat.

"Yes, I found something, but it wasn't what I had expected."

"Oh? Disappointed, were you?" replied Catherine without taking her eyes from the binoculars.

"I think confused is a better word."

"I understand. I've never actually done anything like that myself, although I suppose I could if I wanted to. From what I hear, there are so many to choose from."

Catherine's final remark didn't make sense to Bride. Certainly she was better at this verbal jousting than he, but her words didn't seem to fit into her plan of attack. His pulse quickened. Perhaps he had been mistaken. Was there a chance she *didn't* know about St. Bartholomew's?

"Are we talking about the same thing?" he ventured.

"I should think so."

She turned to look at him with slight puzzlement. "The innkeeper at your hotel, a Mrs. Rumpole I believe...she told me that you had gone over to Covent Garden to buy a watercolor from one of the street artists. She assumed you found a good pub on the way back and that's why you weren't back as yet."

Bride suddenly remembered yet another falsehood he had told Fionnuala Rumpole as he had exited the Dunbarton the night before on his way to meet Colin Crowe. He really needed to improve his amateurish skills at lying and covering up if this was to become a way of life for him.

"Is something wrong?" inquired Catherine.

"Why did you invite me here today?"

"Why? Well, I must admit I don't really know. I suppose I thought you would enjoy the spectacle, that's all."

"If you're still feeling indebted about that pillbox I returned—"

"This had nothing to do with the pillbox," interrupted Catherine. "This was merely a gesture of friendship. Even Royals are permitted to have friends, are they not?" she asked with a smile.

"Yes. Yes they are," said Bride, feeling even guiltier about his skullduggery the night before. But soon he felt a flood of relief as he realized his secret was safe.

"Tell me the truth," said Catherine. "Do you like my new hat?"

The answer was already formed in Bride's mind from the first time he had seen the hat. "No."

It wasn't the answer Catherine had been expecting. She looked wounded as she frowned at Bride. "Honestly, Dr. Bride, sometimes your candor can be quite insulting."

"You asked me a question, I told you the truth. I don't really like the hat. If you didn't want the truth, then why did you ask me the question?"

"I was hoping for some affirmation."

"Meaning *you* don't really like the hat either."

"I didn't say that."

"Don't you want to know *why* I don't like the hat?"

"I'm not sure I can withstand any more of your honesty."

"I don't like the hat because it covers up your face. I realize a proper English lady is supposed to keep her milky white complexion away from the sun, but to me it's like draping a sheet over a new sofa."

"That's what you compare me to? A piece of furniture?"

Bride drew a sturdy breath and looked pointedly at the Princess. "What I'm trying to say is that I'd prefer to look at the face more than the hat."

Catherine started to issue another retort from her defensive position, but thought better of it as she recognized the sincere sentiment Bride was trying to convey with his backhanded compliment. She stared down at her feet like a shy schoolgirl, slowly removed the hat and tossed it aside. She gently smoothed back a lock of hair behind her blushing ear, feeling as though her face was suddenly on full display in a museum.

"The truth is, Professor, I didn't particularly care for the hat myself." She smiled warmly, then raised her chin high like the proud blueblood she was and turned back to look at the field of play.

Only now did Bride fully realize there was a polo match being fiercely contested on the field below. His eyes zeroed in on one player in particular who seemed to be moving faster and more furiously than any of the other competitors. The player beneath the deep purple helmet spun his dapple-gray polo pony back and forth as he pitched from side to side on his English saddle, slashing at the ball with spitfire rage. The man and his steed reminded Bride of St. George slaying a dragon. The player allowed nothing to stand in his way. He bumped the other horses, took unapologetic swipes at their legs, and jerked mercilessly on the reins of his own frothing mount.

"Who is that?" asked Bride as he pointed to the field.

"Which one?"

"Number seven, the madman on the gray horse."

"You mean you don't know?"

"Sorry. I don't follow polo."

"You don't need to. That's Prince George."

Bride blushed with complete embarrassment. No sooner had he been delivered from one hellfire that he found himself plunging into yet another abyss.

"I'm...I'm sorry. I guess I don't really understand the game."

Catherine tossed back her head and laughed. "No need to apologize. George *is* a dirty player. I'm afraid he gets a bit daft in the heat of competition, and unfortunately nobody can say anything about it because he's who he is. Those who dare to complain incur even greater wrath in their next outing. Just be glad his passion is polo and not fencing."

As Catherine's eyes locked onto his, Bride found himself becoming more and more enamored with her understated charm. Under different circumstances, this was someone he might even be inclined to pursue socially. She was that rare woman whom Bride would consider inviting to lunch, or escorting to a film festival or an art gallery. But this wasn't New England. This was Olde England. She was a Princess and all illusions of anything beyond this afternoon ended right there.

"George's behavior only seems strange to you because you don't know him the way we do. The only time you see him in the States is when he's frozen on the pages of *Life* magazine or being interviewed about some honorary degree he's getting from Cambridge."

"That's about to change, isn't it?"

"Yes, and if anyone's prepared for it, it's George. My brother, for all of his faults, is nonetheless a man of tremendous resolve."

"Is that an inherited trait?"

Bride's seemingly innocent question caused a sudden flashing in Catherine's eyes, not unlike the reaction he had seen in Paddy Butterfill when he mentioned the name Bartholomew. Within an instant, however, her expression had returned to normal as she once again watched the polo match.

"As a young boy, George was packed off to Gordonstoun, a very rigid school for wealthy boys that in comparison makes Newgate prison appear like summer camp. But while the other lads were huddled in their bunks crying for their nannies, George was thriving on the challenge. He excelled at everything he did—academics, student government, athletics. He became so proficient at boxing that he beat his instructor to a bloody pulp one day. His classmates didn't consider him to be just another one of the boys."

"They saw him as a man?" said Bride with a nod.

She shook her head and stared into space.

"They saw him as a god. And he knew it. I think that's why he's so miserable now. Except for the few years he spent in the Royal Navy, he's never had the opportunity to do anything of any real significance with his life. He was born to lead, but he's fifty-seven years old and he's never raised a sword to do anything more than cut a wedding cake.

"He was born at a time that made him either too young or too old to fight in a war, not even a minor territorial dispute, and while most men his age would view that as a blessing, George sees it as an opportunity lost. He's a crusader without a crusade. He's socially impotent and for a man of his abilities, that bothers him more than you'll ever know."

"There again, that's subject to change," said Bride.

"We shall see," nodded the Princess. "We shall see."

Bride turned his attention back to the polo match. He found it odd that someone like George who had just declared his intent to become Prime Minister had time for something like polo. Stranger still was that this charter member of the upper crust was now asking for political support from the masses, comprised of dockworkers, miners, masons, and other real men whose jobs required perspiration. He doubted that any of them had ever seen a polo match, much less one on the grounds of Windsor Castle. How could a man whose day consisted of a few chukkers in the morning, tea in the afternoon, and chess and cognac at night possibly represent the best interests of the working class? The paradox was glaring to the American, but nobody else seemed to think that was strange. How very British, thought Bride.

The match ended after several hours with Prince George's team naturally the winner. Despite his less than gentlemanly play, every man on the field came over to congratulate the Prince, even those sporting gashes from George's uncaring polo mallet. It was obvious to Bride that this was not a display of respect or admiration—this was an act of fear.

Bride followed Catherine down to the playing field as George walked off, splattered with mud and sweat but beaming like a man who had just led a successful charge of the Light Brigade.

"Congratulations," said Catherine politely, hugging her brother in a cursory fashion for the benefit of the battalion of Royal Pap rapid-firing their cameras from behind the velvet ropes nearby.

"Thank you. Fourteen to six is a solid thrashing ," boasted George.

"Thirteen," blurted Bride before he could stop himself.

"Excuse me?" said the startled Prince as he pulled off his helmet.

It was the first time Bride had seen Prince George without every hair slicked back into place, and made a mental note of how common he could look. The Prince was smiling, but it was the kind of tense grin that belongs to a man standing on the precipice of losing his temper. He stared at Bride with an intimidating glare in his eyes like someone who had just been accused of cheating in a friendly game of poker. Catherine grew nervous as she watched her brother, hoping he would let the American's remark pass. Bride sensed he was walking in deep woods here, but decided straight ahead was the only way out.

"I thought the final score was thirteen to six," said Bride, starting to feel some of the same fear as George's opponents. "But perhaps I'm mistaken."

George's face softened a bit as the grin on his face took on a more sincere look. "No, I actually believe you are correct, Dr. Bride. It was thirteen, but a rewarding victory all the same."

Bride was thrust into a mild state of shock. Not because Prince George had agreed with him, but because he actually remembered Bride's name. "Wonderful victory," said Bride, putting an end to an awkward situation.

"Well then," said George, "off to spend a penny. I have a speech to give tonight." George strode away in his distinct heel to toe fashion.

"Your brother has quite a presence to him, doesn't he?" said Bride after George was out of earshot.

"He's the Crown Prince of Great Britain. He's supposed to have a presence. What's more impressive to me is that an American professor can stand toe to toe with him and not flinch. That's a rare sight."

Bride blushed and shrugged his shoulders. Princess Catherine had no idea how intimidated he had really been. On the other hand, he felt a growing sense of pride that the Prince had put him to the test and he had passed.

"Would you like to stay for his speech?" asked Catherine.

"I really have to go. But thank you for inviting me. I will always remember your kindness."

"That sounds more like farewell than just goodbye."

"I don't know if I'll see you again."

"Are you leaving England?" she asked with a hint of remorse.

"No, but I need to get back to my original purpose for coming here."

"And what would that be?"

"I came here to trace my ancestry. That's what I was doing the night I first saw you. I've been a little sidetracked since then, but now it's time to get back to it," said Bride as if trying to convince himself that his original mission to England was more important than the mystery he'd uncovered upon arrival.

"It seems to mean a great deal to you."

"It does. And the more elusive the truth, the more it intrigues me."

Bride's mind flashed back to the skeletal remains of the infant he'd discovered the night before, and his irrational impulse during this private moment was to confess his actions and ask Catherine what she knew about the grave. Fortunately his rational mind conquered his primal urges and returned him to the conversation.

"And this pursuit of the truth precludes our meeting again?" she asked.

"Not necessarily, but I don't want to wear out my welcome. I've had three audiences now with the Princess Royal, three more than most could hope for."

"And three is your limit?"

Bride gently shook his head as he narrowed his gaze and looked squarely into Catherine's eyes. "From the moment I arrived in England, I began to discover that I *have* no limits."

A timid smile of relief spread across Catherine's face. "Good. That's starting to sound more like goodbye than farewell."

She extended her hand. Bride returned her smile and nodded as he took her hand and gave it a polite shake.

"Goodbye, your Highness" he told her. Bride held onto Catherine's hand for a fraction of a second longer than proper protocol advised, indicating to her that they indeed would meet again. Just hours before, he had dreaded seeing her. He now left wondering when he might see her again.

Bride made it back to the Dunbarton that night in time to catch the late news on the BBC, which already had the undivided attention of Peter and Fionnuala Rumpole.

As his image shone on the television set in the den, Prince George had completed his transformation from muddy horseman to polished statesman as he sat in one of Windsor Castle's gilded drawing rooms. His chest puffed out of his double-breasted chalkstripe suit as he delivered his first national campaign speech, quite possibly the first speech in his life that really meant anything.

"The task to restore England to its former greatness will begin at Buckingham Palace. If I am elected, and even if I'm not, I will see to it that the Royal Family will pay more taxes. The Chancellor of the Exchequer will be instructed to permit fewer names on the civil list. Traditional perks of the monarchy will be pared down, including decommissioning the Royal yacht. Diplomatic junkets will no longer be financed by the taxpayers, nor will picnics at Ascot, or weekend hunts in the grouse moors of Yorkshire.

"If I am going to lead this country, then I am going to lead by example. The pounds that have heretofore been wasted on the idle rich will be woven back into the fabric of Mother England. Railways will be modernized, shipbuilding will be revitalized, our schools will be upgraded, and our military brought back to high standard. We will deal a crushing blow to terrorism, so that the streets of Belfast and London will be safe once again. The Labourites brought you bankruptcies and repossessions, unemployment and inflation. The Conservative Party will bring you prosperity where there is now poverty, hope where there is now despair, and pride where there is now shame. We will march back to Jarrow and reclaim our wealth, our pride, and our honor. May God bless us all as we embark on the path to glory. Goodnight."

"I'm not bloody believin' me ears!" shouted Rumpole. "He wants the Royals to pay *more* taxes? He's got my vote right there! If he can get that bleedin' lot to pitch in, who knows what he might be able to accomplish!"

"It's just political talk," said Fionnuala.

"It's *all* just talk, love. But for the first time, I actually like what I'm 'earin'!"

Fionnuala picked up the empty teacups on the table and started to head for the kitchen. Only then did she see Professor Bride standing in the doorway to the sitting room.

"Mr. Bride! Did you get a look at that? Bonnie Prince Georgie promising us the moon."

"A born politician," replied Bride, abandoning all hopes of ever getting Mrs. Rumpole to call him "Doctor".

"And how was your day? Did you see your lady friend?"

"Uh, yes, as a matter of fact, I did."

"My, my, keep this up and you might not be makin' it back to the States. Leastways, not alone."

Bride shrugged and forced a smile. It pained him to think that would never be possible.

Chapter Thirteen

Ordinarily, a politician looks ridiculous whenever he tries to create a photo opportunity by donning the appropriate garb in a working-class setting. The hardhats always seem to sit too high, the protective goggles distort the face, or the pristine white smocks stand out glaringly among the soiled ones of the regular factory workers and scream "I don't belong here!"

More elections have been lost through gross miscalculations as to how the candidate will appear at one of these staged media events. If he or she looks idiotic in the hairnet at the canning factory, rest assured he or she will look even worse on the front page the next day.

Which is why the success of Prince George's campaign stop at the local smithy in Stagsden was all the more remarkable. The highly choreographed event was bathed in surreal light. Here was a member of the most famous family on earth putting on dirty brown overalls and hammering new shoes onto one of the local plowhorses as a herd of media captured each bouncing blow of the ball peen hammer. The hundreds of locals in attendance marveled at how well George handled himself, never once considering the fact that he developed his skills while shoeing one of his £15,000 polo ponies.

One of Prince George's seminal experiences during one of his diplomatic junkets abroad was getting the opportunity to meet American President Richard Nixon. George was always impressed that a man of such humble beginnings could rise to be the Head of State, and he could only wonder how far someone with his own high upbringing could go. George was also in awe of how well Nixon moved in all social classes, seemingly equally as comfortable with the ushers in the aisles as he was with the stars on the stage. George began to understand what Nixon already knew—that no matter how rich or how important a person becomes, that man or woman still only has one vote to cast, and since the "haves" are far outnumbered by the "have nots" the smart politician learns how to play the fanfare of the common man. It was to this end that he now found himself holding the hoof of a plowhorse in the Cotswolds.

"What brings you to Stagsden?" asked a voice in the crowd.

The real answer was obvious to anyone who looked at the most recent polls showing the people of Stagsden prepared to vote over-whelmingly in favor of the Conservative candidate. Taking full advantage of a quirky British law that doesn't require a Member of Parliament to actually live in the district he or she represents, the Conservative Party had decided to run Prince George in Stagsden, thus assuring him of a landslide victory. The Prince, however, tried to make his visit there seem more noble.

"The more appropriate question," said George without missing a beat with the hammer, "is why haven't I been here before? When is the last time an MP wandered in your midst?"

"'92" shouted one of the locals.

"Yeah...1892!" shouted another.

George paused from his work and laughed heartily with the crowd. He recognized a cue to take center stage when he heard one. "Exactly my point. Government has lost touch with the working man." The crowd roared its approval. George felt the wave of momentum under his feet and he rode the crest. "Unless we come to know you, we can't possibly know what you need. Parliament is not the backbone of Britain...The Royal Family is not the backbone of Britain...*you* are the backbone and it's high time this nation stood erect and told its leaders to stop talking and start listening!"

The thunderous roar from the gathering was loud enough to spook the poor old plowhorse. George deftly turned and placed his right hand on the neck of the horse and stroked it soothingly. What the cameras didn't see behind George's back was his left hand snatching the bit in the animal's mouth and yanking down hard to bring it back under control.

He turned back to the crowd and smiled. "Apparently this is a Labour horse," he joked. "They're all a bit nervous these days." The laughter again cascaded. George had won them over handily.

The complaisant moment was interrupted when one of the journalists finally dared to ask a serious question. "Now that you're involved in politics, are you prepared to renounce your claim to the throne?"

A hush fell over the gathering. Even the plowhorse sensed it was time to remain perfectly still as Prince George contemplated his reply.

"As I have attempted to explain on several occasions now, there is no need to renounce my claims because I will never become King, at least not anytime soon. But in the meantime, I can't sit idly by and watch my beloved country slip further and further behind. I have fresh ideas and I have the energy to implement them if given the chance."

"Getting back to my original question," continued the reporter, "why *not* renounce if you have no intention of ever ascending to the throne?"

George did his best to mask his growing annoyance with the persistent reporter. "Why should I waste valuable time on a non-issue? Mother and I agree that the sovereignty of this nation is a sacred trust, a job for life, and she has my full support as long as she wears the Crown."

"But I read in the tabs that she's actually quite ill," said the reporter. "Some are saying it might even be cancer."

George scoffed. "Consider the source. We're not talking about esteemed journalists such as yourselves, who will no doubt believe me when I tell you that Queen Alexandra is in much better condition than the Labour Party, and destined to be in power a great deal longer!"

Applause shattered the awkward silence. George had finally managed to fend off the irritating questions and bring the discussion back to his agenda—the election. He would depart Stagsden to rave reviews and he knew that with a few more campaign stops like this one, he would be unstoppable.

◆　◆　◆

Crowe held up his pint of ale and stared at its amber marriage of barley, hops, and malt. "It's about the only thing I've seen lately that has much clarity," he mused philosophically. "Nothing on this island makes sense anymore."

Bride leaned next to him at the railing of the Marlborough Arms pub and nodded his agreement. "I know what you mean. For every answer, there seems to be a dozen new questions."

"I'm assuming that you didn't learn anything new about St. Bartholomew's when you met with Princess Catherine at the polo match."

"How'd you know about that?" asked a startled Bride.

Crowe sipped his pint with a twinkle in his eye. "When are you going to learn, professor, that I am the toll booth operator on the information superhighway?"

"Well needless to say, I didn't bring up the subject."

"Why not?" said Crowe with the incredulity of a journalist who was accustomed to posing the tough questions.

"Oh, and how exactly would that conversation begin? 'Catherine, I was digging around in a graveyard the other night and discovered something peculiar.' I don't think so."

"I thought you two were becoming friends."

"We are, which is maybe why I'm becoming increasingly reluctant to pursue this whole sordid affair. In addition to those bones we found in St. Bartholomew's, I think there's a lot of pain buried there as well. For Catherine's sake, I'm not sure I want to dig it up."

"Chivalry is not dead," chuckled Crowe. "It's not feeling well, but at least it's not dead." Crowe downed the remainder of his pint and motioned to the bartender for a refill. He leaned both elbows onto the bar and squinted his eyes, deep in thought.

"Something's just not right with this whole Prince George thing," said Crowe as the bartender brought him his ale. "It just doesn't quite add up to me."

"I can imagine that seeing one of your Royals seeking political office takes some getting used to," nodded Bride.

"It's not so much that he's taking the plunge. I'm a bit of a modernist, I can accept that. It's the bedfellows he's taken up with."

"What do you mean?"

"If *I* were the Prince, and I'm bloody glad I'm not, but if I were, I would think teaming up with the Labourites would be the more logical choice."

"Why's that?"

"Well, the Tories ran things for decades, and they eventually made a mess of it. Why? Because Conservatives are exactly that—conservative! They don't like change! They don't embrace new ways of thinking. Yet now they're going to hurl centuries of tradition into the Thames. How do they reconcile that? That's what bothers me."

"From what I can tell, Prince George is anxious to bring some changes to Great Britain, and the Conservatives provide him with the quickest avenue to power."

"Yes, but it seems to me that if George is really trying to create some change, he wouldn't align himself with a crowd that is intrinsically opposed to change! It worries me, it does."

"Good point," nodded Bride.

"Maybe you'll find out more when you dine at Kensington."

Bride was confused. "Excuse me?"

"You've been invited to dinner at Prince George's apartment in Kensington," Crowe assured him.

"I was impressed up to this point, Mr. Crowe, but I'm afraid you've tied into some misinformation. I haven't received any invitations to Kensington. Sorry."

"Well not yet. But I saw an advance copy of the guest list and your name was on it. So keep Tuesday night open." Crowe winked and licked off the pale white mustache of ale from under his nose.

Bride was stunned that this man knew more about his comings and goings than he did. And his respect for Crowe's abilities to gather information took a quantum leap forward. "Why in the world am I being invited to Kensington Palace?" Bride demanded to know.

"The same reason you've been traipsing out to Windsor Castle I would imagine. Can't you see it, old boy? You have cracked the inner circle! You're in the Royal fraternity! And do you understand that there are only two ways of getting there? Either you're born into it, or one of the bluebloods takes a fondness to you. In this case, the Princess Royal has her eye on you."

"That's ridiculous! We're friends, nothing more. Besides, Catherine can have any man she wants."

"Yes, but has she wanted one? Since the death of her husband, she hasn't been seen with a single escort at any public function. Suddenly, she's invited the same man to three events in less than a fortnight. Doesn't that tell you something? Open your eyes, man! You don't get invites like that just because they're looking to fill a seat."

It wasn't so much a revelation to Bride as it was his wildest imaginings suddenly melding with reality. If indeed Catherine had developed a fondness for him, then the attraction was most certainly reciprocal. Up to this point he hadn't dared to even *think* of the possibility, but he was overwhelmingly happy to hear it from the mouth of Colin Crowe, a reliable source if there ever was one.

Chapter Fourteen

Elliott Wiggs was not one given to smiling easily, but as he studied the front page of *The Times*, the thin corners of his lips turned ever so slightly upward.

"*The Times* is comparing you to Henry the VI," he said to George, who was engrossed in the morning edition of *The Independent*. "He was the good one, you know."

George showed Wiggs the paper stretched out between his own arms. "Listen to Bevins's column. 'Prince George handled his first national television address like a seasoned veteran of many political campaigns. Above all, his remarks seem to capture the restless pulse of anyone who has ever eaten kidney pie'. I rather like this Bevins chap!"

"It's just the start," said Wiggs like a wise old grandfather. "Just the start."

♦ ♦ ♦

Queen Alexandra hadn't been out of her bedroom in Buckingham Palace for over two months. Doctors had prescribed complete rest to help the aging monarch regain her strength from repeated bouts with pneumonia, but the isolation for the most public of public figures was slowly draining her spirit.

"Good afternoon, Mother," said Princess Catherine as she opened a shutter to let in the rare London sunshine. "Did you sleep well?"

"No worse than usual," replied the Queen as she struggled to sit up in bed. "I'm just glad to wake up. I understand the papers are trying to bury me already."

"Absolutely not!" exclaimed Catherine. She sat on the edge of her mother's bed and gently stroked her forehead. "You have an entire country out there trying to nurse you back to good health. You shouldn't worry about such things. You're going to be fine."

"It's not really me I'm worried about. I'm not afraid of dying. Death comes to all mortals. What concerns me most is the death of institutions."

"What in the world are you talking about?"

"I'm talking about the monarchy. Our life as we know it. I feel that every inch I move closer to the grave, the Crown follows right behind me."

"That's nonsense, Mother! There has always been a King or Queen of England, and there always will be. It's ludicrous to suggest otherwise."

"I used to think that myself, but times have changed. The poor of England now *know* they're poor, and the notion of aristocrats lounging about in castles and palaces can't sit too well. Your brother understands this. Why else would he be launching into this political foolishness?"

"He only wants to make an impact."

"The irony is, it's only going to hasten the demise of the monarchy. He's stepped out onto a playing field where the Labourites don't give a farthing about his Royal blood. They'll make him a laughing-stock, and the derision will spread to the rest of us. Part of me hopes I'm not around to see it."

"Don't talk like that!" pleaded Catherine.

"But it's true. I can't help but wonder to myself if I shouldn't have turned over the throne to your brother earlier. I should have sensed his impatience. Now it's too late."

Alexandra closed her eyes and drifted back to sleep, her only escape from her mounting burdens.

Catherine grimaced as she sat next to the ailing Queen. It pained her to see her proud mother in such a helpless state, and somewhere deep inside, she feared Alexandra's words might be prophetic. She kissed her softly on the cheek and tiptoed out of the room.

◆ ◆ ◆

"You *have* to reconsider!" cried Catherine to George in an angry tone of voice that nobody else in the kingdom would dare to use. "All of this political nonsense is killing Mother!"

"Nonsense?" shot back George above the rising tones of Paganini in the background. "Is that what you think this is? Some new hobby

I've taken up, like lawn bowling?"

The Princess stood over her younger brother as he sat at his study desk in Kensington Palace, delicately wrapping a yellow plume onto a fishing hook with fine green thread. "I perhaps know better than anyone what you are capable of doing, and therefore I feel no less an authority on that of which you are incapable. You can't win, and worse than that, you threaten to destroy all of us in the process."

"I appreciate your undying confidence in me, dear sister."

"Look at you! You're vying for one of the most powerful positions in the free world, and you've spent the afternoon fashioning fishing lures!"

"I find it relaxing."

"Well, you're going to have plenty of time to relax once the general election is over."

Prince George snapped off the thread with his teeth and attempted to tie the end onto the hook. His forefinger slipped as he pulled the thread taut and the barb of the hook sank deep into his flesh. He didn't flinch as he backed the hook out of his finger, unleashing a tiny geyser of blood. "Are you more worried about Mother dying, or losing your Royal allowance?" asked George.

"What a perfectly awful thing to say!" bellowed Catherine.

"You're right. I apologize." George stood up and placed his hands on Catherine's shoulders. Tiny droplets of blood trickled onto her white linen blouse. "Nobody feels worse about Mother's present physical state than I, despite what you might think. But the fact of the matter is she's mistaken. The monarchy will be stronger than ever because for the first time since George III, the Crown will have real power—power to make change."

She looked at George with alarm. "You talk as if you don't intend to give up the throne if you're elected Prime Minister."

"What I'm trying to say is that England needs a real leader and that leader is me—you know it. And if I'm given the chance, I will succeed at everything I promise to do. And by so doing, I will breathe new life into the monarchy and restore some respect, because besides you and Mother, nobody else in the House of Windsor has done much to earn it."

"I suppose this is where I make my entrance," cackled Prince John as he entered the room. He plopped down into the centuries old Chippendale chair and propped his black leather boots onto the priceless French writing table in front of it. "What you fail to understand, Brother George, is that the monarchy is already dead. The ravens have flown the Tower."

George's eyes flashed with anger as he stood angrily in front of his slouching younger brother. "When I appoint a new Secretary of State for environment, I shall see to it that the cleanup of toxic waste sites begins with you."

"George, please!" pleaded Catherine.

John sneered back at his brother, unfazed by the verbal attack. "I really just dropped by to tell you the news."

"News of what?" snapped George.

"My divorce. Jackie and I are finally making it official."

The woman to whom John referred was one Jacqueline Wordforth. Their marriage had been arranged five years before, with the hope and understanding that the Cambridge educated daughter of Sir Michael Wordforth would provide a calming influence for the way-ward young Prince. In fact, the opposite had occurred. John was successful in converting the innocent lass into his religion of moral decay, until she became so proficient that she had no trouble launching a life of debauchery all on her own.

They were still married on paper, but over the last three years, Jackie had been seen sunbathing in Greece more than she'd ever been seen with Prince John, and nearly everyone had forgotten that they were actually man and wife. As long as the subject of divorce was never mentioned, the British public hadn't seemed to mind their obvious separation and allowed the new arrangement to proceed without much furor.

"What!" screamed George. "Why now?"

"We just felt like it was time," John replied casually. "I think we both need our freedom."

"Oh, I see," said George sarcastically. "As opposed to the oppressive state of affairs you both endure now."

John was thoroughly enjoying watching his brother's anger rise. "I knew you would understand."

"He does raise a valid question, John," interjected Catherine. "Why do you suddenly feel the need to do this?"

"Why not?"

George spun around and slammed his hand down on the writing table. "Why not? I'll tell you why not! Because Royals don't divorce, that's why not!"

"You mean they don't divorce when one of them is running for political office and it becomes potentially embarrassing?"

"I mean they don't divorce period!"

"But times are changing, Georgie boy. I believe you recently said that yourself."

"I know you're doing this to hurt my campaign, and it will accomplish that, but I can take it. In fact, as I think about it, a bit of distance between you and me would only enhance my reputation. But I'm asking you to rethink this, or at the very least postpone. If for no other reason, you need to consider Mother. This is going to hit her very hard."

"Oh, like you give a tinker's damn about Mother. The sooner she's boxed up and packed off to Westminster Abbey, the sooner you can latch on to the sceptre."

George was seething venom from every pore. "You're pitiful, do you know that? If it were possible to divorce a sibling, I should initiate the proceedings right now."

"George is right," said Catherine. "We need to worry about Mother."

"Mother has people she pays to worry about her. I need to worry about me, and the sooner I'm free and clear of Jackie, the happier I'll be."

John stood up to leave, but George suddenly rushed up to him and in a fit of temper shoved him back into the chair. The Chippendale tipped over, sending John sprawling onto the floor.

"You are not getting a divorce!" he screamed. "Do you understand? One more word about it and I'll see to it that your allowance is immediately discontinued!"

John slowly picked himself up off the floor. He maintained his air of defiance, but was careful now to keep a safe distance away from his enraged and considerably stronger older brother. "I understand, Georgie boy. Royals don't divorce. We just get rid of our wives the old fashioned way, don't we?"

Every fiber in George's body twitched with anger. One more word out of John's mouth and he would pounce. Catherine quickly took three steps forward to put herself in between them, creating a barrier that would allow John to slink out of the room with his limbs intact.

"So wonderful we can all still get together like this!" said John as he walked out the door. "Just like the old days at Sandringham. Ah, family!"

The nerve endings in George's face were firing involuntarily as he watched John disappear into the corridor. He sucked away a rising droplet of blood on his finger and spat on the floor.

♦ ♦ ♦

Prince John sought immediate refuge in The Crypt, where he was among the first to arrive as the doors opened for the evening. He was soon joined by Nigel Banks-Finch of the *Sun Times* and his open checkbook. They found a couch in a quiet corner and began their sordid business.

"Alexandra...any change?" queried Banks-Finch, skipping any small talk and getting straight to the heart of the matter.

"No. Nothing."

"Then why the bloody hell did you page me?"

"I've got something rich for you."

"How rich?"

"Front page."

"This better be more newsworthy than just you and Jackie getting a divorce."

"It is, but it'll cost."

"How much?"

"A thousand pounds."

"A thousand! Out of the question."

"Fine. If you won't pay for it, I know five other tabs that will, and you can read about it in *their* headlines tomorrow."

The Prince lit a cigarette and sank down into the couch as he stared blankly around the disco with an attitude that said "take it or leave it."

Banks-Finch drummed his fingers as if he was mulling it over, but he knew he was checkmated. He popped open the hasps on his briefcase and John sat forward in Pavlovian response. Banks-Finch fished out ten notes of a hundred pounds each, wadded them together, and jammed them into John's trembling hand.

"This had better be damned good," said Banks-Finch as he tried to regain some semblance of control in the one-sided bargain. He pulled out his pen and pad and stood ready to copy down the expensive information.

"Catherine has taken on a lover," said John with a gleeful smirk.

Banks-Finch began to scribble but only managed to write a capital *C* when he abruptly stopped. He stared at Prince John, angry for several reasons. Firstly, except for Queen Alexandra herself, Princess Catherine was the last of the Royals the tabloids wanted to splash on their front pages. She had earned so much respect and admiration over the years that nobody wanted to read anything bad about Catherine, any more than the tabs wanted to write it.

Secondly, Banks-Finch was incensed that he'd just doled out a thousand pounds for something he didn't believe was even possible.

"Give me back the money!" he bellowed at Prince John.

"Why?" said John. "This is good stuff I'm giving you!"

"It's complete rubbish and you know it. Your sister wouldn't do that. Now give me back the money, or you can forget seeing any more of it from me."

"It's true and I can prove it."

"Is that so?" said Banks-Finch with disbelief.

"He's an American. His name is Bride. Malcolm Bride. He's a doctor of some sort, I believe. She's had him out to Windsor on two occasions, but the press has been so caught up with George's antics that they haven't noticed him milling about."

Banks-Finch narrowed his eyes, trying to discern how much truth was oozing out of Black Jack. He put his pen to his pad and started to take notes.

"Where did they meet?" he asked John.

"Don't know."

"What makes you think they're lovers? Couldn't they just be friends?" said Banks-Finch, not wanting to believe the worst about the Princess Royal. It was an unfamiliar position for a tabloid journalist, but after all, this was Catherine they were talking about.

"He's coming to dinner tonight at Kensington. That makes at least three dates they've had, maybe four. When's the last time someone escorted Catherine more than once? And when's the last time you let the facts get in the way of a good story?"

"Where can I find this Bride chap?"

"He's staying at a B and B in Bloomsbury, not sure of the name. I'll try to find out."

"You do that."

Banks-Finch closed his notebook and tossed it inside his briefcase, quickly shutting it and locking the hasps as if the scandalous information he'd just recorded would try to escape.

He walked away without any acknowledgement to the Prince.

As Banks-Finch moved through the assortment of human pariahs that were filtering into The Crypt, he cringed as he thought about how far his career as a journalist had strayed. But as he entered the London night, those regrets soon gave way to excitement over how pleased his bosses would be if what John had just revealed were really true.

Chapter Fifteen

Prince George and Elliott Wiggs sat comfortably in red leather wing chairs in the Prince's private library in Kensington Palace. The ubiquitous Nick Crumrie stood solemnly next to the blue and white marble fireplace where a tiny statuette of Napoleon stood with his arms crossed. One brass chandelier and hundreds of leatherbound books with gold embossment added the only richness and color to the darkly paneled room.

Their meeting on this night was with a grizzled old northerner named Ian Sturges, leader of the National Union of Mineworkers. With limited education and callous hands, he was the diametric opposite of the two men seated across the room, yet Sturges barely blinked in the presence of their power. Nor did Crumrie's menacing glare faze him. He had faced cave-ins at the collieries of Grimethorpe, violent labor disputes, and abject poverty, so intimidation was not a ploy that worked well on Ian Sturges. With forty years of coal dust permanently ground into the lines of his weathered face, he leaned out of his chair and looked George directly in the eyes.

"So what's the offer?" he growled in a gravel voice that was filtered by years of black soot.

George looked away as he casually twirled the brandy in his snifter, just to remind Sturges who was in control of this meeting. "We convince the High Court judges to overturn British Coal's plan to close fifty mining pits. In exchange, you assure us that the sixty thousand men in your union vote strictly Conservative in the election."

The Union boss narrowed his eyes. Break ranks with the Labour Party? Neither he nor anyone who'd ever washed coal dust out of his trousers had ever considered voting Conservative. It was political heresy. Might as well root for the French in the next World Cup. But fifty mining pits shutting down was a real threat to their livelihoods, destined to cost them their jobs and their way of life. It had appeared to be inevitable, so the Prince's startling proposal seemed too good to be true. "That's an awful lot to be promisin'. How do I know you can make good?"

"Yes, it is quite generous," said George, not answering the real question. "But think of it as a gesture of goodwill."

"Why are you so willing?" asked Sturges.

"This will be a close election in every district," chimed in Wiggs, "especially the western districts. We need every assurance that your union is firmly behind us. We can't have any surprises on election day."

Sturges mulled over the offer. The livelihoods of thousands of union members were firmly in his hands. Normally, he'd want more time to think about such a weighty matter, but he understood these were not men that one puts on hold. He took a deep breath into his coal-blackened lungs and slowly nodded his head. "If you can keep the pits open, I can deliver the votes."

"Consider it done!" said George, rising to his feet and shaking Sturges's gnarled hand. "England was built by the blood and sweat of coal miners, and we shan't turn our backs on them."

Prince George escorted Sturges to the door. "You do understand that there can be no mention of this meeting tonight, don't you?" he told him. "It would substantially weaken our position."

"I understand. I just want what's best for the men."

"Don't we all. Goodnight, Mr. Sturges."

The door closed behind the hulking miner. George and Wiggs paused for an appropriate amount of time, then broke into wide smiles. Obviously the meeting had gone their way.

◆ ◆ ◆

The dining room table at Kensington was set with only six blue and white Minton dinner plates adorned with a band of twenty-two karat gold.

Malcolm Bride sat uncomfortably in his center seat. The guests of honor were a husband and wife of minor nobility from Chelmsford in Essex who seemed intent on laying out every accomplishment in their coddled lives and dropping every name of import they'd ever encountered as if to justify their titles and their invitations to Kensington. When they weren't talking about themselves, the rest of their conversation focused on such weighty issues as the merits of

Belgian chocolate as compared to that manufactured by the Swiss, and the dire need for more pink flowers in the Pond Garden at Hampton Court Palace. Bride was a participant in the discussion only in polite smiles and nods, and about the time the wife issued the declaration that "there is *nothing* worse than rubbery lobster" was also about the time Bride tuned out completely.

Adding to his discomfort was the fact that the tuxedo that had been sent to his room at the Dunbarton earlier that day was at least a size and a half too small. On top of everything, he sensed he was sitting at the junction of studied stares from Prince George on one end of the table and Wiggs on the other.

Ordinarily an invitation to Kensington would be considered a high honor, a coveted opportunity to rub elbows with aristocracy in a more intimate setting, but to Bride, it was becoming a chore. The food wasn't even as good as what came out of the kitchen of Fionnuala Rumpole or the oven of Rachel Mawhinney. The glamour and mystique of royalty was rapidly fading for the American, and it was only the occasional beaming glance from Princess Catherine that allowed him to get through it. How he hoped Crowe was right about her feelings for him.

At the end of the meal, Bride wandered onto the veranda overlooking the massive gardens of Kensington Palace. He secretly hoped Catherine would see him out there and join him for a private moment. When the French doors opened behind him, he smiled to himself and turned around, expecting to see the moonlight glancing off her white silk gown.

Instead, there was Prince George standing next to him with one hand thrust awkwardly into his coat pocket. "Couldn't stand that couple from Essex any longer, eh?" said George.

"I didn't say that," stammered Bride.

"You didn't have to. An honest man wears his emotions like a new derby, and your hat has been on all night."

"I apologize if I was rude."

"Don't apologize. They're yammering twits and we both know it. The only reason they're here is because he employs about a thousand men on a fleet of oyster boats and I need their votes. How's that for honesty?"

"A trait I admire," said Bride.

"Cigar?" asked the Prince, handing a fine Cuban to Bride without waiting for a reply. George carefully clipped the end of his cigar with a gold knife. Bride bit off the end of his and spit the remains out over the veranda. George took out a stainless steel Ronson and held it up to Bride's face. He flicked the flintwheel and a flame of six inches shot out of the lighter.

"Sorry, mate!" said George as he adjusted the height of the flame and lit Bride's cigar. It had all felt according to script, thought Bride. George puffed heavily on his cigar, moistening his lips as he smoked. "So tell me, Dr. Bride," he said between puffs, "as long as honesty is the order of the moment, what are your intentions with my sister?"

Bride nearly choked. It was the last question he had expected to hear and he was not entirely prepared to answer. "Intentions?" he said.

"That's right. I notice you've been spending quite a number of hours in her company."

"Yes, yes I have. But at her request, I might add."

"So I understand, but what troubles me, dear Professor Bride, is that this is not normal behavior for my sister. Which naturally leads me to wonder what's going on between you two."

The Prince's air of condescension and smarmy tone of voice were starting to anger Bride, and that anger was being catalyzed into a growing self-confidence. "Well, not having known your sister until quite recently, I can't speak to that. What I *can* tell you is that what has transpired thus far has been purely Platonic, and I have no reason to believe that it won't remain so, Your Highness."

George could detect a hint of sarcasm and disrespect in the way Bride said *Your Highness*. He was preparing to launch his next verbal attack, but it was Bride who raised his foil first.

"As long as we're being honest, what I would like to know," began Bride with a steady voice, "is what exactly are *your* intentions?"

The Crown Prince wasn't accustomed to pointed questions in one on one conversations, but he was actually enjoying the challenge of a sparring session. "*My* intentions?" said George, echoing Bride's words.

"That's right," shot back Bride on cue. "Tell me about your vision for Great Britain."

"I think that's been made clear these past few nights on the BBC. I want to reclaim the stature this nation once knew."

"I understand that, but what puzzles me is the way you're going about it."

"Oh?" said George with amusement. "And would the American professor care to elaborate?"

Bride puffed on his Cuban, using the time to determine the most delicate way to couch his questions that were certain to irritate the Prince.

"I suppose I don't understand a lot about the English way of life because after all, I'm just an American, but I can't help but wonder about a few things. For instance, you talk quite a bit about energy conservation, but then you drive a gas guzzling Bentley. You voice support for the nature movement, but you still take part in fox hunting. You say you want to lead by example, but as you can see, that wouldn't appear to be the case. But again, I'm an American, and sometimes these things need to be explained to us colonials."

Prince George stared grim faced at Bride as the daggers thrown his way slowly sunk in. Bride sensed that he'd gone too far, but suddenly George broke into a wry smile. "You're a very clever man, Dr. Bride. A wise politician could use an adviser like you."

"From what I see in the most recent polls, you don't really need much advice."

"As you have so graciously pointed out, my politics may need a little fine tuning, but so far I seem to be striking a chord amongst the people. And to answer your original question, my intention is to combine their wishes with my vision."

"And a noble intention it is, if you'll pardon the pun."

The two men leaned against the railing of the balcony and puffed away. The war of words had been a draw.

The French doors to the veranda swung open and Catherine stepped outside from the dining room, shimmering in her white dress. "Is this a gentlemens' only club, or are ladies permitted?" she asked with a smile.

"We'll gladly make an exception," replied George. "In fact, I was just leaving. Don't want to leave Wiggs to fend for himself with the King and Queen of Essex. Goodnight, Dr. Bride. I enjoyed our little chat." George pitched his cigar over the railing with a flick of his middle finger and quickly exited the veranda. Bride and Catherine were suddenly alone, and neither one was quite sure what to do next.

"So, what was your 'little chat' about?" inquired the Princess.

"If you must know, it revolved around you. Or more to the point, he wanted to know about us."

"Us? I wasn't aware that you and I had become 'us'."

"Precisely what I told your brother."

"Very good. That matter is settled then."

The atmosphere on the veranda up to this point had been light-hearted and noncommittal, like a masquerade ball where nobody was admitting their true identity. But still feeling the surge of confidence after his duel with Prince George, Bride felt it was time to take off his mask.

"Is it settled?" he boldly asked the Princess Royal.

Catherine understood the true meaning of the simple question. All of their shared smiles across crowded rooms, their ambiguous question and answer sessions, their hypothetical posturing about love and romance, had been leading them to the precipice of romance. But the Princess stood on the brink and stopped short of taking the next step. She adroitly changed the subject but would soon regret it.

"So how are you enjoying your peek behind the palace walls?" she asked Bride.

"Here again, I have to be honest," said Bride. "It makes me a little uncomfortable, Your Highness."

"The formality?"

"No, the money. I can't believe how much you people spend on, well, on everything. Maybe it's because I'm an American, but I guess I don't understand how your subjects put up with it. There's so much poverty in the world, you don't have to go two miles from here to see it, but you live like...like—"

"Like Kings?" interjected Catherine with a twinge of irritation.

"Exactly. I guess I'm wondering why you even have a Royal Family."

"What you're asking in so many words, Dr. Bride, is why I exist. Is that your question?"

"Not exactly," backpedaled Bride.

"Oh, but I think it *is* your question."

"I didn't mean to offend you."

Catherine smiled to ease the tension. "No offense intended, so none taken. If the ideals of tradition, history, and national pride don't move you to deeper understanding, then perhaps I can put it in terms an American might comprehend. Twelve billion pounds in tourist money doesn't hurt the economy much. And *that*, Dr. Bride, is why I exist."

"Interesting that you mention that," began Bride, sounding like the Amherst professor he was. "Because I read recently that in the years since your mother became Queen, tourism in the United States has increased nearly five times, tripled in France and Italy, and gone up *thirteen* times in Spain. But in that same period of time, tourism in England has actually dropped. So you see—"

"How *dare* you!" she cried out loudly enough for the passersby on Kensington High Street to hear.

It was another classic case of Bride allowing his mouth to speak before his brain had considered the impact of his statement. The rage that welled up into Catherine's face told him immediately that he'd crossed way over the line. She pulled back her right hand, ready to slap him, but held it there as if she realized this was not behavior befitting the Princess Royal.

The French doors to the veranda burst open and Trevor McFarlane's broad shoulders blocked out the following light from the dining room.

"Is there a problem, Your Highness?" snapped Trevor as he glared at Bride, clearly hoping for her command to toss the professor over the balcony.

Catherine still had her hand poised to strike the cheek of the offending American as she trembled with anger. Slowly, she brought her hand down to her side and regained a modicum of her normal composure.

"Dr. Bride was just leaving. Be so kind as to drive him home, will you please?"

"My pleasure," sneered Trevor, and indeed it was.

"Farewell, Dr. Bride," said Princess Catherine without looking at him. The finality of her dismissal was not lost on him. He nodded his head in resignation and quietly exited the veranda.

Bride reluctantly climbed into the backseat of Catherine's limousine outside of Kensington Palace, mentally flogging himself for his bluntness. Trevor slammed the door behind him with purpose, then jumped into the driver's seat and quickly captained the vehicle off the palace grounds.

◆ ◆ ◆

On the ground floor of Kensington, Prince George and Elliott Wiggs had just finished saying their polite goodbyes to the couple from Essex and were witnesses to Bride's sudden departure. Wiggs narrowed his eyes as Trevor's limousine pulled away. He turned to Crumrie, standing in the shadows a few yards away.

"Something about that man bothers me," said Wiggs. "Have him followed until he's back on a plane to the States."

Crumrie nodded and immediately vanished to carry out the orders. Wiggs knew that with Crumrie on the case, Bride wouldn't even make it back to the Dunbarton without watchful eyes upon him.

◆ ◆ ◆

On the veranda above, Catherine watched them drive away. Her anger was slowly giving way to remorse.

Bride wasn't sure he liked Trevor, but he was most certain that Trevor didn't care for him. As the limousine moved swiftly down Knightsbridge toward Park Lane, his suspicions were confirmed as Trevor couldn't contain his contempt any longer.

"You shouldn't be upsettin' Her Highness," he sneered from the driver's seat. "You don't just go poppin' off like that, not to her. Where the hell do you come off bein' so bloody rude?"

"You don't even know what I said!" Bride shot back.

"Don't matter. It had to be somethin' off the beam to make her react the way she did. You need to apologize."

"All I did was point out a few simple facts that can be found in any almanac."

Trevor slammed on the brakes and jerked the car over to the side of the road in front of the Apsley House museum. He spun around from the front seat and stared squarely at Bride, his teeth gnashing with contempt. "It's not your place to be pointin' out anything! And if you know what's good for you, you'll pack your bags and ship out in the mornin'!"

Bride stood his ground with a false air of control, like a man staring into the jaws of an angry Doberman. "You love her, don't you?" he asked calmly.

"What?" snapped the grizzled Scot.

"Catherine...you love her, don't you?"

Trevor was taken aback by Bride's surprise response. "Well of course I do! Everyone loves Catherine!"

"Yes, I know, but I mean you're *in love* with her."

Trevor's eyes flared with a quick temper. "Where do you get off with such tosh?" he bellowed. "This is not about me and Her Highness!"

"Tell me I'm wrong. Tell me you're not in love with her."

"I'm not! I'm a loyal subject, and that's it!"

"I don't believe you," said Bride unflinchingly.

Trevor turned back to face the windshield, gathering his thoughts. He whipped back around to face Bride, his temper seeping out of the whirlpools in his eyes. "You know, mate, I've got 'aff a mind to—"

"To what?" prodded Bride. "Half a mind to what?"

"To take you out and beat you to a bloody pulp, 'at's what!" he barked with nostrils flaring.

"So what's stopping you?" chided Bride.

The American's composure was enraging Trevor. He had only known two worlds, that of a rugged South London youth and a soldier where disputes were settled with might, and now his life in Buckingham Palace, where diplomacy and subordination provided the guidelines.

As he glared at Bride, Trevor found those two worlds colliding. He was a representative of the Crown and was thereby expected to show Catherine's guest the proper respect. On the other hand, he was still very much a man and found it difficult to back down when his manhood was being challenged. Trevor was paralyzed, torn between the law of the land and the rules of the jungle.

"I know what you're thinking," said Bride.

"Oh, do you?"

"You want to take a swing at me, don't you? But you can't, because you're afraid you'll lose your job, isn't that right?"

Trevor didn't answer. He was breathing harder, like a caged animal ready to be unleashed. Bride suddenly opened the door and got out. He walked thirty yards into Hyde Park, pulling off his tuxedo jacket and bow tie as he walked. Trevor remained in the car, more confused than ever.

"Well come on now, I haven't got all night!" yelled Bride from the park. "This is what you want, isn't it?"

Every man has a fuse and Trevor had just reached the end of his. He jerked open the door to the limousine and climbed out, slamming the door so hard that the lock failed to latch. It had been a dozen years since he'd been in a good row and he planned to take full advantage of Bride's open invitation. Off came his hat, his jacket, his tie, and finally his shirt, leaving a trail of discarded clothing on the grass like lovers do on their way to the bedroom.

A streetlamp shone brightly on their arena, silhouetting Trevor's enormous barrel chest against the night sky. An impressive tattoo covering his breastbone depicted the crest of the McFarlane Clan. It was a faded blue likeness of a barechested and bearded man, with a sword in his right hand and a crown to his left. Across the top was written the motto, *This I'll Defend.* The skin on Trevor's forearms and biceps were badly scarred by third degree burns, a war wound surmised Bride. These were the markings of a man who welcomed a dangerous challenge.

Bride had rolled his sleeves up over his elbow and was stretching his neck muscles when Trevor squared up in front of him. The two combatants engaged in the ritual of slowly circling each other before they came to blows. Trevor had his arms down by his waist with his fingers stretched wide open like a wrestler preparing to grapple, while

Bride's fists were raised in an awkward bareknuckled stance like a gentleman boxer who had learned to fight by looking at pictures of John L. Sullivan.

"You started this, let's not forget that," said Trevor.

"I started it, and I intend to finish it," said Bride.

"You? Do you know who you're takin' on here, mate? I was a sergeant in the Royal Scots. I hardly think a schoolteacher is gonna be much of a match for—"

He never finished the sentence as Bride struck him on the jaw with a quick jab. Trevor rubbed his chin, more out of shock than from pain. Bride had suddenly adopted a more conventional pugilistic pose with his left hand protecting his chin and his right fist cocked and ready for action. His head was bobbing, his shoulders swiveling and his feet moving with speed and grace like somebody who should be named "Sugar" or "Kid".

"Boxing team, Columbia, 1964," taunted Bride. "While others were out dancing, I was skipping rope."

Trevor suddenly broke into a peculiar grin. Not only was this going to be a fight, it was suddenly going to be against a formidable opponent, and something about that excited him.

He lunged at Bride in an effort to tackle him but was met with an uppercut to the chin as Bride landed a solid blow and sidestepped him. Trevor grinned and again attacked with his head down like a raging bull. Bride avoided his charge and fired off a combination of accurate rights and lefts to Trevor's ironclad midsection.

Trevor sensed that simple brawling wasn't going to work with the quicker and more nimble professor. He balled up his fists and prepared to wage hand to hand combat.

To Bride's fifty-seven year old body, the next four minutes seemed more like forty. They locked up like bull terriers in a vicious fistfight that covered half an acre of Hyde Park. Blood was drawn, clothes were torn, and hair was yanked out by the roots as the two warriors battled with blind fury. The older Bride was quickly running out of energy and decided it was time for a knockout blow. His intention was to butt his head against Trevor's forehead with reckless abandon, worrying about the consequences to his own skull at some later time.

Unfortunately, Trevor had precisely the same idea and executed it simultaneously with Bride's blow. The result was something akin to two trains colliding head on and both fighters stumbled backwards in states of half consciousness.

Without a word being spoken between them, they knew the fight had ended. A few dazed moments were spent inspecting wounds and gathering up missing shoes, then staggering back across the lawn to the limousine.

Trevor reached the car first and popped open the trunk. He reached deep inside it and fished around for something. As Bride stood next to him, he realized it could have been a tire iron Trevor was looking for, or possibly a gun, but Bride didn't care. He was too tired to move.

What Trevor finally pulled out of the trunk was a bottle of Glenlivet. He screwed off the top and tossed it aside, indicating they wouldn't need it again. He tossed back a mighty swig of the liquor and wiped his mouth with a bloody hand. He held out the bottle to Bride who gladly accepted the closest thing he was going to get to first aid. Together they sat down on the rear bumper of the limousine and handed the bottle of Scotch back and forth.

"Apology accepted," said Trevor.

Chapter Sixteen

Bride walked down the corridor of the Dunbarton towards the front door, the taste of Fionnuala's English breakfast still fresh on his tongue. He had no way of knowing that he had just enjoyed his last good night of sleep and his last quiet meal for some time.

He opened the door to Gower Street and had only managed one step before a photographer confronted him with a lens that was long enough to perch a dozen pigeons. The motordrive whirred relentlessly as the photographer took aim at Bride, who was exceedingly uncomfortable with the unwanted attention. The last time he'd been photographed was for the faculty section of the Amherst yearbook, and even that was an unpleasant experience. This was persecution by comparison.

"Who are you?" he demanded from the photographer, but his only response was the snapping of more pictures. At this point, Bride did all the wrong things. He instinctively covered up his face and retreated back into the relative safety of the Dunbarton, looking as guilty as the Ripper.

Once inside, he turned his back to the door and blocked it with his full wingspan, as if the assailant were going to come charging through with cameras blazing. He stood there panting with fear and no idea of what to do next.

Bride saw an open window at the end of the corridor and made a mad dash for it, not knowing that the photographer had long since departed the premises. He scrambled out of the window and across the tiny courtyard in the rear of the townhouse where Fionnuala had just finished hanging the morning laundry. Bride scaled a small wooden fence and dropped onto the cobblestone alley below. He ran as quickly as his leather soles would take him over the slippery cobbles, occasionally glancing back to see if he was being pursued.

The alley emptied out into Torrington Place, where Bride slowed from a run into a brisk walk so as not to draw attention to himself. He mingled in with the morning crowds on Tottenham Court Road, satisfied that he'd given the mysterious photographer the slip. He had no idea why he'd been photographed or even why he'd fled like a criminal. Nor did Bride have any way of knowing that by the same time tomorrow, he would no longer be able to walk the streets with anonymity.

The world around Malcolm Bride had been moving so quickly in recent days that he felt the need to come to a place where time stood still on canvas. The cuts and contusions from his scrap with Trevor McFarlane the night before were still fresh on his face as he wandered through the maze of corridors at the National Gallery in Trafalgar Square.

He entered an exhibit hall upstairs and there on the wall was a painting that spoke to him. *Christ Before the High Priest* was the name of the painting by Van Honthorst. It showed a priest with his finger raised in an accusing manner as candlelight illuminated the book in front of him.

Bride sat down and studied the work of art, attempting to understand its true meaning. It raised the central question in his mind; what is truth? He didn't know anymore. Truth had lost its way in a maze of deceit and dead ends, and Bride was ready to backtrack through the hedges and never enter again. Did it really matter who was buried in the unmarked grave at St. Bartholomew's? Had he never stumbled upon Princess Catherine that night in the cemetery, would the course of history be changed one iota?

He thought about his own life, where his own personal truth had been altered when he learned he was adopted. What if he hadn't made the discovery? Would he be a considerably different person? No, thought Bride, as he tried to convince himself that real truth wasn't always meant to be uncovered.

But he stared again at the painting as the high priest prepared to pass judgement on Jesus Christ. Here was someone who hadn't bothered to learn the truth about the man from Galilee and sentenced him to die on a cross. It was a mistake the world has been paying for ever since.

Bride hung his head between his knees, unable to decide which fork at the crossroads to take. Go forward or go home, those were his choices. Whichever path he chose, he would have company, because across the exhibit hall, Crumrie blended into the woodwork.

◆ ◆ ◆

The afternoon edition of the *Sun-Times* landed with a thud at the newsstand on Oxford Street. The two-inch headline read:

MOURNING HAS BROKEN

Accompanying the text was a file photo of Princess Catherine, and a five by seven color photo of Malcolm Bride, frowning with dismay and holding his hand up in a feeble attempt to fend off the probing eyes of a camera lens.

Under the byline of Nigel Banks-Finch was a sensationalized account of the budding romance between the Princess Royal and the American history professor, peppered with phrases like "stolen moments" and "secret lustings". The skeleton of the story was based primarily on the information that Banks-Finch had purchased from Prince John, but the flesh was the writer's own creation. It was a black and white case of where the truth mattered little and circulation mattered most.

It's an odd phenomenon in Britain that many people will publicly declare that they care very little about the comings and goings of the Royals, but then consume with voracity any juicy little tidbit that pertains to their personal lives. This paradox played out as the headline in the *Sun-Times* set off a feeding frenzy that Fleet Street hadn't seen in years. Londoners were literally jumping out of taxis and snapping up the tabloid, some purchasing two at the time as if the edition on the top of the stack had somehow gotten it wrong and required double-checking.

The only real sovereignty possessed by a member of the modern British monarchy is over the enormous cast of assistants, secretaries, equerries, ladies-in-waiting, chambermaids, and butlers that surround them. Any request for service from one of the Royals is dutifully, often blindly attended to, because it gives the members of the staff a sense of purpose and the feeling that they're assisting the Crown, even if it's just posting a letter or turning down a bedsheet. Once an order is given, it remains in place, unquestioned, until the order is rescinded. That explains events such as a fresh bottle of whiskey being delivered every night to a bedroom in Buckingham Palace where the current inhabitant doesn't even drink, just because some member of the monarchy put in the order on a cold winter night a century ago and nobody ever bothered to change it.

One of Prince George's strictest requirements of his equerries was to bring him any periodical that mentioned his name, and now that he was involved in a tight political race, that task was even more important. When the headline about Princess Catherine in the *Sun-Times* splashed down, George's staff scrambled into action to make sure they got it to him before he heard it from another source. Their only dilemma was deciding who should actually present him with the tabloid, because they knew the Crown Prince wouldn't like what he was about to read.

After a brief gathering of the minds, the staff members at Kensington Palace finally decided that the delivery of the *Sun-Times* to Prince George's study should be made by a young butler named Michael who stood only five feet four inches tall. The decision was based on the logic that if Michael lowered his head, the Prince might not be able to see his face and therefore wouldn't be able to recall the bearer of bad news. The decision was nearly unanimous. The one dissenting vote was cast by Michael.

He took a deep breath and picked up the paper to be delivered, walking upstairs like a schoolboy on his way to see the principal. As he neared the Prince's study and the strains of Puccini grew louder, his approach had slowed to resemble a man heading for death row, which was closer to the actual situation.

The original plan had been for Michael to hand Prince George a rolled up edition of the *Sun-Times* in hopes that by the time His Majesty unfurled its pages, Michael might be well out of firing range. But the young butler knew that papers weren't delivered at this hour of the day unless they contained bad news and he didn't want to be remembered as the messenger. A brainstorm of self-preservation suddenly came over Michael as he knocked on the door to the study.

"Enter!" came George's voice from inside over the operatic tones on the radio, already sounding angry and for no real reason at this point.

Michael opened the paper to expose the headline and photos on the front page. He opened the door and stepped inside, holding the paper outstretched in front of him like a newsboy hawking an "extra" on a street corner. The ploy worked. Prince George saw the headline from across the room and the veins in his neck immediately pulsated with tension. He snatched the paper out of the Michael's hand and saw nothing else in the room, including the face of one very clever young butler slipping quietly out the door.

George's fluttering eyes quickly scanned the words of Banks-Finch. He turned to the remainder of the article inside, glossed over the text, then hurled the pages across the room where they collided with *The Collected Works of Shelley* sitting benignly on the bookshelf.

By tabloid standards, the story about Catherine was tame, but by George's standards, it was unacceptable. Over the years he had swallowed the bitter pill that Queen Alexandra and Princess Catherine got all of the coveted media attention. The only time George had been alone in the limelight was after the death of his wife and Sir Nolan in the skiing accident, and the news was less than flattering. Aside from that, the only thing George saw of the photographers was their backs. Finally, with his debut into politics, Prince George was in the spotlight and for all the right reasons. The last thing his political aspirations needed was a distraction like the headline he saw in the *Sun-Times*, and he was determined to give the story a swift execution.

◆ ◆ ◆

Bride turned the corner onto Gower Street and was aghast over what he saw. No less than two dozen reporters, most with dubious journalistic credentials, were camped outside of the Dunbarton. He had no idea why they were there, but realized there must be some connection with the mysterious photographer who had assaulted him earlier that morning. Bride stopped cold in his tracks, but was immediately aware that his actions seemed suspicious and were likely to alert the brigade of paparazzi up ahead that the lamb was arriving for the slaughter. He quickly bent over and feigned tieing his shoe, no small act of theater because he was wearing loafers. Bride peeked casually to see if there was any movement in the ranks and seeing none, he turned back and walked as quickly as he dared toward Tottenham Court Road.

Bride felt like a real bride heading toward the altar, deliberately trying to convince the feet to walk as slowly as possible down the aisle but finding it impossible because the mind was racing a hundred times faster.

The only witness to his narrow escape was the ubiquitous Nick Crumrie, who followed a safe distance behind Bride as he made his way to the Goodge Street tube station. He popped through the turnstile and vaulted down the stairs to the crowded platform below to wait for the underground. He didn't know where he was going, but he knew his destination was best described as "somewhere away from here".

Blending into the crowd and feeling safer for the time being, Bride tried to determine why he was being hunted, and could reach only one logical conclusion; surely someone had discovered that he and Crowe had unearthed the mysterious bones in St. Bartholomew's and he was going to be arrested for trespassing or graverobbing or for whatever English law deemed appropriate. But why only reporters and photographers and no police? Of course, thought Bride, the papers are always onto these things before the authorities because they pay their sources a lot better. It would only be a matter of time before the long arm of the London law caught up to him.

Bride could suddenly hear the piercing whine of approaching police cars echoing down the stairs and resounding throughout the cavernous tunnels of the London subway. Tires squealed to a stop, car doors slammed, and the sound of leather police boots clattered quickly down the stairs.

It was one thing to run from a photographer, quite another to run from police. Bride knew he had been caught. He would offer no resistance. He had never been arrested and wasn't quite sure of the protocol involved, but knew from the movies that it involved holding up his hands. He raised his palms up to his shoulders as he turned to face several bobbies and a man in a trenchcoat who were scurrying his way.

"Clear the area!" shouted the man in the trenchcoat to the crowd gathered on the platform. As if on cue, the crowd began to disperse in typically organized British fashion. There seemed to be a sense of urgency, but the exodus to the stairs was performed without pushing or shoving, the women being politely motioned in front of the gentlemen, as if they were rehearsing a fire drill.

Bride remained frozen in place, waiting for the others to depart and make him easy access to the arresting officers.

The man in the trenchcoat looked at Bride and frowned. "You!" he bellowed. Bride gulped with fear. "Move along now! We've had a bomb threat! Everyone must clear the area immediately!"

Bride still didn't move. He had been so resigned to the fact that all of this commotion was centered around him and his criminality that it took him several seconds to realize otherwise.

"Sir, I'm ordering you to clear these premises!" yelled the man in the trenchcoat once again.

It finally dawned on Bride that the police were responding to a matter totally unrelated to his situation. He sheepishly dropped his hands to his sides, smiled meekly and waved a quick farewell to the man in the trenchcoat as the bobbies quickly cordoned off the station.

Bride followed the other passengers up the stairs and outside, where more police cars and a bomb disposal unit from Scotland Yard were arriving. He was almost in a state of shock, being tossed around in the tornado of uncontrollable events swirling around him. He didn't even realize the only good fortune coming out of the confusion of the last fifteen minutes; Crumrie had lost his trail.

Unable to go home to the Dunbarton because of the throng of media, Bride decided the next best thing was a barstool at the Marlborough Arms. His second black and tan had just about steadied his nerves when another surge of adrenaline rushed through his body.

Colin Crowe had walked through the door and was peering through the smoky air of the pub. Bride had no chance to hide as Crowe's gaze fell immediately his way. He moved quickly across the room and took the American by the arm.

"Come on, you're coming with me," said Crowe emphatically.

Bride didn't move. "Why should I do that?" he said.

"Because I'm the only friend you have on this island. Now come along before we create a scene." Crowe tugged again at Bride's arm, but the sturdy professor refused to leave his barstool.

"This has to do with St. Bartholomew's, doesn't it?"

"You mean you don't know?" asked Crowe.

"Know what? All I know is that I've had photographers chasing me, reporters camping out on my doorstep. I know I'm in some kind of trouble, but I'm not sure how much."

Crowe reached into his back pocket and pulled out a crumpled edition of the *Sun-Times*. He slowly opened it to reveal the headline and photos of Bride with Princess Catherine. Bride sat stunned as he looked at it, slowly shaking his head with incredulity. "I don't believe this," he sputtered.

"Believe it, mate, and it's just the beginning. Now let's get going."

This time Bride obeyed Crowe's directions and allowed himself to be swiftly escorted out of the pub.

Crowe led him across the street to a car park and into his Triumph.

"How'd you know where to find me?" asked Bride as Crowe pulled into afternoon traffic.

Crowe nervously checked the rear-view mirror as he drove. "I took into account that you and I are similar creatures. When something's bothering me, I go hide in one of two places, either the cinema, or the nearest pub. I further took into consideration that you, being an American, have no doubt already seen all the movies currently playing here months ago, which sent me on my pub-crawl. Or, I was just around the corner doing some follow-up on the latest IRA bomb threat to bring the underground to a grinding halt and I stopped in for a pint and just happened to bump into you. Take your pick."

"I'm guessing it was a little of both," smiled Bride. His frown suddenly returned as he stared out the window. "What have I gotten myself into?" he asked Crowe.

"You are officially now the fresh bait for the school of piranha that is the British press, and until something better comes along, you'll continue to be the catch of the day. Which is why you are coming with me."

"Where are we going?"

"I'm taking you to my flat in Marylebone. You can stay there until things die down a bit. I'll see to it that your belongings are discreetly transported from the Dunbarton."

"This is really nice of you."

"Don't think for a moment that this is a gesture born out of chivalry. My motives are completely selfish, I assure you."

"In what way?" asked Bride.

"It's quite simple. If the tabs are stalking you, then I no longer have an exclusive audience with you. I don't know what it is yet, but there's something very important about that grave in St. Bartholomew's and together, you and I are going to find out what it is."

Crowe turned off of George Street onto Gloucester Place and went two blocks north. Without warning, he suddenly yanked down on the steering wheel and yanked the Triumph hard to the right, making a tight U-turn south. Bride slammed against the dashboard.

"What are you doing?" he yelled to Crowe.

"Making sure we haven't been followed," responded Crowe as he watched the side-view mirror to make sure nobody had duplicated his wild maneuver. Satisfied they were not being tailed, Crowe cut over to Upper Montagu Street and headed north to Dorset Square. They drove the rest of the way in silence. Bride could only think that at one point he had decided to abandon the tangled route he was on, but now he was farther than ever down a road that appeared more and more to be one way.

Crowe pulled over and parked. "Come on. We walk the rest of the way."

Crowe led Bride past a crescent row of Georgian townhouses and into an alleyway behind. The trip to Crowe's flat was taking on a distinctive cloak and dagger feel as the reporter lifted two loose boards on a tall wooden fence and guided Bride through the opening.

They proceeded down a narrow sidewalk to a greenhouse that contained the first new leaves of hothouse tomatoes. Crowe took a quick look around to make sure nobody was watching, then motioned Bride inside. He removed a section of wooden flooring in the corner of the greenhouse and revealed a short flight of stairs that led into a tunnel.

"Where are we going?" asked a reluctant Bride.

"To my flat," said Crowe.

"You don't have a front door?"

"Of course I do. And a back door. And then there is door number three, which I reserve for special occasions."

The puzzled look on Bride's face told Crowe that his entryway needed more explaining.

"As I have mentioned on at least one previous occasion," began Crowe, "spies are everywhere. Now if a reporter for a rival media outlet can't track down a story on his own, then what's the next best thing? To track down the reporter who's already on to the story and follow him until he leads you right to it. So, competitive and selfish fellow that I am, I devised a secret access to my flat so that my comings and goings can't be monitored by my rivals.

"I have lamps inside my flat that are timed to periodically go on and off so as to give the impression to the spies lurking about that I'm still inside, when in actuality I'm out haunting the streets of London trying to nail down my story. In this case, I'd rather nobody saw you going inside, and I think you'd agree. Now then, Dr. Bride, if you will follow me this way, and please, try to stay with the group."

Crowe descended the stairs into the tunnel with Bride right behind him. They crept along the dark passageway like Christians in the catacombs until they reached the dim light at the end. Crowe pushed back a large heating vent that swung out on hinges and crawled through the opening into his flat. Bride emerged moments later, relieved to see that he was standing in a living room and not a dungeon.

"It's not much," said Crowe apologetically, "but it's far from the madding crowd."

Crowe's home was not his castle. It was more like his warehouse, filled to capacity with filing cabinets. Each one contained his copious notes on the thousands of stories he'd covered over the years, clearly marked and catalogued according to the year and the subject matter. He was technology in reverse. All the information that could be stored on a single computer hard-drive was contained in a dozen four-drawer steel cabinets in his living room.

Crowe slid open a file drawer and pulled out an overflowing folder labeled "IRA Bombings" and deposited a page of his notes scribbled earlier that afternoon. He slammed it shut, then walked to another cabinet and pulled out a file marked "St. Bartholomew's." Crowe checked his watch. It was 7:34 PM. He counted several beats under his breath and the brass lamp on the end table suddenly clicked on by way of a timer in the wall socket. "Right on time!" he exclaimed with a certain satisfaction.

Crowe cleared away a stack of newspapers off a sitting chair and motioned Bride over to it. He opened the St. Bartholomew file.

"Have a seat, Malcolm. We have a lot to talk about."

Chapter Seventeen

Prince George stood in his sister's bedroom at Buckingham Palace with his eyes twitching in anger.

"You will stop seeing him this instant, and that is an order!" he bellowed.

"Since when were you in charge of my private affairs?" countered Catherine without a hint of fear.

"When your love life threatens my political life, then it becomes my concern. It's bad enough I have to deal with John. The last thing I need is for you to embarrass me."

"Me embarrass *you*?" she asked with laughing disbelief. "That, coming from a man who stands to make a mockery of the Crown by cavorting with politicians? Oh, yes, George, dear me, I can certainly understand how my inviting a friend to dinner is an embarrassment to your exalted position."

"I will not be talked to that way!" he yelled loudly enough for all of the palace staff to hear, even those who didn't have their ears pressed against all the adjacent walls and doors.

"Nor will I," responded Catherine calmly. "I will not forego my own happiness for yours."

The Prince and Princess stared at each other like bull and bull-fighter, waiting for the other one to make the next move. George could see the resolve in Catherine's face. He had seen similar steadfastness in his mother on numerous occasions, and he knew it was an inherited trait. Still, there was too much at stake to let her link to the American remain unbroken. He took two steps closer to Catherine to underscore the threatening words he was about to unleash.

"As you may know, my dear Catherine, I have a certain way of getting what I want, and what I want at this moment is for you to stop seeing Malcolm Bride. Now then, if *you* can't be sensible enough to end this relationship, then perhaps I'll have to send Mr. Crumrie to meet with the good professor and explain my position. Am I making myself understood?"

With that chilling warning, George abruptly turned and walked heel to toe toward the bedroom door. Eavesdroppers on the other side could be heard scurrying away like kitchen roaches as the Prince approached. He took one last look back at Catherine as if to dare her to defy his edict, then yanked open the door and vanished into the hallway.

Despite all of her inner strength, Catherine was beginning to tremble. She had never thought of her brother as an honest man, but she did consider him to be a man of his word.

It was only moments later that Prince George stood in one of the opulent drawing rooms in Buckingham Palace, surrounded by crystal chandeliers, priceless oil paintings, and gilded moldings. The angry scowl he had employed in Princess Catherine's bedroom had somehow evaporated during the trip across the chamber floor corridor and downstairs to the White Drawing- Room where George would present himself as a smiling and gracious host to the fifty people anxiously awaiting his arrival.

It was a charity event for the Save the Children Foundation and the irony of the setting was unending. The Crown Prince was lending his presence to the occasion so that a little publicity could be generated and the increased public awareness might help the charity to raise a few hundred pounds. If George had simply boxed up one of the gold candlesticks or gaudy vases in the White Drawing-Room and sent it over with a nice note, the charity could have sold it for a few thousand pounds and saved everyone the trouble.

For all of his adult life, Prince George had viewed such gatherings as drudgery, part of the job of being a Royal, something to waltz through with a painted smile and the required number of noble gestures. But suddenly these public engagements provided a forum for his political aspirations and all of his remarks were now designed to win votes.

"We are meeting tonight for the sake of children," said George without the benefit of notes. "They are our future and we must invest in them. But we are at the crossroads of what kind of future we are going to provide. Will it be one with jobs? The jobless rate in this country is up over seven percent in the last four years of Labour rule in Parliament. The rate of inflation has increased nearly nine and a half percent in that same period of time."

The people in the audience were starting to squirm. This was not the standard fare for a charity function. A speech under these circumstances was supposed to include phrases like "wonderful work" and "a worthwhile cause", but George was launching into a socioeconomic diatribe and he showed no signs of changing course.

"The budget deficit is now over fifty billion pounds. Fifty *billion*! I submit to you that the Labourites have not been good stewards of our money, and that their wasteful spending habits have put us in the sad state of affairs we currently see."

It didn't matter to George that the Conservative Party he was seeking to lead had historically been free spending while the Labour Party under Prime Minister Roth's administration had actually fought tooth and nail for reduced spending, less government, and lower taxes. Nor did it matter that he had completely abandoned the reason for the gathering at Buckingham Palace that night. He was center stage, the cameras were rolling, and he was relishing the moment.

"It is time for change, and not change just for the sake of it, but meaningful change, a radical departure from the way things have been done. I am willing to risk all that I have and all that I am to see that this comes about. I implore you to join me. Vote Conservative in the upcoming election and together we will forge a bold new Britain for our children! Thank you, and goodnight."

A smattering of polite applause from the stunned audience rippled through the drawing room as George waved goodnight with both hands in a hasty departure. The applause stopped the instant he was gone as the baffled spectators tried to make some sense out of the spectacle they had just witnessed. Their charity event had taken months to plan but in the end there hadn't been a single mention of the Save the Children Foundation in the Prince's remarks. A wasted effort for everyone, except George and his new friends in the political arena.

◆ ◆ ◆

Fionnuala Rumpole had her nose pressed against the window in the third floor of the Dunbarton. On the dark sidewalk below, the throng of media still stood vigil, waiting for the elusive Malcolm Bride to reappear. "It's half past nine and they're still out there!" she said to Peter as he sat on their bed and shined his shoes.

"Is the crowd gettin' any smaller?" asked Peter.

"Don't think so," replied Fionnuala as she made a quick head count. "If anythin', I'd say there's even more than before."

She pulled the curtain closed and joined her husband on the bed. "Who would have ever thought our dear Dr. Bride was up to somethin' like this. I knew he was seein' a lady friend, but the Princess Royal herself!"

"You never know about people," nodded Peter as he spit on the tip of his Oxford and continued to shine.

Fionnuala looked at her hand. "And to think, I've touched the hand that's touched the hand of royalty."

"And who knows what else!" said Peter with a laugh.

Fionnuala slapped his shoulder. "Peter! That's Princess Catherine you're talking about."

"She's human too, you know."

Fionnuala grimaced, not caring to believe in fallen angels. She suddenly noticed that Peter was shining a pair of shoes he hadn't worn since his uncle's funeral two years ago. "Why are you shinin' up your Oxfords? Somebody die?"

"No, nobody died."

"Then why?"

Peter held his freshly shined shoe up to the light and admired the sheen. "If there's going to be T.V. cameras at my front door when I step outside, I want to look me best."

It didn't occur to either of the innkeepers that even if the cameras turned on them, their shoes would probably not be seen on the BBC that night. Fionnuala nodded in agreement and immediately checked the state of her own shoes to see how much work they needed before they were presentable to the rest of the world.

The phone on the nightstand rang and Fionnuala reached over to answer. "This is the world famous Dunbarton as seen on the telly," she exclaimed with an exaggerated Cockney accent. "Mrs. Fionnuala Rumpole, proprietor, speaking!" She looked over at Peter who was enjoying their journey into celebrity as much as she was.

Songbirds and telephone lines are the only things that can move freely about London without regard to traffic, locked gates, and social castes. The other end of the phone call to the Dunbarton was only a few miles away as the songbird flies, but a universe away in all other respects. Nonetheless, the two worlds were now connected.

"I'd like to speak to Dr. Malcolm Bride," came the demure voice of Princess Catherine over the receiver.

"Wouldn't everybody, love!" cackled Fionnuala.

"Please, can you put him on? I'm a friend of his."

Fionnuala's gleeful smirk suddenly vanished and her eyes widened with sudden realization. A blushing blood ran into her cheeks as she recognized the voice on the phone and the equation fell into place. "It's you, isn't it?" gasped Fionnuala. She stood up and curtsied out of respect and habit.

Peter stopped shining his other Oxford and stood up. Even the voice of royalty entering his home was enough to make him rise to attention.

"Yes, it's me," answered the voice on the phone. "Is Dr. Bride there?"

"No, Your Royal Highness. He hasn't been here all day, not with all the clamor and such goin' on outside."

"Do you expect him?"

"No. Someone came earlier today and picked up his belongings. He didn't say where he was taking them."

There was a long silence on the other end, the silence of someone who wasn't sure what to do next. "If you talk to him, can you give him a message?"

"Of course I can, Your Highness. Anything you say." Fionnuala gestured frantically at Peter to bring her a pad and pen, but her one-armed gesticulations were so wild that he had absolutely no idea what message she was trying to convey.

"Tell him," began Catherine in a soft voice. "Tell him...goodbye."

Fionnuala stopped gesturing. She cradled the receiver in both hands, feeling Catherine's pain over the phone lines. "I'll tell him. I will."

"Thank you, Mrs. Rumpole."

The phone went dead. Fionnuala held tightly to the receiver, not wanting to end the moment. She finally hung up as tears started to form in her eyes.

The same scene was being played out in a lonely bedroom of a palace several miles away.

Chapter Eighteen

Crowe entered the front door of his Marylebone flat carrying Bride's suitcases and two fresh orders of fish and chips wrapped up in the afternoon edition of the *Sun-Times*.

"Good news all around. I picked up your things at the Dunbarton without a hint of suspicion, and, even better, dinner is served," he announced as he spread the bounty on the coffee table amid the scattered notes of news stories in progress.

Bride didn't move.

"Come on, mate, you have to eat something."

"I'm not very hungry. Thanks anyway."

"Well then, what can I get you to drink?"

"Not thirsty either."

"Well do you mind if I partake? I haven't eaten all day."

"Go ahead."

Crowe uncovered a bottle of Guinness in his refrigerator and popped off the top on the edge of his countertop. The bottle cap fell to the floor, joining dozens of others that had died a similar death. He took a deep swig of the thick liquid and exhaled with both disgust and admiration for the healing powers of stout.

He sat down across from Bride and dug into the golden fried fish in front of him. "What's the matter, Malcolm?"

"I wish I'd never been to St. Bartholomew's. I wish I'd never seen the limousine pull up that night, never found the pillbox, never met Rachel Mawhinney or Paddy Butterfill or even you for that matter. No offense."

"I sympathize with you, but I must also point out that if you hadn't been in St. Bartholomew's that night, you would have never met Catherine."

"Right. Add another name to the list."

"Oh, but do you really mean that, Professor? Remember, we deal in truth here, and I believe the truth to be that you miss her, and that, more than anything, is why you are refusing to eat." Crowe nodded his head and bit off another flaky morsel of the fish.

Bride sat erect and opened his mouth to protest, but could tell by the look on Crowe's face that the reporter had once again uncovered the story. He slumped back into the chair and nodded in resigned agreement. "The last person I should confide in is a journalist. I might as well take an ad out in the *Sunday Times*. But I suppose you're right. I do miss her. I can't fully explain it, but there's some connection between us, something that draws me to her, as if we were lovers in some past life."

"Perhaps you were."

"Too bad that I don't believe in reincarnation. It would give me some hope for our future. Unfortunately, I have to deal with the present and it's presently a mess."

"When are you going to see her again?" asked Crowe after another taste of Guinness. Bride looked sideways at him with suspicion. "I'm not asking as a journalist. I'm asking as a friend, as someone who truly hates to see love lost."

"The truth is, I don't think I will see her again. I know Catherine well enough to realize that any hint of scandal would really upset her, so the faster I fade into the woodwork, the better it is for her."

"I think you're selling her short. The fact that she's requested your company on so many occasions tells me she must have feelings for you as well, and I wouldn't doubt if she's not sitting over there in Buckingham right now wondering when she can see *you* again."

"Right," replied Bride with sarcasm. "She's pining away over an American she's known for two weeks."

"Only one way to find out, isn't there?"

"What's that?"

"Go see her. I've got the list of Royal engagements right here." Crowe rummaged around in another pile of papers on the floor and pulled out a three page press release. "Let's see, where's a good one for you...ah, here we go, perfect. The Princess Royal will attend a ribbon cutting ceremony at the new ceramic teapot exhibit at Norwich Castle."

"Ceramic teapots?"

"Oh, absolutely," nodded Crowe. "Finest collection in the world from what I understand." He referred back to the press release. "She'll be there tomorrow at noon. You can see her then, and I should think a trip seaside would do you some good. Frankly, you look awful."

"Where is Norwich?"

"In Norfolk, maybe a hundred miles northeast from here. If you take the eight o'clock train, you should get there in plenty of time."

Bride thought it over. He wanted to run and hide from everything around him, but he kept getting pulled back in and he now realized the magnetic force was Princess Catherine. He searched for some excuse not to go. "The media's going to be there. I'll be noticed."

"My good man, you are sitting in the presence of a nationally known reporter who has found his way past security guards, maitre d's, and other assorted nuisances with no more disguise than a driving cap and bifocals. I should think we can come up with a way for you to blend in, especially in the shelter of East Anglia."

"What are you going to do while I'm gone?"

"I'm going to find out what our bonnie Prince George is *really* up to. When a politician sounds too good to be true, he or she usually is."

Bride stood up and looked at himself in the mirror. He *did* look awful. Perhaps a few therapeutic breaths of salt air would do him some good.

◆ ◆ ◆

Prince George was livid as he paced the wooden floors of his study at Kensington Palace. He looked alternately at the ceiling and then at Crumrie, who was hanging his head in an effort to deflect the sting of his employer's glare.

"You *lost* him?" snarled George.

"Yessir," admitted Crumrie.

"How can you lose track of a man who doesn't even know he's being followed? How is that possible?"

"There were extenuating circumstances, sir. The IRA phoned in a bomb threat to the Goodge Street station and I think we all know what sort of confusion results." Crumrie looked over at Elliott Wiggs sitting quietly in the corner, hoping for some support. Wiggs maintained his frigid demeanor.

"Don't give me excuses!" snapped George. "Give me results, or I'll give you a new assignment! We're at a very critical stage right now and we can't afford any problems."

"But with all due respect, sir, we're not even sure if this Bride fellow is up to anything," offered Crumrie.

"Which is precisely why I want him monitored! We know what the enemy is up to. It's the civilians we need to worry about. Now get on with it!"

Crumrie nodded with assurance to his superiors and made a hasty exit from the study.

The hint of a smile creased Wiggs's thin lips. "You handled that well," he told George. "Direct, authoritative, uncompromising. You'll make a wonderful Prime Minister!" Wiggs nodded quietly to himself as he stared into space, perhaps trying to envision the near future.

Chapter Nineteen

Bride dozed most of the way on the train ride to Norwich. He had not slept well the night before, partly out of worry but mostly because the mattress in Crowe's spare bedroom felt as though it were stuffed with wet sand. The train jostled him awake just long enough to catch glimpses of the water meadows of the Stour River in Essex and the flint houses and parish churches of Suffolk. Plump white clouds hung overhead and sunlight bounced off the gardens of hollyhocks, signalling brighter things ahead.

At Stowmarket, an elderly woman boarded and sat across from Bride. She studied him with a scowl on her face and Bride couldn't tell if she thought she recognized him or she didn't like his slumped posture against the window of the rail car. She finally took her eyes off him, but just to be on the safe side, he lowered the tweed driving hat Crowe had loaned him to cover more of his face.

He remained awake for the final half-hour of the trip as the train wound its way through the fens, heaths, and lagoons. The occasional dikes and windmills that dotted the low landscape reminded Bride of his trip to the Netherlands years ago. A nice, simple vacation, thought Bride, where he had taken a few pictures, written a few postcards, eaten a fine meal or two, and returned home without having been involved in a single international incident. It all seemed a lifetime ago.

Bride stepped off the train in Norwich and was greeted by the smell of salt-marsh samphire plants and the breeze from the North Sea twenty miles away, a distinct and refreshing change from the industrialized air of London.

A taxi took him from the train station to the center of town where a 12th century Norman castle stood bravely on a large mound. The medieval fortress was imposing, but it wasn't the structure that captured Bride's attention.

It was the mass of people waiting outside to catch a glimpse of the Princess Royal. The population of Norwich had tripled in the hours leading up to Catherine's arrival and the crowd buzzed with anticipation. Many of them carried banners and placards professing their love for the Princess, while the rest waved miniature Union Jacks.

Bride pulled his tweed cap down to his eyebrows and put on a pair of reading glasses that he could see over, leaving barely an inch of unrestricted vision. He mingled with the onlookers, cautiously at first, but soon realized they were so intent on seeing the Princess that he could have strolled around the town square in nothing more than bedroom slippers and nobody would have noticed him.

What impressed Bride more than anything was how far some people were willing to go to get a glimpse of Her Highness. Several young men had scaled lampposts, clinging to the light fixtures with one hand and their cameras with the other. Along the avenue where Catherine would make her entrance, some people were hanging out of windows, others were perched precariously on ledges, while a few brave souls were resting on the steep pitch of shingled roofs with their feet braced in the rain gutter.

Bride had always sensed the affection the British people felt for the Princess, but until now he had never realized the extent. People were literally risking life and limb just to *see* her, thought Bride. Imagine what they would do to spend an afternoon with her or share a meal, as he had been fortunate enough to do on several occasions.

At precisely noon, Catherine's limousine rolled through the town center of Norwich with Trevor at the wheel. Through the open window in the back seat, she waved to the crowd and made eye contact with as many people as possible so they could take away a personal moment shared with Royalty. To Princess Catherine, it was just another item on her endless agenda, but she beamed with such enthusiasm that the people of Norfolk surely believed they were hosting the event of the season.

The well wishers waved their banners and flags fanatically and hugged each other in celebration over having come this close to a member of the monarchy.

Bride knew exactly how they felt. The depression that had invaded him was temporarily lifted. Just seeing her again, even from a distance, had made him feel better. Then he wondered if she were thinking about him, and his depression began to creep back in. It worried him that a woman could have this effect on him, particularly one so inaccessible.

Catherine's limousine made its way through the sea of people and into the gates of the castle. Trevor jumped out and moved efficiently to the rear of the vehicle to open Catherine's door. She stepped gracefully from the car in a teal blue suit and matching hat, waving warmly to the crowd in the street before being whisked away by a protective museum curator.

Bride's next move was to try to get a message to Trevor. He knew he couldn't speak to Catherine directly, but surely Trevor would deliver a note for him. After all, he'd earned at least that much during their battle in Hyde Park. He fought through the throng and made his way closer to the limousine.

Inside the castle, Princess Catherine was fawning over the unrivalled collection of ceramic teapots, Lowestoft porcelain, and Norwich silver. She understood their importance in terms of British heritage and tradition, not unlike the monarchy itself, although the silverware was showing a lot less tarnish than the Crown these days.

Outside, Bride had made his way to the limousine and stood among several dozen other people who were admiring its polished black lines. Wouldn't they love to know that they were in the company of a man who had actually been *in* the royal carriage? Not only that, he'd sipped whiskey while sitting on its back bumper.

A firm grip suddenly grabbed Bride's forearm and also his complete attention. He looked up in rigid fear as he realized he'd gotten so swept up in his own musing that he'd let his guard down. He turned slowly around and was relieved to discover that Trevor McFarlane himself was holding onto him. The hunted had cornered the hunter.

"I knew you'd come lookin' for her," growled the burly Scot.

"Oh? And how'd you know that?"

"Because you love her."

"But *everyone* loves her, isn't that right?"

Trevor ignored the obvious reference to his own affections for Catherine and led Bride quietly away from the car. "What's with the disguise?" he asked with suspicion.

"I want to get a message to her without the newspapers seeing me. I wanted to tell her I was sorry if I caused her any problems. Can you tell her that for me?"

"You can tell her yourself. She wants to see you."

Elation wrapped its warm arms around Bride and embraced him. An actual chemical change rushed through his body, an experience he'd never felt before but one that seemed perfectly natural.

"When?"

"We're on our way to Sandringham for the day. There's a tavern on Route 47 called The Carvery. Wait outside in the east end of the car park there and we'll pick you up on our way out."

"I'll be there," nodded Bride. "And thank you."

Trevor grunted as he walked away. It was bad enough he was making arrangements for the American and his beloved Princess to get together. It was even worse that Bride was being so damned likable.

Bride walked nearly two miles to The Carvery and stood as innocently as possible in the corner of the parking lot. If he had merely been waiting for the next bus, looking innocent would have come naturally. But knowing he was waiting for a Princess, and trying to appear innocent, he suddenly found it quite difficult. Bride tried at least ten different poses, all designed to convey to passersby that he had absolutely no hidden agenda, but each one made him look and feel guiltier than the one before. His self-consciousness began to wane when he caught a whiff of a shepherd's pie in the kitchen and he realized he hadn't eaten anything since breakfast the day before.

His appetite had suddenly returned and he thought about venturing inside the tavern for a quick bite. He took two steps forward, then realized he might miss the arrival of Catherine's limousine. It would certainly be considered bad form to be inside a roadhouse eating shepherd's pie while the Princess Royal sat idling in the gravel parking lot.

He turned back and headed for the marble stanchion he'd been leaning against, but the aroma of food again wafted in front of his nose. It could be hours before Catherine arrived. And how long could it take to order a simple meal?

He spun back around and took three steps toward the inviting doors of The Carvery. No, no, he thought, it wasn't worth the gamble. He had survived this long without food, he could last a while longer, particularly given the risks and rewards.

He made another about face towards the stanchion and only then did he realize that two elderly gentlemen in the meadow across the road had been standing there the entire time, watching his bizarre dance of indecision. The last thing Bride had wanted to do was draw attention to himself and he'd done everything but fire up a distress flare. He smiled meekly at the two gents, tipped his tweed driving cap, and took a seat firmly on the stanchion. He crossed his arms and vowed not to move a muscle until he saw Catherine's limousine pull over. The elderly men in the meadow shook their heads in bemusement and went on their way.

It turned out that Bride had made the right decision because less than two minutes later the Rolls Royce appeared over the crest of the hill on Route 47. Trevor wheeled the black beauty into the parking lot and barely rolled to a stop as Bride quickly opened the door and hopped in. The limo sped away into the English countryside without a witness to its added cargo.

Bride instinctively slid halfway across the seat as he secured the car door and suddenly found himself pushed up next to Catherine.

"Sorry!" he blurted as he backed away.

They stared at each other like young lovers who had been separated for the summer vacation and weren't quite sure if the spark in their relationship were still there. Bride was shaking with adrenaline as he stared at Catherine's face. He had never seen her look so beautiful.

"Hello, Dr. Bride."

He nodded his hello, unable to speak. He suddenly leaned forward and embraced her. Trevor's foot immediately hit the brake pedal, partly from the instinctive reaction of a bodyguard and partly out of deep-seated jealousy. He resumed normal speed as Catherine and Bride finally let go of each other.

"I'm sorry about the article in the *Sun-Times*. I had no idea—"

Catherine put her finger to her lips and shook her head to cut him off. "If it's anyone's fault, it's mine. As you Americans say, this is my ballpark and I should know the rules. The truth is, it doesn't really matter. I have every right to advance my social life and I think a decade of mourning should be sufficient. If I can live with it, then they should be able to as well," she stated emphatically.

"What's really distressing though is that we're front page news and absolutely nothing has happened!"

"No," replied Catherine. "Not yet."

Bride cocked his head and looked at Catherine, trying to discern the meaning of her remark. She looked back with an impish grin that made Bride forget about all of his troubles, even his empty stomach. The Princess turned her attention to the East Anglia countryside that was whizzing past her window and hummed a gentle tune.

The limousine turned down a wooded road that was alive with the cardinal and lavender splendor of rhododendrons and azaleas. Within moments they arrived on the sprawling grounds of Sandringham, an opulent Edwardian mansion that had served as the country home of five generations of British monarchs. It had been purchased in 1862 to lure a young Edward VII away from the temptations of busy London, and had slowly evolved into a family refuge from the same.

Bride gazed in amazement out the car window and was awestruck by the sheer number of chimneys that poked out of the red-brick monolith, fifteen at least. No wonder there weren't many trees in the area, thought Bride.

"We won't be going inside, I'm afraid," said Catherine as she observed the awe and curiosity that enveloped Bride's face. "It's the tourist season, you know." She leaned forward to talk to Trevor, eschewing the private phone in the backseat that a less personable passenger would use. "Can you take us to the stables, Trevor? And perhaps call up to the kitchen for something to eat."

"Yes, ma'am," said Trevor as politely as possible under the circumstances. It bothered him deeply that he had no choice but to play the part of facilitator in Catherine's romance, but managed to find some shred of consolation in that he had never seen her this happy in all the years he'd worked for her.

The limousine passed by some of the seventy acres of gardens amply stocked with hydrangeas and camellias and rolled to a gentle stop in front of a sign reading "Sandringham Stud". At Amherst, thought Bride, a building like this would have been considered a dormitory complex. But in England, where so many things were larger than life, it was simply a stable.

Bride climbed out of the car and stood ready to assist Catherine, but Trevor had already scrambled back into position at the other door and was gladly performing one of his favorite duties. The bodyguard bowed with a respectful nod to Catherine, shot one last angry glare at Bride, then jumped back in the car and proceeded to the main house.

"Do you ride?" she asked Bride.

He wasn't quite sure how to answer. In his many travels as a younger man, he'd put his backside into the squeaky leather of a lot of saddles. He'd reined in fire breathing quarter horses in Abilene, galloped with the gauchos across the pampas of Argentina, even raced camels across the desert outside of Marrakesh, but he hadn't put a foot in a stirrup in nearly ten years and wasn't sure if riding a horse involved the same luxury of lapsed time as riding a bike.

Bride also knew that the Princess had a reputation as an accomplished horsewoman and he didn't want to boast of his experience and then be shown up out on the trail.

"I've ridden some in the past," he finally replied. It was a fair representation of the truth. Enough to satisfy his sense of honesty, but at the same time ambiguous enough to leave him ample margin for error should he either rise to the occasion or tumble to the hallowed grounds of Sandringham.

"Good. We'll have a go at it then."

Bride followed Catherine to the stables. The smell of fresh manure shot his mind back to the kennel in Yorkshire run by poor Paddy Butterfill. All of that seemed like years ago.

She led him into the tack room, which was filled with the soothing aroma of shiny black leather saddlery. The walls were covered with red, blue, and yellow ribbons of various equestrian events and regal photos of various royal steeds that were clearly better attended to than most humans in the world.

"I'm going to change. Would you care for some other clothes?"

Bride looked down at his corduroy pants and loafers and decided he had a golden opportunity to look incredibly ridiculous. The situation reminded him of one of his colleagues at Amherst who toured the campus on a moped while wearing a three-piece suit and wing tips.

"Is there something else for me to wear?"

"In there. Some of George's things should fit you," she said as she pointed to a dressing room at the end of the room.

"I'll meet you out here in a few minutes."

Bride entered the spacious dressing room and opened the doors to a large walnut armoire. Inside were handsomely tailored riding clothes for all occasions from fox hunts to polo practice. He pulled out a pair of light tan jodhpurs and tried them on. They fit perfectly, as did the faded navy polo shirt. Even the black riding boots slipped onto his feet like they were made for him.

Bride stood back and looked at himself in the mirror. He felt a little awkward borrowing clothing from the Crown Prince of England, but knew he'd feel even worse in the corduroys and loafers now tucked away in the corner of the dressing room.

He admired himself a moment longer in the mirror, stopping to ponder that this ancient looking glass had reflected the faces of Kings, Dukes, and Princes for over a century. He exited the dressing area feeling a bit more regal, even mocking his outfit's owner by jamming the tips of his fingers into his pants pockets and exaggerating the same heel-to-toe strut of Prince George.

Only then did he notice Catherine standing at the other end of the tack room, her mouth agape and her ivory skin even paler than normal. Bride naturally assumed she was in shock over his display of irreverence. He immediately stopped his satirical act and lowered his head in embarrassment.

"I'm sorry," he whispered.

She said nothing, but nodded gently to indicate her forgiveness and walked quietly outside.

On the rare occasions that he allowed himself to think about such things, Bride had always imagined that the perfect woman for him would look just as good in flannel as she would in diamonds.

As Catherine stood outside the stables, that prescription flashed through his mind. Instead of flannel she was dressed in caramel colored herringbone slacks with brown riding boots that came up almost to her knees. Her hair, the color of warm cider, flowed freely around her shoulders and down the back of a white cotton shirt with the two top buttons undone, exposing the top third of an alabaster breastbone. Bride had never seen her look so casual nor more at ease with herself.

"You look...uh..." stammered Bride.

"Different?"

"Yes. Different."

"And is that a compliment?"

"The highest."

Catherine blushed. Her Royal blood seemed to rise directly from her heart through her neck and seep into her face. "We'd better get going."

Bride nodded and followed her to where a stableboy was leading a pair of saddled horses by their bridles. "Good afternoon, Your Highness," said the young man with genuine respect and admiration. "I got Ginny ready for you. Picked out a good mount for the gentleman as well. Hope you don't mind."

"Thank you, Peter," said Catherine. "You're always a step ahead of me."

"Thank you, Your Highness. Have a good ride. I'll be here when you return."

The stableboy gave Ginny a warm rub on the side of her head and turned over the respective reins to Catherine and Bride. Ginny, a smallish chestnut mare, reflected Catherine's personality. She stood calmly as Catherine inspected the saddle, then softly nuzzled her owner as the Princess adjusted the bit in her mouth. Like Catherine, Ginny could be as gentle as a zephyr gliding along the Broads, but also capable of a North Sea gale when her enormous power was summoned.

Rama, the high strung Arabian colt at the end of the reins in Bride's hands, pawed nervously at the ground as he sized up his new rider. He was normally ridden by Prince George and something about Bride seemed familiar to him, but the horse knew this was their first meeting.

Catherine swung gracefully into her English saddle. Ginny didn't move a single sinew.

Bride put his left foot in the stirrup of his saddle and took several bounces on the ball of his right foot. He started to swing his right leg up and over onto Rama's back, but the Arabian moved his hindquarters several paces to the right and preempted the mounting. Bride paused a moment, took a firmer grip on the top of the saddle, and again tried to climb on. Again Rama sidestepped him.

Catherine couldn't hide her smile but managed to bite her upper lip and look away so as not to embarrass her guest any further.

A less experienced rider might have immediately attempted another mounting, but Bride knew the results would probably be the same. Instead, he marched directly in front of Rama, tugged firmly on the bit to get the beast's attention, and stared squarely into his round ebony eyes.

"Now you listen to me, young fellow," said Bride with firm determination. "If God hadn't intended you to be ridden, He would have made you a cow. And if you don't cooperate, I'll see to it that you end up the same way as most cattle I know. Is that clear?"

The display of bravado had really been intended for Catherine's benefit, but Rama seemed to understand the text of Bride's warning as well as the tone. He suddenly stood rigidly at attention and allowed the American to mount him with no further trouble. "There. Now that we understand each other, I think we're in for a good day of riding," said Bride as he patted the horse's sleek black neck.

Catherine gave Ginny a gentle kick in the ribs and the chestnut statue suddenly shot forward as if she'd heard the starting bell at Newmarket as her wispy tail waved a wild goodbye.

Bride sat stunned for a moment at the sudden departure of the two females until Rama turned around as if to ask, "Are we going or aren't we?" Bride bounced his heels into Rama's midsection and the Arabian responded, dashing out of the stable area and chasing after Ginny down the dirt lane. It was more like riding a bike than Bride had remembered.

Rama ran closely to the white wooden fence along the road like a racehorse hugging the rail and within seconds had caught up to Ginny and Catherine. With a grin of mischief, Catherine suddenly pulled hard on the reins to the right and in perfect equestrian form jumped over the fence and into the meadow on the other side.

Bride yanked Rama to an abrupt stop, no small feat for a charging horse on a dirt road. They watched as Ginny and Catherine galloped away with at least one of them laughing as they put distance between themselves and their pursuers.

Bride spun Rama around and gave the horse room to build up speed to vault the fence. Jumping was not an equestrian skill Bride possessed, but he convinced himself that if Rama were up to it, then so was he. He spurred the horse and charged toward the fence. Bride hoped Rama knew what to do when they got there because holding on for dear life was the only thing he was going to contribute to their joint effort.

Ten yards from the fence, Bride lost his nerve. The thought of hurtling through space on the back of an animal seemed suicidal and he knew he couldn't do it. He pulled hard to the right, aborting their mission. If the chase were to continue, they'd have to find another way into the meadow.

Two hundred feet ahead the fence ended and a hedgerow began. In swift collaboration of horse and rider, Rama and Bride sprinted to the end of the fenceline and burst through the hedges. The branches tore at Bride's legs but the exhilarating thrill of the chase swept the pain aside.

Rama's powerful thoroughbred flanks churned like a locomotive as he gained ground on Ginny. Past fields of peas and beans and thickets of blackcurrants they raced as heath cocks scrambled for cover.

Catherine leaned low into her saddle, glancing back at Bride as he steadily closed the gap. She couldn't remember riding like this since she was a schoolgirl and she didn't want it to end. At Catherine's gentle beckoning, Ginny suddenly bore hard to the right and cut into the woods.

Bride aimed Rama at the spot where they had vanished behind the trees and rode directly toward it. He was feeling so confident on his mount now that he forgot to take into account that Rama was at least three hands higher than Ginny and he sat at least eight inches taller in the saddle than Catherine. The combination of those factors, added to the low slung pine branch, was an equation for disaster. No sooner had Rama taken two steps into the treeline than Bride was collared by a branch and sent sprawling backwards to the ground.

He lay motionless for a solid minute as he caught his breath and tried to determine how many bones were fractured. Rama stood over him, not apologetically, but rather with impatience over Bride's failure to scramble back into the saddle and resume the spirited chase.

As Bride slowly pulled himself up and realized nothing was broken, Catherine and Ginny came trotting back through the forest.

"Are you alright?" she asked.

"Fine," he said in a clipped tone as he brushed off some mud. "When's the last time the royal pruners were out this way?"

Catherine covered her mouth in a feeble attempt to hide her laughter but she failed to contain her dancing eyes and bouncing shoulders. Bride looked up at her and feigned irritation, but it couldn't last as he broke into a wide grin. "I suppose this makes you the winner."

"Yes, but you are a gracious loser, milord."

"I try."

"It was time to eat anyway," said Catherine as she swung down out of her saddle.

"Food!" shouted Bride, slapping his forehead with his open palm. "We rode off and forgot lunch!"

"No we didn't," said the Princess with a shake of her head. She stood on her tiptoes and peered out of the woods across the meadow. "I'm having it delivered."

Across the field came a large white and brown spotted dog with a small wicker picnic basket clenched between his teeth. Its breed was unidentifiable but suffice to say that his ancestors had been a hearty mix of shepherd, retriever, and beagle who had combined their genetics to give him the best nose in Norfolk. His olfactive radar had led him over half a mile to Catherine and the moment his eyes made contact with hers he picked up his pace another notch.

"Good boy, Ollie! Good dog!" cheered Catherine. The dog set the picnic basket down at her feet and then leaped up and threw two muddy paws onto her white blouse. She didn't care as she exchanged a frothy kiss with his eager tongue. Bride shook his head in admiration.

"You're amazing. Your considerable influence even extends to the animal kingdom. What's next, a falcon swoops down with a bottle of wine?"

"Of course not. Ollie never forgets the wine."

Catherine pulled out a white linen tablecloth from the picnic basket and spread it across the grass in the shade of the treeline. They enjoyed a feast of turkey breast sandwiches, seedless green grapes, a wedge of Brie, and a split of vintage French Chablis. Catherine offered a hunk of cheese to Ollie and he gladly accepted the tip.

"I'm learning more about royalty every day. Here I've always assumed that a Princess would have a dog like a long-haired dachshund or a whippet or some kind of spaniel with a pedigree as long as your own, and here you are owning a mutt. Another myth crumbles."

Catherine scratched Ollie behind the ears causing his eyes to roll deeply back into his head.

"His real name is Oliver, like the orphan in the musical. I found him wandering out here about eight years ago, starving to death. I guess I've always had a soft spot for strays. Dogs, cats, birds, I've taken them all in at one time or another."

"And people too, I might add," said Bride as he sipped his wine.

"What do you mean?"

"I mean Trevor McFarlane. A nice enough man once you get to know him, but he hardly seems like the kind of candidate for the job he has. Something tells me you rescued him from something too."

"Quite the contrary, Dr. Bride. It was Trevor McFarlane who rescued me."

"Oh?"

Catherine wrapped her arms around Ollie's neck and placed her cheek on the dog's forehead. Her gaze went out across the meadow as she recalled a day from years before. "Are you familiar with the ravens at the Tower of London?"

Bride shook his head. "Not really."

"The ravens first came to the Tower in the early 1600s when the royal kitchens were the only place they could find something to eat. They've been there ever since and now legend says that if the ravens should ever leave the Tower of London, the monarchy will fall, so they still keep eight or so of them on the grounds."

"What's all that have to do with Trevor?" asked Bride with a puzzled look.

"A few years ago I was coming out of the Tower chapel after some sort of ceremony, I've forgotten now, and Trevor was stationed there as a Yeoman Warder."

"Yeoman Warder?"

"A Beefeater. You know, the men in the quaint Tudor outfits that look as though they've just stepped off of a bottle of gin. Anyway, I turned around to speak to someone and suddenly one of the Tower ravens flew up and attacked me. I suppose being in captivity all these years made this particular bird go a little daft and he viciously tore into my flesh like something out of a Hitchcock movie.

"So here I am about to be pecked to death and nobody around me is doing anything to stop it. Suddenly here comes Trevor McFarlane sprinting across the lawn. He shoves me to the ground, snatches the raven right out of the air, and snaps its evil little neck right in half. He tossed it aside like a dishtowel and helped me to my feet, then went back to his post without saying a word.

"Now here was someone who didn't think about the possible consequences of knocking a Princess on her royal rump, much less throttling a national treasure like a Tower raven. He simply saw that I was in trouble and he responded, swiftly and decisively. That's the kind of man I want for a bodyguard and so he's been at my side ever since."

She paused briefly, narrowing her eyes as she gathered her memory. "There's a wonderful inscription at the military chapel in Edinburgh Castle that reads 'the souls of the righteous are in the hand of God. There shall no evil happen to them.' I think whoever wrote that was talking about Trevor McFarlane."

"He loves you, you know."

"Yes, I suppose he does. There's nothing I can do about that. It's daunting, actually."

"In what way?"

"Several years ago I was sleeping in a bedroom at Windsor Castle when it caught fire. I was trapped, absolutely no exit. Trevor fought his way through the flames and rescued me. It confirmed what I'd always known, that he would trade his life for mine."

"I'm beginning to think there are a lot of people who would."

"What makes you say that?"

"After watching those people in Norwich today risking their lives just to snap a picture or even catch a glimpse of you, I can see now how much this country loves the monarchy. I hope the ravens stay at the Tower a long time."

"Thank you, Dr. Bride. So do I." Catherine patted Ollie firmly on the back to signal that his massage was over. He moved aside and laid down as Catherine poured another glass of Chablis.

"Tell me about your father," said Bride.

"My father," she said emphatically like a child repeating an assigned word at the National Spelling Bee. "There's not much to tell really. He was away most of my early childhood and died when I was only fourteen. It's sad to admit, but most of what I know about him comes from things I've read in history books."

"And you can't always believe them, can you?" joked Bride.

"I have chosen to only believe the good things written about him."

"And what were those?"

"Principally that he was a good husband. A *faithful* husband, which is not always the case for consorts to the Queen. My mother was one of the few fortunate members of the Royal Family who actually married for love. She honestly believed my father was sent to her as a divine gift. While other matrimonial unions among the Royals were arranged by the likes of Elliott Wiggs, her marriage seemed to be arranged by God."

"They're not the same person?" mused Bride. Catherine laughed out loud, one of the rare times Bride had seen her lose her composure. "Did Wiggs arrange your marriage to Nolan?" Her radiant smile vanished immediately, but to his surprise, she didn't end the conversation.

"I met Robert when I was twenty-three and he came to Buckingham Palace as the new official physician to the Crown." She shook her head with amusement. "The very first time we met, I had to undress in front of him for a physical examination. No man had ever seen me without clothes on before, and the instant he looked at me I knew no other man would ever get the opportunity because I didn't think I could stand the embarrassment. I found out later that his appointment was the direct result of Wiggs's maneuvering behind the scenes in a grand design to find me a suitable husband. Nolan swept me off my feet and the next thing I know I'm dragging an enormous white train down the aisle at Westminster Abbey."

"Did you love him?"

"I thought so at the time, but my idealism was soon thereafter to be rudely awakened. You see, Sir Nolan didn't share my father's high ideals about monogamy within the confines of matrimony. From the moment I first found out about his numerous indiscretions, I ached inside because I knew I had lost something that could never be found again."

"You're sure about that?" asked Bride pointedly.

Catherine demurely turned away. She was as uncomfortable as Bride when it came to discussing matters of the heart.

"I will make no secret that I have enjoyed your company these past few weeks, Dr. Bride. You are most unlike any gentleman of my acquaintance. But I must admit to you and to myself that part of the reason I've felt so comfortable around you is because I know your stay here in England is only temporary. It's provided a certain safety net for our relationship."

"We can't get involved because there's no time, is that what you're saying?"

She turned back to face him. "What I'm saying is that I'm no longer equipped for romance."

"Why do you say that? You're everything a man wants. You're intelligent, gracious, witty...and if you'll permit me, extremely beautiful."

"You can be quite flattering," whispered Catherine as she blushed and again turned away.

"It's all true and you know it. Which is why I can't understand why you'd say you aren't equipped for romance."

"After I learned of my late husband's affairs, I built a wall around myself and it's been impenetrable by even the most earnest of suitors. You, Dr. Bride, at least made it to the top of that wall, but I must tell you that you are still on the outside looking in."

"Is that the only reason for the wall?" asked Bride.

"What do you mean?"

"I sense there's another source of pain that you haven't told me about."

"I don't know what you mean," she replied with a clipped tone as she stared deep into the surrounding woods.

"I suppose we've come full circle now to our first meeting in the cemetery at St. Bartholomew's. I've tried to get it out of my mind, but I can't help but wonder who it is you were there to visit. I know it's not Nolan."

Catherine turned to him with temper flaring in her eyes. "What makes you think that?" she blurted.

Bride didn't *think* that, he *knew* it, but couldn't very well tell her that he and Crowe had dug up the grave. Fortunately, he had another way around it.

"It's my understanding that Nolan's body was never recovered after the skiing accident, so naturally I'm assuming someone else is buried in St. Bartholomew's. Someone you care about."

Catherine swallowed hard and looked up at the clouds. A single tear began to roll down her cheek. She suddenly brushed it aside and shook her head, forcing her cheekbones to form a wide smile. She had been well trained to mask her emotions and she now put that training to use as she bluntly deflected the question.

"We always seem to be talking about my love life, don't we?"

she said to Bride. "What about you? Tell me about the people who love you."

Bride sensed her unwillingness to talk about St. Bartholomew's and chose not to push it. "There aren't any, really. A few students who have shown some genuine affection over the years, but that's about it. My parents are both dead. No brothers or sisters. Just me."

"Have you ever been married?"

Bride laughed out loud and shook his head. "I haven't even been on a date since the Eisenhower administration."

"And whose fault is that? You're an attractive man...robust, intelligent...intermittently charming," she said with wry smile. "I should think plenty of young lasses would come calling."

"Maybe I just never found the right woman."

They sat silently under the trees staring at each other. Seldom in the history of man and woman had a romance proceeded with such caution. It was as if they were driving down a winding country road through a dense night fog where they couldn't see around the next corner, much less their final destination. They could only stare straight ahead in hopes of remaining on course.

The spell was broken as Rama snorted a few yards away, anxious to run again. Bride and Catherine cleaned up their picnic, put the basket back into Ollie's jaws and sent him on his way. They rode back to the stable side by side as the sun sank slowly into the moors.

"I used to enjoy sunsets," said Bride. "But not this one."

"Why?" asked Catherine.

"Because, your Highness, it means our day is over, and I never know when I'll see you again."

"Catherine," she said softly, looking straight ahead. "You may call me Catherine."

They rode the rest of the way in silence.

Trevor drove Bride to the railway station at King's Lynn where he would catch the last train to London. With a window for his pillow, Bride fell asleep before the departure whistle blew.

◆ ◆ ◆

Nothing makes an underling walk faster to his superior's office than when he has good news to report. Crumrie strode quickly down the upstairs corridor of Kensington Palace and rapped loudly on the door to Prince George's study.

"Enter," came George's voice from inside above the blaring Verdi aria.

Crumrie entered the study and found the Crown Prince sitting in an armchair by the window, staring pensively out at the night sky. George recognized Crumrie's distinctive knock and didn't need to turn around to see who it was. "I hope for your sake this is good news."

"It is, sir. We found him."

George sprang to his feet. "Where is he?"

"He's on a train, returning to London from Sandringham. He's been there all day with your sister."

George's eyes flared with anger. He had issued a direct order for her to stop seeing the American and she had disobeyed. "With Catherine? You're certain about this?"

"One of the gardeners saw her out riding with a man that fits Bride's description. In fact, he was wearing some of your clothes."

"Do you have somebody at the train station waiting for Bride?"

"Better than that, sir. One of my men is boarding the train at Cambridge. He'll follow him the rest of the way, and this time we won't lose him."

"When is Catherine due back at Buckingham?"

"Within the half hour," replied Crumrie with a check of his watch.

"Get my car."

◆ ◆ ◆

It is usually the quick thinking man who manages to escape when he's being chased, but it was actually Bride's dulled senses that would turn out to be his savior as his train pulled into the station.

He awakened with a start when the conductor applied the brakes with a slightly heavy hand, causing the train to lurch to a stop in a series of staccato squeals from metal grinding against metal. Bride had no concept of time nor place as he stood to his feet and followed the other passengers in his berth down the aisle and out the door to the platform below.

He yawned like a lion as he stretched a neck that was locked in place at a forty-five degree angle from an awkward sleeping position.

His senses were gradually getting up to speed as he rubbed his weary eyes and drew two invigorating breaths.

Bride took two steps in search of a taxi stand but suddenly stopped. Something didn't seem quite right. He raised his chin and took in another deep breath of the dewy night. The London air suddenly seemed fresher than he remembered, more like the clean salt air of East Anglia. Now that he took a good look around him, Bride also noticed that the train station wasn't nearly as busy as he would have imagined.

It was only after he walked another ten yards that he saw the large wooden sign hanging above the edge of the platform. Cambridge. He squinted for a better focus but the sign didn't change. Cambridge, as in fifty miles away from London. The lights of the last train out were disappearing down the tracks.

As Bride rode in the back seat down M-11 in a very expensive cab ride to London, he shook his head repeatedly, castigating himself for getting off at the wrong stop.

He had no way of knowing that on a southbound train somewhere up ahead, one of Crumrie's men was walking from berth to berth in a futile search for the elusive Dr. Bride.

Chapter Twenty

It was after ten o'clock but Trevor was still in the garage at Buckingham Palace wiping off the dust of the day's travels from the black fenders of Catherine's limousine. There were other young men in the Crown Equerry normally assigned for such mundane tasks, but Trevor never felt they had the passion to do the job like it needed to be done. If he was going to be seen driving the Princess Royal, then it was going to be in the shiniest vehicle in the fleet of Rolls Royces in the palace garage.

As Trevor polished the Royal Coat-of-Arms on the roof plaque, he heard the squeal of tires behind him. He stood up to see George's familiar Bentley pull in and come to an abrupt stop. Crumrie hopped out of the driver's side and opened the rear door. George stepped out and marched immediately inside. Trevor feared he knew where the Prince was going and there was nothing he could do to stop him.

Members of the Royal Family seldom find themselves alone, even in the privacy of home. There is virtually always a butler, a chambermaid, a lady-in-waiting, an equerry, or other employee of some sort in the same room to attend to each and every need.

Princess Catherine could hardly sneeze without three or four arms stretching out to hand her a tissue, and so it was rare that she was completely alone as she brushed out her auburn hair before going to bed. Just as well that her attendants didn't see the pine needles of Sandringham falling out of her head and start the rumor mill churning again. She was enjoying the solitude as the perfect end to her day, one filled with adoration from loyal subjects, the fresh salt air of Norfolk, and the hint of romance.

As she walked over to her bed, however, the quiet was about to come to an abrupt ending.

George burst into the bedroom and shattered the silence as he slammed the door behind him. "I told you to stay away from him!" he yelled as he stormed toward her.

Catherine was defiant, not moving an inch backwards. "Since when do I take orders from you?" she replied firmly.

George's response was physical. He slapped her angrily across the cheek, the sting of his palm turning her white skin a deep shade of scarlet. Catherine fell back two steps and braced herself on the side of the bed. She was stunned by George's actions, and never having been struck before by anyone, she wasn't quite sure how to react. George took another step closer and raised his hand to strike again.

"You get away from me!" she screamed.

George grabbed her left wrist and tried to backhand her across the face but she blocked his motion with her free hand. He wrestled for control of her flailing arms as she struggled to get free.

A soft voice penetrated the door to the adjacent servant's room. "Your Highness, is everything alright?"

The seconds that followed were tense. George let go of her arm and moved back a step, heaving for breath. He glared at her, concerned over what her response would be.

"Do you need some assistance?" came the voice again from behind the door.

"No, no. Everything's fine. Thank you." She raised her chin and stared over the bridge of her nose at the Prince. "You will kindly leave my bedroom now."

George didn't move. There had been no closure on the business he'd come for and he wasn't ready to leave. She turned her back on him, bravely announcing that she didn't fear him.

"I'm not finished with you," murmured George. He slammed the door on his way out.

Catherine held her hand against her cheek to soothe her brother's blow. She crawled into her sumptuous bed, turned off the light, and gently cried herself to sleep.

Down the hallway, George had regained his composure as he entered the room of Queen Alexandra. There was a young nurse sitting erect in a chair next to the Queen's dressing table, keeping vigil through the night. Prince George held his finger up to his lips as he crept into the room.

"How long has she been asleep?" he whispered.

"Only a few minutes, Your Majesty."

"Could I have a few minutes alone with her?"

"Certainly, sir. I'll be right outside if you need me."

As the nurse moved silently out of the room, George walked over and sat on the edge of Queen Alexandra's bed. She lay motionless, barely breathing and somewhat resembling a corpse at an open viewing with her hair fixed neatly in place.

George was ashamed of what was running through his head as he sat on her probable deathbed. He tried his best to block his thoughts out of his mind, but he couldn't help the way he felt. He knew he should be feeling love for this woman and sorrow over her slow demise, but all he could think was that this frail body was all that stood between him and the throne of Britain. If she was going to die, why couldn't she just get on with it?

"You're not going to choke me, are you?" said Queen Alexandra.

George leapt off the bed with a start. He hadn't expected her to speak, nor had he expected her to so clearly read his wandering mind.

"Mother, you're awake."

"I'm still alive if that's what you mean," said the Queen as she finally opened her eyes and sat up against her pillows.

"Oh, Mother, don't be so macabre. I just came by to check on you."

"You mean you wanted a progress report? I'd say that for every day you keep up this political nonsense, I lose another day on this earth."

"Please don't talk that way," he said. "I was worried about you, so I stopped in."

"I'm sorry. I suppose I'm becoming somewhat cynical these days. I'm starting to realize the bitter irony that I have control over so many things in this world, but mortality is not one of them. You would think the Defender of the Faith would get some sort of special allowance from the Almighty, wouldn't you?"

Alexandra rattled out a pill from the bottle on her nightstand and washed it down with water. She winced with pain, then slid back down under her covers and closed her eyes.

"Actually, I'm feeling a little better. I'm hoping to make some public appearances next week. The people need to see me up and about, I think. It buoys their spirits. So tell me, how is your little campaign going?" she asked.

George ignored the slight dig. "The latest polls show us gaining ground, particularly in the North and West. It's encouraging."

"Yes, I suppose it is." Alexandra sighed heavily. "You used to be such a nice boy, George. So levelheaded. What happened?"

"I grew up, Mother."

"No, no, it's more than that. You changed, almost overnight."

"Perhaps I changed because the world around me changed. Which is why I'm doing what I'm doing now."

"And what are you going to do if you win? Have you considered that possibility?"

"I should hope to rule with the same wisdom you have always shown, Mother."

Queen Alexandra surrendered a faint smile. "You make it difficult to remain angry with you, George. You always have."

"Another inherited trait no doubt."

"Just promise me that you'll look after John and Catherine. They're not as strong as you."

"I will, Mother. You have my promise." George bent over and kissed Alexandra's forehead as she faded back into sleep. He wiped his mouth as he quickly exited the room.

♦ ♦ ♦

Down in the garage, Crumrie puffed on a cigarette as he leaned against the Bentley. For the first time, he noticed Trevor polishing the limousine across the way.

"Working a bit late, aren't ya mate?" said Crumrie.

"Aren't we all," growled Trevor. "What brings you over here at this hour?"

"Official business," came Crumrie's smug reply.

"I'm sure. What's so bleedin' important that it couldn't wait 'til the mornin'?"

"If you know what's good for you, mate, you'll learn to stop asking so many questions."

Crumrie dropped the cigarette in front of him and crushed it with his heel. The meaning wasn't lost on Trevor, but the threat wasn't daunting. He spit on his polishing rag, invoking a little symbolism of his own.

Prince George burst into the garage and marched to his Bentley.

"We're going now," he snapped at Crumrie. The doors slammed and the car careened out of the garage.

Trevor glared at George as he drove past, sensing that the Prince's anger had been vented on Catherine. Through the years his McFarlane clan had devoted themselves to serving their country and their Crown, but at this moment Trevor felt treason in his heart. He would like nothing better than to take Prince George and give him a thorough thrashing.

Since the death of his father, nobody had ever dared to stand up to George. Even Wiggs was losing some of his considerable influence over his protege and if the Prince were to somehow capture the upcoming election, he would be insufferable. Just one good swing was all Trevor wanted. Just one good swing. He spit on his rag and rubbed harder on the fender.

Chapter Twenty-One

Sirens blared from a convoy of police cars as they roared into Covent Garden. Scotland Yard had just received another phone call from the IRA and the bomb squad scrambled into action. The situation was particularly tense on this morning because Prince George was scheduled to speak at Covent Garden within the hour.

A crowd of reporters surrounded the gate that Prince George normally used to exit Kensington Palace. His Bentley turned the corner and rolled swiftly up to the gate. The reporters could see George in the back seat and they clamored for his attention.

"Are you still going to Covent Garden?" yelled a reporter from the BBC through the tinted glass.

The Crown Prince leaned forward and motioned for Crumrie to stop the car. He opened his own door and climbed out to address the media. Whether it was a last second decision or it was by design didn't matter at this point as even seasoned reporters gasped in awe at this departure from the norm.

Even though the Crown remained on the head of Queen Alexandra, George was already talking like a King. Surrounded by a ring of security guards, he swaggered into the gaggle of microphones and spoke with Churchillian bravado.

"I have been informed of the threat on my life by Scotland Yard and here is my response to the cowards who issued it. I will not bend to the threats of terrorists, period. The Royal Family has a rich history of remaining with the ship, if you will, and that's one of the things I *don't* plan on changing. I see today's situation as similar to what we faced during the war when we remained in London despite the air raids. Dictators, terrorists, and other assorted embodiments of evil will try to shake the monarchy, but I assure you, we will not be moved.

"It brings to mind a time when England stood alone against Napoleon and Prime Minister William Pitt warned his people that 'you cannot make peace with dictators—you must defeat them'." George paused dramatically and uttered the most important thing he would ever say. "Now then, if you'll excuse me, the Prince has an appointment to keep in Covent Garden."

That single line would be splashed in the headlines and repeated time and again on the television and radio reports until it echoed throughout the Kingdom. These were the words of a man who was increasingly being perceived as one prepared to stand up for righteousness even in the face of death. The defiant stance would stir the hearts of all Britons who would like to believe they shared the same sense of courage and duty. And above all, George's popularity would take a quantum leap in the national opinion polls.

George saluted the reporters like Montgomery saluted his troops, then ducked back into his Bentley and headed for his threatened destination. He leaned back in the leather seat and lit up a cigar. He had seized the moment and he knew it.

George was greeted in front of the Royal Opera House at Covent Garden by a committee of police officers who wanted to bring him up to date. The small crowd contained behind some ropes couldn't hear their conversation but could see the Prince repeatedly shaking his head at the pleadings of the officers. George would occasionally point to a portion of the stage or motion to other officers to join the roundtable discussion, emitting the body language of a man in control of the situation. Finally the policemen threw up their hands in frustration and the Prince marched regally to the podium.

The crowd, well aware of the bomb threat, roared its approval.

"I intended to use this occasion to discuss education and our nation's need to overhaul the national curriculum," began George, "but I will instead take the opportunity to emphatically state my position on dealing with terrorists. In 1994, the IRA promised a cessation of its guerrilla activities, but in the years that followed, it has continued its murderous ways. I say the time has come for more stringent action. We will fight the devil with his own hellfire if that's what it takes!"

The impromptu news conference outside of Kensington Palace just minutes before had served as the perfect dress rehearsal as George reiterated his earlier statements but this time with more force and dramatic flair. He managed to work in the word "cowards" at least a dozen times during the course of his remarks, firmly entrenching himself as the very opposite.

He left the stage amid a rousing ovation from the other brave souls who had remained in Covent Garden despite the IRA's bomb threat. He climbed inside his Bentley and Crumrie whisked him away without further incident. He had kept his appointment in Covent Garden and the whole world would know about it.

◆ ◆ ◆

Colin Crowe was working on a story involving the Crown Prince, but it had nothing to do with the IRA or Covent Garden. He was seated at a quiet table in The Grenadier near Belgrave Square, buying a lunch of mushroom pie and beef Wellington for an attractive strawberry blonde named Rosalie Linley. She was a flight attendant for British Airways that he'd met years before on a trip to Madrid.

Rosalie had at one time attempted to see Crowe on a social basis but his demanding schedule forced her to abandon any romantic notions and she now viewed him merely as a friend. On this occasion Crowe didn't look upon Rosalie Linley as a friend nor as a lover. Today she was a source.

Over the years Rosalie had proved invaluable in providing Crowe with information about arrivals and departures from Heathrow and Gatwick. Whenever she noticed that one of her passengers was an ambassador, a politician, an entertainer, or someone just acting suspiciously, she would contact Crowe and offer the details. Often it turned out to be nothing, but occasionally Crowe stumbled onto a good story just by knowing where people were going. It always took some digging to figure out what they were up to once they reached their destination, but that was usually the easy part.

Many a clandestine rendezvous had been exposed by Rosalie's discreet observations on board the planes and she had come to enjoy her journalistic sleuthing. She also had a real incentive in knowing there was a free meal on the other end of her reporting at any restaurant of her choosing. She still liked Crowe enough as a friend to go easy on him in her choices and they usually ended up in a quaint setting like The Grenadier. If she had only known how important the information she was about to give Crowe really was, she might have opted for something slightly more upscale like Chez Nico or the Lindsay House.

Crowe's notebook and pen were still tucked inside his jacket because taking notes might draw attention among the sophisticated young lunchtime crowd of businessmen and mews-dwellers. A miniature tape recorder was tucked unobtrusively behind a tall Bloody Mary to capture Rosalie's every word. They spoke so quietly that even the ghost of the dead grenadier who haunted the pub couldn't have overheard them.

"Do you recall their names?" asked Crowe.

"Zholobetsky was one of them," replied Rosalie.

"Vladimir Zholobetsky?" said Crowe.

"I don't know. Their names weren't on the list of passengers. I only saw his last name on his garment bag."

"And what about the other one?"

"I didn't get his name but you could hardly miss him. He was nearly seven feet tall. His legs were so long he couldn't get comfortable, even in first class."

"Malinkoff," said Crowe in a loud whisper directed more to his own ear than Rosalie's.

"Who are they?" she asked.

"Scientists. Nuclear scientists. Formerly of the Soviet Union, now living in Berlin."

"I knew they were somebody important the way they got whisked away at the gate. When a passenger doesn't have to go through customs, I always know my suspicions about him were right." Rosalie took another sumptuous bite of beef Wellington. "So what do you make of it? Does it mean anything?"

"I'm not sure, to be honest with you. But just the bare facts you've given me indicate that something's up."

"How do you know?"

"First off, nuclear scientists don't usually travel together on holiday, so I'm fairly certain they didn't come to England for the tulip festival. Secondly, these aren't the kind of men who can really afford to be flying first class, which tells me that someone bought their tickets for them. I shall now attempt to find out who."

"Will you tell me when you do?"

"Yes, my dear Rosalie, I will tell you." Her eyes lit up. She loved the intrigue of modern journalism. "All you have to do," continued Crowe, "is listen to Radio 4 every day at one o'clock." Her delight evaporated. Just for that, she would order dessert.

That evening in Crowe's flat, Bride watched the news reports on BBC-1 of Prince George's show of strength earlier that day at Covent

Garden. The announcer began the report with figures from the recent polls that showed the Conservatives now even with or leading the Labourites in a majority of the constituencies. With the general election just two weeks away, the Conservative Party's gambit of putting Prince George at the helm had quickly righted the sinking ship.

Though his contact with the Crown Prince had been minimal, Bride couldn't help but feel the private George was distinctly different from the public image, and in this case different was definitely not better. On the sidelines of the polo field or alone on the veranda at Kensington, George came off as egotistical, condescending, and often downright rude. But as Bride listened to him on television in his daring rebuke of the IRA terrorists, George brought forth a persona that was engaging, forthright, powerful, and likeable. His ego translated to self-confidence. His abruptness felt more like determination. At the end of the day, George was immensely likeable as a candidate.

In the span of a few weeks, he had shed his image as a coddled member of the Royal Family and taken on the mantle of a true leader, someone who could indeed play a leading man in the theater of the world. George's ability to pull off the transformation impressed Bride. It also scared him.

Bride's mind wandered to thoughts of Catherine. He wondered why she hadn't contacted him in days, especially after their perfect afternoon together at Sandringham. He had tried to call Trevor but had never received an answer. Something must be wrong, he thought. His guilty conscience flashed back to the lurid night in the cemetery at St. Bartholomew's and hoped that wasn't her motive for not calling.

He also realized this was yet another reason he'd always been reluctant to get romantically involved. There didn't seem to be any hard and fast rules as to how often one half of a romantic liaison should get in touch with the other half, and the wait was killing him.

The front door to the flat swung open and Crowe walked in with yet another greasy meal of fish and chips. If the British fishing and potato industries were in decline, it was no fault of Colin Crowe's. He tossed his keys on the coffee table and spread the golden repast in front of Bride. He noticed the absence of salivation around his American friend's mouth.

"What? It's cheap and it doesn't require utensils."

"And it goes equally well with red or white wine," cracked Bride.

Crowe grinned as he went into the kitchen and dug through the refrigerator. "You know, *Woman's Hour* is looking for a food critic. I'll be happy to pass on your resume." Crowe's smile disappeared as he returned to the living room and saw the face of Prince George filling the television screen.

"I see you're one of the captivated millions," Crowe said to Bride as he cracked open another earthy brown Guinness.

"You have to admit, he shows some real courage," said Bride with a shrug. "I'm not sure I'd be out saying 'I dare you' to the IRA."

"No, which is why you'll last longer on this earth than bonnie Prince George. He seems to be bent on self destruction."

"You say that as if you have further evidence to support that theory."

Crowe nodded as he lit up a fresh cigarette. "I've been a busy boy today."

Crowe sat down on the couch and pulled out his notepad. He took a bite of fish and washed it down with a swig of Guinness, never once removing the lit cigarette that dangled from his mouth. It clearly wasn't the first time he'd done this. He flipped through his notes as the cigarette smoke rose up into his watering eyes.

"Tell me what you make of this," said Crowe. "Two weeks ago, Prince George convinces the miners to back him in the election by promising to keep their pits open."

"Makes sense," said Bride. "Smart politics."

"But yesterday he holds a secret meeting at Whites Hotel in Lancaster Gate with two scientists, Vladimir Zholobetsky and Sergei Malinkoff. At one time, these two men headed up the nuclear energy commission in the former Soviet Union. Now here's my question—if Prince George the politician is truly committed to king coal as an energy source, then what the bloody hell is he doing holding secret meetings with nuclear physicists?"

"I have another question," replied Bride. "If it was a *secret* meeting, how did you know about it?"

"I followed the trail of vodka and caviar. Or, I went to every five-star hotel in the city until I could find a talkative bellboy. Take your pick."

"What's your best guess?" asked Bride.

"I really don't have an answer," said Crowe, reexamining his notes as if the solution might magically appear. "That will require more investigation. But I have reached one conclusion."

"What's that?"

"That our Crown Prince is accelerating his habit of saying one thing and doing quite another."

Bride nodded and glanced over at the television. "I know what you mean."

◆ ◆ ◆

Queen Alexandra lay sleeping as Princess Catherine leaned over her face and checked to make sure she was still breathing, the same way a young mother checks her newborn infant.

The night nurse seated next to the Queen's bed had fallen asleep in her chair, but rather than chastise her for malfeasance, Catherine simply jostled the nurse's knee to bring her back to life. The embarrassed young woman jumped up and pushed her chair back under a desk to indicate to the Princess that she would not drift away from her station again.

Catherine stepped quietly to the doorway of the Queen's bedroom, taking a long look at Alexandra in the crack of light wedging in from the hall. It had become a nightly ritual for Catherine, who never knew when it might be the last time she saw her mother alive.

She returned to her own room and crawled into bed, unable to sleep. It wasn't the first time she had felt lonely. Despite her congenial nature, she really had no close friends. The only person she really wanted to talk to at that moment was Malcolm Bride, but despite her outwardly defiant stance with George, she genuinely feared his reprisal if she contacted the American. Catherine could only pray that Bride would understand why she hadn't called.

Chapter Twenty-Two

"You know I don't pay for information," said Crowe. "I can take you to lunch, but that's about it."

He was sitting at the bar in Steph's on Dean Street in Soho. Next to him at the rail was Prince John, living up to his Black Jack reputation in a leather jumpsuit.

"I know. I don't want money," he said as he stared straight ahead and sipped champagne. His eyes had that glassy look of someone who's had too much drink and not enough to live for.

"Then why did you call me?"

"Because I want to cause trouble." He downed the remainder of the champagne in his glass and quickly poured another from the bottle on the bar, not caring that he spilled at least another full glass by pouring too quickly. He took another swallow for courage. "I'm going to give you the grapes and you will have to make the wine. From what I know about you, that shouldn't be a problem."

"I appreciate the compliment."

"And if you say you got it from me I'll of course categorically deny it."

"Understood. But people in here have seen us talking."

"Doesn't matter. These people hate George as much as I do."

"I'm listening."

"My older brother has quietly been wresting away hundreds of thousands of pounds, perhaps millions by now, of my mother's money. He and Wiggs have her convinced that it's inevitable that the Queen will have to pay even more income taxes and they've further convinced her that she can save a large chunk of that tax if she divests herself of certain properties. George and Wiggs of course act as brokers for all of the arrangements and make a handsome profit."

"Why would he do that? He's wealthy in his own right."

"It's like the mountain, Mr. Crowe. Because it's there."

"And you're upset that he's taking advantage of your mother for financial gain?"

"Heavens no!" answered John with a drunken laugh. "The old girl's worth about twelve billion by now. Losing a few million pounds here and there isn't going to do her bank account any harm. What bothers me is what Georgie's doing with the money he's stealing."

"And exactly what *is* he doing?" asked Crowe.

"He's sunk a fortune into a shipping company that transports uranium mined in Russia through the Baltic and North Seas."

"That's a bit odd for a man who publicly moans about the sad state of the environment," added Crowe, scribbling away. "I may not be fully informed as to the preservationist doctrine, but I'm fairly certain it doesn't involve uranium."

"That's just the tip of the iceberg," continued John. "George is also making inquiries into purchasing land that might be suitable for nuclear reactors. To make a long story short, George is laying the groundwork for a monopoly on nuclear energy in the U.K, and when one stops to consider that one pound of enriched uranium can provide as much energy as a thousand *tons* of coal, it doesn't take long to understand why."

Crowe's mind was racing. He felt as though he was experiencing the early warnings of an enormous earthquake. A chandelier tinkling here, a teacup rattling there, all harbingers of the great shakeup to follow. The Prince's meeting with Zholobetsky and Malinkoff suddenly made sense. They were consultants in the master plan. Everything fit.

Prince George was a man who craved control. What better way to exercise control over a nation than to control its energy supply? But this wasn't really about energy, thought Crowe. This was all about power, and George stood on the brink of a great deal of raw power. As Prime Minister he would have it in government and military, and now in the world of economics he would hold an artery to the nation's heart.

"You're certain about this?" asked Crowe.

"Dead certain," nodded John, enjoying the pun. "I rummage through Wiggs's desk every chance I get. It's all set up through dummy corporations, but all roads lead to Kensington." Prince John downed another glass of champagne, this one in celebration.

Crowe didn't ask another question as he closed up his notebook and wandered out of Steph's. His excitement was molting into fear and mind-numbing dread as he tried to see into the future. He walked to Piccadilly Circus where the neon lights peeked through the descending blanket of fog. The dim rainbow of color in the murky London night mirrored his own mind. He could discern only patches of clarity in an otherwise cloudy soup of recent events. George's radical departure from tradition. John's revelations about the uranium. The nuclear physicists. And the mysterious secret so closely guarded by Catherine that must somehow enter into the equation.

Crowe climbed into his Triumph and drove back to his flat in Marylebone. His mind was hollow and inattentive to his driving. The Triumph found its way home by sheer habit.

Bride was already asleep in the spare bedroom when Crowe returned home from his meeting with Prince John. Crowe opened the bedroom door and the light from the hallway immediately aroused the light-sleeping professor.

"Bride, are you awake?" whispered Crowe.

"I am now," replied Bride with a hint of annoyance.

"I need to talk to somebody."

"Couldn't it be somebody else?" he said, sitting upright. Bride's irritation disappeared when he saw the downcast look on Crowe's face. He pulled down the coverlet and swung his feet onto the floor. "What's wrong?" he asked Crowe with concern.

"You're a student of history. Tell me how a dictator rises to power."

Bride shook the cobwebs of an hour's sleep out of his head and turned on the lamp on the nightstand. "Well, I suppose there have been lots of different ways over the centuries."

"Tell me about modern history. Tell me about Hitler." Bride nodded as he pondered the question carefully. An outline of events was organizing itself inside his head. "Hitler started by attacking the government in his speeches. He promised that the Nazi Party could restore the economy and put people back to work. He vowed to lead Germany to greatness again."

"And where did he garner support?"

"Mostly in small towns and among the labor unions."

"And how did he finally become chancellor?" asked Crowe like a barrister leading his witness.

"As I recall, there were national elections in 1932 and the Nazis emerged as the strongest party with Hitler at the top. After that, he was virtually unstoppable."

Crowe looked solemnly at Bride. "Does any of this sound familiar?" said Crowe. Bride's mind was finally fully awake and the significance of the history lesson he'd been giving Crowe suddenly dawned on him. In virtually every instance, the steps George was currently taking paralleled the same path as Adolf Hitler's rise to power.

Garnering the support of the working man and the man who was out of work with promises of economic boom. Delivering speeches at every opportunity with a theme of restoring the nation to former greatness. Entering the political system to lend credibility to his stature even as he defied existing law. Once in a position of power, he took control of the nation's economy and its military and the rest was a sad chapter in history.

"Oh, my God," said Bride as he began to realize the frightening consequences of George's hidden agenda.

"I can't help but return to the grave at St. Bartholomew's. My gut tells me those bones are involved in this."

"But how?" asked Bride.

"I don't know and I've turned over every cobblestone in London trying to find out. But I know at least one person who can give us the answer." Crowe didn't have to mention Princess Catherine by name. Bride knew exactly who Crowe meant from the look on his face. "You're close to her, Bride. At this point, probably closer to her than anyone in the Kingdom."

"I can't do it," said Bride.

"Well the only other choice is to lean on her driver."

"Trevor McFarlane? I'd have better luck with Catherine."

"Then that's who you approach."

Bride balked at the thought. His relationship with Catherine up to this point had been something of a modern fairy tale. He knew that one mention of the grave would close the book.

Crowe sensed his hesitation but wouldn't relent. "Think about what's at stake here, man! You *have* to do it!" Bride was wavering.

"But I don't know when I'll see her again, or even *if* I'll see her again. She hasn't called me in days."

"So why don't you call *her*? I have about twenty different numbers for Buckingham Palace over there on my rolodex. One of them is bound to get you connected."

"I sincerely doubt they'll let some American stranger just call up and talk to the Princess."

"You underestimate your charm, Dr. Bride. She'll take your call. And when she does, you must do what you must do."

Bride nodded quietly, trying to convince himself that Crowe was right. "Maybe."

"Do you know why nobody stopped Hitler?" said Crowe. "Because nobody knew what he was up to. His greatest stroke of genius, if you can call it that, was to shut down the free press. I can give you one promise. There is one voice on the airwaves that will not be silenced. Goodnight, Malcolm."

"Goodnight, Colin."

Crowe departed and closed the bedroom door. Bride remained on the edge of the bed, staring at the floorboards. The hour of sleep he'd already captured would be the only decent rest he would get that night.

Chapter Twenty-Three

Crowe drove north from London at the crack of the new day to work on his investigation of Prince George's interests in developing nuclear power to fuel Britain.

All afternoon and well into the evening he scoured the countryside and pubs of Lincolnshire to uncover new leads and find sources willing to confirm Prince John's allegations. He found none. Nobody was talking, nobody was listening. His investigation had run into one enormous stone wall that would have made Hadrian proud.

Crowe decided the trail had come to a dead end for one of three reasons; either George had covered his tracks extremely well, or anyone who knew anything was in fear of George's wrath if they volunteered information, or Prince John had simply fabricated the whole story in a desperate attempt to embarrass his brother before the upcoming election.

Crowe had just about convinced himself the latter was true and was making plans the next morning to return to London empty-handed. For some reason, almost by whimsy, he decided to make one more visit to the Register of Deeds in Lincoln.

It was there that Crowe discovered a tiny piece of information that he hoped would be the spark to ignite the second Great Fire of London.

The records showed that a large farm near the seaside town of Mablethorpe had recently been purchased and full payment had been made in cash. That by itself was not overly suspicious, but Crowe noticed the entity making the purchase was listed as Continental Golf Design, Inc. Ordinarily, there would be nothing terribly strange about a company that builds golf courses buying up huge tracts of undeveloped land, but in this case Crowe realized, the acreage was essentially marshland. Great for growing potatoes or tulip bulbs, but completely worthless for building golf courses. The only way it could be done was if somebody were willing to spend millions of pounds to haul in millions of pounds of topsoil, which would make no sense given the ample number of farms for sale further inland that were already on solid ground.

What the marshy tract of land *did* provide, however, was easy access to the water. In fact, it would be an ideal point of entry for freighters from the North Sea or the Baltic.

A lesser reporter might have overlooked the oddity or downplayed its significance, but Crowe hadn't risen to the top of his profession by underestimating the power of minutiae. To him, each investigation was a game of chess in which the taking of pawns could be as important as capturing a rook or a bishop.

With the first clue of his treasure hunt scribbled into his notepad, Crowe raced his Triumph down the motorway back to London.

More dogged detective work with the help of an anonymous source at the Bank of England and he finally traced Continental Golf Design, Inc. through a circuitous route of dummy corporations all the way back to Kensington Palace. Of all things, Prince John had actually been telling the truth.

The timing for his story was perfect. The nation's interest was keenly focused on the approaching elections and every morsel of information pertaining to the campaign was being snapped up. Crowe was about to deliver a meal. It wasn't the feast he had hoped to lay out, but it would be enough to fill them until the next course arrived.

As dusk filtered through the charcoal gray sky, Crowe stepped into his converted taxi cab outside his Marylebone flat and flipped the switches on the generators of the mobile broadcasting unit. Power comes in so many forms, thought Crowe as his equipment hummed to life. A few batteries would be all he needed to take his message to the airwaves and put a chink in the armor of Prince George.

At precisely six o'clock, Crowe got his cue from the station.

"This is David Hemdale," came the familiar baritone voice, "and this is *The World Tonight*. BBC Radio 4 has learned that Prince George has become personally involved in the transport of uranium and the future development of nuclear power plants on Britain's east coast. For an exclusive report, we now go live to Chief Political Correspondent, Colin Crowe."

As hundreds of thousands listened in with their jaws dropping lower and lower, Crowe unveiled his gripping tale. He told of secret meetings with Russian nuclear physicists, of secret land acquisitions, and of millions of pounds taken right out from under the nose of the Queen to finance it all.

If ever there had been nuclear fallout, this was it. Within minutes the television stations, mainstream newspapers, and tabloids were scrambling to play catch up with Crowe's bombshell. "Radio-Activity" was already being typeset in two-inch headlines by more than one journal.

Crowe turned off the power in his mobile broadcast unit and smiled through the smoke of a fresh cigarette. He had broken the story of the century twice now in the span of a month. "Take *that*, Georgie boy," he said happily to himself.

◆ ◆ ◆

Nowhere was the story received with more anger than in Prince George's private apartment in Kensington Palace. Priceless French antiques were upended as he vented his anger with a temper so forceful that even Wiggs couldn't calm him.

"Who's responsible for this? I will have his head!" screamed George like some ancient Tudor King.

"We don't know exactly, but we're trying to find out," replied Wiggs in an unusually calm voice.

"See that we do!" thundered George. "These security breaches are intolerable!" He tossed aside a Victorian chair and stood with his hands on the windowsill, heaving with angry exhaustion. He turned to Crumrie who stood rigidly by the door. "Now!" screamed George. Crumrie looked at Wiggs, who gently nodded his head in support of George's command.

"Yessir," said Crumrie. He exited the apartment. He would take care of it, and he already had a good idea of where to start.

Night had scarcely fallen on Kensington when a mob of coal miners descended on the property with inconsolable anger, yelling "traitor" in one loud voice. They carried torches like ancient Prussian villagers, clanging on the iron gates of George's palace and echoing the betrayal that was felt from the pits of Yorkshire to the Welsh Rhondda Valley. Nuclear power put the miners' livelihoods at risk and they were ready to burn Prince George at the coal-fired stake for reneging on his deal with mining union chief Ian Sturges.

George and Wiggs stood on a palace veranda and stared out at the distant torch fires. Wiggs hadn't survived for over sixty years behind palace walls without an adroitness for political maneuvering, and he knew exactly what the situation called for.

"Denial," he said firmly to George. "We only have to hold them off for three more days."

In less than thirty minutes, a written release was handed through the palace fence to the miner who appeared to be in charge of the protest. The letter dismissed the entire uranium story as "a mixture of fantasy and fabrication from Labour's dirty tricks department," and promised the miners a full hearing on the issue the next day. Appeased for the time being, the miners extinguished their torches and disbanded.

Crowe's news report was also extremely unsettling to Princess Catherine. Her darkest fears that the monarchy would crumble with the inevitable death of her mother seemed to be coming true. She couldn't sleep as visions rushed through her brain of the Tower ravens taking flight over the skies of London to announce to everyone below that the monarchy had fallen.

It was after midnight when Catherine heard her brother's unmistakable heel-to-toe gait stalking down the chamber floor corridor. She hopped quickly out of bed and scurried across the room to her door. As she peered into the hallway, she saw George opening the door to John's room, looking around, then slamming the door in anger.

"George, what are you doing here at this hour?"

"Nothing. Now go back to bed." He stormed past her and vanished down the staircase.

The scene stuck uncomfortably in Catherine's mind. Why was he looking for John? She raced back to her bedroom and placed a frantic call to Trevor.

Prince John had completed his usual nightly migration from Steph's to The Napoleon Club, only drunker than usual. He was stretched out on a chair in the corner of the disco with his head slung back as far as it would go, singing a muddled version of "Britannia Rules the Waves" in competition with the throbbing acid-house music.

Crumrie pushed his way past the doorman and scanned the wild assortment of patrons in the nightclub. Within moments he had discovered his non-moving target. Crumrie brusquely grabbed one of Prince John's bony arms and pulled him out of the bar. The regulars of The Napoleon Club had seen John dragged out in similar fashion before, usually on orders from his mother, and thought nothing of it this time around given his drunken condition.

Crumrie pulled John outside and down the sidewalk to an alley-way off New Bond Street, reminiscent of the days when drunken young men were impressed into naval service. At the end of the alley was a black Rolls Royce that melded into the indigo darkness of night, its Royal crest discreetly covered up.

The door was yanked opened and John was flung inside on all fours. He struggled to regain his balance as the door slammed and locked behind him. He focused his vision, severely impaired by French champagne and Jamaican marijuana, and saw George sitting in the back seat like the Don of a mafia family.

"Georgie boy!" cackled John. "Come out to play, have ya?"

George slapped John across the face with his bare hand.

"Shut up!" yelled George as he boiled over.

John wiped his mouth with the back of his hand and saw the blood trickling out of the corner of his mouth.

"Well look at that," said John with amusement. "It's not blue at all! I must be some sort of fraud!" He licked away the blood from his mouth with a long sweep of his tongue, laughing through a series of involuntary belches.

"You're a disgrace, that's what you are."

"Every family needs a black sheep, Georgie boy. I'm just trying to do my part." He laughed again but immediately stopped as he looked at the rage on his older brother's face. His voice turned morose. "I've always been a disgrace, George. Why did you come out here in the middle of the night to tell me something we already know?"

"I came out here to tell you that starting immediately, you are no longer on the civil list. You are being cut off completely from any further financial support. The days of sponging off Mother are over. Furthermore, your things will be packed up and removed from Buckingham Palace."

"Why?"

"I think you know."

"I must have forgotten. Tell me again."

"There have been leaks to the media about some of my financial dealings, and Mr. Crumrie has evidence that those leaks can be traced back to you." The sloppy grin on John's face suddenly turned quite a bit more sober. He turned away, unable to face his accuser.

"The next few days are critical in my plans and I can't afford these indiscretions. If it were anybody else, I would deal with them quite a bit more harshly, but in your case I think the worst thing I can do to you is force you to develop some responsibility. So, as of this very moment, no more money, no more Royal perks, no privileges, not even entrance through the palace gates. If you insist on being a black sheep, you will do so without a shepherd to watch over you. Now get out."

"You can't do this to me, George!" pleaded John.

"I bloody well do what I want."

"But it wasn't me! I'm not the leak! I never said anything to anyone about uranium!"

"Who said we were talking about uranium?" said George coldly. John took a breath to issue a protest, but the steely glint in George's eyes told him that there was no use in keeping up the facade. He bowed his head, the drunken defiance of a few minutes ago giving way to sober humility.

"George, I'm begging you, give me another chance." George rapped on the window, his signal that the discussion was over. Crumrie snatched open the door and grabbed Prince John's arm, nearly dislocating it from its socket as he pulled him out of the Rolls Royce. He shoved John hard, bouncing him against the wall of the alley and into a pile of garbage. John struggled to his feet and pounded on George's window.

"You bastard!" he yelled, loudly enough for passersby on New Bond Street to hear. They had no idea they were listening in on nobility, but rather assumed it was another quarrel among lovers. "Wait 'til I tell them about the night in the East End with the four teenage lasses! Wonder what they'll have to say about the future Defender of the Faith *then* Georgie boy! What will they say when they find out the Crown Prince has to pay for it! There's plenty more where that came from, Georgie boy! Plenty more!"

John's angry threats were cut short when Crumrie's boot struck him squarely in the ribs. He gasped for breath, staggered backwards and collapsed in the middle of the alley. The boot struck again, this time in the temple. Crumrie hopped in the limousine and drove away, leaving John to gasp the trail of fumes.

Prince George stared coldly out the tinted window of the limousine as it passed by Berkeley Square.

"Crumrie," said George in a controlled voice.

"Yes, Your Highness?"

"Crumrie, you're a military man. Tell me, what's the penalty for a soldier leaking information to the enemy?"

"In times of peace, sir, he's court-martialed."

"And in times of war, Crumrie?"

"He's shot, sir."

George nodded his head and leaned back in the leather benchseat. "Find the leak, Crumrie. And plug it."

Crumrie nodded, grinning at the opportunity.

Back in the alleyway, Prince John attempted to stand up but the pain inflicted by Crumrie's steel-toed boots sent him falling back to the pavement. He was born into one of the highest stations in the free world, but had descended into the gutter like one of the heroin addicts under the arches of Waterloo Bridge. He'd been given everything, too much of everything, and had squandered a bright future into a black hole of nothingness. He could only imagine that somewhere in heaven his father was looking down at him in that alley and shaking his head with disappointment, as he had so many times on earth. He was literally and figuratively at rock bottom.

For the first time in nine years, John said a prayer. He had decided that if he was permitted by the grace of God to survive, he would from that moment forward be a changed man. He lapsed into unconsciousness.

John regained a grain of lucidity minutes later, just long enough to feel a pair of strong arms reach under his midsection and lift him into the backseat of a car. If this was how God claimed the heavenbound, it was awfully pedestrian thought John. Perhaps he was headed in a different direction. His mind went black again.

Chapter Twenty-Four

The morning sun poked a few fingers through the heavy cloud cover and touched the dome of St. Paul's Cathedral. The heart of London was just coming to life as the Cockney pitchmen of Petticoat Lane prepared their stalls for business.

Bankers and stockbrokers in chalk-striped suits climbed out of the bowels of the Liverpool Street tube station and headed for their offices in The City. They didn't break stride when they heard the blast of explosives a few blocks away, assuming it was just another row of ancient flats being leveled to make way for a gaudy new skyscraper.

Minutes later, the sirens of police cars, ambulances, and fire engines followed. A few minutes after that, *Today* on BBC Radio 4 would interrupt an interview with Prime Minister Roth to air a bulletin that an explosion had ripped apart three floors of a brothel off Leadenhall Street, renowned among the upper crust for its quality and discretion.

An hour later another bulletin announced that the IRA had already called Scotland Yard to claim credit for unleashing the bomb. It would be well into the afternoon before the news broke that among the dead bodies pulled out of the rubble was Prince John of the House of Windsor.

◆ ◆ ◆

Princess Catherine laid in bed and wept until she had no more tears to give. Her ladies-in-waiting had tried everything from breakfast tea to cognac but nothing would console her.

As a member of the Royal Family she had been accustomed to tragedy, in fact seeking it out on countless occasions. Trips to mining disasters and plane crashes, hospitals with wounded veterans, and clinics for the terminally ill, on and on in an official capacity of mourner but with her inner emotions stirred by each sad face she encountered.

And if the Princess Royal's public duties didn't keep her dressed in black, Catherine's personal life provided ample more opportunities. By the age of five she had buried her grandparents. As a teenager she stood in Westminster Abbey and watched them lower her father's casket into the ground. The decade of her forties saw the death of her husband and her sister-in-law. And in a quiet corner in the cemetery of St. Bartholomew's Church were the remains of some other unknown tragedy that had invaded Catherine's life. It was becoming too much to bear and her hours of sobbing weren't helping.

Trevor knocked quietly on Catherine's door and was let into the room by one of the ladies-in-waiting.

"You called for me, Your Highness?" he said respectfully. She nodded and signaled to the other women in the room to please leave them alone. "I'm very sorry about John," said Trevor. It was one of the rare times in Catherine's company where he spoke first.

"Thank you. It all seems to be a nightmare and I can't seem to wake up. Please, sit down."

Trevor nervously looked around the room for a chair. He couldn't recall ever having actually sat down in the bedroom of the Princess. He spotted a side chair against the wall and perched on its edge. Princess Catherine pulled the chair from her vanity closer to him and sat down. She spoke in a whisper, knowing full well that the walls were trying to listen.

"I didn't hear back from you so I assumed that you had found John last night."

"I did, Your Highness. Face down in the alley next to The Napoleon Club. I picked him up and brought him directly home."

"Then what?"

"Cleaned him up a bit and laid him right in his bed downstairs."

"Did he say anything about going back out?"

"Ma'am, when I left him he couldn't *move*, much less talk. If he got up out of that bed it was because somebody helped him get out of it."

"Do you suppose it was one of his friends?"

"No, Your Highness. I'm supposin' it was one of his enemies."

Catherine angled her head with suspicion, trying to discern if she fully understood his meaning. Trevor nodded his head to let her know there was no miscommunication between them.

Catherine's lips quivered as it all sunk in. She suddenly leaned

over and wrapped her arms around Trevor like a child hugs her father. She burst into tears, her sobs muffled in the broad shoulders of
a McFarlane. He held her tightly and fought back his own tears from
seeing his beloved Princess in so much pain.

◆　◆　◆

George stood grim-faced amidst the bombed out rubble of the
brothel. He was wearing khaki pants and a sport shirt as if he'd been
suddenly called away from something and had been too hurried to
change clothes.

A wall of microphones and an army of reporters stood in front of
him, including Colin Crowe. Several thousand people stood behind
police barricades on the other side of the lane. Bobbies and
plainclothed bodyguards were thick among them.

"Cowardice!" roared George. "Pure and simple cowardice! And
we must stand here at death's door and ask ourselves why? Why are
they doing this? Why have these cowards taken the life of a brother I
loved very deeply? Because they can see the new age dawning on this
country, the new order that I am ushering in, and they don't like it!

"But I promise you that they can't stop us, no more than they can
stop God's sun from rising in the morning. My rage does not only
come from the loss of my brother. No, my rage represents the rage of
all England! The rage of all free people everywhere! In two days, you
can vent your rage by going to the polls and voting Conservative! Together we will crush them, swiftly and mightily, that is the vow I make
to you as your leader."

Raucous applause reverberated up and down the street as the
Prince waded through splintered floorboards to his waiting limousine. Even some of the reporters allowed themselves a moment of
ovation. George left them with a brief salute and vanished into his
car. Crumrie slammed George's door, took one last look at the pile of
rubble through his sunglasses, then stepped around the hood to the
driver's side and climbed in. The limousine roared away as if to signal
there was much work to be done and the bonnie Prince of Wales was
by God speeding off to do it.

His Highness Prince John was buried the next day among the Victorian statues in Highgate Cemetery where he would be the second
most famous resident next to Karl Marx. It was an unusual place for
nobility to wind up but Prince John was the black sheep to the bitter
end. It was according to John's wishes that he be buried close to the
artists and musicians of Hampstead Village, and few people in the

palace minded that he would be interred in relative obscurity.

Very few people outside of London's underground culture turned out for the funeral procession. As the casket passed down Swain's Lane there were nearly as many bodyguards for the Royal Family members as there were mourners.

Queen Alexandra was escorted from her limousine by equerries on either arm. Her face was heavily made up to hide the dark lines and circles of sickness, like some aging film star. They kept her well away from the cameras, knowing she wasn't ready for a close-up.

Prince George stood stoically at the graveside, occasionally shaking his head with anguish as the photographers focused in. He wiped away moisture from his cheeks that would appear on the evening news that night to be tears, but were in reality drops of rain that had begun to fall at Highgate.

Princess Catherine was among the very few who shed real tears. At one point, her eyes locked onto George's and a silent anger poured out and bored into his soul. In that instant, Catherine's eyes conveyed everything she was feeling towards her brother: rage, disdain, and above all, blame. Trevor's theory that John's presence at the brothel that night wasn't of his own doing kept running through her mind, and she couldn't help but wonder if George were somehow involved. George looked away, unable to face his sister any longer.

A minor clergyman had been dispatched from the Anglican Church for the unenviable task of performing a sacred religious ritual over the dead body of an avowed sinner. The result was a generic service that was delivered as if the priest had a tight schedule to keep.

The eulogy consisted of an ethereal free-form poem, written and read by one of John's tattooed friends. It made absolutely no sense to anyone who heard it, but when it was mercifully over they all nodded in polite agreement with whatever sentiment it was intended to convey.

There were a few uncomfortable moments at the conclusion of the ceremony when nobody quite knew what to do next. George finally gave a nod of his head as if to say "that's that" and headed back to his limousine as the rain began to fall harder. Such was the life and death of Prince John. Shallow, misunderstood, and to many, inconvenient.

The bodyguards retreated to their cars and whisked George away in a caravan of staff cars. Queen Alexandra was carefully escorted back into her limousine, looking increasingly feeble from the strain.

The other onlookers gradually backed away and disappeared into the mist. Only Catherine remained behind, with Trevor a few yards behind her. She knelt next to her brother's grave and said a prayer, then looked skyward through the stinging rain as if she were providing God with a reference for John's admission into heaven. She thought she had no more tears left, but somehow found a few more.

Chapter Twenty-Five

In an odd twist of fate, Crowe's news flash about George's interests in uranium and nuclear energy would actually aid and abet the Prince's steady rise to power.

In reaction stories on the BBC evening news that night, modernizers and industry leaders were calling him a visionary. A sizable number of Liberal Democrats were now leaning in George's favor as the candidate most capable of leading the country into the next century on equal footing with the United States, Japan, and Germany. Even some leading environmentalists were admitting that nuclear power might be safer and certainly cleaner than the millions of tons of coal that were burned every year.

George had intended to meet with Ian Sturges and followup on his blanket denial about his involvement with nuclear power. After all, he had used the miners' backing as a springboard into politics and he didn't want to lose their support on the eve of the election. But as he watched the BBC broadcasts that night and weighed the favorable public opinion, he decided to handle the miners in the same manner as any seasoned politician—he ignored them.

The voter turnout for the first national election in six years exceeded all expectations. Prince George's entry into the race had created new interest in politics and record numbers of Brits turned out to cast their ballots.

In exit polls from the Isle of Lewis in the Outer Hebrides to the Isle of Skye in the English Channel, the clear majority was voting for the Conservatives.

By 5:00 PM, well before the polls closed, the blue and white headline sheet of the *Evening Standard* was stapled up on the newsstand on Charing Cross.

CONSERVATIVE LANDSLIDE!

George would win in his district by an eight to one margin, by far the most lopsided race in the entire House of Commons.

It was George's stand against terrorism that had carried the day. In refusing to buckle under to IRA terrorism, George had found a popular note among the voters and he'd carried the tune for weeks as he rose to the top of the opinion polls. His now famous line, "the Prince has an appointment to keep in Covent Garden," had become part of the political lexicon, a national rallying cry against everything that was wrong with modern Britain.

The uranium scandal had cost him the votes of sixty thousand miners, but all of that was quickly forgotten. He was now a mere formality away from being installed as Great Britain's new Prime Minister.

George sat on Queen Alexandra's bed in Buckingham Palace. He had victory parties to attend, but he wanted to make sure he got in a visit to his ailing mother before he went out on the town. Wiggs had assured him it would look good in the morning newspapers, and George actually wanted the opportunity to gloat a little bit.

His election victory was his first bona fide accomplishment that hadn't been the direct result of some privilege extended to him by his mother. It wasn't an heirloom handed down, or some ceremonial rite of passage like his investiture as the Prince of Wales. This was all his doing, and though it wasn't the military conquest George longed for, it was the next best thing and he intended to savor the victory cigar.

"I thought you might want to congratulate me," said George as he took Alexandra's feeble hand.

"For what? Forging the nails for my coffin?"

George let go of the Queen's hand, stunned by her reaction. He had fully expected his mother to show some pride in what he'd been able to do, or at the very least a small amount of contrition for having doubted him. The monarch's next words would shock him even further.

"George, of course you realize who formally appoints the Prime Minister?"

"Of course," he replied, looking away with a certain loathing disrespect. "You do."

"Yes, and as Head of State, I won't permit you to take the position. It is my sovereign right and also my duty. I know you better than anyone under the sun, and I know you are not equipped to run this country."

George rose angrily from the bed, his temper flaring like a blacksmith's fire. "You can't do that!"

"I can. I will. I must."

"The people won't stand for it, Mother!"

"Don't try to match me in a popularity contest, George. That's one race you can't win."

"Why now, Mother? Why didn't you say anything about this before?"

"Because I didn't think it would come to this. Frankly, I didn't think you could win. But since you have surprised us all, I hope you will be content to represent your fine constituents of Stagsden." Queen Alexandra closed her eyes. Discussion over.

"We will just see about that," raged George. "We will just see."

He stormed across the room and reached for the doorknob, preparing to slam it shut with all his anger, but as if thunderstruck by a novel idea, George suddenly changed his mind. He slowly pulled the door closed, as the narrowing sliver of light from the hallway illuminated a large feather pillow on the floor next to Alexandra's bed. The latch gently clicked into place. The room darkened.

Minutes later in the corridor, George turned to the night nurse waiting for him to leave so she could return to her station. "The Queen requests that she be permitted to sleep alone this evening," George told her. "No offense to you, but she doesn't seem to rest as well with someone watching her. You understand, of course."

She nodded and departed as George managed to feign a warm smile through clenched teeth.

That same smile would remain on his face throughout the evening as he hopscotched across London to celebrate the election. But the anger inside him grew more and more intense as he thought about Queen Alexandra's declaration. He had not come this far to stop now.

Chapter Twenty-Six

The world may not have come to a complete stop but it certainly slowed down on a gray London morning in June of 2002. A lady-in-waiting entered Queen Alexandra's bedroom at Buckingham Palace and found her beloved sovereign pale and motionless.

The Queen had passed away in her sleep sometime during the night. She had apparently suffocated in the large feather pillow found next to her head, too weak from fatigue and medication to roll back over when her breath became short. She died as she had lived, in regal posture, troubling no one with cries for help.

Her children were summoned to her side. Catherine arrived immediately from her suite on the bedroom floor of Buckingham Palace. She wept unabashedly, racked with guilt that she had fallen asleep the night before without making her usual check on her mother.

Prince George arrived quickly from Kensington. He paused at the door as he entered the bedroom and saw the Queen on her deathbed. He finally ventured closer to her and placed his arm on the shoulder of the weeping Catherine. She turned and recoiled, perhaps sensing his mixed emotions over the death of the reigning monarch. An image flashed through her mind of George gleefully dashing out to the Tower of London for a fitting of the Crown of Edward the Confessor.

George instead made his way to the Regency Room where he went before the television cameras and announced to the world the passing of the Queen. In a collected manner, he read a statement that didn't seem all that hastily prepared.

According to her wishes, Queen Alexandra was buried without a public viewing. She understood her place in the hearts of her subjects and declared in her last will and testament that "any prolonged period of mourning will only lead to a national state of depression. Take solace in knowing that the Lord God Almighty will watch over you as He is watching over me".

The funeral procession from Buckingham Palace to Westminster Abbey was witnessed by over two million spectators, many of them sobbing uncontrollably as the shrouded wooden burial coach rolled by.

Millions more, like Fionnuala and Peter Rumpole, sat in front of their television sets and wept.

Alexandra was laid to rest next to her parents.

If ever the case to retain the monarchy was to be made, it would be made on this day. The Queen was indeed a symbol of national unity and her loyal subjects were now united in sorrow.

Chapter Twenty-Seven

Bride felt like a prisoner under house arrest as he paced back and forth in Crowe's flat, following Crowe's explicit instructions to stay there. He looked at the clock on the desk, *6:38 PM*. Another day of vacation had slipped away.

He had spent most of the day watching the television coverage of Queen Alexandra's funeral, maudlin enough but made almost intolerable for him by the constant pictures of Princess Catherine weeping. How badly he wished he could be there to console her. Bride wanted that more than he had ever wanted anything in his life.

Bride went to Crowe's refrigerator, hoping that food might take his mind off his problems. All he found was a jar of mustard and eight cold bottles of Guinness. He reluctantly took one out and opened it.

Over the centuries, seldom has alcohol led to clearer thinking, but one swig of the earthy brown stout suddenly brought everything into focus for Malcolm Bride. His thoughts were crystallized into a simple conclusion; it was time to go home. He missed American beer, inferior though it may be, he still missed it. He missed his apartment, his bed, the Boston sports page, his students, something other than fish and chips for dinner, and all the other familiar things in his life.

Bride realized his adventures with Colin Crowe and the outrageous theories they developed about Prince George were really just a diversion to keep him from his real purpose for coming. He resigned himself that it must be destiny that he would never find out his heritage. Something was trying to tell him to give up his search, and finally he was ready to listen.

The only drawing card that England still held for him was Princess Catherine, and she was clearly unattainable. The longer he allowed himself to pursue her, the greater his heartache would be when he ultimately failed. It was time to pack up and go home.

Suddenly infused with a clear plan of action, Bride walked quickly over to Crowe's desk and flipped through his rolodex. He found a phone number for the main exchange at Buckingham Palace and dialed. "I'm trying to reach Trevor McFarlane. Would that be possi—?"

He hadn't even finished the word "possible" before the operator had switched him over. Bride couldn't believe it was that easy. No long winded explanation, no secret password, not even a chance to tell a lie.

Trevor was shining his boots when the phone rang in his quarters. "McFarlane," he answered in an official sounding voice.

"Trevor? It's me, Malcolm Bride."

"Oh," came the gruff reply.

"I wanted to call you."

"About what?"

"I'm leaving. Going back to Boston."

"Smart man. 'Ave a nice trip." Trevor started to put the phone back on the receiver.

Bride could sense he was about to hang up. "Wait!"

"What?"

"I wondered if you could tell her goodbye."

"I'll do it," said Trevor flippantly. His irritation was increasing the longer the call went on. Playing conduit between Bride and Catherine was almost more than he could stand and he was thankful this would be the last time he would be forced to do it. "Will there be anythin' else for ya today?"

"No, no, that's it, just goodbye. And goodbye to you too. I know you don't really like me much, but I always thought you were a good man. She's lucky to have you. Well, I guess that's it. Goodbye."

Trevor was suddenly embarrassed that he'd been so cavalier. He felt Bride's pain over Catherine, as he'd felt it so many times himself. He took a deep breath and shook his head, almost as if he were disappointed in himself for caving in to sentiment. "Dr. Bride?" he said quickly into the receiver.

"Yes?"

"How much longer will you be in England in case she wants to return your call?"

"I'm hoping to leave day after tomorrow. When do you think she'll call?"

"Don't know that she will. That's up to her. Lot goin' on in her life right about now. But I'll be sure and give her the message."

The phone went dead in Bride's hand. He slowly hung it up, feeling sick to his empty stomach.

Crowe burst in through the front door, smacking a fresh pack of cigarettes against his palm.

"Come on, we're going out," snapped Crowe as he tore open the pack and coaxed out a smoke. He was in a foul mood. He had spent the day trying to resurrect the story on George's uranium interests, but had failed to find a single fresh lead. Not a very impressive showing for the reporter who had become the toast of journalistic London.

"Where are we going?" asked Bride.

"Someplace to eat. Anywhere that doesn't serve fish." Crowe looked at his watch. *6:45.* He cocked his head and rolled his eyes upwards as if waiting for something to happen. The light in the hallway clicked on from the automatic timer.

"That's the best thing about England. Everything runs on time! Come on now, let's go."

They exited the flat through the secret tunnel to the greenhouse and walked down the alleyway behind.

"I've reached a decision," said Bride.

Crowe blew a plume of cigarette smoke high into the air. "In regards to what?"

"I'm going back to the States."

Crowe stopped cold in his tracks. "What? You're joking."

"No, I'm serious. There's no reason for me to stay here anymore."

"But I need you! We're *so* close to cracking a major story! You can't leave me now!"

"I have to be honest with you. I'm not convinced there really is anything to all of this. I just think we've both let our imaginations get away from us."

"What? What about the bones in St. Bartholomew's? That alone should tell you we're on to something!"

Bride shook his head. "When in doubt, I go with my gut feeling, and right how, it's telling me to head home."

Crowe narrowed his gaze and studied his American friend to see how serious he really was. He took a long draw on his cigarette and blew the smoke out of the side of his mouth.

"Let's go somewhere we can talk."

They reached the end of the alley and walked across the street to where Crowe's Triumph was parked. Crowe reached for his keys and started to open the passenger door for Bride when suddenly a white van appeared on the street and screeched to a stop in front of them. The side door slid open and two men in black ski masks jumped out, both waving pistols. One of them cupped his hand around Crowe's mouth and jammed his gun into his neck.

"What about this one?" said his partner in a thick Irish accent as he trained his gun on Bride.

"Him too," came the order from the first man as he shoved Crowe into the van. They grabbed Bride and dragged him inside as the van sped off and the door slammed shut. The entire operation had taken less than ten seconds.

Bride and Crowe leaned against the side of the van wall with terror in their eyes and their hands held up over their shoulders.

"Don't look at us!" barked one of the men in the ski masks. They quickly obeyed and stared at the floor of the van as it rumbled through the city streets, turning at nearly every corner to disorient the captives inside. Black blindfolds were quickly tied around their heads.

"What do you want?" asked Crowe.

"Shut up!" yelled the man in the mask. He raised the butt of his gun as if to strike Crowe but didn't follow through.

They rode in silence for what seemed an eternity to Bride. It was ironic, he thought, that he couldn't wait for the van to stop even though he believed that in all likelihood he was being driven to his death. He was certain that whatever he and Crowe had stumbled on had touched a nerve too close to Prince George and George was going to close the book before they could write the final chapter. How fitting that an adventure that began for him in a cemetery was going to end up with his own burial.

It suddenly occurred to him that when one is about to die, he's supposed to ponder all of his regrets, all of the things he wanted to do but never got around to finishing. He'd lived a full life and at this moment Bride could only think of two things he wished he had done. He wished he'd found out who his real parents were so if he were fortunate enough to make it into heaven, he might look them up. And he wished he had kissed Princess Catherine. He felt about her as he'd felt about no other woman he'd ever met, but he'd never had the courage to express it. And now it was too late.

"We're here!" yelled the driver of the van. One of the masked gunmen slid back the door and jumped out. He ran up and unlatched the deadbolt on a small garage and swung open two large wooden doors. The van pulled in and parked as the wooden doors were closed behind them, plunging them all into an eerie darkness.

"I suppose you're wonderin' what this is all about," said the first man to Crowe in a calm Irish brogue.

"So tell me," answered the reporter.

"All these bombings they're linking to the IRA? It's not us."

A flood of relief poured across Bride's taut body. For the first time since he'd been thrust inside the van he didn't firmly believe he was going to die.

The man in the ski mask continued. "The bomb in the pub that killed the Tory leaders, the supposed threat on Prince George's life when he was speaking at Covent Garden, the explosion in the brothel—we're not responsible for any of it! We'll admit to maybe 'alf of the bomb threats in the tube stations, but that's it! Somebody else is behind the rest of this and they're blaming it on us."

"Why are you telling *me*?" said Crowe.

"Because right now you've got this whole country listening to your every word, that's why. If they hear it from you, they know they're hearin' the truth."

"And why do you want them to know?"

"Because George is usin' this to wreak havoc on what we're trying to do. Every time there's a bomb scare, he uses it to blast off on the IRA. Sinn Fein and Prime Minister Roth are trying to negotiate another cease-fire, but this is making life very difficult for us."

Crowe sensed he was no longer in mortal danger and got bolder with his questions. "How do I know you're telling the truth? How do I know you're not just saying this to deflect some of the public anger all of this has stirred up?"

"You don't, but if you're as good a reporter as I think you are, I know you'll check your sources. Meanwhile, consider these two points. First of all, why would we attack people from the Conservatives when it's the bloody Labourites that's causing us the most trouble?"

"I didn't think the IRA cared who it blew to bits these days, just so they were British," said Crowe with the arrogance of a prisoner at the gallows.

The man in the mask bristled at the jab, leaning closer to Crowe and snorting like a bull pondering a charge. He collected his anger and pulled away.

"Alright then, think about this," said the man in the mask. "Does it not strike you the least bit odd that Prince John, a flaming homosexual, died in a brothel?"

"I considered the irony momentarily," answered Crowe. "But my sources inform me that particular establishment was, shall we say, staffed for any eventuality?"

"Well, obviously your sources didn't dig deep enough into the rubble."

"What do you mean?"

"I mean that every female pulled out of the heap was a working girl. Every male they recovered was a customer—a john. One of those johns was a gay Prince, who died in a brothel full of women!"

Crowe's mouth slowly fell open. He couldn't believe that important fact had eluded his grasp. As soon as his embarrassment subsided, he would indeed be double-checking his facts, but that information alone was enough to make him believe his IRA kidnappers.

"I strongly suggest that you tell that to the world," said the kidnapper, "or we will be meeting again. And it won't be as pleasant." He banged on the side of the van. The doors to the garage were flung open and the van lurched into reverse.

They drove in silence for a few minutes, twisting and turning along the city streets and narrow alleyways, as Crowe reorganized his thoughts with the new information from his kidnappers. He never had to ask himself the question "if not the IRA, then who?" because the answer was already formed. Who would profit most from all of this? Deep down, the Brit in him didn't want to believe the answer, which was simultaneously unbelievable yet undeniable. The rise of Prince George would tolerate no obstacles.

The van suddenly pulled to a stop. The door slid open and Bride and Crowe were nudged along by the barrel of a pistol.

"Get out, and don't look back!" The two prisoners obeyed the command to the letter as they jumped onto the sidewalk. The van wheeled away around the corner and disappeared just as suddenly as it had arrived. Bride and Crowe removed their blindfolds and adjusted their eyes to the hazy sunlight.

"You still with me?" said Crowe.

"Still with you," nodded Bride.

"Good. Question now is, where the hell are we?" said Crowe as he lit up another cigarette.

Within seconds Crowe realized they were on the north end of Portland Place, just up the street from BBC Broadcasting House.

"Come on. We need advice from a higher authority," he told Bride as they jaywalked through traffic to the other side of the street.

They walked two blocks to All Souls' Church directly across from Broadcasting House. Crowe took four quick puffs on his cigarette before crushing it under his heel and heading inside.

Choir singers were on their way out the front door, having just finished a late rehearsal for Radio 4's *Daily Service*. Crowe and Bride slid by them with a friendly nod but without any words being spoken.

Crowe felt safe and secure inside a church, but was strangely uncomfortable around devout Christians. In some ways he felt as though they might look down on the individual religion he had created for himself, a theology that condoned smoking, drinking, and late nights with attractive young women. Fortunately, he also believed that God understood.

Crowe gave a reverent nod to the large oil painting of Christ in the front of the church and took a seat in a rear pew where Bride joined him. They were the only mortals left in the church.

"Still think there's nothing to it?" said Crowe in a whisper. "Think about what those men were saying. They're accusing dear old George of murder."

"They didn't say that."

"But they were thinking it, and so are you. George stages all of these IRA bombings to make himself look courageous, and it works so well that he takes out his own brother by the same method. Brilliant. Evil, but nonetheless brilliant."

"We're in too deep," said Bride, hanging his head.

Crowe paused and drummed his fingers on the pew cushion. "I know. Now I'm trying to decide if the story of the millennium is worth getting killed over."

They both leaned on the pew in front of them and stared straight ahead, deep in their own thoughts. Bride didn't know if this was an avenue he wanted to explore. Every time he had tried to step off the mysterious path he was walking, some outside force had seemed to intervene and pushed him further along. This time, he finally decided, he would resist.

Bride looked over at Crowe who simultaneously looked back. They had scanned their own private thoughts and reached different answers. Crowe would go on, Bride would go home. They shook their heads silently to each other, took one final look at the painting of Christ, then walked arm in arm out of the church.

Chapter Twenty-Eight

From the moment that news of Queen Alexandra's death spread across the kingdom, one question had followed immediately behind. Would George abandon his political aspirations and ascend to the throne, or keep his implied promise to not seek the kingship?

After several days of silence, George had finally made his intentions clear. As he spoke into the BBC camera from his Kensington Palace drawing room, it was not the answer his national television audience was expecting.

"After extensive introspection, counsel from trusted advisers, and hours of prayer," said George solemnly, "I have reached the conclusion that it is in Britain's best interest that I fulfill my responsibility as rightful heir and ascend to the throne. In light of recent political developments, I realize this decision may be met with some controversy. However, I cite a thousand years of British tradition that mandate this bold course of action.

"For the time being, I will continue my involvement in the House of Commons for one reason and one reason alone. This nation is at a critical stage and needs strong leadership to guide it through to new prosperity. I intend to provide that leadership. This was my beloved mother's dying wish, and with your help and the grace of God, together we will fulfill that promise. God Bless the British Commonwealth, and may God Bless all of you. Goodnight."

Prince George, soon to be King, folded up the single sheet of parchment in front of him and grimly departed the room. The instant the BBC camera went off, the heated debate began. For weeks, George had told the British people that it was time to reject tradition and allow a member of the nobility to seek political office. He had insisted that his ascension to the throne was a moot point, a possibility so remotely off in the future as to not be worth considering.

Now he was doing a complete turnabout and embracing the very conventions he had discounted. In essence, he was making a mockery of all of the people who had voted for him, yet he had cleverly done it with one hand on the Bible and the other hand waving the Union Jack. As the war of words over his ascension escalated, George would find millions of Brits willing to give him the power to lead. Those who opposed him would find there was little they could now do to stop him.

"We're almost there," said Wiggs with the eager grin of a man who couldn't wait for the next step. He sipped his warm cognac and sat back in the soft leather wing chair. The teacher was pleased with his pupil's television performance just moments before. "There will be a tremendous furor over your speech tonight, but it will die down, just as it did after you announced your entry into politics. And at the end of the day, there's nothing the Labourites can do about it.

"The Conservative MP's are firmly behind you now and it would be suicidal for them to abandon the very man who led them to victory. No, there will be no stopping us now. Everything we've worked for is only a few ceremonies away. Before week's end you'll be crowned King. As soon as Parliament sits again, you will appoint yourself as Prime Minister, thereby reuniting the British monarchy and the head of government."

"The Divine Right of Kings," nodded Prince George. He stood across the room from Wiggs in his Kensington Palace study and slowly nodded his head. His eyes danced wildly as he stared out the window into the faint night sky and dreamed of the possibilities. "As it should be."

"As it should be," repeated Wiggs. "Absolute power is within our grasp, George."

George turned his head halfway around without moving his body. "Did you say *our* grasp, Wiggs?"

Wiggs smiled as he swirled his snifter in front of his eyes and stared through the amber legs of his cognac. "*Your* grasp, George. *Your* grasp."

George nodded and turned back as if to say "that's better."

"It's all coming true, Wiggs. Just as you said."

"Yes, but the next few days are the most critical of all. Until the Coronation Ceremony, there must be absolutely no ripples in the waters, nothing to give Labour any ammunition to change the course of history. One misstep threatens to destroy everything. Once the Crown is on your head, the situation won't be quite as delicate. You will have the power to crush any opposition and with Crumrie as your Secretary of State for Defence and myself as Chancellor of the Exchequer, you won't even have to get your hands dirty. But until you hold that sceptre, not a wrong foot forward. Is that understood?"

"Understood."

Chapter Twenty-Nine

Crowe spent the next morning trying to call in favors. His first visit was to a tiny coffee shop on Birdcage Walk where he happened to know that Inspector Clive Hobday stopped for a cafe au lait every morning on his way to New Scotland Yard.

Hobday was a stout man with the ruddy face of an alcoholic that made him appear considerably older than his forty-seven years. The food stains on his faded trenchcoat and the worn heels of his shoes were telling signs of a twice-divorced bachelor who cared more about the sports scores than fashion.

Hobday was sitting at the counter sipping his hot brew when he saw Crowe walk in and scan the room. Hobday immediately tried to hide behind his newspaper but he was too late. The eagle had spotted his prey and was moving in for the kill.

"Morning, Inspector," said Crowe as he sat down next to him.

"Not today, Crowe, I don't have time for you."

"No time, you say? Now isn't that odd. Scotland Yard had time for me when I knew the whereabouts of two art thieves. Scotland Yard had time for me when I had an exclusive interview with a Libyan terrorist. But now suddenly, as you sip your coffee and browse through the cricket scores, Scotland Yard doesn't have time for me. Yes, I would say that is a bit on the odd side, wouldn't you agree, Inspector Hobday?"

Hobday rattled his newspaper with irritation, then finally set it down and turned to Crowe. "What is it *this* time?" he asked in anguish.

"Now that's more like it!" chirped Crowe. "Did you want to order me a coffee while we talk?"

"Don't push it."

"Alright, alright. I need to ask a few questions."

"About?"

"About the IRA and all the activity lately."

"Wouldn't know about that."

Crowe scratched his head. "Again, that strikes me odd. You are head of Scotland Yard's anti-terrorist squad, are you not? I should think you would be the leading authority on the subject."

Hobday exhaled loudly and rolled his eyes in exasperation.

"What exactly is the point of this conversation, Crowe?"

Crowe's flippant attitude immediately disappeared, displaced by focused seriousness. He leaned closer to Inspector Hobday. "I have reason to believe that all of the bombs and all of the bomb scares the last few weeks that everyone is attributing to the IRA aren't really their doing at all. Now then, am I the only one who thinks so?"

Hobday looked away and blew on his coffee before taking a sip. He shook his head. "Sorry, Crowe. I don't know anything about that."

"Come on, Hobday, just the way you're acting tells me that you do."

"I don't, and that's that," said Hobday in a hushed voice. "I have to go now." Hobday tossed a pound note on the counter and didn't bother to wait for change. Crowe knew he had hit a nerve but would have to dig deeper.

◆ ◆ ◆

With the cascade of major events in London, the free press had completely forgotten about Malcolm Bride and he was once again free to roam the streets of London without feeling like the scarlet letter was emblazoned on his back.

He was feeling better about his decision to leave England and return to Boston, having finally resigned himself to the fact that he wasn't going to tie up any loose ends. His ancestry would remain a mystery, as would the bones in St. Bartholomew's. Worst of all, he would leave Princess Catherine without getting to say goodbye, left only to admire her now on magazine covers and souvenir coffee mugs.

He didn't think he could pack his bags without stopping by the Dunbarton on Gower one last time, not only to say goodbye to the hospitable Rumpoles but also to retrieve two pairs of shoes from the closet in Room One that Crowe had missed in his haste to gather up his belongings.

He gingerly pushed open the heavy oak door to the Dunbarton, tinkling the bell as he had on his initial entry there weeks before. The biting smell of tar from the men fixing the asphalt on Gower was replaced with the aroma of Fionnuala's fresh bread as he stepped into the creaking hallway. The vase on the sideboard had recently been replenished with fresh daisies.

"Hello?" he called down the hall.

"I'm comin', I'm comin'!" came Fionnuala's voice from the kitchen. She burst into the entry hall, wiping her hands on her apron. She stopped cold on the Persian rug when she looked up and saw the professor standing in front of her with a broad smile.

"Are you the lady of the house?" he said with a grin.

"Mr. Bride!" shrieked Fionnuala and she rushed up to hug him. "What brings you 'round here?"

"I came by to say goodbye. I'm leaving tomorrow to go back home. Oh, and to get a couple of pairs of shoes I left here."

"Back to America, is it then?"

"I'm afraid so. London is a little too...eventful."

"It's been one 'ell of a summer, eh, Guvnah? Wouldn't surprise me if Tower Bridge fell right into the Thames. Wouldn't surprise me one bit. Oh, dear God, I nearly forgot! You had some messages while you were away."

Fionnuala rummaged through the doors of the sideboard and fished out an envelope. She handed it to Bride as she provided information of the contents inside. "One is from a Professor Donald Lawrie, ringing you up from St. Andrews as I recall. Said it was urgent, but I didn't know how to get hold of you, so whatever it was may have come and gone. The second call was from a chap by the name of McFarlane. Didn't leave a first name. Said he was lookin' for you and this was the only place he knew to call."

Bride looked at the messages inside the envelope, debating which call to return first. His mind told him to contact Donald Lawrie, but his heart persuaded him otherwise. "When did McFarlane call?"

"This morning. Woke us all up. Odd sort of fellow. A bit gruff. Friend of yours, Mr. Bride?"

"Uh...sort of," he replied with his mind still on the messages in his hand.

Fionnuala gave Bride a studied look. He had all the appearances of a man who had been up all night. Tired, wrinkled, and unshaven. He was a far cry from the robust professor who had first entered the Dunbarton in a crisply starched shirt under his coat and tie.

"Mr. Bride, I don't usually go pokin' me nose into other people's business, but are you in some kind of trouble?"

She had finally gotten his full attention. He thought it over a solid ten seconds before answering. "No. Not anymore. Tomorrow, I'm leaving trouble behind on the runway at Heathrow."

Bride declined Fionnuala's invitation to stay for breakfast. He retrieved his two pairs of shoes from Room One, hugged her goodbye, and exited back onto Gower Street.

Bride poured his coins into the pay phone in the Goodge Street tube station and dialed Trevor's number.

"McFarlane," came the familiar terse reply.

"Trevor, it's Malcolm Bride. I had a message to call you."

"She wants to see you."

He trembled with anticipation. "When?"

"Eleven-thirty. Can you make it?"

Bride checked his watch. It was only 8:35. Plenty of time to return to Crowe's flat, clean up, and meet Catherine. "Absolutely. Just tell me where."

"Under the gazebo."

"I'll be there."

The circuitous trip from Bloomsbury back to Marylebone on the Northern, Central, and Bakerloo tube lines couldn't go fast enough for Bride. At each transfer, he walked to the front of the first railcar as if he would arrive appreciably sooner by doing so.

Through the fence in the alleyway, into the tunnel in the greenhouse, and out through the heating vent in the living room he made his way back into Crowe's flat.

Once inside, Bride blazed into action. He still had two and half hours to go before his appointment with Catherine, but he didn't want to take any chances. If he started right now, he figured, he would have plenty of time to recover from any nicks and cuts his trembling hands might inflict while shaving.

As he hurriedly shed his clothes, the message from Donald Lawrie fell out of his pants pocket. He scooped it up and headed straight to the phone to place a long distance call to Scotland. As the connection went through, he made a mental note to reimburse Crowe for the toll.

The phone rang at Lawrie's office desk in McIntosh Hall in St. Andrews as he took the last bite of a buttery breakfast scone. "Hello?" said Lawrie with his mouth still full.

"Donald?" said the voice on the other end. "This is Malcolm. I'm sorry it took me so long to get back to you but—"

"Malcolm!" shouted Lawrie as he sprang to his feet and choked down the remainder of the food in his mouth. "Where are you?" he asked with urgency.

"I'm in London until tomorrow, then—"

"Don't say another word!" warned Lawrie as he interrupted.

"I want you to go to a pay phone, one that's nowhere near where you're staying. I have something to tell you and I don't want to take a chance that someone's listening in."

Bride was confused but not completely surprised. After everything that had taken place in the last few weeks, nothing was astonishing anymore. "I understand," said Bride. "I'll call you back in thirty minutes."

Bride hung up, starting to really feel pressed for time. He showered and shaved without bloodshed, threw on his only clean shirt and pants, and tied his necktie as he wriggled into his loafers. He brushed his teeth as he combed his hair.

His mind was so preoccupied with thoughts of seeing Catherine again that Crowe's warnings to remain carefully hidden from view were long forgotten as he walked straight out the front door of Crowe's flat in search of the nearest taxi.

As he ran to the street corner and jumped in the first cab that rolled down Montagu, it suddenly occurred to him that he might have made a mistake. He sat lower in the seat, hoping he hadn't.

"Where to?" asked the driver.

"Uh..." Bride hesitated, trying to think of a safe place from which to call Lawrie. "Charterhouse Square," he finally decided for no real reason. The taxi driver nodded and took off.

Bride never saw the black sedan pulling into traffic behind them.

Bride's mind began to wander as busily as the London traffic around him. What could Lawrie possibly need to tell him that demanded such secrecy? Surely it must have something to do with their discussion about the mysterious grave in St. Bartholomew's, but what could his friend have learned? And hadn't Lawrie himself warned Bride to stay away from the subject? What was he doing delving into the forbidden?

Bride decided that Lawrie's natural instincts to learn and acquire knowledge must have consumed him, just as they had pushed Bride to do things he knew he shouldn't. After all, Lawrie was a professor of anthropology. It was his nature to dig. What had he uncovered? Bride was about to find out.

He stepped out of the taxi at Charterhouse Square, not far from the plague pits where the bones of countless thousands were resting uncomfortably. He walked briskly to the bright red telephone booth in the middle of the sidewalk, unaware that the black sedan that had been following him was still on his trail. He poured a handful of twenty pence pieces into the payphone and dialed Lawrie's number.

"Bride?" came Lawrie's hushed answer on the other end. He had drawn the blinds in his office and sat hunched over the phone receiver in his darkened office.

"It's me," acknowledged Bride. He was whispering, even though he was behind closed doors. It seemed like the proper thing to do.

"Are you taking notes?"

"No," answered Bride as he felt around in his breast pocket for a pen.

"Good. Don't write any of this down." Bride stopped searching for a pen.

"What's going on, Donald? What is it?"

"Listen carefully," said Lawrie. "I'm not sure I have the courage to say this more than once."

"It's something to do with St. Bartholomew's, isn't it?"

"I'm not sure, but here's what I've found out. Try as I might, I couldn't get our discussion about Sir Robert Nolan out of my mind, so I did a little independent research."

"I knew you couldn't walk away from it," laughed Bride.

"It's the curse of all educators, I suppose. Anyway, I did some poking around and found an old newspaper article that said that at the time of his death, Sir Nolan had been working with none other than *Basil Jeffery*!" Lawrie waited for Bride to respond to his dramatic presentation.

"Who?" asked Bride.

It was not the reply Lawrie had expected and he was visibly crestfallen over the lack of impact his bombshell had delivered.

"Basil Jeffery! Surely you've heard of him!"

"Sorry."

"Basil Jeffery won some awards a few years back in the field of cytogenetics...heredity, that sort of thing, specifically in the realm of hemophilia. I got to know him a few years back at a seminar on the dating of archaeological specimens through serology, so last week I went down to Edinburgh to speak with him. I, of course didn't breathe a word about our discussion a few weeks back, but I did pry a little more into his relationship with Sir Nolan."

"And?"

"Brace yourself for this. Jeffery had persuaded Nolan to give him some blood samples from members of the Royal Family for his research, figuring that as their physician, he could do it discreetly with no questions asked.

"Nolan gathered the samples and performed some simple tests on them, then called Jeffery to tell him that apparently something was peculiar about the samples. He promised to bring them to Edinburgh for further testing, just as soon as he returned from a ski trip to Austria. As we know, Nolan never made it back. On top of all that, Jeffery traveled to London and inquired about the samples and couldn't find them. Nor could he locate any of Nolan's files on the subject."

"And what do you think that means?"

"I don't know, I just find it all to be a bit queer, don't you? And when I started plugging it into our hypothesis about George and the avalanche and everything else, I must admit I got a little goose flesh."

"I see what you mean. If you put it in our context, it doesn't sound like a coincidence."

"Not at all," agreed Lawrie.

"So why didn't this Basil Jeffery follow up on it?"

"Apparently he did for a while, but you see, Jeffery's considered a bit of an eccentric. Some even call him a crackpot, and nobody was willing to take him seriously. After a while, he gave up and went back to his laboratory."

"Did you find out anything else?"

"To be frank, Malcolm, I lost my nerve. If there's something going on here, I really don't want to be the one to unravel it. I'll leave that up to you. From this point forward, you're on your own."

The phone clicked twice in Bride's ear, indicating that he needed to put in more money. He fished around in his pockets for more change but before couldn't find any. The line went dead before he had a chance to say goodbye.

Bride stepped out of the phone booth and wandered down the street, trying to make sense out of yet another obscure piece of the puzzle. He had so much information in his head. Most of it, he decided he was probably better off not knowing. He felt as though he were holding a ticking bomb and he would either diffuse it or make that one false move and snip the wrong wire. He forced his mind to return to the more pleasant subject of Catherine.

◆ ◆ ◆

Crowe's busy morning continued. His next stop was at the headquarters of MI-5, the counterintelligence unit responsible for Britain and Northern Ireland. It wasn't an encouraging sign to the reporter when his second stop of the day was also his last resort, but that was the sad state of affairs Crowe found himself in. If Hobday from Scotland Yard wasn't forthcoming with information, Crowe knew he had little chance if any of extracting it from the bunkers of MI-5. Still, he had to exhaust all avenues if he was going to be able to break the story because he knew that quoting a kidnapper in a ski mask who claimed he was from the IRA was not generally recognized as solid journalism.

He stood nervously in the lobby as he waited to speak with Gregory Lawford, a former high school classmate of his who had worked his way up the ranks in the secretive organization. Lawford seemed to remember Crowe as one of the few boys in school who didn't ridicule him mercilessly about his crewcut and short trousers. As repayment, Lawford would occasionally provide Crowe with information that no other reporter could obtain through ordinary channels.

Crowe couldn't see the cameras and recording devices watching him as he waited, but he knew they were there and it made him uncomfortable. In a subconscious attempt to look better for whomever was watching him, Crowe smoothed back his hair that hadn't been combed as he'd rushed out of his flat early that morning.

Lawford burst through the security door into the lobby, looking very much the stiff intelligence officer in his navy suit, black-rimmed glasses, and slicked-back hair.

"Good morning, Colin. This way."

Lawford ushered Crowe into a spartan conference room with stark white walls, a table, and two chairs. For the first time since he'd set foot in MI-5 headquarters, Crowe sensed that he wasn't being monitored. "Now then," said Lawford. "Why are you here?"

From his past dealings with Lawford, Crowe had learned to get directly to the point. If Lawford could help him, he would. If not, the meeting was over without any chitchat or nostalgic visits back to their school days. Crowe pushed the envelope slightly as he phrased the question, pretending to know more than he really did.

"I've learned from two sources that the recent bombs attributed to the IRA are actually the work of someone else. Do you know who's really behind them?"

Lawford clamped his lips together as if to keep top secret information from suddenly leaping out of his mouth involuntarily. He pulled off his glasses and stared squarely into Crowe's eyes to see if he'd blink, the standard MI-5 litmus test for discerning how much someone really knows. Crowe was ready for Lawford's silent interrogation and he didn't back off. His heart pounded with excitement as he could sense that Lawford was on the brink of telling him what he wanted to know, but still he didn't blink.

Lawford put his glasses back on and sat back in his chair. He exhaled through his nose and drummed his fingers on the table. Crowe wanted desperately to coax him on to open up, but knew the decision was Lawford's alone to make and anything Crowe might say would break the spell. Lawford opened his mouth, ready to verify the story, then suddenly shook his head.

"Classified. Can't help you."

The fact that Lawford had hesitated for so long before answering wasn't like him, Crowe's first solid clue that he was well traveled down the right track. And if there wasn't a file on the subject at MI-5, Lawford wouldn't have told him "classified", he would have simply told him "no". He decided to press his luck a little harder.

"Look, I already have enough for a story, I just want to get the facts right. I want to let people know that the authorities are on top of this. I don't want to give *all* the credit to Scotland Yard."

Lawford pulled off his glasses once again and chewed on the end of the frames. One of the two things he despised most in the world was people thinking MI-5 wasn't doing its job. The only thing he hated worse than that was people thinking Scotland Yard was doing it better. Crowe's bluff worked.

"You won't quote me?" asked Lawford. Those were the magic words that every reporter wanted to hear. Crowe whisked out his notepad and clicked open his pen. "The fact of the matter is," began Lawford, "is that I honestly don't know. We have launched an investigation but it's based solely on suspicion, nothing on fact as yet."

"Suspicion over what?" ventured Crowe.

"Motive. Firstly, why would the IRA want to kill the leaders of the Conservative Party? Doesn't add up. It's the Labourites they should be going after. After all, it's the ruling party that's mucking up things in Ulster, not the Tories. Secondly, since when did the IRA start targeting the Royal Family? Despite their tactics, the leaders of the IRA are public relations minded and I can't think of a faster way to turn absolutely everyone against you than to knock off one of the Royals."

Crowe nodded as he scribbled. "So if not the IRA, then who's behind it?"

"Can't say."

"Is that 'you can't say', or 'you don't know'?"

"Both. Just ask yourself this question, Colin. Who has the most to gain? Think about that."

Lawford stood up and opened the door to the conference room, indicating that the meeting was adjourned. He hadn't told Crowe everything he'd wanted to know, but he'd provided confirmation enough to break the story.

As Crowe drove home to his flat, he asked himself the very question that Lawford had posed. Who *did* stand to gain the most? The answer he kept getting was unthinkable but at the same time unavoidable. Prince George himself was clearly the major beneficiary. The bombings had initially provided him with an opening into the Conservative party, then a platform for garnering votes, and finally a chance to appear to be the bravest knight in all of England.

Crowe knew an allegation like that would be hard if not impossible to prove, but in two hours when he would file his report on *The World at One*, he'd at least get the wrecking ball swinging in George's direction.

◆ ◆ ◆

Inspector Hobday perspired heavily as he put ten pence into the pay booth and dialed a number he knew by heart. He looked anxiously around him through the glass panes of the phone booth as his forehead wrinkled from his troubled mind. The party he was calling finally picked up. Hobday didn't even have to identify himself.

"You may have a problem," he said with a deep worry in his voice. "Colin Crowe came 'round this morning asking questions. He knows about the bombings. I'm not certain how he knows or how much he knows, but he knows. And he was just over at MI-5 pokin' about."

There was a long pause on the other end. Hobday wiped away the beads of sweat forming under his nose. "Yes, I think that's the best way to handle it."

The line went dead. Hobday hung up the handset and cleaned off his fingerprints with his handkerchief, then wiped his sweaty forehead and exited the phone booth.

Chapter Thirty

Bride took a cab from Charterhouse Square over to Bloomsbury, trying to put Lawrie's information about the blood into some meaningful context. What can you learn from blood samples? You can tell if someone has a disease they don't want revealed. Probably not enough to kill someone over. You can tell who's related to whom, who is the parent of whom.

Bride started to weave a new scenario. What if George fathered a child out of wedlock but nobody knew about it? The illegitimate child was hidden away, cared for by some nanny somewhere. But the child becomes ill and is brought to Nolan for healing. He can't do anything and the child dies. Nolan performs the autopsy and makes a note of the little lad's blood type. The child is buried in St. Bartholomew's and Catherine goes to visit the grave on occasion because she has a good heart and thinks someone needs to remember the child even in death.

Everything's fine for a few years until suddenly Nolan extracts a blood sample from George's Royal arm and compares it to the deceased child. They match. Nolan confirms that George is the father of the child. Not a terrible sin in most people's view, but in the eyes of the Anglican bishops, not such a good thing for the Defender of the Faith and future King to have on his resume. Nolan threatens to blackmail George, and George has him killed.

What about George's wife? Where did she fit into this? Either she knew about the whole mess or he was simply sick of her and knew divorce wasn't an option. The proverbial two birds with one stone, or in this case, two problems with one avalanche.

Bride went back over the incredible tale he'd just concocted in his mind and tried to poke holes in his own theory. He couldn't. It was an even wilder and more elaborate version of the hypothetical scenario he'd created with Donald Lawrie weeks before, but this time it made even more sense.

As he paid the taxi driver and stepped onto the sidewalk on Great Russell Street, Bride shook his head in disbelief over his own runaway imagination. It was like a bad dream and it was getting worse. A nice vacation had slowly turned into some Shakespearean tragedy.

His nose guided him into a nearby pub called the Museum Tavern where he would kill the last hour before his meeting with Catherine over a ploughman's lunch and a cold glass of cider. He sat in a booth by the window and ate, staring outside as if the answers to a cauldron of questions swirling in his head would be written in the gray skies above the British Museum.

He was physically exhausted but his brain was still flashing with sound and motion like the midway of a carnival. He was not at a cross-roads in his life but rather a corniche, winding along a steep alpine cliff where one wrong turn would send him plunging over the side. He and Colin Crowe had enough pieces of a sordid puzzle that they could bring down the Crown Prince of Great Britain.

It would unfold like any other story that had been dragged through the modern media mill. First there would be scandal, and then there would be denial, then more investigation, more scandal and more denial as the media and the authorities pecked away at the truth. And in the middle of the firestorm would be a mild mannered college professor who didn't even like to be quoted in the student newspaper. Was he ready for that? Bride couldn't imagine how *anyone* could be ready for that.

He'd always felt sorry for people, regardless of their misdeeds, who were swept up into the tornado of tabloid journalism, swirled around until the twister ran out of energy and eventually deposited along the wayside. His own brush with the British tabs had been emotionally wrenching and they never fully extended their claws into him.

Then Bride stopped to consider his options. What if he didn't say anything and let George continue his ways? George was either going to be a powerful leader who would indeed restore lustre to Great Britain, or he would become a despot who would bring tyrannical fear back to another European nation. Imagine how much suffering would have been avoided had somebody risen up to challenge Hitler or Stalin or Mussolini before they seized absolute power. Slay the kit before it becomes a mauling tiger.

On the other hand, supposedly wise men saw fit to crucify Christ before his full bloom.

Bride felt like Atlas with the weight of the world on his shoulders. He wasn't far off. He tried to organize the clues in his head into some kind of framework. A Princess makes secret visits to a child's grave. The sexton who most likely buried the child is an insane recluse. The husband of the Princess is doing research involving the blood of the Royal Family when he's killed under mysterious circumstances.

The muddled landscape seemed to be coming into focus but Bride still couldn't form a clear picture. He tried to make a case to his rational mind that all of these various events could in fact be completely unrelated, but his gut instinct quickly overruled. He knew there was some connection, and deep inside he desperately wanted to uncover it. But his rational mind was still begging him to walk away, to just get back on that airplane the next day and leave it all behind.

Bride closed his eyes and pressed his fingers hard against his temples, hoping to quell the maelstrom swirling through his mind.

As if by miracle, the turbulence that churned inside him began to calm. There was a sudden peacefulness that began to pour through him, bathed in a soft light that begged to show him the way down the dark road. The vast ocean of recent events was being distilled into something that started to make sense.

Bride recalled Crowe's words as they had sat together in the church. *"Was this worth getting killed over?"* Bride wondered how many things in this world *were* worth getting killed over. He thought about Trevor McFarlane, who stood ever ready to trade his life for the Princess he served. Was it worth it? Probably. He thought about his adoptive father who had gone to foreign soil and risked his life to fight fascism, and Barrie Mawhinney who had made the ultimate sacrifice on a stormy beach in Normandy. Was it worth it? Absolutely.

The name of Bostonian Paul Revere popped into his head, a man who had risked his life to battle the heavy imperial hand of King George III. Was it worth it? No question. History was repeating itself and Bride knew he couldn't stand in the way of it coming full circle.

But was it worth it? There would be only one way to find out. After his meeting with Catherine, he would cancel his flight home and see his journey through to its duration.

Having made a decision he felt he could live with, Bride opened his eyes and tipped his head back to finish off the last of his cider. It was only then, through the concave reflection of his glass that he noticed the dark sedan parked across the street. The driver was clearly watching everyone who went in and out of the tavern. Bride was seized with adrenaline. He didn't know who it was, but he was certain he knew what the mystery man was doing there.

As casually as his rubbery legs would let him, Bride made his way over to the bar where the publican was wiping off the taps.

"Excuse me, sir, but is there a back door here?"

"What's wrong with the front one, mate?"

Bride's answer was quick. "My boss is headed this way and I'm supposed to be home sick today." His lying was getting more accomplished all the time. The bartender winked and nodded his head.

"Say no more, say no more!" he whispered as he motioned Bride around to the inside of the bar. "We usually reserve this for men with angry wives, but we'll make an exception here." The bartender reached down to the floor and pulled on a brass ring embedded in one of the floorboards. He gave it a yank and a trap door opened. A short stepladder led down into the basement.

"Thanks," said Bride with a furtive glance to the door to enhance his story. He stepped through the opening in the floor and scrambled down the ladder.

"Just watch your step, mate!" called the bartender after him as he vanished. Bride maneuvered through a maze of hoses that led from aluminum kegs to the taps above. He pushed open a narrow wooden door and found himself at the bottom of a stairwell in the rear of the pub. He wasted no time in sprinting up the steps two at a time and fleeing down the alleyway. He wouldn't stop running for five blocks, where he hid breathlessly in a narrow alley between two townhouses.

The driver of the black sedan outside of the Museum Tavern would not like what he saw when his patience wore out and he finally ventured inside ten minutes later, or more precisely, what he didn't see.

Bride had peered out of his hiding place enough times to ensure himself that he was no longer being followed. He wiped away the perspiration from his brow and checked his watch. *11:26.* He had four minutes to cover the final few blocks to the sycamores of Bedford Square and still be on time.

Weeks ago the Private Park sign had made Bride stop and ponder the moral and social ramifications of breaking the law. This time he completely ignored the sign as he scaled the iron fence and dropped to the other side.

He moved quickly to the gazebo where Catherine was already sitting. She rose anxiously to her feet and stepped toward him as he rushed to embrace her. She buried her face in his shoulder as they clutched each other, their rigid fingertips pushing firmly into each other's backs. They held on without a word being spoken, breathing more and more rapidly in synchronization as their pulses quickened. In a world that seemed to be spinning wildly out of control, finally they had something to hold onto.

Catherine pulled her head back and looked up at Bride, more vulnerable than he had ever seen her. Their eyes met and the passions that had been simmering ever since their first encounter in the park were ready to be unleashed. They moved closer, their faces inches away. Bride placed a comforting hand on Catherine's cheekbone and caressed it with his thumb, wiping away a single tear that had rolled halfway down her face. She closed her eyes and tilted her chin slightly higher. Bride leaned over and kissed her softly on her lips with more emotion than he had ever known.

Bride had always remembered his very first kiss. It was on a humid Boston night in the summer between the fifth and sixth grades and even though he had to stand on the bottom rail of a split-rail fence just to reach the mouth of a girl who was nine inches taller than he, that first kiss had always stood the test of time as the best one he could remember. Finally, forty-five years later, it had been surpassed, but only by perfection. A delicate touch of the lips just long enough to join two hearts, but not so long as to spoil the moment. Bride would be content if this was the last kiss he ever experienced.

Catherine finally pulled away and led Bride by the hand over to the bench in the gazebo. She gently stroked his hand as she searched for the right words.

"This is not what I most want to say to you, Malcolm, but there is no choice in the matter. You need to leave England at once. I want you to go back to Amherst and forget about everything you've seen and done here."

"I can't do that."

"You must! Forget about St. Bartholomew's, forget about George, and forget about me."

"Forget about you? That's impossible."

"Then the impossible is what you must do. I fear the consequences if you don't."

"What are you trying to tell me, Catherine?"

"I'm telling you that your life is in danger and if you don't get out now, you might not get the chance later."

"Why do you think I'm in danger?"

"Because you're too close."

"To what? To you?"

"To George."

"George?"

"George craves power, and he'll stop at nothing to get it. I don't want to see you trampled in his wake."

"Like Nolan? Like John?" he said pointedly. Bride's remark caught Catherine off guard. It wasn't really a question but rather a statement that indicated that Bride already knew a lot more than Catherine thought he did.

She pulled her hand away. "Why would you say that?" she asked coolly.

"Because I think we both know John's death was no accident."

"I still don't know what you mean."

"Yes you do. You know John didn't go to that brothel on his own. Someone took him there. And it wasn't the IRA that planted that bomb, either."

Catherine's lips quivered. She had been trying to deny the awful truth to herself but she couldn't fight it any longer. Still, she controlled her emotions without confirming to Bride that he was on the right track.

"I don't have all the parts of the equation yet, but here's what I think," continued Bride. "I'm guessing that John found out about George's little secret, and rather than risk exposure, George had him killed and made it look like the IRA was responsible. The same thing happened to Sir Nolan when he found out about the secret."

"And what secret is that?" probed Catherine.

"The child."

"The child?"

"The child you visit in St. Bartholomew's."

Catherine's Royal blood flushed into her cheeks, turning her face a deep crimson. "What makes you think there's a child buried there?"

"I just do."

"And who's child is it?"

"I don't know who the mother is, but I think we both know who the father would be."

Catherine's forehead wrinkled in puzzlement. They seemed to be reading the same book but weren't on the same page.

"Who?" she asked.

"George, of course."

"George?" she said with her confusion increasing.

"Let's drop the cat and mouse game, shall we? Here's what I know. George fathered a child out of wedlock some years ago and Nolan found out about it when he was gathering blood samples for Basil Jeffery." Catherine's look of shock told Bride he was on the right track and he pressed on.

"Soon thereafter, Sir Nolan disappears and George's secret is again safe. Then recently, John somehow stumbles onto it and we know what happened to him. You still visit the child's grave because, well, that's the kind of decent person you are."

"But you're also saying that makes me the kind of person who would keep silent about murder. An accessory, if you will."

"I can think of a half dozen reasons why you wouldn't say anything, but one reason stands above the rest. You're such a good person that you can't bring yourself to believe that others are capable of such evil. But now you have to face the facts. Am I right?"

"No, you are not right." The Princess crossed her arms and looked away. She looked up at the giant sycamore in front of her, pondering her next step. She turned back to Bride, her defenses dropping only slightly. After a long pause, she spoke again. "But you are close. Too close. Which is why you *must* leave England!"

"I'm not leaving England until I find out. I'm going to keep digging."

"You are digging your own grave, Malcolm! You don't understand what you're getting into! I beg you to stop!"

"If you want me to stop, then why don't *you* tell me the truth, Catherine? I need to know the *truth*."

Bride sat up straight on the bench and put his strong hands on Catherine's shoulders. He craned his neck forward until his eyes were only inches away from hers.

"Why did you really call me here? Just to say goodbye? Just to tell me to leave? No. You called me here because you *want* to tell me the truth, don't you? You want the truth about your brother to come out, but you can't do it alone because you know the consequences will be overwhelming, so you've turned to me for help. Isn't that right?"

Catherine hung her head. Bride was precisely right. She had held a secret deep in her heart from the time she was a small child and had managed to keep it hidden away for over fifty years. She had come to deny it to herself for so long that it no longer seemed like reality. Even with the death of her husband, she hadn't wavered. But things had changed rapidly in recent weeks and her reasons for keeping the secret no longer applied.

It was an enormous weight she had carried for half a century and at long last she wanted desperately for someone to take the millstone from around her neck, or at least share the burden. She knew it wasn't coincidence or serendipity that Professor Malcolm Bride had seen her in St. Bartholomew's that foggy night weeks ago. She believed and understood that it was divine providence, a merciful act of God.

The Almighty had sent this man to her in order to deliver her from her private purgatory. Yes, she wanted to tell him—desperately. Her entire life had been marked by fear and dread that the dark secret that hung over the House of Windsor would be revealed, but suddenly she felt relief as if she had been touched by the healing hands of God Himself. She nodded gently to Bride. She was ready to talk.

"March 16, 1945. What does that day mean to you?" began Catherine.

"That's my birthday. How'd you know that?"

"Because it also happens to be the exact date of birth of Prince George." Bride cocked his head in puzzlement. Why would she point out a coincidence like that at a time like this?

"I'm confused," he said. "What do you mean?"

"March 16, 1945, is the day it all began, for both of us, actually." Catherine stared into empty space with glassy eyes as she reconstructed the events of the last five decades. "The war in Europe was raging. The people of England were still clinging to life in the rubble left by months of bombing by the German Luftwaffe. Their morale had been stretched to its limits and nobody knew if they could withstand much more.

"During all of this death and destruction, there was one beacon of hope. One event to take people's minds off their terrible troubles. Queen Alexandra gave birth to a son. It was a difficult labor that lasted well into the night, but she made it through and gave her country an heir. His name was George."

Catherine swallowed hard, struggling to continue the story. She began to speak as if she were far removed from the scene, like someone describing strangers encountered in a dream.

"The next morning while George was sleeping, a very young Princess waited for the baby's wet nurse to leave the bedroom, then crept in to look at her new brother. She knew she wasn't supposed to be in his nursery, but she couldn't help herself. The baby slept so peacefully, unaware that someday he would sit on the throne of Britain.

"The little girl bent over his bassinet and picked him up like one of her dolls, rocking him back and forth, but he started to cry. She heard footsteps coming down the hallway and she put the baby back in his bed, then ran and hid behind the heavy curtains, frightened that she was going to be discovered. The wet nurse entered the room to check on the baby. She picked him up to comfort him, but then—"

Catherine stopped in midsentence, unable to continue. She was breathing harder, on the brink of mild hysteria as the events of over fifty years ago came rushing back into her memory. Bride clutched her hands and whispered with reassurance, "It's alright. I'm here."

Catherine nodded and fought hard to continue. "The nurse lost her grip. The baby fell to the floor. It was an accident. A horrible accident. She screamed as she scooped him up and held him to her chest, but the baby wasn't crying. Something was wrong, terribly wrong.

"She put him back in his bassinet and immediately ran out of the nursery. Moments later she returned with a man. He examined the baby and then ordered the wet nurse out of the room. He stood over the child, just shaking his head. He suddenly wrapped the child in a blanket and dashed out of the room through the door to the back staircase. That afternoon Queen Alexandra was feeling well enough to see her son and he was brought to her room, but it wasn't the same baby that had been in the bassinet. It wasn't the same baby."

Catherine shook her head in anguish. She closed her eyes and took several deep breaths as if she was coming out of a hypnotic trance. She looked exhausted as she turned to Bride with a more lucid gaze, her mind having returned from a morning of terror in 1945 to the relative safety of the present moment.

Bride's brain was racing so wildly he couldn't keep up. A thousand new questions erupted in his mind. "Who was the man who came into the nursery?"

"Wiggs. Elliott Wiggs."

"Are you telling me that the Crown Prince of England died and Wiggs replaced him with another child?"

Catherine nodded her head as tears from the memory of unspeakable sins welled up in her eyes.

"And the dead Prince is buried in St. Bartholomew's?"

Again she nodded, closing her eyes as she stoically raised her chin, bracing herself for more questions. It was more than catharsis, more than purgation. It was an exorcism of ancient demons that had haunted Catherine's soul. She would need to summon every ounce of her embattled inner forces to endure it.

"And where did Wiggs find another child?"

Catherine paused a long time before answering.

"There was a lady-in-waiting at the palace who had gotten pregnant out of wedlock. Her father was a minister and she feared his wrath, so she was hidden away at St. James's Palace to wait out the delivery. With the air raids going on over London, St. James's was deserted except for a few servants, so nobody suspected a thing. She gave birth to twin boys. The day was March 16, 1945."

Bride's heart nearly stopped. Realization spread across his face. March 16, 1945. His birthday.

"And the lady-in-waiting's name, was Bridget Allison. My God," exhaled Bride, the oath barely audible. Catherine nodded.

The blurry kaleidoscope inside his mind had finally been twisted far enough to bring brilliant color into sharp focus. The history of a half century ago suddenly meshed with the events of recent weeks like the planets of the solar system rotating into alignment. Reasonable deduction would fill in the blanks as Bride rapidly put the outline together in his head.

The true Crown Prince of England died before he was a day old. Fearing a crushing blow to the nation's morale in the middle of war, Wiggs arranged a replacement. Not even Queen Alexandra herself was told of the deception. Paddy Butterfill dug the child's anonymous grave in St. Bartholomew's and went insane harboring the secret.

Bridget Allison gave up one of her babies and when the other one was old enough to travel, she was shipped off to the United States. She died en route and Alfred and Maria Martelli took her infant into their home. They raised him as their own son, John Martelli, who would one day call himself Malcolm Bride.

"You wanted the truth?" said Catherine, "There it is. Now take it with you and leave England."

Bride shook his dazed head. He was in shock. He remembered how he had felt the day he found out the Martellis were not his real parents, and now it seemed to pale in comparison to this mind numbing revelation.

"When did you realize that the other brother was me?"

"When I saw you in George's riding gear at Sandringham, I noticed the resemblance and began to have suspicions. I couldn't believe it, but nor could I dismiss it, so I had Trevor check into your immigration records to find out your date of birth. That's when I knew."

"But you weren't going to tell me."

"No. I wasn't. But since you know, consider yourself a lucky man. You came here seeking your past and now you've uncovered it, for better or worse. Go home and live in peace."

Bride sat silently for over a minute, still trying to fathom everything he'd just heard. "Who was my real father?" he asked her.

"I don't know. I doubt he even knew he'd gotten Bridget pregnant."

"When did George find out about all of this?"

"I'm not entirely certain. Somewhere around the time he was fifteen he began to wonder out loud why he didn't resemble either of his parents or his siblings. Suddenly his questions stopped, and coincidentally George's relationships with the rest of the family members took on a definite chill. He changed, virtually overnight, and I can only assume that Wiggs pulled him aside and told him the same story I've just told you."

"And does he know that *you* know?"

"Deep down I think he suspects, but the subject has never been broached."

"And so the secret remained safe," said Bride. "That is, until Sir Nolan stumbled onto it."

"Yes."

"It *was* the blood sample, wasn't it?"

"Yes."

"Here I've been thinking all along that George feared the blood samples would prove that he was related to a child he'd fathered, but actually he was afraid they'd show to whom he *wasn't* related—his own mother! Not one drop of nobility in George's entire cold-blooded body, and that knowledge cost Nolan his life."

"That was never proven."

"But you know in your heart that George had him killed. Just like he had John killed."

"No, I don't."

"Why are you denying it to yourself? Your brother is a murderer!"

"You don't understand!"

"Well then explain it to me! Why are you keeping his secrets for him?"

Catherine gently shook her head, as if she would like to hear a reasonable explanation herself. "When you're a young girl and you witness something as horrid as that, all you can do is hide under your bed at night and pray that it goes away like the thunder of a summer storm. But it never does go away, and as you get older, you begin inventing better reasons why you should keep it inside you.

"I suppose my biggest fear was that if George were no longer the true heir to the Crown, then John was next in line. I loved my young brother very much, but I don't think I need to elaborate on the dire consequences of John ascending to the throne. The good of the Commonwealth has to come first. I don't think this country could survive a blow that severe."

Bride scoffed. "You're not thinking about the country, Catherine! You're thinking about yourself! You don't think the *monarchy* can survive it, and you're scared about what's going to happen to *you*, isn't that it?"

"Stop it! Just stop it! I will not be talked to that way!"

Bride backed down. "I'm sorry. But it's the truth."

"Listen to me, Malcolm! This is a deadly game you're playing and as much as I respect your abilities, I don't think it's a game you can win! George has his people watching you almost everywhere you go. You are in grave danger, even more so after this meeting, and every minute you stay in England the situation worsens! Now go!"

"See? You're proving my point! You know your brother is a dangerous man, and he has to be stopped. You *know* that! If he ascends to the throne, he'll have a firm grip on absolute power and then he *can't* be stopped!"

"But what if he *can* do all the things he says he can do? What if his vision for Britain is the right one?"

"Come on, Catherine, you sound like Neville Chamberlain talking about Hitler! I know you love your country and you want what's best for the people, but we both know that George isn't the answer. He's a murderer, Catherine! You have to stop him!"

"Don't you understand? I'm not capable of doing it!"

"Yes you are! In fact, you're the only one who is! There are people willing to *die* for you, Catherine."

"I don't know," she whispered, shaking her head. "I just don't know."

"We need to get going, Your Highness," called out Trevor. He appeared seemingly of nowhere. Catherine backed away from Bride. "He's right," she said to Bride as she checked her watch. "I'm speaking at a luncheon in Knightsbridge and it's bad form to be late."

"But when will I see you again?"

There was no reply as Catherine turned away and Trevor's burly arm escorted her out of a gate to her limousine. Trevor closed her car door, then shot an ugly glance back at Bride before circling around to the driver's side and climbing in.

Bride watched the Princess depart, the ache of separation already setting in. What a unique woman, he thought. She held the course of British history in her delicate palm, yet seemed more concerned that she didn't keep others waiting. There was nobody else like her on earth. Maybe that's why he loved her so much, thought Bride.

He sat down on the bench in the gazebo and closed his eyes, savoring the moment of their first and perhaps only kiss. He was still able to detect the fragile scent of her perfume clinging to the air of Bedford Square.

Bride suddenly snapped backwards. A sharp sting tore in his right shoulder blade. A millisecond later he heard the percussion of a single gunshot cracking from the east end of the park. He clutched his bleeding shoulder in disbelief, then instinctively dove to the ground.

Another gunshot ricocheted off the bench. Bride looked up from his prone position and saw the same man who had been watching him inside the Museum Tavern. The assassin pointed a gun at Bride, trying to get a better line of sight between the iron bars of the fence.

Bride scrambled to the back of the gazebo and kicked out a section of the wooden latticework, then crawled on his belly through the opening. Hunched over, he wound his way through a protective gathering of sycamores, then charged through the gate and staggered across the street, grabbing the searing pain in his shoulder.

A pair of washerwomen poked their heads out from a townhouse window overlooking the park to investigate the commotion down below, fully expecting to see nothing more than a delivery truck backfiring. When they saw the man in the suit running with a revolver in his hand, their shrieking disappearance back into the townhouse told the gunman that a phone call to the police was only seconds away. He reversed his course and disappeared into the backstreets of Bloomsbury.

Bride simply ran. He didn't know where he was going, but he was determined to get there as fast as he could.

He turned down an alleyway and ran the next hundred yards, constantly turning around to see if anyone was still chasing him. He finally slowed to an awkward walk as the rush of adrenaline fueling him gave in to the burning pain of his gunshot wound.

He staggered into the backyard of a well kept townhouse and intended to knock on the door for assistance, but suddenly thought better of it. He was so far in over his head now in this whirlpool of trouble, he couldn't see the point of dragging anybody else in to drown with him. Instead, he yanked a freshly washed bedsheet off the clothesline and left a five pound note sticking out from underneath a nearby flowerpot.

Bride returned to the alley and pulled off his jacket and dress shirt, now soaked with blood. He could see in the reflection of a window on a parked car that the bullet had exited the top of his shoulder without doing any major damage. He wrapped the sheet around his shoulder blade and pulled tightly on both ends to stop the bleeding, then put his jacket back on and kept running.

At the end of the alley was a bicycle, propped up against the side of a building and chained to an aluminum downspout. Bride was about to add stealing to his growing list of recent crimes as he yanked on the rain gutter and split it apart at the seams. The chain slid free and within seconds Bride was pedaling away, one hand on the handlebars, the other clutching the bloody sheet under his jacket.

Chapter Thirty-One

J t was 12:48 in the afternoon when Crowe finally finished pounding out his story on the manual typewriter in his flat. He'd only given his producers on *The World at One* the broad strokes about his story but guaranteed them it was worthy of being their lead item. Given his track record they had no reason to doubt him.

Crowe's report wasn't as detailed as he would have ordinarily wanted, but he didn't think he could wait any longer to break it. For one, he couldn't be certain that rival reporters hadn't already picked up the scent and might beat him to the punch. In the back of his mind he also knew that the longer he held the story, the more danger he was inviting.

The words he had typed out on the portable in front of him would be more than just another thorn in the side of Prince George. The story was infinitely more powerful than the news about the uranium. This was essentially an accusation of murder. Crowe didn't have enough information to convict, but there was certainly enough for an indictment. He knew that once the flesh was opened, the rest of the media would descend like jackals and the bloody truth would come out one sensational story at a time. If George was going to stop the verbal explosion, he would have to snuff out the fuse that was Colin Crowe.

It was now eleven minutes before his one o'clock deadline. Crowe snatched the story out of the typewriter carriage and headed for his front door.

"Oh my God!" yelled Crowe as he opened the door. There stood Bride on the front porch, bloody and exhausted, unable to take another step. "What happened?" said Crowe as he rushed out to assist him. He saw the stolen bicycle toppled over on the sidewalk and assumed Bride had been in some kind of traffic accident.

Bride swallowed hard, laboring to draw three deep breaths. "There's something I have to tell you." He fell forward and collapsed into Crowe's arms.

"Not now! We have to get you to a hospital! Come on."

Crowe wrapped Bride's arm around his neck, uncaring that blood was getting all over his herringbone sportscoat. Crowe checked his watch. Ten minutes to one o'clock. He spirited the wounded American down the sidewalk and into his black taxi cab that had been converted into a mobile BBC radio unit.

Bride laid down in the backseat amongst the radio equipment, his mind fading in and out of blackness. Crowe stomped on the gas and raced through the streets of St. Marylebone like it was the Grand Prix of Monaco. Six minutes later, he squealed to an abrupt stop in front of the clinic at Bedford College in Regent's Park. He blasted the car horn several times to summon help, then jumped from the car to help Bride out of the back seat.

"I have to tell you something," murmured Bride as Crowe stood him up. A nurse came running out of the clinic to assist him.

"It can wait," said Crowe.

"No! It can't!" bellowed Bride, wincing in pain.

Crowe turned his attention to the nurse as she took Bride's other arm and helped him down the walkway. "I'm Colin Crowe, BBC Radio 4, and this is a friend of mine."

"What happened to him?" asked the nurse, trying to get a look at Bride's bloody shoulder.

"I don't know exactly. I think he fell off a bicycle. Anyway, he's lost a lot of blood."

"I didn't fall off a bicycle!" slurred Bride.

"Don't try to talk, mate. You're delirious."

"No, please listen to me!" he cried out with all the strength he had left.

Another nurse rushed up to help as they carried Bride through the door of the clinic, relieving Crowe. He checked his watch as the nurses laid Bride down on a bed and went to work on his wound. Three minutes before airtime.

"Now listen to me, Malcolm. I have to step outside and deliver my report. I'll be back in five minutes and we can talk then. In the meantime, you let these people take care of you."

Crowe rushed back outside and walked briskly over to his car. He climbed into the back seat and maneuvered into position behind his microphone. His hand trembled as he glanced one final time over the typewritten story he held in his hand. He took three deep breaths to steady himself, then reached down to flip the switch to the power generators for the mobile transmitter.

The last thing Colin Crowe would see on this earth was a flash of bright light. The massive explosion would shatter windows in the clinic and rock the foundations of every townhouse around Regent's Park. Cowardly dynamite had won again.

Shrapnel from the radio equipment was still raining down as Bride pulled away from the two nurses and ran to the window of the clinic. He saw the burning mass of twisted metal outside.

"Crowe!" screamed Bride as he staggered toward the doorway. "Crowe!" he cried louder as he tried to go outside, but his sudden burst of adrenaline had been used up. He collapsed on the sidewalk as the smoke that signalled Crowe's assassination twisted higher into the London sky. The ashes of Crowe's story floated benignly away. Bride succumbed to unconsciousness.

Bride never heard the sirens from the police units and fire engines that responded to the explosion. He didn't remember the nurses hoisting him back into the hospital bed and pumping six pints of whole blood into him. He had no recollection of the anesthetic being applied to his wounds, or the stitches that now closed the bullet hole in his shoulder blade. For the moment, he didn't even remember the tragedy befalling his friend Crowe.

When he finally awakened four hours later on the stark white bedsheet in the clinic's recovery room, he couldn't decide which ached more, his shoulder or his pounding head.

He scanned the room trying to find someone who could tell him anything about his current situation, beginning with basic information such as where in the world was he? Everyone around him appeared too busy to ask. He swung his bare feet onto the floor and tested his balance with a few small steps. He was actually moving fairly well for someone who had taunted death earlier that afternoon.

Still groggy, he steadied himself and started to head to the nurses' station at the end of the corridor, but suddenly stopped in his tracks. There, inquiring about something to the duty nurse, was a man Bride vaguely recognized. He couldn't immediately place where he knew the man but something instinctively told him the stranger was dangerous.

The man nodded politely to the duty nurse and started to walk toward the recovery room. Bride ducked behind a partitioning curtain and silently observed the mysterious man walking from bed to bed, inspecting the sleeping patients. It suddenly rushed into Bride's head where he'd seen this man before. It was at Kensington Palace. Bride didn't know his name was Nick Crumrie, but he knew the man was an assistant to Prince George. It was all he needed to know to realize he had to flee the clinic immediately.

Crumrie stepped behind another curtain and Bride could see the bottom of his legs as he approached the head of the next bed. Bride moved swiftly but silently out of the recovery room, his escape aided by the quiet of his bare feet. He walked down the corridor as inconspicuously as possible for a man with no shoes and a huge bandage covering his shoulder.

"Sir? Excuse me, sir?" called out the duty nurse.

Bride ignored her completely as he headed directly out the exit.

"Sir!" yelled the nurse as she scrambled from behind the counter and ran after the escaping patient.

Bride was already out of the doors. He yanked up a wooden stake from a small sapling in the front yard of the clinic and ran it through the curved handles on the side-by-side doors, buying him extra time as the nurse gave chase.

Only then did Bride look across the street and see the wooden police barriers encircling the charred remains of Crowe's taxi. Several bobbies stood guard as a man in a white shirt and thin black tie snapped pictures from several different angles. Another man was taking measurements of some sort and jotting down notes.

Bride froze as the horrible experience of several hours before came rushing back to him. His memory of the day's events returned to him in reverse chronology like someone sandblasting away layer after layer of old paint from a clapboard house. The fire that engulfed Crowe's taxi, the enormous explosion that rocked the clinic, Crowe tossing him in the back of the car, the bloody ride home on the bicycle, the shot that rang out in Bedford Square, and at the bottom of the chain of events, the incredible story of deception told to him by Princess Catherine.

The nurse rattled the door behind him and yelled through the glass. "Sir, open this door!"

Bride snapped back into reality. He shook his head to clear away the awful memories, then ran across the lawn of the clinic and vanished around the corner.

Crumrie heard the nurse's yells as he stood in the far end of the recovery room. He sprinted back down the corridor and saw the nurse jerking on the barricaded door to no avail. "What's going on here?" said Crumrie.

"One of our patients...he ran off!"

Crumrie knew immediately that the patient she was talking about was the same one he'd come to see. With the expertise of a trained martial artist, he raised his leg and thrust it sideways like a piston, snapping the wooden stake on the other side and springing open the doors.

He rushed outside and scanned the area for Bride but there were no signs of him. He glanced over at the bobbies across the street and quickly turned his head, briskly but casually disappearing to his car.

Bride ran awkwardly down the alleyway behind Crowe's flat, his shoulder aching deep under several layers of bandages. He was so intent on watching everything around him that he didn't see the sliver of glass directly in his path. He sliced open a gash on the bottom of his bare foot and someone else's donated blood dripped out onto the pavement. He took one look and kept running. There was no time for first aid now.

Bride entered the flat by way of the tunnel in the greenhouse and popped through the heating vent into the darkened living room.

He wasn't sure why, but he felt as though he didn't have much time to waste and he quickly went about the business of grabbing all of the items on the mental checklist he'd assembled in his head on the way over.

He made his way quickly into his bedroom and retrieved his passport and money from underneath the mattress. If he was going to get out of England, he couldn't do it without them.

He grabbed a pair of socks out of his suitcase then ran to his closet and grabbed another pair of shoes, now happier than ever that he'd taken the time to retrieve them from the Dunbarton. As he sat on the edge of the bed and put on his socks, the blood from the cut on his toe began seeping through. Putting on his shoes was more of a struggle with his bandaged shoulder. He managed to get the first one onto his good foot and was reaching for the other shoe when he heard the front door of the flat rattle.

Alarmed, Bride picked up the shoe and stepped quietly down the hallway to the living room. The door rattled again, this time more vigorously. He heard something enter the lock, not a key, but a tool of some kind. After a few seconds, the lock had been successfully picked and Crumrie crept inside.

Bride ducked for cover, crouching behind one of Crowe's filing cabinets as Crumrie moved cautiously through the dusky room.

Crumrie pulled a gun from his waistband and held it tightly in his outstretched hand. He suddenly noticed the heating grate standing open from the tunnel and upon closer inspection, saw the trail of blood droplets that led down the hallway. He grinned eerily and sidestepped his way to the bedroom, flashing his gun around each corner.

Bride tried to seize the opportunity to escape. He yanked on his other shoe and took one step towards the front door. He froze in his tracks as the floorboard underneath his foot squeaked loudly. The sound of Crumrie rummaging around could still be heard in the back bedroom.

There were several more things Bride needed to retrieve before he left and he knew he could find them in Crowe's desk. He tiptoed gingerly toward the desk and slowly pulled open the top drawer. He took out an envelope, a book of stamps, and a small tape recorder not much bigger than a pack of cigarettes.

Crumrie had followed the trail of spattered blood into the closet, then back to the edge of the bed. By this time he realized the bloodstains had changed pattern and he began to retrace the dabs of blood that had oozed through Bride's sock.

Bride shoved the items from Crowe's desk into his pocket and started for the door, but could suddenly hear Crumrie's footsteps steadily approaching down the hallway. He was trapped. He could make a quick charge for the front door, but given his list of handicapping ailments, he didn't think he could outrun Crumrie. Even with a sizable head start, he knew how quickly a bullet could catch up. He frantically searched for a place to hide.

Crumrie's senses were fully heightened as he moved back into the living room. He knew he wasn't alone as he followed the incriminating trail of bloodstains, his eyes darting back and forth from the floor to the shadowy room around him. The trail of blood ended at the filing cabinet where Bride had been hiding moments before. Crumrie held the gun with both hands and kicked the top of the cabinet, sending it crashing to the floor. Years of Crowe's carefully collected notes spilled out around him, but there was no sign of Bride.

"I know you're in here!" Crumrie called out into the darkness. "I can feel it!" The maniacal grin returned to his face as he stalked around the living room. Crumrie could detect the faint odor of perspiration in the room and drew several deep breaths through his nose to hone in on the source of the smell like a bloodhound. He suddenly noticed the top drawer on the desk was standing open and it struck him that it had been closed when he had first entered from outside. He moved three steps closer to Crowe's desk, unaware that Bride was crouched underneath in the gap between the legs where the chair slid in.

Two steps closer he came to Bride, just inches away now. All he had to do was look down and the hunt would be over. But Colin Crowe, always one to have the last word, would get a final say in this matter even from beyond the grave.

At that very moment, the lamp behind Crumrie clicked on as the timer Crowe used to fool his rivals had done so once again. Crumrie spun around and reactively pumped three bullets in the general direction of the lamp, shattering it on the third shot.

Bride summoned all of his strength and courage and shoved the desk chair forward as hard as he possibly could, ramming Crumrie in the back of the knees. Crumrie crashed face forward onto the floor as Bride burst out of his cramped hiding place. The assassin scrambled to his feet and turned to fire his gun but Bride was waiting for him. He snatched Crowe's portable typewriter off the desk and slammed it across Crumrie's forehead, driving him to the ground with a bloody gash splitting open over his eyebrow. Crowe had firmly believed the old adage that the pen was mightier than the sword, and in a variation on the theme, he was proven correct once again.

Bride didn't wait around to see how much damage he'd inflicted on Crumrie. He stumbled toward the door and was almost outside when he spotted the keys to Crowe's Triumph hanging on a peg next to the hat rack. Bride grabbed the key ring and fled outside, not bothering to turn around to see Crumrie slowly pulling himself to his feet.

Bride stood in the middle of the street and scanned the curbsides for Crowe's parked car but couldn't immediately pick it out in the approaching darkness. He spun around in terror as the front door to Crowe's flat banged open and Crumrie stood under the transom, wiping blood from his eyes and wavering like a heavyweight boxer who had just lumbered to his feet after narrowly avoiding a knockout.

Bride was truly at a crossroads. He had to go one way or the other to find Crowe's car to escape and he had to get it right on the first try because Crumrie was rapidly regaining his full faculties.

He wasn't going to rely on deduction to help him figure out where the car was, nor would he take a chance on pure luck. Bride had led a good life, marked by decency, integrity, and kindness. If everyone lived their lives like Malcolm Bride, there would be no crime, no prejudice, no hatred, no desperate grabs at power, no wars. Up to this point he'd never asked for anything in return for his inherent goodness, but now he was calling in a marker.

"God help me," prayed Bride aloud. Something told him to go to the right. He couldn't explain it, and there certainly wasn't time to question it as Crumrie staggered down the walkway. He simply trusted his feelings, turning to the right and running as fast as his slashed foot and aching shoulder would take him.

He clutched the belongings in his bulging pockets to keep them from falling out as he ran down the row of parked cars, occasionally turning back to see Crumrie gaining on him.

Bride was quickly approaching the end of the street and still no sign of the Triumph. Could his instincts have been wrong? Did he speak to God but the Devil answered? His faith in the Almighty was in serious jeopardy as he turned the corner, only to have it fully restored. In the last space on the street sat Crowe's Triumph, a four-wheeled chariot waiting to deliver him from evil.

Bride found new energy to sprint to the car as Crumrie was closing the gap. He fumbled through the keys and finally found the one with the word "Triumph" engraved into the black plastic covering on the end. He shoved it into the door lock but it stuck halfway in. Upside down. He jerked it back out, turning to see Crumrie closing to within fifty yards. He tried again and the key slid in. He yanked open the door and scrambled inside as Crumrie continued to stagger after him.

In his panic, Bride had made a crucial mistake. The American suddenly realized he had jumped into the left-hand side of the car. The passenger side in England. The steering wheel was on the other side of the Triumph's cramped cockpit.

Crumrie was within thirty yards now, wiping away a red river of blood from his eyes as he raised his gun to shoot.

Bride had been through hell that day but he wasn't ready for heaven. He lunged across the stickshift between the bucket seats and landed hard on the other side behind the steering wheel. He rammed the key into the ignition and pumped the gas as the Triumph's engine struggled to rise to the occasion.

Crumrie was ten yards away. He stopped and held his gun with both hands, taking dead aim at Bride's head through the windshield. He fired.

The windshield shattered just as the Triumph lurched forward and smashed into the car in front. Crumrie fired again as Bride jerked the shifter into reverse, slamming into the car behind him. Shards of glass and bullets were flying. Bride ducked his head, shoved the shifter forward and stomped on the gas pedal as he popped the clutch. The tires spun wildly, sending up a rooster tail of black smoke, then suddenly grabbed the pavement and launched the Triumph forward like a Brahma bull charging out of a rodeo pen. Crumrie dove out of the way, narrowly avoiding serious injury as the Triumph roared past him.

Bride sat up and battled to regain control of the runaway vehicle, sideswiping a car on the other side of the street. He somehow managed to keep it aimed forward down the street.

Crumrie rose to his knees and fired five more shots into the back of the car as it careened away, but couldn't stop it from vanishing around the corner. His superiors would not like his report.

Chapter Thirty-Two

Bride's first inclination was to drive as far away as a tank of gas would take him, but he slowly realized that Crumrie's wide dragnet would quickly be thrown out to look for him, and a Triumph with no windshield and a raft of bullet holes wouldn't be that hard for one of his minions to spot. He had to find a safe haven as quickly as possible, and he immediately knew where he would go. If he were going to put an end to Prince George's murderous rise to power, then he would start at the beginning.

The Triumph rolled to a stop on the narrow service road next to the cemetery at St. Bartholomew's, the gravel crackling underneath the tires just as it had the night Princess Catherine had arrived. Bride turned off the headlights that bounced off the blanket of thick fog. He climbed out of the car and peered into the mist, scanning the headstones to make sure nobody was watching. He quickly determined that he was alone with the spirits.

Bride stepped through the iron gate and walked through the long grass between the graves. He had never been so glad to be alive. Reverently he approached the tiny unmarked plot under the yew in the corner of the cemetery. The bones below the surface held new meaning to him now.

They belonged to a child who had been destined for the throne of Britain, but whose brief life had taken a different track. He would never feel the weight of the Crown on his head or the ermine of the King's robes. He never even felt the touch of his own mother's hand. Only the moist peat of St. Bartholomew's remained to embrace him. There were so many reasons that necessitated bringing George to justice, but at that moment, Bride decided that if for no other reason, then he would do it to avenge the death of the innocent Prince buried beneath his feet.

He sat down in the moist grass and took Crowe's tape recorder out of his pocket. There was an hour long cassette in it, ample time for Bride to recount his incredible journey that began fifty-seven years ago. He cleared his throat, pressed the "record" button, and began.

"Hello, Donald," said Bride into the microphone. "This is your old friend Malcolm. By the time you receive this tape, there's a good chance I won't be around anymore. I'll have disappeared, probably without a trace. Hopefully that won't happen, but if it should, I want you to know why. Do you recall our conversations about Basil Jeffery and Sir Robert Nolan?"

With that preface, Bride proceeded to dictate everything he knew to that point about Prince George, Elliott Wiggs, and Nick Crumrie. He tried to be meticulous in detail as if he were writing the chapters of a history book. The story began with the death of the real Prince George during the war and ended with Bride's harrowing escape from Crumrie just an hour before. The tape was nearly full when Bride finally signed off.

"Everything I've told you in this tape is what I hope to tell the world, if I can stay alive long enough to do it. If I don't make it, then it's up to you. You have to be the one to spread the truth. Sorry to do that to you old friend, but you're the only person I know on this island who I can trust. Well, that is, you and Princess Catherine, but I don't hold much hope of seeing her again. I'll do my best to get you off the hook, but if I can't, then I'm leaving history in your hands. The world is depending on you to follow through. God be with you. Your friend, Malcolm Bride."

He clicked off the tape recorder and reflected on everything he'd said. All in all, he was pleased with his recapitulation of the bizarre events. He knew Donald Lawrie was one of the few people who would believe such a wild tale, and he had a good feeling that the Scot would accept the challenge of convincing the rest of the world if it came down to it. He put the tiny cassette tape into the envelope he'd taken from Crowe's desk and addressed it to his friend in St. Andrews, then covered the top right corner with more than enough stamps to make sure it would get there.

Bride left the cemetery on foot, leaving the Triumph parked on the gravel road. He flirted with the notion of leaving a taunting note on the dashboard for Crumrie, certain that he'd be the first one to arrive, but decided he had more important items on his agenda and he'd better get to them.

Bride walked several blocks to a quiet avenue and found a mailbox. He dropped the letter to Donald Lawrie inside, heaving a sigh of relief that George's secret was no longer his alone to keep.

He walked to the end of the street and blended into the shadows of a lamppost next to a stop sign at the intersection. He was too weak to walk where he was going, and didn't dare try the underground for fear of getting trapped. He needed room to maneuver in case something went wrong with his plan and so a taxi was his only choice. At the time he had been running from the tabloid reporters he had hated the invasion of his privacy, but now he was thankful for the experience for he had learned how to hide out in the middle of a city and this time it might save his life. He only wished that it was still microphones and cameras pointing at him instead of snub nosed revolvers.

He waited patiently as several available taxis came and went, waiting for the right one to approach. At this point, he trusted nobody. He was struck by the irony that here he was trying to save the world, yet he was suddenly on the fringes of misanthropy, trusting no one. His paranoia wasn't without foundation, however, because everyone who passed by was potentially an agent of Prince George. Bride would at least try to improve his chances by getting into the right cab.

Finally one pulled up that fit his criterion: a woman driver. Bride knew that a condescending misogynist like George would never trust a woman to carry out his bidding. Nor, thought Bride, would a woman of any sense want anything to do with a tyrant like George. It flashed through his mind how different and how much nicer the world would be if women were in charge. Territorial disputes might well be settled over lunch instead of over bloody battlefields.

He stepped out of the shadows and flagged her down. He moved cautiously closer, sizing her up before committing himself. She rolled her window down just a crack in an equal display of distrust.

"BBC Broadcasting House?" he asked with the implied questions of "do you know where it is?" and "can you take me there?" built in to the tone of his voice.

The driver looked at Bride with the careful eye of someone who had more than once left potential muggers standing on the street corner without a ride in *her* cab. Bride flashed a weak smile, an expression that begged for mercy from a Good Samaritan.

"'Op in," she finally said with a nod of her head, unlocking the door to the back seat.

Bride climbed in and sunk low into the seat. He was hoping for a brief respite to collect himself, but he wouldn't get it. London cabbies come in two varieties; the kind who don't say anything, and the kind who prattle on incessantly. Bride found himself in the company of the latter.

"A bit late to be goin' to Broadcasting House, ain't it? I imagine they've been closed for some time now," said the woman behind the wheel.

"I work there," answered Bride tersely, hoping to end the conversation right there.

"Do ya now?" she said, impressed. "Doing what?"

"I'm a...consultant...on American affairs." The lies were just rolling off his tongue now without a hint of remorse.

"For which part?"

"Radio 4."

"Really! So then you knew him."

"Who?"

"Crowe. Colin Crowe. Tragic what happened today. Tragic."

Bride could only nod his head and stare blankly out the window. She had no idea how tragic it was.

"They won't stop at anything, will they?" continued the driver.

"Who?" was again his reply.

"The bloody IRA. All the news reports says it was them that's claimin' responsibility. I'm tellin' ya, they got no conscience, that lot. They're supposed to be doin' all this in the name of religion, but if you ask me, God's got nothin' to do with 'em. They're murderers, that's what they are, nothin' more. They just keep killin' until they get what they want. That's why I cast my vote for George. He'll put a stop to 'em, you'll see."

The irony of her declaration was almost more than Bride could stand. He wanted to lean over the back seat and shake her while screaming "you don't understand!" into her ignorant ears. He managed to control himself. The time for elucidation of the masses was coming.

The taxi was still several blocks away from Broadcasting House when Bride motioned to her to pull over.

"This is fine right here," he said.

"But we're not quite—," she protested.

"I know, I know. I like a brisk walk before I go in."

"Fine then, suit yourself. At'll be four pounds twenty."

Bride handed her a ten pound note. "That radio of yours get

Radio 4?"

"Tuned to it right now," she nodded.

"Good. Make sure you listen tonight."

Bride stepped from the cab and walked to the mouth of an alleyway between two old buildings. He stood silent and motionless like the Ripper waiting for his victim. His eyes panned the boulevard, observing the night around him. No other cars were on the street, no other pedestrians. He felt confident he hadn't been followed.

He moved quickly down the sidewalk and covered the final few blocks to BBC Broadcasting House in short order, ignoring the gash in his foot and the thudding ache in his shoulder.

He arrived at the front door and pulled out Crowe's key ring. It took him four tries but he finally found the right key for the heavy deadbolt lock. He took one last look over his shoulder, acknowledged the presence of All Souls' church across the street as if someone were watching, then slipped quietly inside.

The lobby was empty. The words inscribed above, *all things foul or hostile to peace may be banished hence* seemed to cry out to him and bolster his courage for what he was about to do.

Bride wasn't quite sure where he was going, but it hadn't stopped him before and he proceeded forward into the corridor. He crossed through the vacated newsroom and made his way closer to the studio, a small cubicle behind a large pane of glass.

The sweeping secondhand on the clock overhead was five seconds away from exactly 11:30 PM. Broadcaster Peter Highsmith punched on the cartridge for *Sailing By* and twirled the long whiskers of his beard as he looked over the marine forecast for the next morning. Bride moved stealthily towards the studio, unobserved by the announcer inside as he leaned over his microphone.

"Gales near Plymouth and Biscay tomorrow... Southampton, Brighton, good becoming moderate," announced Highsmith with reassuring confidence.

Bride stepped closer, his heart leaping against the inner wall of his chest.

"Back with a preview of tomorrow's programming, right after this," said Highsmith as he deftly punched on a cartridge with several commercials. The red light went off and the amber light that told him he was off-air clicked on. He sat back, pushed his square wire rimmed glasses up onto his forehead, and rubbed his weary eyes.

Bride crept closer to the door of the studio. This was his chance. He reached for the knob, his hand trembling with fear.

"What are you doing?" yelled a voice from across the room.

The security guard walked quickly in Bride's direction. It was extremely rare that he got any suspicious activity on his late shift and he intended to pursue the matter vigorously. Bride had still not answered him. "I asked you a question, sir. What are you doing here?"

Bride reached into his pocket and pulled out the handheld tape recorder he'd taken from Crowe's flat. "I found this on the sidewalk outside," said Bride. "I was just going to return it to that gentleman in there when he got a break, then be on my way."

Bride handed him the tape recorder. The guard examined it and noticed the tiny BBC sticker on the side. He narrowed his eyes and looked up at Bride. "How'd you get in here?"

"The other guard let me in."

"What other guard? I'm the only one on duty at night."

Bride had finally run out of lies. He'd been caught and there was only one way out. "Well then who's that man down there in the hallway?" he asked as he pointed to the door to the newsroom.

The security guard turned his head. Nobody was there. He started to turn back, never really seeing the roundhouse punch that had made Bride the star of the Columbia boxing team. Bride's fist landed squarely on the guard's chin and he slowly tumbled over like the center mast on a capsized sailboat.

The commotion in the newsroom caught Highsmith's eye in the broadcast booth. He stood up and peered out of the glass into the darkened newsroom.

Bride began motioning frantically to Highsmith. "This man's having a heart attack!" he yelled.

Highsmith couldn't hear a word through the soundproof glass panel, but the desperate look on Bride's face told him the situation warranted further investigation. He slipped off his headphones and cracked open the door leading to the newsroom. "What's the problem?" he asked.

"Heart attack!" hollered Bride as he stood over the guard and feigned administering medical attention. "He just keeled over!"

"My God!" yelled Highsmith as he charged out the door and knelt down next to the guard.

In the same rush of wind, Bride sprang to his feet, bolted past Highsmith, and slipped into the announcing booth. He had already slammed the door and locked the deadbolt by the time Highsmith could turn his head.

"Hey! What are you doing? You can't go in there!" yelled Highsmith as he pounded on the glass. Bride cupped his hand to his ear as he looked at Highsmith through the glass, shrugging his shoulders to indicate he couldn't understand what he was saying. Bride quickly shoved a monstrous metal desk against the door and wedged two desk chairs behind it. The drawbridge to his castle was up and nobody was getting inside.

He turned to the control panel and stared at the dozens of toggle switches, looking for the one that would take him to the airwaves. He started flipping every switch in front of him, watching the amber light on the wall.

"Stop it!" screamed Highsmith as he pounded on the glass.

Bride ignored his pleadings and kept flipping the switches. Finally, the amber light faded and the red light blazed to life. Malcolm Bride was on the air. He picked up the microphone stand off the side of the desk and cleared his throat.

"My name is Malcolm Bride. Dr. Malcolm Bride. I was a friend of Colin Crowe, and it's to his memory that I will dedicate my first and only radio broadcast."

Bride looked over at the glass window and noticed Highsmith was gone, presumably to contact the authorities. "I don't know how much time I'm going to have on the air tonight, so I'll talk fast. You probably won't believe a thing I'm about to say, but I can assure you it's all true and everything can be verified. If enough of you out there hear it, he can't stop us all. It's not exactly a *Book at Bedtime*, but I think it's a story you'll all want to hear."

Bride took a deep breath and gathered his thoughts.

"The 'he' I'm referring to is Prince George himself. He is in fact a Prince in name only. There isn't a drop of Royal blood in his miserable body. He's as common as you and me. In 1945, there was a lady-in-waiting at the palace who gave birth to twins. One of those twin boys was me. My brother is the man you are about to anoint as your King. At the same time, there was a tragedy behind the palace walls. Queen Alexandra's son, your true Crown Prince, died when he was less than twenty-four hours old."

For the next ten minutes, Bride proceeded to regale his radio audience with a story that would surpass any tale the walls of the Tower of London could tell. Having recently had a rehearsal in the tape he made for Donald Lawrie, Bride smoothly and succinctly recapped the substitution of babies by Elliott Wiggs, the payoff of Paddy Butterfill, the murders of Sir Nolan and George's wife, the bombings and fake bomb threats blamed on the IRA, John's murder, and finally Crowe's recent death in the afternoon.

His only glaring omission was the name of Princess Catherine. Deep down, he felt she was a silent accomplice in all of this, but even deeper than that, he could understand her motives and could forgive her.

"And so now you know. The secret that has cost lives, including that of Colin Crowe's, is now a secret we all share. Crowe believed that journalism is the voice of freedom and he vowed that his voice would never be silenced. He should have been the one to do this tonight, but since he couldn't be here, I hope I've made good on his promise."

The window to the announcing booth suddenly shattered and a thousand angry shards of broken glass poured in on Bride like jagged hailstones. Crumrie stood on the other side of the fractured pane, his gun still smoking from the bullet he'd just fired. Bride clutched the microphone and backed as far into the corner of the booth as the cord would let him.

"He's here!" Bride screamed frantically into the microphone. "He works for Elliott Wiggs! He's going to kill me! He's standing right here with a gun! He's going to kill me!"

Crumrie vaulted through the broken window and dropped softly into the announcing booth. He had a wry smile on his face as he dusted a piece of glass off his shoulder.

"They can't hear you, Dr. Bride. I'm afraid you have an audience of only one."

Crumrie held up a handful of electrical cables with freshly cut wires sticking out of the ends.

"Fortunately, Mr. Highsmith had the presence of mind to run and yank out the cables to the transmitter, effectively cutting off your power. Unfortunately, I had to perform the same operation on Mr. Highsmith."

Bride's heart sank to the depths. His electronic lifeline was in Crumrie's hands, and now too was his life. He set the dead microphone on the desk.

"Now then, Dr. Bride, I think you'll want to come with me. I've got somebody who wants to talk to *you*."

The security guard whom Bride had knocked cold minutes before had regained consciousness and struggled to his feet. He was still groggy as he saw the two men inside the broadcast booth.

"Hey!" he said as he moved in front of the broken window.

In one swift and fluid motion, Crumrie whipped his arm across his body and fired a single shot into the guard's chest, knocking him to the ground again. This time he wouldn't be getting up. The gun was immediately aimed back at Bride.

Crumrie pushed aside the metal desk in front of the door and slid back the deadbolt. He waved his revolver at Bride, motioning him through the door. "Let's go."

Bride readily obeyed.

Chapter Thirty-Three

For the next ten minutes, Bride knew exactly where he was. He was crammed into the trunk of Crumrie's car. Where he was going remained a mystery, although several sonic clues managed to penetrate the trunk.

At one point, Bride could detect the faint sounds of a tugboat's horn, and he knew he wasn't far from the Thames. Moments later, he could distinctly hear the chimes of Big Ben at midnight, the twelfth peal noticeably louder than the first as Crumrie's car drove closer to the Houses of Parliament.

The car slowed to a stop. Crumrie's door slammed and Bride could hear his footsteps approaching the trunk. A gun barrel was the first thing Bride saw as the trunk lid popped open.

"Out," ordered Crumrie.

Bride climbed out of the trunk and quickly tried to get his bearings. He was in a dark alley next to the river, with a bridge overhead. No other landmarks were visible in the dense fog. Crumrie grabbed his arm and led him down the alley where a black limousine blended into the black bricks behind it. He politely opened the door like a valet and motioned Bride inside.

Bride climbed in the car and found it was as dark as the trunk he'd just left. What little light there was in the alley was completely blocked out by the tinted windows of the limousine. He sat motionless in the dark trying to determine if he was alone. He sensed he wasn't.

A match struck on the other side of the limousine and for an instant, Bride could see George's face through the flare. George held the match up to a long Cuban cigar and turned the packed tobacco at the tip into a soft ember that provided the only light in the car.

"Good evening, Dr. Bride," said George.

"It's actually morning," came Bride's reply.

"Ah yes, so it is. Always on the side of correctness, aren't you, Bride?"

"Do you have something to say?" said Bride with bold disdain. He wasn't yet beyond fear at this point, but was determined that George wouldn't get the satisfaction of watching him squirm.

"Yes, actually I do have something to say. I would really like to apologize."

Bride was slightly stunned. "Apologize? For what?"

George took a puff on his cigar and shook his head with a hint of ruefulness. "One doesn't do away with his own brother without some expression of regret, I should think."

"How thoughtful of you, George. How very British. Did you extend the same courtesy to Prince John?"

"No, but as you know, he wasn't my real brother. I realize your sarcasm in this case, but my sentiment is genuine. You are my flesh and blood brother, my twin no less, beginning life together from the same womb. The thought that I'm going to be responsible for ending your life is...unpleasant."

"Yes, murder can be distasteful at times. However, I would think with all of your practice that by now you'd be immune to those nagging feelings of remorse."

"There is no choice, don't you understand? I didn't set this course, I'm only following it, and if death is one of the signposts along the way, then so be it. Death made me a Prince. Death will make me King."

"You don't want to be a King, George. You want to be a dictator. The name Hitler comes to mind."

"Even Hitler did some good things. He built the autobahn, you know."

"The autobahn, huh?" said Bride sarcastically. "Well, I guess that about evens up the ledger on him."

"Actually, I prefer comparisons to Napoleon. He got a little greedy in the end, but he accomplished a fair amount before then, the Napoleonic code and all that. I don't intend to repeat his mistakes, only his victories."

George rolled down the window and tossed the cigar outside. He leaned forward, staring at the floor of the car and wringing his hands.

"I tried to get you to stop. I desperately wanted you to return to America and live out your life in peace, but you wouldn't quit, would you? You just *had* to keep pressing the issue. I suppose that's one more trait we have in common. Actually, I rather admired your determination to get to the heart of the matter. Between you and dear Mr. Crowe, you almost had the whole story put together."

"Almost?"

"You got a little off track on the uranium story. True, I do intend to reap handsome profits from nuclear energy, but it's really a different sort of power I intend to develop."

"Meaning?"

"Strategic power, Malcolm. Enough to make Britain the most feared nation on earth, even more than your United States. The Russians are having a virtual fire sale on the nuclear arsenal they stockpiled during the Cold War, and I intend to take advantage of their bargain prices."

"So *that's* why you brought in the Russian scientists? To be your buyers?"

"Precisely. Oh, you do possess a keen mind, Malcolm! If only you had been intelligent enough to leave well enough alone. Everything would have turned out for the best! You see, I have dreams for England! You want to study history, but I want to *make* it!"

"And the end justifies the means. Is that what you're telling me?"

"In this instance, yes. And you, sadly, are the last hurdle before I reach that end. And that is why I wanted to apologize. Strange words to hear from your executioner as you step on the gallows, I understand, but I *am* sorry."

"I'm sorry too," said Bride.

"About what?"

"That I'm still going to ruin your plans."

"What do you mean?"

"I mean that I recorded everything I know about you and mailed the tape to a trusted friend. The rest of me may be gone, but my voice will live on to tell your dirty little secrets."

"I see," said George. He reached into his breast pocket and pulled out an envelope. "Do you mean *this* tape?"

Bride was aghast. By the faint light from the alley that came through the half open window, he could see the address of Donald Lawrie written on the envelope in his own handwriting. The game was over. He thought he had the King in checkmate but in one stunning move he had slipped away. His trump card had failed to take the trick. Crestfallen, Bride slumped against the seat of the limousine. George tucked the envelope back into his pocket.

"You don't seem to understand. I own this country, and everything in it."

"So that's it," said Bride in a somber voice. "You win."

"I'm afraid so."

"I can only wonder about one thing."

"What's that?"

"What would have happened if Wiggs had put *me* in that bassinet and sent you off to America. Would things have turned out differently?"

George pondered the question, gently shaking his head.

"We'll never know, will we?"

The two men sat in silence, both trying to look into the future of Great Britain. One brother with excitement over the possibilities, the other brother with dread.

The quiet was broken as George rapped on the window. Crumrie was instantly there, opening the car door and pulling Bride out by the arm.

Crumrie marched Bride back to his car at gunpoint. "Turn around and lean against the car," he ordered.

"And let you shoot me in the back?" scoffed Bride. "I don't think so. If I'm going to die, then my killer is going to watch."

"Oh, I'm going to watch alright, don't worry about that. But you're not going to die here, not in a dark alleyway. George wants you to go out with as little pain as possible."

Crumrie reached into the back seat of his car and pulled out something that resembled a long jumprope with enormous white handles. Attached on each end of a six-foot rope was a large block of salt two feet square. Each end of the rope was threaded through a hole that had been drilled through each salt block, then knotted at the tip to keep it from sliding back out. Crumrie draped the contraption over his shoulder and motioned Bride with his gun.

"Let's go," grunted Crumrie.

"What's that?" said Bride, pointing to the rope with the blocks.

"You'll find out soon enough. Now move."

They trudged down the alley until they came to a long flight of stone stairs that led to the bridge above. Bride didn't know it at the time, but he was on the north end of Blackfriars Bridge, not far from Fleet Street where the newspaper presses were sleeping through the biggest story in modern British history. He could just barely make out a portion of the dome of St. Paul's Cathedral and wondered if anything saintly was looking back.

They got to the top of the bridge and stood in the shadows at the far end as several cars passed by. Bride considered yelling for help but thought better of it. Crumrie had been ahead of him every step of the way and Bride figured anyone else he drew into this mess would probably be killed as well. Hopefully, the long list of the dead would end with him.

Crumrie removed the rope from his shoulder.

"So you're wonderin' what this little contraption is, are you, mate?" he asked Bride.

"The thought had crossed my mind."

"I call it a 'jump rope'. The salt blocks here on the end drag you down to the bottom of the river, then eventually dissolve away. The rope floats free and you float to the top where everyone thinks you did yourself in by jumping off the bridge."

"Ingenious," said Bride with a nod. He was genuinely impressed. "But what's to keep me from untying the rope once I'm in the water?"

"You won't," smirked Crumrie. "Now bend over." Bride shook his head.

"No."

"Bend over, mate, or I'll shoot you through the brain right here. Drowning is what George wants for you because it's a much better way to go, but I'll tell you right now it doesn't matter to me."

Bride thought it over and was forced to agree with his intended killer. From everything he'd read, drowning was indeed the best way to die aside from passing away in your sleep. On the other hand, drowning would take a lot longer and would prolong the agony. It may be painful but at least a bullet was quick about its business.

The bottom line, decided Bride, was that dying was dying and in the long run it really didn't matter much to the person on the receiving end. In this case, however, it did seem to make a difference to at least one of the killers. If George wanted Bride to drown, then Bride wanted to make sure that was the one way he *wouldn't* die. And since it was clear to him that he wasn't going to be allowed to gently slip away in his sleep, then one of Crumrie's bullets was his only option. And if Bride could go out having fought the good fight to stay alive, at least there might be some investigation into his death.

Bride nodded and bent over. Crumrie looped the weighted rope around Bride's neck and twisted it down the length of his arms.

Another car drove past their hiding place at the end of the bridge and Bride used the shield of noise to slip one of his shoes off the back of his heel. Crumrie kept his gun trained on Bride's head as he watched the car drive away into the mist rising from the Thames. In the split second that it took Crumrie to turn back, Bride flipped his loose shoe high into the air with a quick flick of his ankle. A second later it landed on the pavement behind Crumrie and he spun around to challenge whatever had dared to intrude on his mission.

The instant Crumrie turned, Bride lunged forward and kicked him in the rib cage as hard as his exhausted body would allow. Crumrie crashed onto the street and Bride attacked again, kicking angrily with both legs, although he moved slower than usual with an extra forty pounds of salt blocks dragging behind him.

Crumrie had already let Bride slip through his hands on three occasions that day and he wasn't about to allow a fourth. He mustered enough strength to whip his legs onto the back of Bride's knees and put him on the ground. One quick pistol-whip to the temple and Bride was unconscious. Crumrie struggled to his feet and pointed his gun at Bride's head. His finger quivered on the trigger. He squeezed it back a millimeter, then slowly let off, realizing George would be able to hear the gunshot and would know Crumrie had disobeyed his orders.

Crumrie shoved the pistol into his waistband and picked up Bride in a fireman's carry, wincing in pain from a broken rib or two. He walked twenty yards out onto Blackfriars Bridge and laid out Bride's limp body onto the ledge, took a quick look in either direction, then put one hand under Bride's shoulder and another under his legs and rolled him off the side.

Bride hurtled impotently toward the Thames with only a hundred yards of thick London fog to slow his descent. He plunged feet first into the choppy water, the deadly blocks of salt splashing next to him an instant later.

Crumrie leaned over the edge of the bridge and listened for the sound of the splash and the silence that followed. He would finally have a good report for his superiors.

The weight of the heavy salt blocks dragged Bride quickly to the bottom of the river. Whether it was the chill of the water or the impact of his entry, something coaxed Bride back to consciousness. He immediately knew he was submerged, breathless, and drowning. He fought hard to remove himself from the yoke that weighed him down, twisting and turning like a shark trapped in a fisherman's net, but his struggle was futile. He was out of air, his limp body now suspended in water, waving aimlessly back and forth like seaweed.

At that moment, a feeling of euphoria slowly came over him as his body resigned itself to a watery grave. Fear vanished, even though he knew he was moments away from dying. He felt warm and comfortable, like an infant wrapped up in his mother's protective arms. But in the very foundation of his soul he knew he shouldn't be feeling that way. He wasn't ready. Too young. Too alive. He had unfinished business, both large and small. He had classes yet to be taught. Remote destinations yet to be explored. He had always wanted to learn to play the piano. He wanted to try fly fishing. He had an Empire to save. And for some odd reason, it occurred to him again that he would never again kiss Princess Catherine. But there he was on the bottom of the river, an obituary waiting to happen.

Something suddenly grabbed the back of his shirt collar and jerked him mightily towards the surface. Bride assumed this was the initial phase of his ascension, but then immediately he saw a thick arm reach down and grab his belt buckle. He peered through the murky river water and could make out the chiseled face of Trevor McFarlane, his eyes wide open and his cheeks bulging with reserved air like a trumpeter. Trevor's powerful legs kicked hard through the water as he pulled Bride upward.

Within seconds Trevor had broken through the surface and he sucked hard for air as he furiously treaded water and fought to keep the drowning man's head above the chop. He pulled the yoke off Bride and let it float harmlessly to the bottom of the Thames. Bride wasn't breathing so Trevor clamped his nose shut with his fingers and blew two quick blasts of his own breath down Bride's windpipe. No response. Trevor drew more foggy air into his lungs and again blew it into Bride's mouth. Bride instantly coughed and spit up water. Trevor gave him two more breaths. Bride coughed some more, then finally began to breathe on his own.

Trevor flipped Bride onto his back, ran his arm under Bride's armpit and across his chest, then scissors kicked toward the shore, struggling for every yard across the swift current. He finally reached the embankment and dragged Bride up onto the slippery green rocks. By the time they escaped from the water, they were two hundred yards down river from Blackfriars Bridge.

It was nearly ten minutes of coughing and spitting before Bride could manage to speak.

"Where did you come from?" he murmured to Trevor.

"I been following Crumrie since darkness fell. Figured he was lookin' for ya and he'd lead me right to ya."

"You almost let him kill me!"

"You forget, mate, I was raised on this river. As soon as I saw him bring out that yoke, I knew what he had planned for ya, so I run on down to the riverbank and dove in to wait for ya. You damn near landed on top a me, ya did!"

"Don't you think you cut it a bit close?" asked Bride with a little annoyance in his voice.

"Sorry. Couldn't find ya right off. The water was a little murky tonight, wasn't it?"

Bride suddenly caught himself. Here he was, angry with the man who had just saved his life. He leaned over and shook Trevor's beefy hand, the hand that had reached out and pulled him back when he was already one step through the gate of heaven. "Thank you," he said quietly.

"Don't thank me. Wasn't my idea. Just following Her Majesty's orders, mate. Just following orders."

Bride wouldn't let go of the brave Scot's hand. Bride had known brilliant scholars, Nobel prize winning scientists, revered statesmen, but he'd never met anyone he respected more than this anvil of a man forged from a mighty river and a bloody battlefield. Bride knew that Trevor loved Catherine, yet he had just risked his own life to save a man whom he perceived as a rival for her affections. Chivalry was truly not dead.

As Bride sat on the riverbank with Trevor and watched the Thames harmlessly rush past him, he knew for certain that however evil that evil might become, goodness would always prevail.

The chimes on Big Ben had struck one o'clock in the morning before Bride was strong enough to get to his feet. Trevor helped him up the rocks to the footpath next to the river. They headed west, back toward Blackfriars Bridge.

"Where are we going?" he asked.

"Got to hide you until it's safe to get you out of the country."

Bride stopped walking. "Out of the country? I can't leave yet!"

"You don't have a choice here, mate."

"But what about George! He has to be stopped!"

"Maybe so, but not by you."

"And why not?" said Bride indignantly.

"'Cause you're not capable, 'at's why! Ever since ya poked your nose into things it's been a bloody disaster. How many more people are ya gonna get killed before you realize you're no match for the man!"

Bride hung his head. Trevor was right. From the moment he found Catherine's pillbox in the cemetery at St. Bartholomew's, Bride had been the captain of an ill-fated ship that couldn't sail out of the hurricane. There were no passengers left to bail. Bride wasn't facing mutiny, but rather harsh reality that he would never reach his final destination and it was time to turn back. Someone else would have to navigate the treacherous waters later.

"Then who will stop him?" said Bride with resignation.

"Her Majesty, Princess Catherine."

"She can't do it, you *know* that! She said herself she doesn't have the strength."

"The woman has more strength than twenty men, she just doesn't know it yet because she hasn't been put to the test. But it's there, and she'll find it, just like her mother did."

"But when?"

"When the time's right."

"But you can't wait! Tomorrow he's crowned King, and then it's too late. You can't give a man like George that much power and then try to take it away from him. He'll crush anyone who tries! This is how dictators operate!"

"It's no longer your concern, Dr. Bride. All that's left for you to do is to get out of England while you're still alive, and if you don't follow me *right* now, I'll throw you back in the river meself."

Bride had no choice but to follow. He exhaled with the frustration of a man who had been climbing a mountain for weeks only to realize he would never reach the summit. He trudged on with only one shoe.

Within minutes they were back underneath Blackfriars Bridge. Trevor scanned the area to make sure they weren't being followed, then led Bride over to a metal grate embedded in the asphalt. He yanked the grate open to reveal a deep ventilation shaft with a ladder leading straight down into blackness. He motioned Bride to climb down.

"Let's go. We 'aven't got all night."

Bride trusted that Trevor knew what he was doing and obeyed his command. Halfway down the ladder, Trevor stepped in after him and pulled the grate back over the top of the shaft.

Thirty feet down into the bowels of the shaft, Bride touched bottom. He stood to one side and could feel the dampness under his stocking foot. The cement sides of the walls were moist and cool and covered with slick algae. Water dripped somewhere nearby and the echoes rushed through the ventilation shaft as they made their escape to the street above.

Bride's eyes began to adjust to the blackness as Trevor arrived at the bottom. He felt along one side of the shaft wall like someone trying to find a light switch in a pitch black bathroom.

"Where are ya?" Trevor muttered as he felt his way forward. "Been awhile since I been down here," he said apologetically to Bride. "Ah, there she is." He yanked on a handle and opened a small door about three feet square. A faint light trickled through the opening.

"Follow me," he ordered Bride as he squeezed his bulky frame through the opening. Bride followed him through the door and into a cavernous room that reverberated with the echo of Trevor shutting the door behind them.

As Bride's eyes adjusted to what faint light was available, he could make out the rough shapes of old subway cars. Dozens of them were harbored in the dank tunnel with years of mildew sandwiched between layers of dust.

"Where are we?" whispered Bride in the darkness.

"Another graveyard," answered Trevor. "This one for railcars. They keep the old ones here for spare parts. Used to come in here and play when I was a boy. Smoked me first cigarette right over there." Trevor flashed a rare smile, then wiped it away as he recalled his purpose for being there. "Come on, we got a ways to go yet."

Trevor stepped onto a stretch of empty track and Bride followed immediately behind as they continued deeper into the tunnel, feeling their way along the rails.

Within a few minutes the tunnel widened again into another large room. Parked on the four rows of parallel tracks were eight flatbed railcars from a freight train, but it was too dark for Bride to see anything farther than two steps away.

"Now where are we?" asked Bride.

"This is the garden," replied Trevor.

"Garden?"

"'At's right." Trevor walked up to one of the flatbeds and pulled at something in the darkness, then turned back to show it to Bride. "Mushrooms. Perfect place to grow 'em and the perfect place for you to hide. You get hungry, you got plenty to eat. Now stay put until I get back."

"Where are you going?"

Trevor took five steps and disappeared into the darkness.

"To get everything ready to get you out of here," echoed his voice down the tunnel.

"When are you coming back?"

"Wait three hours. If I'm not back by then...wait some more."

"Trevor?"

"Yeah, mate?" came his distant reply.

"Thanks for everything. I mean it."

There was no reply. Bride could only hope that Trevor had heard him.

Bride turned around and felt his way to one of the railcars. He reached up and touched one of the wooden flats filled with soft dirt and moist mushrooms. It was the closest thing Bride had seen to a bed in a long time so he hoisted his exhausted frame onto the flatbed and laid down on the spongy mattress of fungi.

His wounded shoulder throbbed with a dull ache and his feet were sore and battered but the pain wouldn't keep him awake. He was fast asleep before Big Ben announced the two o'clock hour.

Chapter Thirty-Four

*T*revor was still in his wet clothes as he stood in his quarters in Buckingham palace and dialed the phone. Catherine immediately picked up on the other end, in bed but wide awake in the middle of the night.

"Yes?" she whispered, knowing right away who was calling her.

"Safe," was Trevor's secretive reply. One could never be certain who was listening in, even in the dead of night.

"In the garden?"

"Yes."

"Well done. Very well done. Goodnight."

"Goodnight, Your Majesty."

Catherine hung up her phone and breathed a sigh of relief. She pulled her knees up under her chin and wrapped her arms around her legs, rocking back and forth with worry.

Trevor pulled off his soggy shoes and peeled off the wet shirt that was clinging to his barrel chest. He rolled his aching neck from side to side, then stripped off the rest of his clothes and crawled into bed. All things considered, it had been a good night.

Trevor had trained himself to be a light sleeper so that he would be immediately alert and available for service at a moment's notice, even in the dead of night. When a knock came at the door of his quarters in the darkest hours of morning, he was instantly vigilant as he stepped softly to the transom and put his ear against the door.

"Who is it?"

"It's Prince George. May I have a word with you?"

Trevor was seized with alarm. There could be only one reason the Prince was coming to see him at 5:30 in the morning on the day of his coronation.

"Is it possible, milord, for this matter to wait 'til the morning?" he asked as politely as possible. He hated Prince George but this was no time to be antagonistic.

"Open the door, McFarlane. Now."

Trevor knew there was no way out of his predicament. He'd been given a direct order from the man who would be King of Britain and to disobey would mean immediate dismissal, perhaps worse. Odd reasoning from a man who had just spent his evening thwarting George's evil agenda, but Trevor wasn't thinking clearly in his panic. And after all, there could be some other explanation for George's unexpected visit.

"Yessir." Trevor turned the knob on his door and had barely opened it a crack when Crumrie burst in and shoved an eight inch knife under his neck, one swift swipe away from severing his carotid artery. He backed Trevor against the wall as George followed him into the room and quietly shut the door behind them.

"We've been a busy boy tonight, haven't we, Trevor?" said George as he picked up the wet shirt from off the floor. "A little midnight swim?"

"What's all this about? I was washing Lady Catherine's car and got a little careless with the hose, that's all."

"Washing her car, were you?" said George. "Now that's odd. We saw her car parked a few blocks away from Blackfriars Bridge. Is that where it got so dirty?"

George raised his eyebrows as if waiting for a reply but not really expecting to get one. He held the wet shirt up to his nose and breathed deeply like someone inspecting a fine Bordeaux. "Ah yes, the Thames. I would recognize her anywhere. Ironic, isn't it? If the manufacturers had listened to me and stopped dumping into her, the water wouldn't smell this way."

"What do you want from me?" said Trevor through his gritted teeth.

"I have given you considerable rope over the years, McFarlane, only because I know how much my sister cares about you. But I'm afraid now that same rope is going to hang you. That is, of course, unless you choose to cooperate."

"Cooperate how?"

"Tell me what I need to know."

"I'm not sure what you mean, sir."

Crumrie shoved the knife harder against Trevor's neck, slicing open a thin line of flesh that dripped blood onto the steel blade.

"Where is he?" snapped George, no longer even attempting to sound genteel.

"I suppose I don't have much choice, do I?" muttered Trevor as he glanced down at the knife wedging up against his neck. "Alright then, I'll tell you. He's in the trummadafuh." Trevor's voice trailed off at the end of his sentence, making his last words unintelligible. George stepped several paces closer.

"What did you say? I can't hear you."

"Well if you took this blade off me throat, I might be able to talk a little plainer," mumbled Trevor.

George nodded to Crumrie to relax the pressure on the knife blade. "Better?" asked George.

"Better."

"Now then, you were saying?"

"Here's what I was saying..."

Trevor's forearm shot upward and caught Crumrie square under the chin, sending him flying against the wall. He grabbed the wrist that held the knife and slammed it against the wall until it dropped from Crumrie's hand and fell harmlessly to the floor. A swift knee to the groin put Crumrie on his knees in agony.

Trevor turned on George, snorting with aggression. He grabbed him by the lapels of his jacket and butted his forehead squarely against the Prince's face, opening a cut over the rim of George's eye. His feet still moving like a trained boxer, Trevor backed away as his instinct to attack was momentarily overridden by the stunning realization that he had just drawn blood from the future King of England. His eyes raging with anger, Trevor exhaled like a medieval dragon as he formulated his next move.

Trevor was suddenly tackled from behind by Crumrie, sending them both crashing forward at George's feet. Crumrie staggered up first and whisked out his revolver, his finger slipping quickly in front of the trigger. Trevor was a man of action who had always solved his problems with brute force, but that was no longer an option in his current dilemma. He slowly raised his head and gazed up at George, who lorded over him with disdain. With a flash of lucidity uncommon to his nature, Trevor now realized what he must do.

Ignoring the open muzzle of Crumrie's revolver, Trevor lunged forward and buried his face into George's sternum, his teeth gnashing like the lion in his heart. The blunt handle of Crumrie's revolver smashed into his temple, sending him careening back onto the floor. Trevor knew another step would be fatal. He got to one knee, swallowed hard and pounded his midsection like a man who'd just consumed a stiff drink, then raised his burly arms in surrender.

George bitterly wiped away the blood from his eye with Trevor's wet shirt. He looked over at Crumrie as the rest of his face twitched with deep anger.

"Get it out of him! I don't care how you do it, but you get it out of him! Malcolm Bride doesn't leave England alive." George stormed out of Trevor's quarters, slamming the door hard enough to knock a mirror off the wall.

Crumrie massaged his chin where Trevor had just rearranged a few pieces of bone. He sat on the bed across the room and reflected on what he was about to say.

"Listen mate, we've had our differences over the years, I realize that, but we've managed to get on, haven't we? I don't want to kill you. I mean, I would consider us friends, wouldn't you?"

"I suppose."

"Then take a friend's advice. At the end of this day, George is going to be King. Now he's a little put out with you right now, understandably so, but you have a golden chance here to make him very happy, and I promise you he won't forget that.

"You're a smart man, McFarlane. You need to stop and see which way the wind is blowin' and then let it help you along. Once that crown sits down on George's head, things are goin' to be a lot different around here and if you haven't pitched your tent in George's camp, you'll live to regret it. That is, if you live at all. Now what do you say? What's it gonna be for you? I really don't see that you have much of a choice."

Trevor took a deep breath as he mulled over Crumrie's advice. "He treats you well, does he?" he asked Crumrie.

"Like a King," said Crumrie with a chuckle. Trevor slowly nodded. He had come to a decision.

"And if I tell you, you'll let me go?"

"Of course. Like I said, we're friends, aren't we?"

Trevor smiled and nodded. "You wouldn't be able to find him on your own," he told Crumrie. "I'd have to lead you to him."

"Now that's a smart move, McFarlane. Very smart. And just in case you change your mind and think about doin' something stupid, just remember, I haven't killed anyone all day and that's got me a little peevish." He waved Trevor toward the door. "It's gettin' late. Let's go."

Trevor pulled himself up and led Crumrie out the door.

◆ ◆ ◆

Prince George leaned inches away from the mirror in his palace apartment, seething with anger as he examined the cut over his eye. He would have more pictures taken of him that day than on any other in his life and this was the last thing he needed. The small gash wouldn't require stitches, but it was noticeable enough that he would need to think of a good excuse as to how he got it. Something noble like fending off a palace intruder seemed like a good idea.

He began to undress, unbuttoning his jacket as he kicked off his shoes. He suddenly noticed that one of the monogrammed gold buttons from his jacket was missing, probably a result of the struggle in Trevor's quarters. The loss was upsetting to George because the solid gold buttons had been a gift from the King of Sweden on the occasion of his investiture as Prince of Wales. They were not only extremely valuable, but also irreplaceable.

He made a mental note to send Crumrie to look for it as soon as he returned from his mission to locate Bride.

He finished undressing and prepared for bed. He laid down on the soft mattress and willed himself to sleep. He had an exhausting day ahead of him and would need to take full advantage of the last few minutes before daybreak.

◆ ◆ ◆

Trevor walked several paces in front of Crumrie as they made their way through the dark tube tunnels near Blackfriars Bridge.

"How much further?" asked Crumrie.

"Almost there, mate. Almost there."

Trevor led Crumrie through a maze of abandoned railcars, pushing away a balustrade of spider webs that clung to the dank cinderblocks. They came to the end of the room where a small door was recessed into the wall. It took Trevor several mighty tugs before he could get the door to open for him. It led into a narrow subway tunnel, barely big enough for anything more than a railcar and a few brown mice scurrying on the bed of the track.

"He's through there," said Trevor as he pointed through the opening of the door. "Down about fifty yards."

"How do I know he's in there?" said Crumrie with suspicion.

"Fair question," nodded Trevor. "Listen." He cupped his hands around his mouth and drew a deep breath. "Bride?" he hollered down the dark tunnel. "Bride? Can you hear me?"

Bride lurched out of his restless sleep on the bed of mushrooms. He could hear Trevor's robust voice reverberating off the walls, but couldn't determine from which direction it came. The echoes through the labyrinth of the underground made it impossible to pinpoint the sound's origin.

"Trevor?" hollered Bride in response. "Is that you?"

Trevor stood in the narrow tunnel and nodded silently to a smiling Crumrie as Bride's distant voice bounced off the walls. "Yes, it's me," he yelled back. "Stay where you are! I'm coming to get you!"

"Alright, I won't move!" answered Bride. He hopped off the flatbed and swept away the potting soil clinging to his clothes.

Trevor moved aside and made a motion for Crumrie to pass by.

"You go on in and do what you need to do. If it's all the same to you, I'd rather he didn't see my face."

Crumrie's face broke out in a contemptuous sneer as he pointed his gun at Trevor. "Don't think so, mate. There's been a slight change of plans."

Trevor's broad shoulders sagged as he sensed betrayal.

"What? What are you talking about?"

"You fool! Did you really think I was going to let you walk away?"

"Hey! We had a deal!" said Trevor.

Crumrie waved his gun to prod Trevor down the tracks. "It's a changing world we live in, McFarlane. You really need to keep up."

"I thought we were friends."

"Friends? That's a good one! That's rich, that is! Now quit stalling and get going. I have an appointment to keep."

Trevor glared angrily at Crumrie, then took a quick glance at his watch. It was just past 6:00 AM. He exhaled loudly with the breath of a beaten man. "I should have known you'd get the better of me. I should have known." He checked his watch again, then started down the narrow tunnel with Crumrie a few paces behind him.

Bride stood leaning against the flatbed railcar, waiting patiently for his rescuer. He picked a mushroom and ate it to quiet the growling in his stomach. Suddenly, he felt the flatbed shake a little bit, then a rumbling under his feet like a small earthquake. He sensed a subway car approaching somewhere nearby as the rumbling gradually intensified.

Trevor had led Crumrie eighty yards down the confining subway shaft.

"How much further?" asked Crumrie impatiently.

Trevor bent down and felt one of the rails along the bed of the track. "Won't be long now," replied Trevor.

By this time they could feel the tiny rumblings that Bride had experienced moments before, getting stronger by the second. Deep into the tunnel, the leading edges of a bright light began to appear. The rumbling under their feet grew even stronger.

Trevor stopped in the middle of the tracks and held up his wrist to get a long look at his watch. "You're right, Crumrie, it *is* a changing world. But you know one thing that's never changed? The tube always runs on time." He looked up and smiled at Crumrie. "Waterloo line. Right on schedule."

Terror had swept down and clutched every fiber of what little soul Crumrie had left. His eyes were wide open as the rumbling violently shook the ground under his feet.

"You bastard!" he screamed at Trevor, his voice competing with the growing howl of the approaching train. Crumrie turned and tried to flee back down the tunnel like one of the mice under his feet, but stumbled on the uneven trackbed and scrambled on his hands and feet to keep his balance. He righted himself and took two more steps, but was stopped in his tracks as Trevor tackled him from behind and held onto his legs as the trackbed shook violently beneath them.

The bright beacon on the front of the speeding subway car lit up the approaching track down the tunnel. The conductor looked up in horror as he saw the two men on the ground in front of him. He reached for the brake but there was no chance of stopping.

Bride couldn't hear the screams above the roar of the subway car in the adjacent tunnel. Within seconds, the sound died down and the rumbling subsided. He wouldn't find out until much later that Trevor McFarlane had died a hero's death, serving his Princess and protecting the Crown until the bitter end.

From the moment Crumrie had burst into his room and held a knife to his throat, Trevor had known his time on earth was not long. But if a good soldier was going to die, then he was going to take one of evil's emissaries with him. Someone else would have to draw swords with Prince George. Trevor had done his part and had done it well. The McFarlane clan could be proud of its brave son.

Bride waited nervously next to the flatbed, sensing something was terribly wrong. The rumbling had stopped, replaced by an awful silence. He had continued to call out Trevor's name, but his own echo was the only response.

Time was growing short. In a few hours, George would be crowned King of Britain, uniting the throne and the head of government into one omnipotent man. Once he seized that power, the task of bringing him down would be impossible. Bride knew he had to reach Catherine before the Coronation Ceremony and persuade her to disclose the truth about the Crown Prince.

He finally decided he could wait no longer and attempted to get his bearings in the catacombs of the London underground. He ventured back down the tunnel, one carefully placed step at a time, trying his best to retrace his path to the ventilator shaft where he and Trevor had entered the dark maze. The initial search proved futile and despite his nap on the bed of mushrooms, his energy reserve was almost depleted. He sank down on the cold floor and rested his exhausted body, feeling like one of the coal miners after a cave-in—lost, frightened, and very much alone.

The conductor on the Waterloo line had radioed for emergency help within seconds after running over the two bodies in the middle of his track. He was beside himself with grief but managed to gather his wits long enough to relay accurate directions that would lead the paramedics to the scene of the tragedy.

Within ten minutes the ambulance had rolled up to the Blackfriars tube station and rescue workers were racing on foot down the tunnel with flashlights and life-support equipment. They would soon discover the latter wouldn't be necessary.

Bride heard the faint whine of the ambulance sirens filtering into the tunnel where he was sitting. Within minutes, he could make out the sounds of muffled voices as paramedics shouted instructions to each other up and down the adjacent shaft of the Waterloo line.

A wave of adrenaline poured into his depleted limbs and he scrambled to his feet with rising spirits. He raced down the tunnel in the direction of the voices emanating from the other side of the wall. He abandoned all notions that he was supposed to be in hiding, knowing that he wasn't going to get out of that tunnel alive without outside assistance. He felt he had to take a chance that the ambulances were summoned by Trevor, not knowing that in an awful way, he was right.

"Help!" shouted Bride at the wall in front of him. He continued to hear a flurry of activity on the other side, but nothing that resembled a response to his plea. "Help!" he shouted louder, but again his voice seemed to be absorbed by an unforgiving wall.

If Bride could have seen to the other side, he would have witnessed six paramedics in the middle of the grim task of removing two mangled bodies from the train tracks. The medical equipment had never made it out of their packs. Bodybags were stretched out on the trackbed as the paramedics attempted to remove as much of the carnage as they could.

Trevor had been knocked to the side of the tunnel at impact and his muscular frame, though punctured and bloodied in places, was essentially intact. Crumrie's body had been dragged well down the tunnel and was virtually unrecognizable as a human form.

Bride ran back to one of the abandoned railcars. He grabbed a piece of sheet metal dangling loose from the side of a car and tore it away from the rusty pop rivets. He searched the ground around him until he found a two-foot section of steel pipe. He rushed back to the sound of the voices with his props, knowing they might be his only chance of survival.

He leaned the top of the piece of sheet metal against the stone wall of the subway tunnel and smashed it repeatedly with the steel pipe like a Chinese drummer. A thunderous noise blasted through the underground as Bride rhythmically and relentlessly beat on the metal.

He stopped for a moment, breathing hard and sweating as he listened for a response. Still nothing. He raised the pipe to strike again.

"Who's there?" came a muffled voice from the other side.

Bride's heart soared. He dropped the steel pipe and pressed his face against the wall of the tunnel.

"Help me!" he shouted. "I'm trapped!"

"Stay where you are!" replied the voice. "We'll send someone in to get you!"

They were almost the same words he had heard Trevor shout to him not a half an hour before. He slumped to the ground and closed his eyes, waiting for his rescuers.

Within minutes two paramedics entered Bride's tunnel through an access door and shone their flashlights on him. He was shoeless, wearing wet clothes, and covered with dirt from sleeping on the flatbed of mushrooms. For all they knew, he had been down there for months.

"Thank God!" murmured Bride as he rushed to embrace his rescuers. "You have to take me to Buckingham Palace! I need to see Princess Catherine!"

"Of course you do," replied one of the medics. "Why don't you just come with us and we'll take care of everything." The man took Bride by the arm and tried to lead him back through the access door.

Bride jerked his arm away and backed up. "No, you don't understand! It's absolutely crucial that I speak with her!"

"We'll take you there, mate, just as soon as we clean ya up a bit. We can't be havin' tea with Her Highness lookin' like that, now can we?" Again the medic attempted to take Bride by the arm, but was violently rebuffed.

"You're talking to me as if I were crazy, but I'm not! If you can't take me to see her, then at least let me get a message through to her!"

Bride's pleas were dismissed as the incoherent ramblings of a man in shock. Before he realized what was happening, his arm was swabbed with alcohol and a paramedic was jabbing a needle full of sedative into his bloodstream.

Soon after he was being whisked away by ambulance to the Royal University College hospital on Gower Street, just blocks from where he had begun his journey at the Dunbarton.

◆   ◆   ◆

There was considerable debate amongst Princess Catherine's assistants as to whether or not a message as upsetting as the one they had to deliver shouldn't wait until after the Coronation Ceremony. The Princess was going to be highly photographed that day and she needed to look her best and after all, Trevor wasn't going to get any worse than his present condition in the next six hours. Finally, however, it was decided that Trevor's lifelong service had earned him special consideration, and the assistants convinced themselves that the Princess would be strong enough to handle the grim news.

When the phone call was patched through to her chambers, Princess Catherine was surrounded by a swarm of ladies-in-waiting preparing her for the coronation. As she listened to the worst news imaginable, her milk white complexion blanched a shade paler. She stared straight ahead through a thin layer of tears and although her chin was quivering, she held it higher as if to tell the Grim Reaper himself that she could not be defeated, no matter how many times he came calling on her.

"Thank you," she murmured into the receiver. She gently placed it back on the phone and stood up, swallowing hard. "I need to go out for awhile," she quietly told her attendants. "You all may leave. I can dress myself."

There was an awkward pause among the ladies-in-waiting. They knew something was terribly wrong, but aside from keeping their mouths shut, they weren't entirely sure what to do. They froze in place and did nothing. Catherine could see their indecision and prodded them along.

"One of you tell the Crown Equerry that I'll need a driver sent around immediately."

One of them nodded and beckoned the others to follow her out the door. Catherine wept.

Trevor's body laid stretched out on the examining table in the coroner's office. The blood had been wiped clean from his skin, but it was still difficult to look at him, even for the veteran medical examiners.

Catherine was escorted into the room by the chief coroner. She looked exceedingly ordinary in a tan raincoat and a pale blue scarf over her hair.

"Can you positively identify him?" asked the coroner.

Catherine approached cautiously as she braced herself against the visual impact of Trevor's dead body. She winced in pain at the sight. There was no need to answer the coroner's question.

She stood by his side and reverently removed her scarf. She extended her trembling hand and caressed his cool forehead, now a yellowish gray in color.

Her fingers touched lightly onto his bare chest. For the first time, she saw the tattoo of the McFarlane crest with the bearded man holding a sword in his right hand and a crown in his left, with the words *This I'll Defend*.

She moved slowly to the end of the examining table and saw something that nobody else had ever seen before. Inside the arch of Trevor's left foot was another tattoo, crudely drawn as if the owner was also the artist. In small indigo letters was her name.

She gently held his unresponsive foot in both hands as she knelt down at the end of the table. She bowed her head and quietly repeated the words inscribed in the military chapel at Edinburgh Castle.

"The souls of the righteous are in the hand of God. There shall no evil happen to them. They are in peace." She rose up and stepped back from Trevor's lifeless body.

"Do you know who's responsible?"

"No, Your Highness. That's all being handled by Scotland Yard. There was, however, one oddity I feel I should ask you about."

"What's that?" she said.

The coroner stepped over to a countertop and picked up a small plastic bag. Inside was a solid gold button.

"We found this in his stomach. It's certainly not what killed him, but as you might imagine, it's a bit out of the ordinary, even in this line of work. Can you shed any light on the matter?"

Catherine took the bag from him and examined the button inside. She turned it over and saw the monogram that was etched into the gold facing. It was all she could do to hide the fact that this was not the first time she had seen it.

Chapter Thirty-Five

Coronations in Great Britain are bittersweet occasions. The celebration of a new sovereign only comes on the heels of the death of his or her predecessor. With the throne being turned over from Queen Alexandra to Prince George, this coronation was more bitter than sweet. It really wasn't so much that they disliked George, but simply a case of an act that was difficult to follow.

George had accelerated the preparations for the Coronation Ceremony on the veiled excuse that it would help take the national mind off its troubles. In truth, he could simply wait no longer to clutch the Royal Sceptre.

The Royal State Coach pulled out of the quadrangle at Buckingham Palace at 10:30 on a dreary London morning that reflected the mood of the Commonwealth. Prince George, soon to be King George the VII, was the only passenger in the ornate coach. Eight sturdy Greys strained together to pull twenty-four feet of gilded carriage weighing over four tons.

An escort of officers from the Commonwealth and Colonial contingents, as well as the King's Bodyguard of the Yeoman of the Guard, followed alongside the Royal State Coach. Legions of Horse Guards, Grenadiers, and marching bands followed ahead and trailed behind.

Twenty thousand sailors, soldiers, and airmen lined the route, flanked by an equal number of police from all across Britain. At least seven hundred thousand spectators stood on the street or hung out of buildings, a sizable number but notably quite fewer than had turned out to witness Queen Alexandra's funeral procession just days before. Flags, pennants, canopies and flowers lined the route, but looked more official than spontaneous.

George, wearing a crimson outer robe and his Cap of State, was jostled around inside from the lack of shock absorbers on the enormous vehicle. It would take thirty minutes to travel less than two miles from Buckingham Palace down the Mall, through Trafalgar Square, past Northumberland Avenue and Victoria Embankment and finally to Westminster Abbey in Parliament Square. Even after five decades of waiting, the last half hour seemed to George to take an eternity.

Bride sat barechested on the edge of an emergency room bed as a nurse applied fresh bandages to the wound on his shoulder. With the help of some strong industrial coffee, he had shaken off the effects of the sedative and regained most of his strength. His first thought was to get out of wherever he was and contact Princess Catherine.

"What time is it?" he asked the nurse as he shook the cobwebs from his dulled senses.

"Twenty past eleven," she said as she wrapped more tape around his shoulder blade.

"I need to go," he said as he stood up to leave.

"But I'm not finished, sir!" pleaded the nurse.

Inspector Clive Hobday of Scotland Yard suddenly walked into the emergency room where Bride was being treated.

"Malcolm Bride?" he called out halfway across the room.

"Yes?" answered Bride.

"Inspector Hobday, Scotland Yard," said Hobday as he pulled out his wallet from under his trenchcoat and flashed his identification. "Need a word with you if you're up to it."

Bride's suspicions were instantly aroused. Why in the world was someone from Scotland Yard coming to talk to him? He couldn't trust anyone anymore, not even the police.

"Actually, if this could wait, I'd appreciate it. I was just on my way out." Bride tried to brush past him but Hobday grabbed his arm and held it tightly.

"That's unfortunate, because I'm going to ask a few questions anyway," said Hobday. "Sit down."

Bride obeyed, finding a chair next to the door. "What kind of questions?" he asked Hobday.

"Such as, what were you doing in that tunnel?"

"I was sightseeing. I'd been on one of those walking tours and wandered off from the group." Bride was now lying to police without hesitation.

"I see," said Hobday, not believing a word of it. "And I suppose you have *no* idea what went on in the adjacent tunnel, do you?"

"No, I don't," came Bride's terse reply. "May I go now...*sir?*"

Hobday took a deep breath and motioned for the nurse to leave them alone. The instant she was gone, Hobday stood in front of Bride and loomed over him with as much intimidation as he could muster.

"Look, mate, I know more about you than you think. We ran a spot check on you and your name turned up in our computers as having recently been mentioned in the tabloids in connection with Princess Catherine. And now her personal bodyguard is dead and you just happen to be 'sightseeing' in the next tunnel."

Bride's jaw dropped. "Dead?"

"That's right. Dead. They were hit by the railcar."

Bride's heart suddenly beat faster. Had the inspector said 'they', as in more than one? His mind raced as he tried to piece together the bits of the puzzle his ears had gathered in the tunnel. He had definitely heard Trevor's voice calling out to him, then the subway rumbling through, then silence until the paramedics arrived. And now the inspector was talking about more than one man killed in the tunnel.

It all distilled into one conclusion; Trevor had come back for him and been followed, probably by Crumrie. If that was the case, if Crumrie *had* come after Trevor, it meant that Prince George knew he was still alive and therefore still a threat.

"I told you before, I was only sightseeing. Now if you don't mind, I really need to get going."

Bride stood up from the chair but Hobday shoved him back down and leaned in even closer.

"Now you listen to me, Bride. I know you're involved in this somehow and if you don't cooperate, I'll run you down to the Old Bailey right now and shackle you up for murder."

Their eyes locked onto each other like two fencers with their foils crossed. Bride was breathing hard. He finally turned away and stared at the floor. After a long reflective pause, he finally nodded his head.

"Alright, alright, I'll tell you the truth. But you might want to take your coat off and have a seat because this is going to take a while."

Hobday smiled in victory. "Now that's more like it." He looked around the room for another chair and pulled it up directly across from Bride.

With his head still hanging toward the floor, Bride rolled his eyes upward, studying Hobday's movements. They were not the eyes of a defeated man. They were alert and darting, flaring with anger. The death of Trevor McFarlane had infused him with incredible new energy and resolve, as if Trevor's spirit had supernaturally transferred his immense courage and strength before floating away. Bride understood what had to be done and knew he was the only one left to do it. In the names of Crowe and McFarlane, he would mount a final charge.

Hobday started to remove his trenchcoat. Bride sat poised but motionless like a leopard on the hunt, waiting for the right moment to pounce. Waiting, waiting, waiting.

As Hobday pulled his trenchcoat over his shoulders and momentarily pinned his own arms in the sleeves, Bride seized the moment and sprang from his chair. He hurled the steaming coffee from his cup into Hobday's face, then bowled over the inspector with a flying bull rush, blasting him backwards over his chair. The back of Hobday's head snapped hard against the tile floor and although still conscious, he was several moments away from regaining his full faculties.

Bride yanked open the door and fled down the hospital corridor like a mental patient escaping his security ward, knocking people and equipment out of the way rather than running around them.

He burst outside onto Gower Street and knew immediately where he was. He'd fled through this neighborhood on more than one occasion in recent weeks and for once he felt as though he held the advantage.

Bad timing was about to enter Bride's life once again. A young bobby turned the corner, relieving his frustration by raking his baton against the railings of the iron fences in front of some of the townhouses on Gower. He was still angry that he hadn't been selected to guard the route of the Coronation Ceremony.

He looked up just in time to see a frantic man with no shoes, no shirt, and a bandaged shoulder come racing out of the emergency room. The young bobby would never be a candidate for detective, but even he knew this was not the ordinary checkout procedure at University College Hospital. He struggled to return his baton to his belt, then fumbled in his effort to locate his whistle. He shoved it into his mouth and blew, only to discover he'd put in the wrong end. He finally got matters straightened out and let loose with a series of shrill blasts.

Bride spun around at the sound of the alarm, then immediately fled in the opposite direction.

Instead of giving chase, the bobby removed his whistle and cupped his hands around his mouth. "Stop!" he yelled at Bride. Through the ages of law enforcement, that command has never once succeeded in arresting a fleeing suspect. History repeated itself at that moment as Bride ignored the bobby's request, darting into an alleyway and disappearing from view.

Inspector Hobday burst out of the doors of the hospital, still rubbing the swollen knot on the back of his scalp.

"That way!" yelled the bobby, pointing in the direction of Bride's escape. He still hadn't moved from his position.

Hobday ran across Gower Street in pursuit. He instinctively ducked into the same alley and caught a glimpse of Bride hopping over a short wall behind one of the townhouses.

◆　◆　◆

All of the nobles of the realm were gathered at Westminster Abbey for the anointing and crowning.

George was met at the west door by the Earl Marshal and escorted inside the hallowed arches of the church by a procession of clergy and nobles. The Great Proceeding brought in the regalia of swords, orbs, and sceptres that had been transferred from the Tower of London and placed them on the high altar.

George stepped up into an area in front of the Abbey called The Theatre and sat in the Chair of State. He couldn't help but sneak a glance at the throne that awaited on the dais behind him.

Princess Catherine, her eyes swollen from tears and lack of sleep, sat in a private box to the right of the altar. Her mind was numb from her private pain, barely able to distinguish that the pomp around her was being played out in reality and wasn't the product of some hallucinatory nightmare.

Princes of the Blood, Members of Parliament, admirals, generals, privy councillors and members of the Coronation Committee found their seats in the gallery, as did members of the diplomatic corps, ministers from British countries overseas, and distinguished members of the public. The heart of the ceremony that every ruler of Britain had taken part in was set to begin.

The Archbishop of Canterbury stood in front of the altar and called out to the people, "Sirs, I here present unto you King George the Seventh, your undoubted sovereign. Wherefore all you who are come this day to do your homage and service, are you willing to do the same?"

"God save the King!" came their practiced response.

Princess Catherine shifted uncomfortably in her seat, realizing some terrible act was being initiated, but incapable of summoning the strength to move against it.

Elliott Wiggs sat across the transept, carefully studying the Princess Royal.

♦ ♦ ♦

Bride crept across the rear terrace of the Dunbarton and slipped quietly through the back door. He made certain to lock it behind him. The wooden floorboards in the hallway seemed to creak louder than ever under his bare feet.

Peter Rumpole emerged from the den where he had been watching the coronation on television. "Can I help you?" he asked before seeing who it was. He stepped into the hallway and saw the bandaged American gasping for breath. "My God! Dr. Bride, what 'appened?"

"I'm in trouble," gasped Bride.

"I can plainly see that! What sort of trouble?"

"It's better that you didn't know. You just have to trust me that I'm doing the right thing and I need your help."

"You got it," said Rumpole without hesitation. "What you need?"

"Shoes and a shirt to start with."

"Right then. Go in and have a seat by the telly. I'll be back straight away."

"Thanks. And hurry if you can. There isn't much time."

Bride started into the den. Rumpole had just turned toward the stairs when they heard a loud rapping on the back door.

"Go!" whispered Rumpole, motioning Bride to continue on into the den. "I'll handle this!"

Bride moved swiftly into the den. He saw George's face filling up the television screen as the BBC cameras beamed the Coronation Ceremonies to the rest of the world. The hands on the wall clock registered 11:31 and seemed to Bride to be churning around the clock face at ten times their normal speed.

The knocking at the back door had grown louder and more frantic. Rumpole picked up a broom from the corner of the hallway as he approached the door. For some reason he felt the prop made him look less suspicious. He opened it to reveal Inspector Hobday, sweating hard in his coffee-stained trenchcoat and panting for breath.

"Inspector Hobday," he wheezed. "Scotland Yard. I have reason to believe a fugitive from justice is on these premises."

"Fugitive?" said Rumpole as innocently as possible. "From justice?"

Hobday pushed his way past Rumpole and entered the hallway. He poked his head through the open door of Room One, hunting for Bride like a Gestapo agent.

"That's right," said Hobday. "A fugitive from justice."

"A fugitive from justice," repeated Rumpole. "What do you know about that? We've had a lot of different sorts of people come through the Dunbarton over the years, but I don't ever recall hostin' a fugitive from justice."

Rumpole moved casually in front of the entryway to the den, sweeping nonexistent dirt off the floor. "I remember once we had a tailor from Hong Kong, but never a fugitive from justice. We've also had—"

"Shut up!" roared Hobday. "You're interfering with official police business."

Rumpole nodded and continued to sweep the floor, hoping his presence would keep the inspector from entering the den. Hobday headed toward the entry and Rumpole moved nonchalantly in front of him as though he were reaching for a particularly elusive piece of dust, effectively blocking his path.

"Excuse me," said Hobday.

"For what?" replied Rumpole.

"I want to get by."

"By what?"

"By you! I want to look in this room."

"This room?"

"Yes! I want to inspect this room!"

"Well, you being an inspector and all, I suppose that would make sense, yes."

"Now *will* you excuse me?" said an exasperated Hobday through gritted teeth.

"Uh...yes. Yes, of course." Rumpole swallowed hard as he stood aside and let Hobday pass. "But I don't know why you would want to go in there. Nothin' in there but the telly."

Hobday stepped cautiously into the den. The faint sound of a floorboard creaking grabbed his attention and he froze in place, trying to pinpoint its origin. He slowly drew his gun from his shoulder holster and wrapped his finger around its well-worn trigger.

Bride lay as motionless as possible on the floor behind the couch, knowing that the slightest movement of any muscle translated into a telltale squeak that jeopardized his hiding place.

Rumpole stood in the entryway in horror as he noticed the very tip of Bride's toe sticking out from behind the couch.

"I can see your foot!" he blurted out.

"What?" said Hobday, spinning around in anger to face Rumpole.

"I said, I can see you're *good*. Very thorough."

Bride had gotten Rumpole's cryptic message. He gingerly pulled his incriminating leg closer to his body. The floor did indeed creak, but at that very moment, Prince George's voice on the television boomed out as he repeated the word of declaration in which he promised to rule according to the laws of the land. He had covered Bride's tracks.

Hobday scowled at Rumpole and turned back around, moving closer to the couch. One more meter and he would be able to see him. He took another step.

"*Peter!*" came a shattering scream from upstairs. "*Peter! Quickly!*" It was Fionnuala's frantic voice.

Hobday and Rumpole raced out of the den and into the hallway where Fionnuala was bounding down the staircase with an armful of dirty bedsheets. Her face was alive with terror.

"Peter, there's a strange man in Room Seven!" I went in there to clean and there he was! Call the police!"

"No! No need to call the police!" said Hobday in a hushed warning. "I'll handle this."

"Who are you?"

"Inspector Hobday, Scotland Yard. Now where did you say this man was?"

"Room Seven."

Hobday nodded and charged up the staircase with his gun drawn, stopping to peer around each corner in a proper police approach.

Rumpole ran back to the den. "Dr. Bride! Quickly!" he called out.

Bride scrambled to his feet and followed Rumpole into the hallway. Fionnuala opened the bedsheets in her arms and pulled out a fresh shirt and a pair of shoes, handing them to Bride with a gleeful wink.

"Might get further with these."

Bride pulled on the shoes and quickly buttoned the shirt.

"We'd give you the keys to our car, only we don't own one," she whispered.

"That's alright, you've done more than enough." He hugged them both in his strong arms. "I won't forget you." Bride opened the front door a crack, looked both ways up and down Gower Street, then slipped outside.

"And we won't soon forget you, Mis...I mean, *Doctor* Bride," said Fionnuala with a wink.

Bride shot her a toothy smile as the door closed behind him.

"Need more guests like him," nodded Rumpole as he wrapped his arm around his wife's waist and softly kissed her forehead. "Livens up the old place."

It would be over three full minutes before Inspector Clive Hobday realized the Dunbarton only had six rooms to let.

Chapter Thirty-Six

George sat in King Edward's Chair as the Archbishop of Canterbury anointed his hands, breast, and head with sacred oil.

He donned the Stole of Armill and the Imperial Mantle with its golden eagles woven into the fabric, the vestments of both a cleric of the church and a ruler of his realm.

Catherine's mind was slowly regaining clarity and she surveyed the gathering in the Abbey. Everyone's eyes were riveted on George except for those of Elliott Wiggs, who was still transfixed on Catherine. His stare frightened her. It was as if Wiggs were trying to pierce her thoughts, wondering if she were going to do anything other than just sit there. Catherine looked away, her heart beginning to pound as her senses came closer to full focus. She wondered the same thing as Wiggs.

◆ ◆ ◆

Bride cut down Chenies Street to Tottenham Court Road and headed south toward Oxford Street. Ordinarily, a man frantically sprinting down the sidewalk would draw some attention, but the streets were alive with people who had turned out to watch the coronation procession and no activity on this morning seemed terribly unusual.

As he bolted through traffic onto Charing Cross Road, he saw the clock outside the tube station. 11:39. He would never make it to Westminster Abbey in time on foot. Even a taxi cab would get mired down in the crush of traffic fanning out from the Abbey.

A police car sat parked in front of a pub with its door flung open.

The officer belonging to the car was on the sidewalk trying to convince some drunken youths with assorted unnatural hair colors to take their reveling back inside. One of the youths was proving to be particularly uncooperative and the discussion was heating up.

Bride saw the open door of the police car as his window of opportunity. He moved quickly down the street and slid easily behind the wheel. He had the car in reverse and was backing away before the officer noticed the hijacking was taking place.

Bride flipped on the wailing sirens of the police car as he sped through Soho, ignoring all traffic lights and speed limits. The law no longer mattered to him. Only the truth.

The car barreled across Coventry and raced toward Trafalgar Square as the statues of Lord Nelson and Charles I down Whitehall watched his progress with varying emotions.

Bride had hoped to cut over to Northumberland Avenue and onto the Victoria Embankment, but the route was sealed off to traffic. Lingering spectators from the procession still clogged the area. Bride leaned on the horn to try to part the sea of humanity, but further progress was hopeless. He slammed the stickshift into reverse.

♦　♦　♦

The Jewelled Sword of State was girded around George's waist by the Archbishop with the charge that it be used to defend the right, protect the Church, the poor, and the helpless. For one brief instant, the hypocrisy of the ceremony touched Catherine. Here was a sword designated to assist the poor, yet it had a hilt covered with diamonds, rubies, and emeralds, housed in a scabbard made of gold. To many, it would seem to symbolize everything that was wrong with the monarchy. But her entire life had been dedicated to the institution, and so many of her decisions had been based purely on the notion that the good health of the monarchy was in the best interest of its subjects, and deep in her heart of hearts that is what she still believed.

Regardless of who sat on the throne, Britain without a King or Queen was like a body without flowing blood to keep it alive.

The Jewelled Sword was removed and set on the altar to symbolize that the full power of the throne would be used to defend the Church.

Princess Catherine turned away, afraid to question any more aspects of her own existence.

♦　♦　♦

Bride spun the police car around and weaved his way through

traffic back across Trafalgar Square, scanning the spokes of avenues for an alternate route to the east. A tour bus pulled in front of him and he jammed on his brakes, narrowly avoiding a broadside collision. He blasted the driver with his horn, but suddenly stopped when he saw a bobby quickly approaching his car. Whether it was his civilian clothes or an emergency radio call from the officer who owned the car he was driving, Bride knew from the bobby's face that he had been found out.

Again he jerked the stickshift into reverse, backed up twenty yards, then thrust it into first gear and careened forward past the bobby. Up onto the crowded sidewalk he drove to get around the bus, then bounced back onto the pavement. He glanced in the rear view mirror to see the bobby still racing after him.

William IV Street was coming up on his right as Bride sped back up Charing Cross. He pulled hard on the steering wheel and squealed around the corner, feeling a certain satisfaction that he was relying on raw instincts to guide him to Westminster.

Unfortunately, while those instincts had been born in England, they were bred in America and that was about to work against him in a profound way. As Bride had wheeled onto William IV Street he had instinctively pulled into the right hand lane, in direct opposition to the oncoming traffic. By the time he saw the car in front of him it was too late. In a violent exchange of grillwork, both cars were rendered inoperable.

Bride jumped out, ready to apologize, until he caught a glimpse of the earnest bobby still giving chase on foot. Bride bolted onto the busy sidewalk and tried to blend in to the crowd.

◆   ◆   ◆

George was given the Swords of Spiritual Justice and Temporal Justice as a pledge of kind and fair dealings in both religious and civic affairs, and finally Curtana, a sword from which the point had been clipped off. Curtana was the Sword of Mercy, intended to signify that justice will not be harsh. If anything symbolized modern England, the ancient sword with the broken tip was it.

The Archbishop carefully placed the Orb in George's right hand. On top of the golden sphere was a large amethyst supporting a cross that symbolized Christ's domination over the earth. Resting in George's trembling hand, it seemed to take on a more earthly meaning.

The Coronation Ring was then placed on the fourth finger of George's right hand by the Archbishop as a promise that all duties of the sovereign would be attended to.

George put a red glove on his right hand to grasp the Sceptre with the Cross, nearly three feet of solid gold topped with the Star of Africa, a diamond weighing over five hundred carats.

"Receive the Royal Sceptre," exhorted the Archbishop, "the ensign of kingly power and justice." George held on to the symbol of Royal authority as if he would never let go.

♦   ♦   ♦

Bride had managed to elude his pursuer as he covered the final half mile to Westminster Abbey on the power of two weary legs. The closer he got to the spires of the church, however, the thicker the security became. Barriers had been erected on every street to keep the exuberant crowds at bay. Police were posted every ten feet around the perimeter of Parliament Square, with clumps of uniformed guards at each entrance to the Abbey.

There was no way inside.

Big Ben called out the noon hour.

♦   ♦   ♦

On a cushion of cloth and gold, the Archbishop held the Crown of Edward the Confessor, named for the most religious of all British rulers.

"O, God, the crown of the faithful," recited the Archbishop. "Bless we beseech Thee and sanctify this, Thy servant George the Seventh and as Thou dost this day set a crown of pure gold upon his head, so enrich his royal heart with Thine abundant grave, and crown him with all princely virtues, through the King eternal, Jesus Christ our Lord. Amen."

George gazed at the circlet of gold, the rosettes of precious stones reflecting in his zealous eyes. He was so close, it was all he could do to keep himself from snatching it off the cushion and thrusting it onto his head.

Catherine's mind was racing, knowing the crown was not following bloodlines, but still uncertain if this weren't a suitable destiny after all. Despite everything George had done, despite every evil sin he had committed, she still respected his abilities and held fast to a hope that he could change the course of modern England for the better. She was trying to look into the future, to weigh everything in the perspective of the larger picture. Catherine quivered noticeably in her seat, but was otherwise paralyzed.

♦   ♦   ♦

Bride stood helplessly among the cheering masses outside Westminster Abbey, knowing the hourglass of opportunity had only a few grains of sand left. So many times he had tried to divorce himself from all of this and every time some reconciliation within his soul had dragged him back into it. He had to convince himself that there was a good reason for his being there, that some higher purpose was still to be served. There was no longer a choice to be made, but rather a destiny to be followed. He no longer felt pulled, but rather led, and he had to trust that whatever forces were at work were going to guide him through the last steps of his journey.

On the outer fringes of the crowd, Bride spotted a Horse Guard. His mount was nervously turning in circles, clearly spooked by all of the activity surrounding him. The Guard's full attention was devoted to keeping his horse under the reins as Bride waded over to him through the throng.

◆ ◆ ◆

George slowly lowered his head, fighting his overwhelming eagerness. The moment he had waited for, the moment he had yearned for, the moment kept from him for so long, had finally arrived. The Archbishop of Canterbury raised the crown and slowly lowered it onto the head of King George the VII. He raised his head and ascended to the throne.

Everyone inside the Abbey leapt to their feet and cried out "God save the King!" Everyone except Catherine. She hung her head, ashamed that her uncertainty had not translated into action. If past sins were meant to be corrected, she had allowed the opportunity to pass her by.

A flourish of trumpets was accompanied by a flashing of gold as the assembled barons and marquesses put on their own coronets. Outside the Abbey, at Tower Hill, and in Hyde Park, cannons thundered a royal salute to the newly crowned monarch.

King George was lifted onto the throne by the princes of the Church and nobles of the realm. They paid homage to him and with a rolling of drums, another blast of trumpets as the words "God save the King! Long live the King! May the King live forever!" echoed through the arches of Westminster Abbey.

King George surveyed the scene in the church and like God examining his creation, he saw that it was good. He had achieved his goal of absolute power.

George allowed himself a brief glance at Elliott Wiggs, who smiled almost imperceptibly and returned a single nod of his gray head.

Of all of God's miracles, perhaps the greatest one is that the hand of the Almighty didn't reach down from heaven, pick up one of the swords from the altar, and smote King George VII as he sat high on his throne in the House of the Lord.

♦   ♦   ♦

Bride approached the mounted Horse Guard from the blind side and without hesitation reached up and grabbed his belt, yanking him down on the ground. He snatched the reins as they dangled free and swung up into the saddle.

"Hey!" shouted the Horse Guard but his voice was lost amid the din of the celebration.

Bride took control of the animal, jerking hard on the reins so that the horse felt the bit in his mouth. He spun the steed around and galloped away behind the last row of the crowd. Even with the pandemonium surrounding him, Bride knew he only had precious seconds before someone in authority noticed him. It was now or never.

He brought the horse to a stop thirty yards behind a barrier set up for crowd control. The horse pawed at the ground and dipped his head up and down like a wild stallion, mirroring the nervous energy that was enveloping his rider.

Bride drew a deep breath, knowing it might be among his last. He jabbed his heels deep into the animal's rib cage and held on for dear life. The horse galloped hard across the pavement as Bride's heels exhorted him to run faster. They approached the barrier at breakneck speed and the horse didn't even think about balking. Together they soared over the barrier and landed on the other side as the horseshoes sparked on the pavement. Bride flew high up out of the English saddle, banging his chin hard against the animal's neck.

With only one leg in the stirrup, he battled to hold on with every ounce of energy left in his tired body. After several seconds in which he was wildly out of control, he managed to right himself.

He jerked the reins hard to the right and aimed his transport toward the front door of the Abbey. He dug in his heels and charged toward the entrance.

Only now did the multitude of guards lining the entryway notice the intruder on horseback, but it was too late for them to do anything about it. Bride sped by them in a rush of wind, lowering his head to make sure he cleared the low transom.

He burst into the Abbey and galloped freely down the black and white checkerboard aisle, the hoofbeats thundering through the arches above and jarring the graves of Dickens, Chaucer, and Kipling below.

"Stop him!" yelled Bride as he rode all the way to The Theatre at the front of the Abbey where King George was sitting on his throne.

The dozens of security personnel instinctively reached for their weapons, but not a shot was fired. Some of the veterans held their fire as they realized an errant bullet meant a dead nobleman somewhere in the Abbey. The younger guards were paralyzed by shock.

It was one of those moments where the events taking place were so bizarre and so unexpected that nobody was quite sure how to react. It was the first Coronation Ceremony for almost everyone in attendance and they weren't entirely certain that this wasn't some planned part of the proceedings. For a brief eternity, they looked on in disbelief like a circus audience that had just seen a trapeze artist plunge to his death. It was simply too much for the senses to comprehend.

Even Princess Catherine, who knew exactly why Bride was there, sat riveted in her seat.

King George understood completely the disaster that was about to unfold in front of him. He leaped from his throne and his first expression of leadership was murderous.

"Shoot him! Shoot this man!"

The guards still didn't move, their fingers collectively frozen on their triggers. Their reluctance to open fire was buoyed by the fact that Bride was clearly unarmed and wasn't actually posing a physical threat to King George.

"Your King is a murderer and a fraud!" countered Bride.

George grabbed the Jewelled Sword of State off the altar and wrapped both hands around the diamond-studded hilt. He lunged at Bride and swung viciously at his legs, but sliced only air as the experienced horseman deftly maneuvered out of his way.

"As King of Britain, I order you to kill this man!" bellowed the new sovereign.

"There's not a drop of royal blood in his bones and I can prove it!" yelled Bride.

By this time, the rational minds of those gathered in Westminster were realizing something was horribly wrong. They began stirring in their seats, on the brink of mass hysteria.

Amid all of the confusion, one clearheaded and brave security guard had crept up behind the dais and hid directly behind the Coronation Chair. He suddenly burst forward and took a flying leap at Bride in the saddle. They tumbled together onto the dais as a swarm of guards immediately descended on the intruder.

"Kill him!" screamed George as the guards wrestled Bride into handcuffs. "I command you to kill him!"

The legion of guards began to drag Bride away from the dais when suddenly another voice rang out.

"Let him go!" came the directive. The voice belonged to Princess Catherine, who now stood boldly erect in front of the throne.

The guards and everyone else in Westminster stopped cold. A hush swept over them.

"This man is telling the truth," said Catherine. "Your King *is* a fraud. And a murderer. And a host of other things that are unmentionable in a house of worship."

"That's treason!" screamed George in a fit of rage that caused his crown to tilt slightly to one side.

"No, George. That's truth." She pointed to Bride. "He speaks it, and finally now I speak it."

Catherine raised her gloved hand high in the air. Between her thumb and finger she held the gold monogrammed button that Trevor had bitten off of George's dinner jacket.

"This button belongs to you, George. Do you know where I found it? In the stomach of Trevor McFarlane, who was murdered early this morning. This button is Jonah. Out of the belly of the fish, and here to deliver his message. Do you want me to continue?"

George gazed at the gold button like a vampire staring at a silver cross. He was unable to speak or move as the lunacy inside his head gradually seeped out through his eyes.

"The ravens may be departing the Tower," continued Catherine. "The monarchy may fall, but the truth has finally shone through. I shall let providence take it from here."

George stood conspicuously alone on the dais, trembling involuntarily. He retreated several steps and collapsed into the throne. It would be the last time he would sit there. The Jewelled Sword of State, intended to defend the right, slipped out of his hand and fell to the floor with a deadened thud.

Elliott Wiggs slipped unnoticed out of the back of the Abbey and disappeared into the throng of people still cheering in celebration, ignorant of the apocalyptic cataclysm that had just taken place inside.

Chapter Thirty-Seven

Wiggs drove sixty miles southeast of London to a small village on the English Channel called Beachy Head. He stood on a precipice known as the "Devil's chimney" that loomed high above the white chalk cliffs and stared down at the foaming waves swirling and crashing onto the jagged rocks five hundred feet below.

In the Sussex countryside leading up to the edge of the sheer cliffs one could still see remnants of the dragon's dentures that had been embedded to stave off Hitler's tanks. The Nazi invasion never materialized, and now another threat to the Commonwealth had been thwarted.

Wiggs braced himself against the cutting wind. His mind traveled a half century back in time to the fearful nights of the German air raids on London.

He retraced the memories of a brief affair with a lady-in-waiting at Buckingham Palace named Bridget Allison, recalling with clarity the morning she told him she was pregnant with twins. He remembered booking her passage to the United States, convincing her that she had rescued the morale of the British people by giving up one of her precious boys.

His happiest days had come soon thereafter as the young Prince George grew and matured. Wiggs had encouraged the Queen's husband to travel extensively during that time so that he and the Crown Prince could spend more time together. For over fifty years he had orchestrated the rise to power for one of his twins and earlier that day they had stood together on the brink of omnipotence.

Now Wiggs stood on the edge of a treacherous cliff, having seen one son fall at the hands of the other. Wiggs jumped to a coward's death.

In the days and weeks that followed, Catherine revealed every sordid detail of George's life.

He was found guilty of murder and remains incarcerated in Newgate Prison, where he receives no special consideration.

Inspector Clive Hobday occupies a cell in the floor below for his assistance in the death of Colin Crowe. The leak at Scotland Yard is now plugged.

Princess Catherine became Queen Catherine I in what history will remember as the most joyous Coronation Ceremony the British people have ever experienced.

Her first official act as sovereign was to erect a modest new headstone at the anonymous grave in St. Bartholomew's, marking the resting place of her brother, the true Crown Prince.

Trevor McFarlane was buried in the plot next to him with full military ceremony. Sir McFarlane was posthumously honored with knighthood for his service to the Crown.

Malcolm Bride returned to America and took a brief leave of absence from teaching until the cavalier spotlight of the modern media moved on to someone else. Upon his return to Amherst, he established a journalism scholarship in the name of Colin Crowe.

He and Queen Catherine still correspond regularly.